*By Vanessa Hua*

Deceit and Other Possibilities

A River of Stars

# A River of Stars

# A River of Stars

A Novel

# Vanessa Hua

Ballantine Books
New York

Copyright © 2018 by Vanessa Hua

Published in the United States by Ballantine Books, an imprint of Random House, a division of Penguin Random House LLC, New York.

Title page art from an original photograph by iStock.com/spondylolithesis

BALLANTINE and the HOUSE colophon are registered trademarks of Penguin Random House LLC.

LIBRARY OF CONGRESS CATALOGING-IN-PUBLICATION DATA

Names: Hua, Vanessa, author.
Title: A river of stars : a novel / Vanessa Hua.
Description: New York : Ballantine Books, 2018.
Identifiers: LCCN 2018009300 |
ISBN 9780399178788 (hardback)
Subjects: LCSH: Chinese women—United States—Fiction. |
Immigrant women—United States—Fiction. | Pregnant
women—United States—Fiction. | Parenthood—Fiction. |
BISAC: FICTION / Contemporary Women. | FICTION /
Literary. | GSAFD: Suspense fiction
Classification: LCC PS3608.U2245 R58 2018 |
DDC 813/.6—dc23
LC record available at https://lccn.loc.gov/2018009300

Ebook ISBN 978-0-399-17880-1

Printed in the United States of America on acid-free paper

randomhousebooks.com

9 8 7 6 5 4 3 2 1

First Edition

*Book design by Virginia Norey*

*To my husband*

# A River of Stars

# Prologue

Scarlett Chen could keep a secret. It was everyone else she couldn't trust: not the passengers in her row, not the flight attendants, not anyone who might give immigration officials a reason to turn her away.

As the plane descended into Los Angeles, she tightened her lips. She didn't want to get airsick and risk someone examining her too closely. She had to look *pangzi,* like any other well-fed Chinese tourist on her way to the Vegas slots. Pressing her fingers against the window, she marveled at the glittering Pacific and the mountain ridges pinched like dumplings. At sunset, the gold, slanting light had transformed the coastline into something more beautiful, more possible than anything China had to offer.

When the flight attendant announced the local time, she could have just as well said midnight or six in the morning. After traveling for nearly an entire day, Scarlett had lost all sense of the hour. It felt strange to arrive at almost the same moment she'd left Shenzhen, as though clocks had gone out of order when she crossed the international dateline.

She had been much too nervous to sleep on her first trip outside of China, her first time on a plane. She checked her passport, burgundy embossed with gold stars, to reassure herself that the visa hadn't disappeared. In the photo, her eyes were wide and startled by the flash, and if you knew where to look, you could make out the new softness under her chin.

She fastened her seatbelt, low beneath her swollen belly. Her mouth had gone unbearably dry, but it was too late to hit the call button to ask for water. Her ears were popping from the change in altitude. Soon the plane would be on the ground, and what she could deny while aloft she now had to accept: she would go through the rest of her third trimester far from her lover, far from all she'd ever known. Taking a deep breath and closing her eyes, she tried to collect herself.

She'd always been solitary, by circumstance and by nature. In the village, the other families had been wary of the power that her mother held over them—and by association, Scarlett. She had never mastered circuitous feminine chatter, lacking the time, patience, or inclination to learn, and now Scarlett would be cloistered among wealthy, pregnant wives who would surely disdain a mistress.

With a jolt, the plane landed, its tires bouncing and squealing on the tarmac. A few passengers jumped into the aisle, yanking open the overhead bins to get their bags, determined to deplane first. They couldn't escape the peasant within: the elbowing, pushing, and shoving necessary to get ahead in a country of billions.

A squat man stumbled and nearly toppled into her row, and she lurched in her seat, shielding herself. Flight attendants shouted at him, ordering everyone to sit down until the plane stopped taxiing. Scarlett didn't need to rush. Her lover had insisted that she check her luggage, worried that she'd endanger their baby by lifting a suitcase above her head.

In the terminal, she smoothed her flowing tunic and hitched up her baggy pants. She rinsed out her mouth at the bathroom sink and ran her fingers through her hair, trying to look respectable. As she waited in line at passport control, she fought the urge to rest her hands on her belly. Despite the air-conditioned chill, Scarlett was sweating. She fanned herself. Studying the line of booths, she prayed she'd get an officer who wouldn't ask too many questions—one who wouldn't recognize the signs that betrayed the latter stages of pregnancy: the pimples on her chin, and the flashes of heat and wooziness that hit without warning. Her bump remained hidden and her paperwork was in order, she reminded herself, even if she was bending the rules on her visa. When the officer waved her over, she strode toward him, her gaze direct and her head held high—just like she'd been told, just like she'd practiced.

He looked through her passport. "First time in the U.S.?"

Scarlett nodded. "Yes." She held herself so tightly she felt she might snap.

"Why are you visiting?" he asked. "How long do you plan to stay?"

Her baby kicked her in the ribs, so hard she almost swayed on her feet.

# Chapter 1

When Boss Yeung first told her about Perfume Bay, she'd tossed the brochure onto the dashboard and reached for a slice of dried mango. Shaking his head, he took the bag, but before he could stop her, she snatched a slice of chewy sweetness. During her pregnancy, he'd begun scrutinizing her, prescribing advice—some backed by science but most by superstition—to protect the baby. She shouldn't eat mangoes, as their heat would give the baby bad skin; no watermelon, whose chill would cool her womb; no bananas, which would cause the baby to slip out early. No water chestnuts, mung beans, or bean sprouts, either. The list of traditional prohibitions grew each time she attempted to eat.

As he drifted into the next lane, she told him to keep his eyes on the road. He gripped the steering wheel and told her his plan: he wanted to send her and their unborn child halfway around the world to Perfume Bay, five-star accommodations located outside of Los Angeles. After she delivered, staff would file for a Social Security card, birth certificate, and passport for the baby. Their son—his sex recently confirmed—would give them a foothold in America.

"Eventually he could sponsor our green cards," Scarlett had responded. "For now, you'll get rid of me. Clever plan, Boss Yeung."

At the factory, she called him Boss Yeung, and she kept it up in private, too, a reminder that she was a deputy manager, and not a *xiaojie*—a mistress, a gold digger from a disco or a hostess bar. They passed factories covered in grimy white tile, built on land that had been fields when she arrived here as a teenager. People from around the country had moved to the Pearl River Delta, just across the border from Hong Kong, to make their fortunes, and the factory girl you snubbed might someday become your manager.

Boss Yeung reached into the glove box for a brand-new U.S. atlas that he must have hand-carried from Hong Kong. Hope unfurled in her chest. She always navigated on their weekend drives, and with this gift, she pictured them traveling across America together.

"Whatever hospital you'd deliver in would be top-class," he said.

"The hospitals are good in Hong Kong, too," she said. Unlike in China, the government wouldn't hassle her there for being an unwed mother, wouldn't fine her or force her to terminate her pregnancy. Women there could have as many children as they wanted.

Boss Yeung frowned. Hong Kong was also home to his wife and three daughters.

"It doesn't matter how good the hospitals are in America, if I end up in jail," she said.

She had conceived even though Boss Yeung had pulled out, evidently not soon enough. For once, the method had failed them. Her periods had never been regular, and she'd been into her second trimester before realizing her nausea wasn't the stomach flu and her heartburn wasn't from the stress of trying to meet production goals.

On the radio, a newscaster announced that the U.S. embassy was evacuating American tourists from Egypt. Boss Yeung stabbed his finger at the radio dial. "The U.S. would save our son."

"From Egypt? Why would I—why would he go to Egypt?"

"From anywhere. The U.S. would get him out of trouble anywhere."

That was when Scarlett had realized just how much his son meant to Boss Yeung, reviving the dream that had died with the birth of his daughters: an heir to carry on his legacy. He had never shared this dream with her, for a boy in his image, a prince of the family. He was almost sixty, she was thirty-six. If Scarlett carried a girl, would Boss Yeung have sent her to Perfume Bay? No. He'd waited to book her stay until he knew she was having a boy, but objecting to such a preference would have been like objecting to gravity.

He sped up, picking off tractor trailers and buses, which still gave her a thrill. Faster and faster they went, getting so far ahead it seemed they might have the road's end to themselves. With him behind the wheel, she might go anywhere. He put his hand on top of hers, lacing their fingers together, and she tucked her head against his shoulder. She never felt more complete than when nestled against him. If she didn't have this baby, she might never have one, not with Boss Yeung or with anyone else.

On her own, Scarlett could have expected deference and attention. One pregnant woman gets a seat on the bus, the front of the line at the bathroom, and good wishes from strangers who pat your bump, ask how far along you are, and guess if you are carrying a boy or a girl. At the sight of a fertile belly, the most hardened can't help but hope for the future, can't help but long for their past.

A dozen pregnant women are a different matter.

You quarrel over who gets the most comfortable seat at dinner, who eats the last of the tofu stew, and whose aches are the most deserving of sympathy.

Deep into her eighth month of pregnancy, she had thought the other guests at Perfume Bay would lose interest, but they wouldn't stop picking on her. Now she found herself squeezed into the corner of the couch by an equally round Lady Yu. Their feud had started over Scarlett's accommodations at Perfume Bay, where she had the most luxurious quarters. Lady Yu had demanded the room, which had a view of the foothills, a massage chair, and a marble Jacuzzi, but apparently, Boss Yeung had more *guanxi* here.

On television, the Hollywood sign appeared, iconic letters that stood a few kilometers away yet seemed distant as the moon. After Scarlett turned up the volume, Lady Yu grabbed the remote and switched the channel.

Because Scarlett never bragged about Boss Yeung's position, because she never mentioned him at all, the other guests found her suspect. She was a threat, not because she'd go after their husbands, but because she represented any woman, every woman who could. It didn't matter that her lover was a stranger to them. Mistresses weren't supposed to have children who competed with theirs.

Lady Yu had made clear that she considered Scarlett and the baby she carried lowly as turtle's eggs. Nothing was more despicable than a turtle—dragging itself through the muck—except its spawn. A nurse arrived to drop prenatal vitamins into their mouths, their faces upturned to her like chicks getting fed. The pill tasted of iron and rotting leaves. Scarlett swallowed and gagged, felt the pill coming back up but chased it down with a few sips of lukewarm water. Her insides would roil all morning.

She had arrived a few weeks ago, and at any given time at Perfume Bay—three white stucco townhomes converted into a compound by ripping out the adjoining walls—about a dozen guests from China and Hong Kong were pregnant, and another half-dozen or so were recovering. The babies slept in a former dining room where a crystal chandelier hung over the bassinets. Cartons of diapers, crates of formula, and sacks of wipes jammed the garages, and closets had been remodeled into bathrooms.

Lady Yu led the Shanghai clique of spoiled wives, who were perhaps only a generation or two removed from the countryside. In Scarlett, they despised who they might have been.

Scarlett changed the channel back.

*"Mei you wenhua,"* Lady Yu shouted. *"Nong min."* Low-class! A peasant! She hurled a magazine at Scarlett, missing wildly and hitting the television.

*"Tuhao,"* Scarlett said. An insult for the newly rich, with more money than manners.

Stung by the insult, Lady Yu heaved herself up and slapped Scarlett.

Scarlett rocked back in disbelief, putting up her hands to protect her belly. Her mother used to slap her, but no one else, not in decades. Lady Yu smiled smugly, the sort who beat her servants. Scarlett grabbed a pillow and smacked it against Lady Yu's head. When Lady Yu clawed at her, Scarlett grabbed her wrists and forced her arms down, twisting almost hard enough to sprain. Their screams set off one baby, then all ten babies in the nursery next door, howls that picked up with the speed and power of a tsunami.

The owner, Mama Fang, rushed in, trailed by nurses, to separate the mothers-to-be, clucking that they shouldn't exert themselves, they should consider their babies, and sent them to their rooms. At Perfume Bay, the mothers were treated like children, so that their children would obtain the most precious gift of all: American citizenship.

After Scarlett left China, she and Boss Yeung had grown apart, talking only every few days on video calls. Without proximity, without work in common, they discussed nothing but her pregnancy, and how irresponsible she was. Tonight, his bullfrog voice rumbled over the crackly Internet connection. "Have you eaten?" he asked. He sat in his office, his own lunch, a chipped plastic bowl of rice and soup from the factory cafeteria, untouched on his desk.

She hesitated. If she told him she fell asleep and missed dinner, he would chide her for denying their son nutrition. Sequestered at Perfume Bay, she'd become a modern-day concubine, her existence reduced to a single purpose: to produce the heir.

If she couldn't please him while pregnant, she never would as a mother. She'd lose any chance of a future together. Mama Fang had promised not to tell him about the catfight in her daily report, but would expect a favor in return. Boss Yeung adjusted the webcam. Scarlett turned her head to hide the bruise blooming on her cheek. She had been drawn to his intensity, that seriousness of purpose. He could be decisive to the point of brusqueness, a trait she had recognized in herself and had admired in him until he started turning on her.

On the video call, his handsome face pixelated, breaking up, as though in a time-lapse film of decay. He was insisting on the name Yaoxi for their son, which meant "to shine on the West."

"I'll call him what I want," Scarlett said. The baby's birthplace shouldn't define him. She wanted him free to go anywhere, to be anyone, and hadn't yet picked a name. Settling on one would define a life that still felt limitless.

He thumped the desk, and the chopsticks clattered off the bowl. The screen locked up, freezing his expression into a snarl. Scarlett steeled herself. During her pregnancy, he had grown accustomed to giving her orders, and he wouldn't stop after she delivered, not unless she stood up to him now.

When the video transmission resumed, Boss Yeung stared at Scarlett, and she quickly brought up her hand to cover the swelling and the inky bruise.

"What happened?" he asked. "To your face."

"Nothing." She dropped her hand, her cheeks hot. "The connection's bad."

"You fell."

She nodded. Better if he believed her clumsy rather than violent.

"Selfish," he said. She understood. If she'd been more careful, if she'd been thinking about their son, she wouldn't have fallen. "I won't let you ruin him." With a hiss of disgust, he logged off.

He wasn't the usual factory boss, paunchy and red-faced from too much drink, sunburned from golf, with a clutch of fawning concubines, one for every night of the week. With high cheekbones and deep-set, watchful eyes, he had the look of a Mongolian warlord. Scarlett curled onto her side, pinned down by her belly, feeling as though she might never rise again. She'd pictured herself someday with a settled life, with a husband—someone solid as Boss Yeung, if not him exactly—a home, and a family. Now someday had arrived with nothing except the baby.

The pregnancy had come between them. She buried her face into the pillow. She couldn't escape Perfume Bay's bitter scent of herbs, which reminded her of her mother's foul medicinal brews. A lifetime ago, she'd stopped relying on Ma, and yet now she wanted her mother's fingers cool against her cheek, applying a poultice that would harden against her skin, crack off, and relieve the pain.

Something scratched the walls of Perfume Bay, branches in the wind or a burrowing rodent that would gnaw at Scarlett in the dark. She had been dreaming of spies peering into her window, of cameras hidden in the overhead light, of an eye in the sky. After a hard kick from her *xiao dou*, her little bean, Scarlett gasped. Did Little Bean dream of what lay beyond the murk? More kicks pummeled her from the inside, and she pressed her hand against an unyielding elbow or knee. Back and forth they pushed until the baby squirmed away, and they both drifted off to sleep.

The next morning, the nurses passed around the newborns just back from the hospital. For Scarlett, Perfume Bay had been a crash course in motherhood. She'd learned that while each newborn was much like the others, with a scrunched monkey face and oversized, lolling head topped by an identical blue-and-red striped knit hat, each little roly-poly body wrapped in an identical blue-and-red striped receiving blanket, she was still expected to exclaim superlatives for each one.

The other guests gasped at the bruise on her cheek, which looked even worse today, and Countess Tien fussed over Lady Yu. Although Scarlett tried to appear unbowed and unapologetic, she seethed at herself for losing her temper. *Diu lian*, loss of face, shameful to fight with Lady Yu.

Scarlett didn't say the courtly titles she'd given the other ladies out loud, but she could think of them no other way. Her secret taunt, for how they carried themselves like descendants of the royal line. With her bejeweled hands, Lady Yu cradled Countess Tien's baby. Her pinched features softened as she touched his nose. "What a noisy thing!" she said, careful not to attract the attention of jealous spirits with praise. She could soothe the fussiest infant, while Scarlett's own lack of interest in children seemed a personal failing.

In her two decades away from her home village, she hadn't spent much time with children, and their laughs, their screams, and their whines seemed to belong in a realm that she watched but did not herself inhabit. New waves of teenage migrant workers arrived daily in the factory cities, and after a few years, some returned to their provinces to marry. If they came back to the city, their children remained in the village, in the care of grandparents. They saw their children only during the Spring Festival, crawling one year, running the next, and they brought them toys and clothes that were already outgrown upon arrival. The fate that Scarlett's baby would have had, if Boss Yeung hadn't been the father.

Bundled up, in slippers and a Perfume Bay velour tracksuit, Countess Tien had taken the most traditional precautions to rest in the month after delivery, forgoing showers and outings, as though she were living in the Ming dynasty, without the benefit of indoor plumbing, clean water, or science. Precautions Boss Yeung wanted for Scarlett, too.

Countess Tien fretted whether her son's wife, decades from now, would demonstrate proper respect to her. "She won't look after me, not like a daughter."

"Who says a daughter has to look after her mother?" Daisy slouched in a chair in the corner. Privately, Scarlett agreed, even though Daisy was their collective nightmare, the troubled teen that their babies each had the potential to become. Her parents must have sent her to Perfume Bay to hide her condition. She twirled her pigtails. "Mine can go to hell."

Neither she nor Scarlett were moneyed married wives, not like the other guests. Surprisingly nimble late in her third trimester, Daisy had the build of a gymnast but for her basketball belly. From behind, she didn't look pregnant, not like Scarlett whose hips, buttocks, and thighs had swelled like a bear fattening for hibernation. After Daisy had been caught sneaking out, Mama Fang had installed bars on the windows of her room.

Everyone ignored Daisy, and the theoretical daughter-in-law continued to vex Countess Tien. "What if she turns my son against me?"

"Disown him," Lady Yu declared.

Mama Fang peered over her bifocals at Countess Tien. "To please your son, she'll have to please you."

On the muted television, children danced, the girls in sequined crop tops and miniskirts over shorts, and the boys in tracksuits. Lady Yu pointed to the center of the stage. "That girl has glasses!" Chinese parents were blunt when it came to calling out physical imperfections in children. Their weight, their eyesight, their teeth, assessed like any other possession.

Countess Tien's baby farted, loud as a bicycle horn, creating the snickering commotion that Scarlett needed to excuse herself. When the other guests engaged in mind-numbing talk of colic remedies, potty training, and educational toys, she wanted to flee. Motherhood and its self-sacrifice still seemed remote.

She began edging off the couch, but Mama Fang stopped her, depositing the baby into her arms. "You need practice." Relentless, she reminded Scarlett of those cunning grannies in the ancient tales, who enabled liaisons between maidens and masters, traded gossip for taels of silver, the go-betweens who weren't the villains or the heroes but upon whom the plot hinged.

Mama Fang carried three passports—U.S., Panama, and Hong Kong—and like a movie action hero or container ship, freely chose which flag to fly. On that premise, she'd founded Perfume Bay, because what parents wouldn't give a child every advantage within their reach?

She instructed Scarlett to support the head of the baby, who had the unfocused stare of a coma patient. He was exceptionally unattractive, with pin-thin limbs and a face mottled with autumn leaves of eczema. Scarlett clasped him against her chest. If she proved herself adept as a mother, Boss Yeung might turn reasonable. If he gave her a chance, she would offer him one, too.

The baby wore a 24-karat gold pendant stamped with his Chinese zodiac sign, the year of the snake. For their child, Boss Yeung had sent one fashioned out of a U.S. gold coin and embossed with bald eagles, one clutching branches in its talons and another roosting in a nest. Ugly and gaudy, it belonged around the neck of a chain-smoking Macau gambler, not their son.

The pacifier fell out of the baby's mouth, and when she tried to catch it one-handed, the baby slipped from her grasp. Thump. Facedown, spread-eagle on the carpet. Silence, utter silence, until he shrieked and everyone shouted at once: *Aiya! Gan shenma!*

Countess Tien wept, asking if he'd been hurt, if he'd have a flat nose. The other women leaned away, as if Scarlett were diseased. She bit her lip, dismayed. Mama Fang scooped him up and checked him over. He wasn't bleeding. He'd suffered a fright, nothing more. "Babies are sturdier than you think," she said lightly. "He has iron bones. An iron head."

Knotting her hands, Scarlett squeezed until the bones ground together. Her hands had been busy and useful until she became pregnant, and the pain now cut through the numbness that had settled over her at Perfume Bay. Countess Tien kissed the top of her baby's head and insisted on going to the emergency room. Mama Fang summoned the van to take them there, arranged for an herbal potion to calm the countess, wrapped the baby in a red quilted blanket, and as she followed them out the door, distracted him with a rattle drum, the tiny beads pattering like rain.

# Chapter 2

Inside the examination room, the tech squirted warm jelly onto Scarlett's belly, tattooed with the dark line of pregnancy. Scarlett had requested an ultrasound a week ahead of schedule because she yearned to see her baby. The local clinic had Chinese doctors and staff, and the tech, Gigi, was originally from Chengdu. Within minutes, she'd shared her life story, how she'd come to Los Angeles on a special nursing visa, how her wages kept her family's hotpot restaurant afloat and her brother in school.

Scarlett soon stopped listening. She had to leave Perfume Bay before she went crazy, before she hurt anyone else. She had a temper, but she'd never been one to catfight. Always restless, she was now skidding out of control, a scooter on gravel. She'd dropped a baby! She wanted to fly to Hong Kong and decide what to do next, but if she stayed here beyond her thirty-sixth week, which began in a few days, no airline would let her board.

Mama Fang held everyone's wallets, passports, and their cash in the safe in her office, part of her pledge to take care of every detail. That meant Scarlett couldn't pay for the fare and couldn't leave the country. And if she asked Boss Yeung for a ticket, he'd refuse.

The waxy tissue paper on the exam table crinkled beneath her. She would have to think of another way to find help, to play the part of a pregnant woman in distress. She could hitch a ride to the airport, but still, what of the ticket and the passport? Her mother would have to go into debt to assist her, if she could get in touch with Ma at all. She'd given her mother a mobile phone, but Ma always kept it turned off; she didn't know how to check her voicemail although Scarlett had shown her dozens of times. Ma didn't know she was in America. Except for Boss Yeung, no one else in China did, either, not her co-workers, not her neighbors.

The tech circled the wand around Scarlett's navel. In China, Boss Yeung had bribed the nurse with a *hong bao*, a red envelope of lucky money, to give a secret sonogram. Her mystery, put on display. The government forbade sex identification, to prevent parents from aborting girls.

When told they were having a boy, Boss Yeung had bowed his head and clasped his hands to his mouth, speechless. His face had seemed almost young, and so unguarded she wanted to run her thumb along his jaw, to stroke the curve of his brows and down his nose and press this memory into her flesh. She'd never made him so happy, and never would again. After that day, after he'd peered inside her, he acted as if he had a right to her every thought, to her every move.

This machine was much fancier, with a large screen bright as a winter moon. Her baby would be bigger now, his features defined, his limbs longer, and body plump, in her second sonogram, the last before he emerged from between her legs.

She wished she could have told Ma. Her mother worked at a family planning clinic, tracking pregnancies throughout the district. The people had to sacrifice, *chi ku*, to eat bitterness for the sake of their country, and the more you defied Ma at the clinic, the harder she struck back. To enforce the one-child policy, she escalated her punishments: she issued fines to the schoolteacher who refused to urinate in front of her during the pregnancy test and to the teenager discovered in the fields screwing a man who wasn't her husband. If you didn't show up for your abortion, she locked up your parents in a dank cinder-block cell beside the clinic.

If anyone found out that her own daughter was pregnant and unmarried, Ma might lose the grim job that had sustained her as

Scarlett never had all these years. If Scarlett had gone to her for help, Ma might have forced her to end the pregnancy.

"How much does Mama Fang charge?" Gigi asked. Having shared the details of her finances, she had no qualms asking about Scarlett's.

"Twenty-five thousand dollars." Years of Scarlett's salary.

"*Waaah!*" Gigi exclaimed. She pressed the wand down hard against the lower curve of Scarlett's belly. "So expensive! You know, you can deliver for free."

Scarlett winced from the pressure. "Free?"

"Some people just go to the emergency room when they're in labor. The hospital can't turn you away, even if you can't pay. Even if you're not an American."

She had to be wrong. Boss Yeung wouldn't have spent so much on Perfume Bay if labor and delivery services were free in the United States. A black-and-white blur appeared onscreen, and Scarlett felt like a bride in an arranged marriage just before the red silk is lifted to reveal her husband's face. What if the tech found something wrong, what if his arm had shriveled, a hole was hollowed out of his heart, or a cleft palate twisted his lips? With each pass of the wand, Scarlett glimpsed a fish-bone spine, the cap of the skull, and the limbs folded like an umbrella, in a silvery shaft of light. The blobby images had little relation to the kicks and flutters deep within her, the secret connection that she and the baby shared that no machine could record.

"She's a swimmer," Gigi said. "Really moving around today."

*She.*

The other sonogram. "They said I was having a boy."

Mistakes happen all the time, Gigi said. "It can be hard to read."

"Maybe you made a mistake."

"Not today." Gigi pointed an arrow at the baby's crotch, at the three white lines that marked her sex. "Not this far along. She's practically posing for us."

Gigi showed her the baby's face, ghostly through the static, a broadcast from a distant planet: the pointed chin, Scarlett's, and the squat nose, Boss Yeung's. The tech hit a button and the machine spat out grainy images.

Scarlett couldn't breathe, couldn't move. If she so much as turned her head, she might topple off the exam table. She stared at the three lines, the sonogram exposing the parts she'd never gotten a clear view of on herself, exposing yet another daughter for Boss Yeung. A girl. A girl like her. Sharing her blood, her breath, her flesh.

If—when—Boss Yeung disowned his bastard, her daughter would need every privilege American citizenship afforded her. Scarlett couldn't risk him summoning her back to China and demanding a refund from Mama Fang. She reached for her purse, on a shelf by the examination table, and dug around until she found the velvet box. Her T-shirt slid onto her sticky belly, clinging and clammy.

"Are you sure it's not a boy?" Scarlett pulled out the gold necklace.

"A girl." Gigi nudged the arrow again. "Three lines."

Scarlett turned her cheek into the light, toward Gigi. The bruise from the catfight was fading but visible. She wanted the tech to understand the danger she was in. "It's a boy." The heavy pendant swung through her fingers, twisting and glimmering.

Gigi slipped the necklace into her pocket with an ease that made Scarlett wonder if the young woman had taken gifts from other expectant mothers with secrets of their own. "Congratulations."

On Thursday, at six A.M., on the ninth day of the seventh lunar month, Lady Yu had an appointment to deliver her son, a day shy of her thirty-ninth week. Almost all the women at Perfume Bay booked their C-sections in advance. Some like Lady Yu had previously given birth via C-section, and others wanted to remove the pain and unpredictability of going into labor and make sure their child's birthday fell on an auspicious date.

The mothers-to-be wanted to ensure their children weren't born on the *seventh* day of the seventh month, the night of the Magpie Festival. On that day in the village, Scarlett and the other girls used to pray for a good husband, newlyweds wished the gods would grant them a happy marriage, and elders told children the legend as romantic as it was tragic. Long ago, two lovers—a humble cow herder and a weaver girl, a fairy in disguise—were torn apart when the Goddess of Heaven, the fairy's mother, scratched her hairpin into the night sky, welling up a river of stars to separate them. Once a year, on the night of the festival, magpies would soar to the heavens, hovering wing to wing. The lovers crossed the universe on this quivering bridge of feathers and reunited for a kiss.

Lady Yu didn't want her son's fate linked to this day. Although he might not marry until two or three decades from now, she would align the heavens in his favor. After all she'd spent on fertility treatments, she considered Perfume Bay a bargain: giving your child U.S. citizenship at birth for twenty-five thousand dollars, compared to the hassles of the green-card program she'd heard about that required you to invest a half-million dollars, create at least ten new jobs, and then wait a few more years to obtain U.S. citizenship.

She wasn't planning to emigrate, but wanted her family to collect passports as they might Ferraris or residences in New York and London. No riches cleared smoggy skies, no riches protected against tainted milk, no riches safeguarded against the poor who might rise again in China. Only your child's American citizenship defended you from all your present and future ills.

On Tuesday evening—two days before the scheduled C-section— Nurse Sun wanted to send Lady Yu to the hospital because her blood pressure had risen and her feet had become puffy as steamed bread. Scarlett wondered if their catfight had caused the symptoms. Lady Yu refused to go. She didn't have a headache, blurry vision, or pain on her right side, none of the riskier signs of preeclampsia. "The baby will wait," she said at dinner, imperious, as though she sat in a sedan chair and not on a donut-shaped hemorrhoid cushion. Lady Yu wasn't going into the operating room today, not on the unlucky seventh day of the seventh month, and not when her physician was unavailable.

Mama Fang hardened her jaw. She didn't like being challenged, but must have understood that if Lady Yu enjoyed her stay, she would bring in many new customers. Scarlett stirred her soup, spongy fish bladders and lily bulbs boiled with pork bones. She was long accustomed to eating every part of the animal, but this menu—

despite its benefits to pregnant women and new mothers—must be hard on the delicate stomachs of the other guests.

Countess Tien massaged her hands, complaining her fingers ached. She'd developed her own physical therapy for the baby Scarlett had dropped. For an hour each day, she pinched her son's nose to straighten it, as he flailed his arms and legs in protest.

A crash outside made everyone jump in their seats. Mama Fang's lanyard snagged on the spindle of her chair, jerking back her head. Rubbing her neck, she set the keys on the counter before peering out the patio door.

"Hello? Who's there?" She disappeared outside.

"Did you see him? That man?" Countess Tien said. "I saw his reflection in my window the other night."

"*Nali!*" Nothing, Lady Yu said. "You're dreaming."

The keys to Mama Fang's office. To the safe. To freedom.

Before Scarlett could brush against the keys, push them behind the hot water dispenser to fetch later, Mama Fang returned. She washed her hands in the sink and slipped the keys around her neck. "Raccoons. Knocked over the can. Garbage everywhere."

Scarlett bit back her disappointment. As much as she wanted to flee Perfume Bay, she had to remain here until after delivery. Boss Yeung could love a daughter; she'd seen the softness in his face when his eldest called. When Scarlett and the baby returned to China, he would forgive the misfortune of her gender.

Scarlett's ambivalence about the pregnancy had been a kind of grief, she had come to see. Because Boss Yeung had claimed the boy wholly, it felt like she'd already lost the baby. A daughter was hers to protect.

Mama Fang ladled soup into Daisy's bowl.

"More soup?" the teenager asked.

At least it wasn't a dish that tasted like baby food; many meals at Perfume Bay were steamed and mashed. The cook's constant boiling soured the air with wine, ginger, and vinegar, and fed mold that slicked the kitchen walls. Daisy pushed her bowl aside, sloshing soup onto the tablecloth, and tucked back her overgrown bangs. Her barbs were hollow and halfhearted, tinged with misery after her failed escape. The other guests wanted nothing to do with her.

Daisy's jailbreak must remind them of their own captivity, a condition they'd rather not consider closely.

Daisy needed a mother in a house full of mothers and mothers-to-be. Scarlett tried to catch her eye, puckering her mouth to show her shared distaste for the soup. The teenager flipped her off. Brat.

After dinner, Mama Fang followed Scarlett, asking how she felt, how she slept. As much as she hovered during the day, she typically didn't come into their rooms. She led Scarlett to bed, tucking pillows around her to take pressure off her joints. "Sleep with one between your legs, one behind your back, and between your arms. Feels like someone's holding you. When men aren't around, women find a way."

Mama Fang sat on the edge of the bed, wafting a granny's scent of medicinal herbs. "Strong women, like you. Like us."

Scarlett tensed, wondering why she'd taken this sudden interest in her.

"You left home young, didn't you?" Mama Fang asked. White roots peeped out from her hairline, above a forehead smooth as tofu pudding. She might have been in her mid-fifties. Judging from her hands—thick and strong from hard labor that probably started when she was a girl—she hadn't led a pampered life. If Papa Fang existed, he never visited, and Mama Fang never spoke of him. Maybe, before founding Perfume Bay, she'd run a brothel. Maybe she'd been a rich man's mistress and cashed in jewelry to open the center.

"Young as Daisy," Scarlett said. "Younger."

"Me too." Mama Fang said she had worked as a maid in the home of a wealthy Hong Kong family. "It was—"

"The others here, they never worked," Scarlett said.

Mama Fang pursed her lips. She didn't expect to be interrupted. Yes, yes, she said, and continued her story. She'd been very lonely, but the family's son was kind to her. After he'd gotten her pregnant, she gave the baby to his family. "I did it for my boy," Mama Fang said. "You can do it for yours."

Too stunned to speak, Scarlett let the words sink in.

Boss Yeung wanted to raise the baby, Mama Fang said, and give him a life of comfort and security. "You'll be free," Mama Fang said.

Free, along with a twenty-thousand-dollar gift for her sacrifice and for her silence.

Scarlett knew at once he'd been too much of a coward to ask himself. He must have enlisted Mama Fang, who would perform any service, sell anything, anyone for an additional fee.

"He—" Scarlett couldn't bring herself to say more, but Mama Fang seemed to understand.

She put her hand on Scarlett's arm. Her touch was more comforting than Scarlett would have expected.

"You can travel," Mama Fang said. "Buy a condo or open a shop with the money."

For once, she hadn't sounded so grasping. She also must have been a woman scorned, paid off by a wealthy family, and she was offering advice to her younger self. Her voice softened. "If you want to become a partner at Perfume Bay, I welcome you. You, me: there's so much possibility."

Scarlett's shock turned to rage. Mama Fang was counseling her with one hand in Scarlett's pocket and the other in Boss Yeung's. Flailing like a dung beetle, she tried to sit up, resisting Mama Fang's attempts to help her. Scarlett hated her. She hated him. She hated herself for being tempted by what this money could buy: a new car, time off for a year or more, and an apartment for Ma who could quit her job at the clinic. Fantasizing only for a moment, but still a moment. In suspecting she might be a gold digger, Boss Yeung had turned her into one. She swung her legs around, her joints creaking, feeling jumbled as a bundle of sticks.

They both stood. "My daughter, you don't need to be ashamed," Mama Fang said. "Some women aren't meant to hold babies."

"I'll learn." Scarlett choked out the words. "You said I'd learn."

"After what happened, the honorable Master Yeung worried about his baby, but I told him we're monitoring you closely." Mama Fang sighed, seeing Scarlett's outrage. "I had to tell him. The bill, for the emergency room. For the tests. If he had you declared a threat to your child, you'd lose your son."

*Your son.* Boss Yeung didn't know Scarlett carried a girl. As soon as he did, he and his money would disappear. He'd end Scarlett's stay at Perfume Bay. She had to get as much as she could from him before he discovered the truth. Mama Fang studied her as though Scarlett were a salt-and-pepper crab and she wanted to extract every last morsel out of her.

"More," Scarlett said. "I want more. If you get me more, then—"

Mama Fang took out a red envelope from her jacket pocket, bulging with hundred-dollar bills. If Scarlett signed the papers giving up her rights by tomorrow, she'd convinced Boss Yeung to add a three-thousand-dollar bonus. "To show he's taking care of you."

She must have secured a bonus for herself, too. She placed the envelope in Scarlett's hand, closed her fingers around it, and gave what she must consider the highest compliment of all. "We think alike. Never settle for the first offer."

Scarlett forced herself to smile and clasped her hands with Mama Fang's. At that moment, she heard the door slam, then someone blunder down the hall, with heavy footfalls that sounded like the erratic raps of a ghost. In the hallway, they found Lady Yu barefoot and groping the wall. She was panting, heaving, and she stank of vomit. Mama Fang touched her arm, and Lady Yu collapsed and slid to the floor. Other guests closed in, a tangle of bellies and arms. Mama Fang shouted at them to get back and when they withdrew, Lady Yu was grimacing, moaning with her eyes closed, pounding the heel of her palm to her forehead as if she might knock out the pain. Mama Fang's bifocals had fallen to the floor, and a cracked lens had popped out of the frame. Nurse Sun ran in, huffing, the pink tunic of her uniform covered in spit-up.

"Call an ambulance!" Countess Tien shouted.

"911," Daisy said. "Call 911."

Mama Fang didn't want to get authorities involved, Scarlett could tell, when she announced that she and Nurse Sun would take Lady Yu. Except that Mama Fang couldn't drive, because her glasses were broken, and Nurse Sun, the only one on duty, didn't know how. She was the youngest on staff, a newlywed and new to the United States, and her husband drove her to and from work. The babies, unattended in the nursery, started wailing. Mama Fang dangled the keys and asked if anyone knew how to drive.

Scarlett owed them nothing. Not Mama Fang, who'd sold her out, not Lady Yu, who'd schemed against her. Scarlett wanted the police to expose Mama Fang and shut down Perfume Bay, but if she didn't drive—now—Lady Yu and her baby might die. She took the keys from Mama Fang. Outside, she hoisted herself into the old van, the seat an uninterrupted expanse from door to door, long and wide enough for someone to take a nap. She'd never driven a vehicle this big, ungainly as an ox. After pulling up to the front door of Perfume Bay, she had to pee. She'd developed the bladder of an incontinent granny. She hobbled inside, where Nurse Sun was trying to maneuver the wheelchair through the living room. Every time the nurse bumped into furniture, Lady Yu slipped toward the floor. When Scarlett emerged from the bathroom, Nurse Sun had her arms around Lady Yu's waist. From behind, Mama Fang had hooked her arms under Lady Yu's shoulders.

They followed Scarlett to the van, Mama Fang climbing beside her into the front passenger seat, and Lady Yu leaning on Nurse Sun in the back. The other guests gathered in the headlights, clutching babies rescued from the nursery. They feared for their friend, and feared for themselves even more, realizing, as Scarlett had, the danger they were in as pregnant women. She, like everyone else here, had believed herself safe, yielding to the illusion that giving birth was under her control, if only she ate a certain combination of foods, swallowed certain herbs, and performed certain exercises. In truth, their bodies had been overtaken.

The residential streets of this hilly neighborhood were dark, without streetlights, and when Scarlett made a right turn out of the driveway, the front tire jumped the curb, throwing everyone back in their seats. By tomorrow, she'd have a bruise on her chest where the seatbelt held her. In pregnancy, blood seemed closer to the surface of her skin, as close as her emotions, pumping like a fire hose through her body. Lady Yu groaned noisily. Overwhelmed, Scarlett screeched to a halt and took her hands off the wheel. If she got into an accident, if the police pulled her over, she'd be detained and possibly arrested. What if she was deported? Her daughter would lose her chance for American citizenship.

"Breathe," Mama Fang told Scarlett. "In through the nose. Out through the mouth. Breathe." She repeated, Scarlett followed and eased off the brake. Traffic was light, and with each block, her speed and confidence grew.

At the hospital, Mama Fang dashed into the emergency room, and orderlies emerged with a gurney to fetch Lady Yu. When an ambulance appeared in her rearview mirror, Scarlett drove the van into a red zone and left the engine running, rather than find a parking spot. She didn't know how long Mama Fang would be inside the building. She hit the wipers, which sprayed and swept the windshield clean, and turned on the radio, spinning the dial until she landed on a rock music station. She adjusted her seat, belt, and mirrors, feeling like an astronaut harnessed in a space capsule before blastoff.

The car behind her honked and she pulled ahead, pushing lightly on the gas. The van glided to the end of the aisle, all but driving itself. The engine throbbed through her, power restrained, though at the ready, urging her on. America called to her: the land of cars, of fast highways that opened up the country that she'd always wanted to explore, the country where she could make a life for her daughter. She could keep going, she *would* keep going, over the speed bump, out of the parking lot, onto the street, and into the unknown.

Heading east, she hit all green lights, the road stretching endlessly ahead. Unrolling the window, she let in the breeze and drummed her fingers against the side of the van. Each beat matched her pounding heart. She brushed her hand across the red envelope stowed in the inner pocket of her tracksuit jacket and then accelerated, the lights around her blurring into stars.

# Chapter 3

**The Grand Canyon** beckoned. Las Vegas, San Francisco, New York, and the White House, every destination Boss Yeung had promised they would visit together. The names sounded like an incantation—Niagara Falls, Yellowstone—and were the closest to marriage vows that would ever pass between them.

New York had the Statue of Liberty, the Empire State Building, yellow cabs, and a Chinatown, where people could tell her how to find housing, a doctor, and other services for those underground, but the drive to New York would take at least five days, likely more. Her back ached, as if clamped in a vise, and she needed to pee again. The baby rode on her bladder, and in her travels, she'd have to stop as frequently as a city bus in rush hour. And what if the van's engine died, stranding her along the side of the road?

A car honked and she sped up. She couldn't risk getting pulled over by police. She squinted at a sign on the intersection. None of the words were familiar and she couldn't tell what direction she was headed. Las Vegas was east of Los Angeles, wasn't it? She'd changed planes there, waiting in the terminal long enough to try a slot machine that ate her dollar. Housing would be cheap and plentiful—she'd seen the grid of subdivisions across the desert from the air—but she didn't want to give birth in a city built on illusion and loss. Her daughter might as well stake a claim to a mighty city, a storied city known the world over, even if Scarlett moved on soon after.

*After.* She couldn't predict the outcome of the next hour, let alone the next month, the next year, the decades in which she would be watching over her daughter. She rolled up her window. She couldn't stay in Los Angeles. Mama Fang must have contacts among the Chinese here, the shop owners and restaurateurs who would keep an eye out for a hugely pregnant woman in exchange for a reward.

She choked back a sob. Despite everything, she wanted nothing more than to fall asleep in the passenger seat while Boss Yeung drove, the heat turned on high, music low, her head against the cool glass. He'd been rugged, resilient as a mountain. It would be a very long time, if ever, before she might be a passenger again, before she would ever feel so protected. If only she hadn't agreed to come to Perfume Bay. Far from him, she had become a line item, a unit of sale. If only he hadn't listened to his friend Uncle Lo—an investor in Perfume Bay and founder of a media empire that spanned Asia and beyond—who'd recommended sending her here.

The golden arches loomed on the corner, familiar like nothing else had been all night, and Scarlett turned into the lot. Due in less than a month, she couldn't get far, not tonight, not when exhaustion drew her under. Not for a while, and the loss of the road trip she'd considered just now was a disappointment as great as any she'd already suffered. Boss Yeung would never accept her refusal of his bribe. Men like him were used to taking what they wanted, and she knew he'd come after her. She'd put as much distance as she could between herself and Perfume Bay, and decide tomorrow where she might find safe, secret harbor.

McDonald's was crowded, though it was past nine. Perfume Bay served dinner early, to ensure early bedtimes, and the full tables reminded her that the world she'd left had carried on. In the bathroom, she splashed water onto her face, trying to wake up. The bruise from her catfight with Lady Yu was fading away, but her eyes were puffy, and she was moonfaced, haggard. She'd aged a decade in a day.

Maybe she should have a Coke. A Coke! Above the counter, the menu dazzled, with pictures of hamburger buns puffy as blimps, and drinks glistening with condensation like morning dew. Her mouth watered. Pointing to what she wanted, she ordered a soda and a small bag of fries, and paid with a hundred-dollar bill from the wad tucked into her jacket.

She should tape the money into the waistband of her underpants. No thief—no one but a doctor or nurse—would root near her crotch and risk a baby tumbling out. Stepping away from the counter, she greedily dug into the fries, scorching her fingers. The scent was golden as a day at the beach, a scent that coated her tongue with the savory promise of grease and held both the wonder of the first bite and the satisfaction of the last. The salt was gritty against her tongue, the fry crisply giving way under her teeth, the fluffy interior a starchy cloud of potato, the taste of earth and sea.

She gulped the Coke, sweet and bubbly, a kick to the brain. A switch flipped and color returned to her black-and-white world. How muted, how miserable she'd been at Perfume Bay! She hadn't consumed caffeine in months because coffee, tea, and soda were forbidden. Fried foods, too. According to the tenets of Chinese medicine, such dishes stoked internal fires, causing nosebleeds, blemishes, and worse. Superstition. Or maybe not? Scarlett had been uncertain enough to obey.

With each bite, she cursed Boss Yeung. With each bite, she cursed Mama Fang, and by the time she reached the exit, she'd finished the bag of fries. She returned to the counter and ordered another—supersized. Glorious: the glossy red box, striped yellow-and-white inside. When she'd first arrived in the factory city, fast-food trash had awed her: the shiny wrappers and waxy cups were finer, brighter than anything in her village. Even into her twenties, sometimes she'd pretended she was eating at a McDonald's in Manhattan or Paris, as if the golden arches were a magic portal that she might slip through to the other side of the planet. She now knew escape never came as easily as closing your eyes and wishing yourself elsewhere.

Another customer waited for her order. Her son, standing beside her, might have been eight. They both had the same stocky build, the same narrow nose. His head bowed, his eyes locked on his comic book. "Boy or a girl?" the woman asked.

That much, Scarlett understood. Girl, she said. Sharing the news for the first time, she felt a fluttering excitement. So much of her pregnancy had been in secret until now.

"A girl!" The woman offered what must have been congratulations.

After pumping ketchup on top of her fries, Scarlett left McDonald's with lightness in her step. A stranger wishing her well turned her hopeful she might find her way in the world again. She licked her fingers, savoring the sweet tang. The van's alarm went off, bleating and insistent, and she fumbled for the keys, the noise escalating. To her shock, the rear doors opened and out slid Daisy.

Scarlett called her name, but Daisy took off running. She went after Daisy in a ridiculous low-speed chase, two women late in their third trimester, ungainly, treading water on land. Joints jangling, hips off-kilter, Scarlett felt like a hula hoop swinging out of control. Panting, they stopped after a few meters, eying each other. Daisy bristled with flight and fight. Scarlett broke the standoff by tipping her take-out bag toward Daisy, who glanced around with suspicion until she couldn't resist. She stuffed fistfuls of fries into her mouth, her eyes closed in ecstasy. During the commotion at Perfume Bay, she must have sneaked into the van.

"Where were you headed?" Scarlett asked.

Daisy didn't answer. She was American by birth. Her parents had been living in Illinois when she was born, while her father studied for his engineering doctorate. The family returned to Taiwan when Daisy was two months old and hadn't been back to the United States since. Lady Yu and Countess Tien had considered her a snob, in that enmity between mainlanders and those whose families fled across the straits to Taiwan after the civil war.

She was the youngest guest at Perfume Bay, and used to attend a fancy international school in Taipei, where the latest American slang circulated in the hallways, where admissions required every student to hold a foreign passport, keeping out locals without the resources to give birth to their children abroad, without second homes in Los Angeles and New York. The kind of school found in cosmopolitan cities where Boss Yeung had wanted to send their son.

In this, Daisy seemed as privileged as the other guests at Perfume Bay. But like Scarlett, she'd kept to herself, never spoke of her baby's father, and never spoke of future plans. They were alike in their defiance and determination, and maybe in other ways, too. Daisy drained the Coke.

"Meeting someone?" Scarlett asked, over the squawk of the drive-through speakers. The headlights of a passing car strobed over her face. "Is someone coming for you?"

Daisy eyed her, probably deciding whether she could trust her. The teenager attracted trouble and sought it out in equal measure. Scarlett would have to drop her off at the Taiwan consulate, where officials could tame a wayward minor. Daisy opened her mouth, as if to plead—and then vomited: the fries, the Coke, her fear, everything that must be churning inside her.

If Scarlett had been maternal, if she'd been sisterly, she might have gathered up Daisy's hair and rubbed her back, but she did not. She turned away from the mess, gasping, trying not to vomit herself. Daisy shuddered and stepped away from the pool on the asphalt. She wiped her mouth with the back of her hand, sipped the Coke, and grimaced.

The McDonald's security guard ran up. He asked her something in English and stared at her cup. He must suspect that she was drunk.

Daisy straightened and made what sounded like an apology. He rubbed his scraggly blond goatee, and asked another question. Did he say "doctor"? Probably he'd asked if she needed a doctor.

Daisy shook her head. When he noticed Scarlett and her pregnant belly, he did a double take. Two pregnant women, in matching velour sweat suits with the Perfume Bay logo. Daisy carried high as the prow of a ship, Scarlett low as a turtle.

The guard studied them. He might have been trying to figure out if they were mother and daughter. Friends? Sister-wives or lovers? He would remember later if police came looking for them, if their disappearance hit the news.

"Mexico," Scarlett blurted.

"Mexico?" the guard asked.

Daisy gave her a quizzical look. In Chinese, Scarlett told her to ask for directions. They couldn't get across the border without their passports, but she wanted to throw off authorities.

The guard was shaped like a gourd, his pale cheeks dotted with zits, his complexion wan under the parking lot lights. After pointing down the road toward the freeway, he returned to his post by the door. Burping, Scarlett tasted fries, simultaneously savory and disgusting. She—and the baby—were hungry again. Later, she promised her daughter. More and more, she talked to her. She couldn't understand what the baby was saying or thinking, or feel what she was feeling, and the baby wouldn't remember her time in utero. But Scarlett wanted to imagine the mind of her daughter in ways she was sure her own mother had never tried to imagine hers.

Back at the van, they discovered it listing heavily to the right, the front tire sunken and torn away from the rim. Did someone sideswipe it or try to steal the tire?

"You hit the curb," Daisy reminded Scarlett.

Scarlett frowned, her body clammy. A pinball of a headache bumped around behind her eyes, the fries too rich after months of dining like a nun. She jerked open the back doors. No spare was visible, not on the door, not on the floor, and she cursed Mama Fang's stinginess.

Daisy trailed her fingers on the floor mat and tugged on the corner. Losing her grip, she stumbled backward. Scarlett caught her. "You'll end up like Lady Yu." Convulsing, rushed to the hospital and sliced open, her baby yanked out.

The mat, now askew, revealed a wheel tucked into a well. Together, they could pry it out. They'd have to squat and lift at a time when merely walking tested their balance. Daisy started to sob, leaving Scarlett at a loss, irritated that she had to contend with this girl's misery, too.

The guard came to their rescue, carrying a tall cup of lemon-lime soda. To settle Daisy's stomach, he said, while he worked on the tire. "Sorry we don't have ginger ale."

"Could I get a bottle of water?" Daisy asked. Her tears stopped. It seemed she'd been trying to get his help by crying melodramatically. "I'm really thirsty for water. The sweet might make me sick."

He jogged toward the door, and Scarlett scolded her. "Can't you take what's offered?"

"Everyone thinks asking for help puts you in debt. It's the opposite," Daisy said. "If someone helps you once, he'll keep helping you. He would have done the same for you, if you'd asked."

"Only if I were your age. Probably not then, either."

The guard disappeared inside the McDonald's, the door slamming behind him. "He's not keeping track of every little thing," Daisy said. "He's telling himself that I'm worth it, and wants to keep helping me. Otherwise, he's an idiot for helping me at all."

"You think Mama Fang isn't keeping track?" Scarlett asked. Her temples pounded.

"I don't owe her a thing." From her backpack, Daisy dug out a stack of passports and thumbed through them, the sound of the sliding covers like cards shuffling, the sound of possibility.

In her haste to get to the hospital, Mama Fang must have left her office unlocked. Daisy handed Scarlett her passport and then smiled, more resourceful than she seemed.


An hour later, when Daisy plucked the cheapest cellphone from the rack at the discount superstore, the clerk tried to convince her to upgrade. With his cloying cologne, slicked back hair, poufy white shirt, and thin mustache, he resembled a pirate.

"You'll be taking a lot of photos of the little one. You don't want to miss a thing."

They ignored him. Scarlett was sick of the clerk, of Mama Fang, of everyone who preyed on pregnant women to turn a profit. The loudspeaker blared an announcement. Daisy translated: the store would close in fifteen minutes, and shoppers should complete their purchases.

They had to get back on the road, but Daisy wanted to get a message to the father of her child. Just like her, he was ABC—American-born Chinese—though he'd grown up in a suburb outside of San Francisco, she told Scarlett. They met while he was attending a summer language program in Taipei. "I have to find him." She gripped the cellphone still encased in clear plastic.

As they passed the cosmetics aisle and its scent of possibility and hope, Daisy ducked in, murmuring she wanted to clean up before she sent her boyfriend a photo. Scarlett caught sight of herself in a warped plastic mirror, her skin greasy and hair stringy as a mop. Boss Yeung wouldn't recognize her; she hardly recognized herself. As a teenager, she used to change her style—panda-bear mascara, doll-pout lips, glam-rock aqua eye shadow, pants studded with rhinestones—to release the different selves clamoring within her. Pregnancy was a different costume altogether, one she couldn't shed at will. The taut belly she'd expected, but not the black line that bisected her. Even her feet became alien, swollen and creased.

Standing side by side, they stared in the mirror, their image blurred as if under water. When Scarlett tentatively smoothed Daisy's rumpled hair, the teenager swallowed, her eyes wet. They looked at each other, and in silent understanding, Daisy reached for a makeup tester. First the toner that she swept over Scarlett's face. Poured onto the white cotton pads, the toner had the grassy fragrance of purity and new beginnings. Scarlett sighed.

Although Mama Fang didn't prohibit makeup, the women of Perfume Bay didn't bother. They also didn't have to worry about keeping up with the latest fashions or maintaining their hair coloring, manicures, and pedicures, all those time-consuming grooming rituals forbidden because of the chemicals. Not like Mama Fang, who wore permanent makeup, her eyebrows plucked and shaved off and tattooed in surprise, and her dark-rimmed eyes with the furtive look of a raccoon. Given the chance, Scarlett would have slashed her face with red lipstick in revenge.

Daisy smoothed cream on the puffy skin below Scarlett's eyes and brushed powder over her face. A ticklish ritual, a blessing, to mark their return to the human race. She stroked Scarlett's wayward brows with the tip of her finger, slicked on cherry-scented pink gloss, and brushed on blush. Scarlett exhaled. "I could fall asleep standing up."

The loudspeaker crackled again: five minutes until closing. Scarlett applied Daisy's makeup quickly, with a heavy hand, and they both looked again into the dimpled mirror. Scarlett touched her own cheeks, caught herself and smiled, embarrassed to be primping. Daisy didn't know Scarlett's story, and Scarlett didn't know hers, but tonight their paths had merged.

Scarlett draped her hand on her belly, where her daughter was drumming out the song of her arrival. Soon. Soon. Soon. Stay inside, she told her daughter, where she could keep her safe, where she could keep her to herself.

The snack bar by the entrance had a popcorn machine, the smell of a movie theater, fake butter and salt. At the checkout, Daisy tore open the package to reach her new phone, ran her fingers over the buttons, and snapped a photo of herself from the waist up, in profile, and emailed it to her boyfriend. The response was immediate, as if he'd been waiting for her. She read the message and her excitement winked out. She showed it to Scarlett: *Error. Address not found.* She tried again with a messaging app, and then another, but couldn't find him.

He'd disappeared.

In the passenger seat, Daisy yawned and rubbed her eyes. Scarlett didn't know how she could take care of her daughter, let alone a teenager, too—a teenager who was also expecting. For more than half her life, Scarlett had been on her own. If Scarlett had gotten pregnant at Daisy's age, she never would have made it to the city. Her mother would have insisted she marry, sentencing Scarlett to a life in the village, or else she would have ended up at the clinic, getting scraped out. Either way, she would have lost the nerve to leave home.

Scarlett pulled out of the parking lot. As ably as Daisy had handled herself tonight, Scarlett wouldn't let the teenager slow down her escape from Boss Yeung. Daisy would have to find her boyfriend on her own. Scarlett suspected that soon enough, Daisy would move on. Reunite with her parents back home and leave her son with them, cared for by a team of *ayis*, while she resumed her life at school. Daisy didn't belong on the road, on the run. With a deep sigh, the teenager slumped over asleep, her mouth slack, her hands limp. In the light of morning, she would understand that fulfilling her prison term at Perfume Bay served the interests of all concerned. The van gently rocked, the engine rumbling in a lullaby. Scarlett turned down the radio and drove back the way she'd come.

The van slowed and Daisy jerked awake. Just after midnight, they were across the street from Perfume Bay. Scarlett hit a button to unlock the doors. "I'm sorry," she said, her voice hoarse with the ferocity of a mother.

Daisy unbuckled her seatbelt and lunged across the bench seat—her belly clearing the dash by millimeters—and hit the horn, three long blasts. "I'm not going back."

"You have to." Scarlett shoved Daisy's shoulder. Reaching her leg as far as it could go, Daisy stomped on the gas, jerked the steering wheel, and the van plowed into the neighbor's mailbox. A crash, and the mailbox toppled and scraped against the bumper. Scarlett hit the brake. More lights blinked on down the street. The front door of Perfume Bay swung open and Countess Tien peered out, cradling her wailing son. The other guests followed.

With Mama Fang still at the hospital and no one telling them what to do, they seemed lost as children in a fable. Daisy hit the gas again, and the wheels spun in place on the lawn, throwing up loamy earth and grass that spattered against the windshield. Deeper and deeper the tires sank. Scarlett released the brake and the van jounced onto the street. Daisy's foot slipped off the accelerator, and her hands flew up to protect her belly.

"Stop! Stop at once," Countess Tien shouted.

Scarlett took control, hitting the gas, tires squealing, stinking with burning rubber, and Daisy braced herself against the dashboard. The engine strained and then stampeded, hurling them forward. She'd have to struggle to force Daisy out of the van, and police might already be on the way. They peeled around the corner and took the next freeway on-ramp. Scarlett pounded on the steering wheel, furious. "You do whatever you want, because you know your parents will save you. The police will come after us."

"The police will come after Mama Fang." Daisy hastily explained that last week, when she'd run away to find her boyfriend, the neighbor across the street had taken her in. What was going on, he had asked. Why were there so many pregnant women at the house all the time?

"A hotel," she told him.

"Here?" he asked.

"For pregnant women."

He scowled and told her Perfume Bay's overflowing septic tank had spilled filth onto the adjoining lawns several times, stinking up the neighborhood.

Mama Fang had to be breaking the law, cramming too many guests into Perfume Bay. Daisy asked to borrow the neighbor's phone, but when she called her boyfriend's number, it wasn't in service. She had punched it in again, trying not to panic. Maybe his parents had canceled the account.

She'd looked back at Perfume Bay. "You want her out? I can help you. I'll get pictures from inside the house, and then you can take me to the bus station. Please?"

Sighing, he'd rummaged in a kitchen drawer and returned with a disposable camera. But when she tried to sneak back inside, Mama Fang had been waiting for her.

As Scarlett accelerated on the freeway, Daisy hastily buckled her seatbelt. "Remember the trash cans that fell at dinner?" Daisy asked.

"The raccoons."

"I bet it was the neighbor."

No one but Daisy had suspected he was going through the garbage to collect evidence. No one but Daisy had known he was spying on Perfume Bay and following the van on the way to the clinic. No one but Daisy had known, and she said nothing.

"After tonight, the neighbors will call the police," Daisy said. "Mama Fang will be ruined."

"You don't know that! You don't know a thing!"

"Mama Fang jailed us. Now we'll shut down Perfume Bay."

The other guests had conspired against them, fallen silent or turned their backs when they'd entered the room, Daisy said. They'd called Scarlett a *xiao san*, a little third. A mistress, a third party, small in every way: a young woman with a selfish heart and a lesser status. Surely, Scarlett must have heard them whispering. They'd called Daisy *xiao dangfu*, little slut.

Mama Fang would be unaware of the havoc they'd wreaked. By tomorrow, police would swarm Perfume Bay and take her in for questioning. By tomorrow, these pampered women and their spoiled babies would be forced onto the street.

As Daisy mimicked Countess Tien's high-pitched, haughty tone, they laughed, united against the world. Scarlett felt like a bottle of champagne shaken up, and yet she knew she could not let loose. Daisy was a danger to herself, to her son. She was rash, as rash as Scarlett when she'd left home for the factory city. Rash as when she'd started an affair with a married man. Rash as when she'd stolen the van and driven it into the night.

As they descended the steep mountain pass out of Los Angeles, the pains began. At first Scarlett blamed the change in altitude. She swallowed, her ears popping; they'd gained and lost more elevation than she realized. The winding road left the dun-colored hills and flattened out into a wide valley. How long the day, how vast this country. For now, despite her reservations, she'd accepted Daisy as a passenger. An unspoken agreement, by its nature nebulous and temporary, but all the agreement they needed to get through the first leg of this journey. Something or somebody must trouble Daisy back home, and Scarlett did not want to deliver her into harm.

They decided to drive to San Francisco, which had many Chinese, offering safety in numbers. Unlike Los Angeles, in San Francisco Mama Fang wouldn't have her fingers in every pot. They could hide from Boss Yeung while searching for Daisy's boyfriend. San Francisco, with its soaring Golden Gate Bridge and cable cars climbing over the hills, had the beauty and charm Scarlett wanted associated with her daughter.

Cars and semi trucks roared past, but she couldn't risk breaking the speed limit. A cramp hit, her pelvis clenching in a way that was familiar, though with an intensity that was not. Beads of sweat popped out on her forehead, and she took deep breaths as the tightness passed. She couldn't be going into labor. She wasn't ready to receive her daughter, not without a home safe from Boss Yeung, not without a name for her in Chinese or English. Her entire body ached, ever since they'd woken up at dawn in a warehouse parking lot in the outskirts of Los Angeles.

She turned on the radio, skittering through static to find a singer with a nasal twang strumming a guitar. She'd heard from the other guests at Perfume Bay that she had hours during a first-time delivery before she might start to push. Hours in which she might speed to safety. A day could pass between the first contraction and when the doctors would admit you to the hospital.

The tightness bore down, a screw turned once more, her pelvis a rag twisted into knots, her belly hard and immobile. She gasped and hunched over, trying to shrink herself, shrink the pain. The contraction hit before the song had ended, the intervals coming faster now. For much of her life, Scarlett had bluffed her way into jobs in which she lacked experience and credentials. Now her ignorance terrified her. If something was going wrong inside her, she wouldn't know. What if the umbilical cord knotted around the neck of her baby and the doctors had to cut her out?

Scarlett had never witnessed a birth firsthand, but back in the village, she'd overheard the screams of her neighbors, seen the blankets afterward covered in blood and shit. Sometimes after much pushing, the baby didn't come and the limp, howling mother would be packed off in a cart to the hospital. Sometimes mother and child returned. Just once, neither. Twice, the women returned alone, with empty arms and hollow eyes.

She never should have left Perfume Bay and the world-class services that Mama Fang provided. Daisy's hands hovered, ready to grab the wheel, while Scarlett steered the van to the next exit and parked on a dirt road fronting the fields. A hundred meters away, workers hunched over, weeding.

Had she been in labor since last night? Her trouble sleeping and the soreness in her body—had those been signs? The time she thought remained until delivery, gone in an instant. She doubled over the steering wheel, gripping until her knuckles turned white. Daisy rolled down her window, waving and shouting, "Help! Help!" at the workers. When she tried to honk the horn, Scarlett grabbed her wrist.

"Not here," she gasped. Not in the van, not in the fields, worse off than Ma, worse off than a peasant in the most modern country in the world. She slid out of the van and staggered to the passenger side, her thin bedroom slippers kicking up puffs of dust. "Drive."

"I can't," Daisy said.

"You have to."

"I've driven a moped, but—"

"You have to."

Daisy could only reach the pedals with the tips of her pointed toes. She slid down in the seat and stretched out her arms like a race-car driver. Barely able to see over the dash, she gunned down the dirt road, the van jouncing. Scarlett rocked against the door and bit her tongue. Blood flooded her mouth, the sinister taste of copper. "Where are you going?"

"Finding a place to turn around," Daisy said. The narrow road bordered fields that stretched toward the horizon, nowhere to swing the van around. She couldn't U-turn. She had to reverse, pull up, reverse and pull up. Each jolt shot up Scarlett's spine. Daisy overshot the road, and the rear left tire slipped onto the edge of the ditch. The windshield tilted up, the sunshine white and blinding, and she hit the gas.

"Stop!" Scarlett's alarm turned into agony.

"The freeway's ahead," Daisy said.

They were fighting for control of the steering wheel when a body hit the windshield. Scarlett covered her face with her hands. She couldn't bear to see the blood, the brains. The van rolled to a halt, the engine sputtering, and Daisy laughed. The laugh of a madwoman, of a murderer, sliding into tears. Through the grimy windshield, Scarlett glimpsed a faded plaid shirt, blue jeans, and straw, a bale's worth of straw.

# Chapter 4

Scarlett wrapped her arms around her belly. What if . . . what if the baby . . . ? From deep within, bubbles exploded. Her daughter was hiccupping, safely suspended in the warm dark. Her contractions ended as abruptly as they had begun. Because she'd changed position after hours of driving, or because her body wanted to remind her that labor—false or not—remained out of her control? She slumped in her seat. Daisy tugged on Scarlett's track pants, her hands frantic, as if she feared she'd have to catch the baby sliding out from between Scarlett's legs, wet and red on a slick of blood.

Scarlett batted her away. "Stop. It stopped." She felt oddly humiliated, heat rising in her cheeks. She hoped when the time came, she could tell the difference between a false alarm and an imminent birth. She got out and dragged the mutilated scarecrow from the windshield. She was intact and so, too, her baby. She squinted, shading her eyes with her hands, and checked the van, which wasn't leaking any fluids.

She rubbed her belly. Her daughter wasn't kicking much at least, maybe lulled by the rocking motion of the van. The workers nearby continued stuffing lettuces into bins strapped at their sides, but they might have radioed their supervisor. She and Daisy had to leave. They switched seats, Scarlett at the wheel. She checked the

traffic and got onto the freeway. Soon the van grew heavy with momentum, as if she were being shot from a cannon, a sensation at
once frightening and reassuring. Set in motion, she couldn't be
stopped, not by Mama Fang, not by Boss Yeung.

Last summer, in a manager's meeting, Scarlett had come to Boss
Yeung's attention by speaking up and suggesting the factory use
scraps as packing material. A cost-cutting measure. He'd nodded in
approval and asked her to remind him of her name. A rare honor,
and as they moved down the agenda, she could tell everyone at the
meeting was studying her.

Cowlicks swirled his thick hair like the whorls of a hurricane.
She'd quickly caught herself and turned back to her notes. Not for
the first time, she'd been staring at him, but she was too old for
crushes, and he was too old for her.

After the meeting, in the hallway that ran along the shop floor,
she told a co-worker about her lessons at Phoenix Driving School
that Saturday. She noticed Boss Yeung off to the side, listening—to
her! He carried himself purposefully, with an economy of motion.

He said nothing, but when she arrived at the school, he was
seated in the waiting room. What a charge she'd felt, jolted alive.
He wanted to check out the school's methods, he said. "You don't
want to start any bad habits."

Scarlett pushed the memory away. The engine vibrated through
her, numbing her bottom as she went rigid with concentration, holding steady on the gas pedal. Her right leg quivered with fatigue, and
she rolled her shoulders back. Discomfort would keep her alert, not
drowsing like Daisy. The teenager startled awake every few minutes, struggling to watch over Scarlett as Scarlett watched over her.

"Have you picked out a name?" Daisy asked.

Scarlett didn't have the luxury of thinking that far ahead.

"You can't know until you see them," Daisy said. "I have a list. A
short one."

A list. Scarlett was less prepared than a teenager for the birth of
her daughter. When she tried to come up with names, her mind
blanked. At Perfume Bay, the guests turned the selection into a
game. Lady Yu had narrowed her choices to Stanley, in honor of
Morgan Stanley, or Warren, after Warren Buffett, excellent role

models for her son. Countess Tien had been partial to the name Kingsway, in the hopes he might follow the "king's way" or Goodwin, to ensure his every victory.

"If I was having a girl, I'd call her Marie," Daisy said.

Scarlett didn't reply. She wasn't asking for suggestions.

"Marie Curie." Daisy said the name with a reverence Scarlett didn't know the teenager possessed. She listed Madame Curie's achievements: the discovery of radium, two Nobel prizes, and a portable X-ray machine she drove onto the battlefield.

Was Daisy a future scientist or a teenager in search of a hero? Maybe both. Unlike Scarlett, she'd had her choice of idols.

"What are you having?" Daisy asked.

"A girl." Scarlett straightened. Each time she admitted it, the hazy edges of her daughter sharpened.

"Lucky! I wanted a girl," Daisy said. "Even though people say that girls steal your beauty."

"You don't get to choose," Scarlett said. All children stole the bloom from their mothers, more so than from their fathers, who could escape moments after conception.

"My parents tried twice," Daisy said. "But . . ." In the silence that followed, Scarlett guessed that Daisy had a younger sister, not the brother her parents had wanted.

After Scarlett, her parents had also wanted a son. He arrived too small and too early and died within the hour, the same year Ba returned from the mines and wasted away. She had always wished for a sibling to help her bear the burden of Ma, her temper and her expectations. With a younger brother or sister, Scarlett might not have kept to herself so much, without a friend to call upon for help. She might have had more patience with Daisy, with most people.

Early afternoon, and they were only halfway to San Francisco. In a couple of hours, traffic would thicken, but for now, the road ahead was smooth and fast as a jet runway. Get to Chinatown, and then she'd know what to do. Even though Daisy couldn't reach her boyfriend, William, by phone or via social media, she vowed to find him on campus. The assurances seemed as much for herself as for Scarlett.

Scarlett stopped listening, emptying herself into the monotony of the crumbly dirt and prickly withered grasses dry as the Gobi Desert. The emptiness of the landscape made her uneasy, this undeveloped stretch of golden hills. By her village, the steepest slopes were terraced, every bit of land cultivated, and factory cities in southern China grew so large that they merged with their neighbors.

Roadkill sprawled at the shoulder—a raccoon or puppy—a stuffed bear, its head nearly torn off and fur spattered in engine oil. She circled her palm on her belly, uneasy, her fears rising like floodwaters. She wanted to deliver in a clean hospital with skilled nurses and doctors, but what if she couldn't gain entry? What if authorities checked the plates of the stolen van, and she went into labor in jail? On the road, with only a vague destination in mind, their possible futures multiplied, the worst scenarios as palpable as the best.

Daisy stifled a sob. For all her bravado—stowing in the back of the van, coaxing the security guard—the teenager had to be terrified, far from home, cut off from her boyfriend and about to become a mother. Scarlett should rub her back, but she felt paralyzed. She feared she lacked the kindness, the tenderness that her own baby deserved. Maybe like so much else, she had to pretend until what felt awkward became second nature. She touched Daisy's arm, and the teenager stiffened. It seemed her family wasn't one who hugged and kissed, either.

"The disconnected number," Daisy said. "What if—if—if he's—gone."

"People change their numbers all the time," Scarlett said. "They lose their phone, get new ones."

"He always had his phone with him." Daisy smiled. "One time, when he answered, it was echoing. I could tell he was in the bathroom."

"You'll find him. If he wants to be found."

Daisy gasped. Scarlett shouldn't have taken such a harsh tone, but the teenager needed to hear what no one else would tell her.

They both fell silent. As they approached the pass, winds buffeted the van, rattling the windows. A mattress reared up on the roof of a sedan behind them, straining against the strap, about to take flight. Scarlett clenched her hands on the wheel to keep the van from swerving into the next lane. Around her, drivers did the same.

"Look," Scarlett said.

*"Wah!"* Daisy exclaimed.

On the ridge, wind turbines marched across the hillside, giant pinwheels twirling against the indigo sky, the bright white propellers a mesmerizing blur not quite of this world.

Chinatown disappointed her: the sidewalks mobbed with matrons toting pink plastic shopping bags, the tenements squat and dingy, and saggy panties hanging in the windows. The neon-lit malls and high-rises that crossed the skies in Shenzhen and Dongguan were imperial by comparison. Daisy was unable to hide her apprehension, and Scarlett wondered if the girl would call home for help rather than stay in this ghetto. The street grew so steep she could only see sky through the windshield. She felt dizzy, as if the van, its engines roaring, might take off into the air and rocket to heaven.

Scarlett was used to nosing cars into traffic, pushing through as she might with her elbows at a wet market, but she'd never driven a barge of a vehicle—or tried to park one. That spot was too short, this one next to a fire hydrant, that one a driveway. The van was elephant-wide, elephant-long, and if she attempted to parallel park—she'd never learned how—she'd drive onto the curb, plunge into the crates of bok choy and spiky durian, and slam through the fish tanks.

Daisy pointed at a spot ahead, a miraculously long one Scarlett could pull into. No—a bus stop. They'd get towed. Scarlett fought the urge to scream, feeling trapped. She was cotton-mouthed, her bladder throbbed, and she was going to piss herself if she didn't find a toilet in the next few minutes. Daisy tapped on the window, at a sign above, *P* for parking. Scarlett drove the van into the dark maw of a garage, hit the button for the ticket, and slowly descended down the spiral ramp, trying not to clip the side mirrors against the walls. She found a spot in the corner, parked across two spaces to prevent herself from getting boxed in, and turned off the ignition. She felt as a seafaring voyager must, grounded on the beach, about to take her first shaky steps on land.

From the underground garage, the elevator rose up until reaching the surface, its doors parting onto Portsmouth Square. First they'd find a bathroom, and then ask around for a place to stay. They entered the park thronged with gamblers: men squatting with their cards, onlookers huddling around them. To the right of the elevator, Scarlett discovered a dead end stacked with cardboard boxes towering above her head. Daisy gasped. An elderly woman slumped in a wheelchair, her eyes glazed and her gray hair tangled, her body musty with dried sweat, with neglect. "Are you okay?" Daisy asked.

The woman didn't move, didn't speak. She was drooling, her mouth open. She must have been abandoned by her daughter, granddaughter, some caregiver eager to escape this mute burden while running errands or gossiping. "Do you need water?" No answer. Daisy waved her arms toward the plaza, trying to catch the attention of whoever was watching over the woman, but no one started toward them.

Where was her family? Maybe she'd never had children or they were long gone. Or maybe she had beaten or starved her children, and now she was getting what she deserved. It was none of their business, and they couldn't help her. Getting to San Francisco had taken nearly everything Scarlett had left in her.

Daisy, who'd never had to fend for herself, could afford generosity and goodwill. Scarlett brushed her hand against her belly, wondering if she'd go into labor in five days—or in five minutes. They had to consider their babies first. No one else would. Her bladder was about to burst, and she tugged on Daisy's elbow.

Daisy jerked away. "We can't leave her."

"She's not ours to take," Scarlett said. Daisy wasn't selfish as she'd thought, but softhearted, which carried its own perils.

Sunshine blasted onto the woman's face—had she been here all day? Scarlett wheeled her into the shade of an overhang, and Daisy blotted at the drool on her chin with a paper napkin. The abandoned woman seemed an ill omen. If people here so easily ignored her, why would they help two strangers?

After a trip to the plaza's ghastly, brimming portable toilets, Scarlett studied the crowd. The back of her neck prickled, and she felt eyes upon her—a wizened old man in a checkered cap walked briskly across the plaza. He was watching her. She looked away, letting go of the breath she didn't realize she was holding. Boss Yeung couldn't have found them yet, not unless he had spy satellites and government agents at his disposal. No one knew they were here. No one knew who they were. No one knew that Scarlett had been a scorned mistress, Daisy an exiled daughter, and no one would ever have to know again.

She closed her eyes and let the neighborhood wash over her: the sound of traffic, the scent of exhaust, fresh ginger, and a whiff of garbage. By a bronze statue of a galleon atop cresting waves, a group of ladies played cards. Their laughter mean-spirited, their eyes appraising, their hair coiled in tight perms, they seemed the sort who would love to gossip about two pregnant women in matching velour tracksuits and slippers. She and Daisy would attract attention anywhere they went. Maybe Scarlett could throw Mama Fang off. Pretend that she and Daisy had parted ways, forcing that scheming woman to launch two different searches. Or she could make Mama Fang think they were elsewhere, in Chicago or Boston. Call her, tell her the van had died and that they'd been robbed, and beg her to fetch them from Reno, from Phoenix, from San Diego, all the cities in the shotgun scatter where they could have ended up. All the lesser cities whose names she had memorized from the atlas Boss Yeung had given her. But how? She feared Mama Fang might trace their call through technological sorcery. She had to be panicking, Boss Yeung furious. Maybe regretful, too.

Scarlett lifted her chin. Let them stew.

In the playground, a granny pushed a little girl in a swing. With thick round glasses and beaky nose, the old woman resembled an owl.

"Is this the best park for kids?" Daisy asked her. "How old is she?"

The granny didn't answer. She might be hard of hearing, or

maybe she only spoke Cantonese; its sharp tones—love songs that sounded like arguments—sliced through the air in this neighborhood.

"We're new." Scarlett asked where they might find a rental. The granny shrugged, said she didn't know, and turned away. Her indifference stung. At the factories, girls from Scarlett's province used to make room for her at their table in the canteen, even if she never went out shopping and strolling with them, even if she spent her meals studying, flipping through flash cards, and never joined their gossip. Even if they weren't friends, they might have cousins in common, and as children, they had toiled and slept under the same big sky.

The granny pulled the little girl to her feet and started to lead her out of the park. The girl stomped her feet and refused, and when the granny tugged again, the girl thrashed and knocked over a toddler boy who started bawling. The granny ducked her head and dragged away the girl, now shrieking. Once she'd been an infant, like the baby inside Scarlett. All that work to keep her alive. How many baths, how many meals, how many diapers, how many fevers, how many tears—only to have your child grow up and flee into the world, with all its dangers and temptations that you'd tried for so long to keep out.

Daisy walked toward the women in sturdy shoes and sensible slacks dancing in unison under a trellis, their silk fans swishing like koi. They practiced the same steps over and over, as if preparing for a performance. Undeterred, she inched closer, causing the woman on the end to stumble to avoid swinging the fan at her. The leader— her hair dyed jet-black, cut into a severe bob—barked at her to get back in line and glared at Daisy.

Scarlett would try the knot of men in the corner in windbreakers, shiny slacks, cheap loafers with athletic socks, and bowl haircuts. Bumpkins. As she approached, a pockmarked man hissed with disgust and tossed aside his cards. He lit a cigarette and regarded Scarlett with suspicion. Apparently women weren't welcome at this particular game, which gave off a seedy air, as if the men were clustered around pictures of naked centerfolds. As Daisy set off to buy a bottle of water, Scarlett watched the game, which had been popular at the electronics factory. She never played and had considered it a waste of time until she and Boss Yeung spent a rainy weekend at the beach. He taught her how to cheat: how to shuffle, to keep the top card for yourself, nudging it slightly aside. How to mark your cards with your fingernails with the barest crescent, the way she marked his back, scratching in wide, slow arcs.

"Is this how you win at cards?" she had asked.

"I want you to protect yourself. To know it when you see it." Boss Yeung disdained gambling—slot machines and the horse track— but considered cards a game of skill.

She'd learned how, though she knew she'd never play cards with anyone except him, and in the end, she hadn't caught the clues that would have revealed his intentions toward her.

Here, she quickly spotted a man cheating. His stubby finger nudged the top card, lightning fast, and he told joke after filthy joke to distract the other players. They were calling him Shrimp Boy, maybe because of his bulging eyes. She should walk away—weren't these men getting what they deserved with their idle games? But she couldn't stand Shrimp Boy's smug grin. And if she helped another player, wouldn't he help her in return? The next time, just before Shrimp Boy shuffled, she caught the eye of the pockmarked man. She cast her gaze at Shrimp Boy as he flicked the top card.

The pockmarked man scowled and challenged Shrimp Boy, and all at once the men were scuffling, a finger thumped against a chest, a shove against the shoulders, with the clumsy menace of bears forced on their hind legs. Scarlett backed away. With one arm, she shielded her belly and with the other, the roll of bills in her jacket. They could turn on her next, push her down and steal her money.

Then the men were laughing, backslapping, telling ten generations of the other's ancestors to fuck off. Maybe they'd played cards so many times that occasional cheating livened up the game. But then she noticed the old man in the checkered cap she'd seen earlier. The others were calling him *Sifu*, master, a title of respect for his skills and experience. He settled the tempers of the two men, cajoling, joking, reminding them of the bites they'd snatched from each other's bowls over the years.

Daisy returned with a bottle of water. The pockmarked man gave her an oily smile, eying her ballooning breasts and the curve of her belly, irrefutable signs of her fertility and her lack of innocence. "Did you find us a place to stay?" Daisy asked.

"I have just the place for you." The pockmarked man laughed and elbowed Shrimp Boy. He spoke in Cantonese, which Daisy didn't understand, but his crude tone couldn't have been clearer. Daisy reddened.

"The only company you keep is with your hands," Scarlett shot back in Cantonese, one of the insults she'd picked up at the factory. Shrimp Boy roared. Though she should have held her tongue, she'd been bullied for too long. The next time the pockmarked man saw them, he'd know not to harass them, not to catcall or follow them.

"He uses his right hand during the week," Shrimp Boy said. "Left hand for special occasions. Calls it 'going to the disco.'"

"Whores," muttered the pockmarked man.

Daisy kicked over the cardboard box serving as their table and playing cards fluttered into the air. *Aiya!* Scarlett hooked her arm into Daisy's. The men gaped but did not fight back against the crazy pregnant women who might spew afterbirth in retaliation.

"Women get like this," the pockmarked man said, "just before the baby comes."

"Your mother's still like that." Shrimp Boy grinned, and with that, the men returned to insulting each other.

Scarlett dragged Daisy toward the elevator to the parking garage, fuming at herself. That girl was a lit match to Scarlett's spilled gasoline. Daisy's temper must have caused her parents so much grief. At the edge of the park, they passed a dozen women sitting cross-legged on mats, wearing sun hats big as flying saucers. Their heads bowed, their hands clasped in meditation, beneath a portrait of the Celestial Goddess printed on a vinyl banner. She resembled Imelda Marcos turned into an interstellar ambassador, with flowing purple robes and a diadem twinkling on her forehead like a third eye.

Boss Yeung's wife also devoted herself to the Celestial Goddess, meditating five hours a day, abstaining from meat, dairy, garlic, and onions, and contributing to her master's charities: vegan restaurants, a line of cubic zirconium jewelry, and a satellite television network. Believers claimed they'd been cured of cancer, been re-united with loved ones, and come into enough money to pay off their debts. Mrs. Yeung must have prayed for a son. But if the god-dess had intervened, she had a sense of humor—getting Scarlett pregnant instead.

Who knows, his wife might even join protests like this one, along with her regular attendance at retreats hosted by the goddess. "Stay or go, she's not really there," he'd once said of his wife. Gone, even when he was in the same room with her. Had he loved her until he lost her to another plane of consciousness, or was it until she failed to produce an heir? Had she always been softheaded, or did she only seek out the assurances Boss Yeung no longer offered her?

A woman with a vampire's aversion to the sun—in a giant visor that obscured most of her face, flowing pants and tunic, and long white gloves to prevent her skin darkening like a peasant's—was handing out flyers to passersby. Scarlett turned away. "I wish you safety and happiness," the woman said. "Do you know you will need to do one thing if you would like to have a safe and happy fu-ture?"

Scarlett didn't answer. When they finally reached the entrance to the garage, she jabbed the scuffed down button. She wasn't leaving, but she didn't know where else to go. Berkeley wasn't far, Daisy said. She'd checked the map, and they could walk around campus to find the father of her child.

"I'm not driving," Scarlett said sourly. She passed her hand over her face, the smell dusty and metallic, the smell of discomfort and disorder.

"We can sit down, get something to eat, and then we can go."

"I'm not going. You can."

The elevator chimed and the doors opened. They didn't get in. It was obvious that Daisy didn't want to part ways yet, not with the clouds gathering in the early evening and the winds starting to whip up, not on the first night in a strange city. Scarlett regretted her threat. She did and she didn't want to be alone.

The elevator doors closed. Turning away, Daisy winced at the sight of the granny still sitting in the wheelchair. She had fallen asleep. Daisy walked over and tucked the lap blanket around the granny, and when she stirred, Daisy patted her withered hand.

Scarlett and Daisy turned at the sound of footsteps—the *Sifu*, who introduced himself as Old Wu. "You're related to Granny Wang?"

"No more than you," Scarlett said.

"You were kind to help her." He'd seen them earlier, he said, wheeling Granny Wang into the shade. Old Wu explained that even after her stroke, she'd had days when she could still get by with her cane, days where she remembered your name. Bad days, too, where she slept most of the time and couldn't make her legs go. The neighbors took turns wheeling her into Portsmouth Square, for the sunshine, for the sound of the children and their laughter to heal her. If her daughter found out, she'd force Granny Wang to leave Chinatown and move to a distant suburb where you had to drive from place to place, where the shops didn't stock dried shrimp and bitter melon, where your grandchildren chose their devices over you, and there were few Chinese—a fate worse than death. It was worth lying to your flesh and blood to maintain your independence.

Old Wu seemed to take this sort of proprietary interest in his fellow residents, whether they'd been here a day or a decade. He cocked his head at Scarlett, smiling, and she could have wept, the tumult of the last twenty-four hours catching up to her. Boss Yeung no longer loved her; maybe he never had. She swayed, weak in the knees, and had to steady herself on the railing.

"Do you need a seat?" He reached for a cardboard box.

"I've been sitting all day." The jumbled pile of boxes teetered in the breeze. "I doubt anything is sturdy enough to hold me up."

He smiled again, and she felt emboldened to ask where they might stay the night. Evergreen Gardens, he answered quickly, where a room had opened up down the hall from him. A reasonable price, with a landlord who didn't ask much of you, if you didn't ask much of him. Their first night in Chinatown, they curled like shrimp, back-to-back, with borrowed extra pillows propped between their legs. The cotton sheets were scratchy, spotted with faded stains and reeking of mothballs, and the mattress on the floor was mushy as a toadstool. She and Daisy kept tumbling into the hollow down the center, arms brushing backs, feet grazing legs. "Sorry." "Didn't mean to—"

As the transgressions multiplied, they stopped apologizing. Scarlett's skin crawled. Before getting pregnant, she'd slept on her back, her arms and legs spread like a starfish, in the same position until morning. Boss Yeung complained, but it had never driven him out of bed. At Perfume Bay, she'd grown accustomed to sleeping on her own again, in the soothing hush of the suburbs after nightfall.

Here the walls were thin enough to hear a fart next door, here shouts and laughter floated up from the street. She squirmed. She'd gone soft, weakened by age, by pregnancy. She used to take pride in her ability to nap in any position, in any condition, on a bus, in the canteen, leaning against a wall for a few minutes. She rubbed her fist in the small of her back, trying to ease the ache. Old Wu had lent her a jar of Tiger Balm, the menthol and camphor cure for every ailment from a cold to an amputation.

She and Daisy washed up under a dribbling shower, but had to change back into their Perfume Bay tracksuits, musty with sweat and smoky from dinner. With a roomy waistband and matted velour, the tracksuits were slovenly and yet infantile, designed for those who couldn't be trusted with zippers or buttons. Scarlett wanted to toss it, torch it, but she was too practical for such a dramatic gesture. She had to make the money last; she couldn't count on finding Daisy's boyfriend. She had to sell the van, at a bargain price to any buyer willing to overlook the missing papers, lost front license plate, and cracked windshield. She wasn't yet sure if mothers could deliver for free, or if they might get charged for medical supplies, the bedpan, the pads, whatever she and Daisy might need during their stay at the hospital. Tomorrow, Scarlett would start asking about where to give birth. The ultrasound technician had sounded so sure that hospitals couldn't turn you away, but what if she'd been wrong?

She'd parked in a dim corner of the garage, which seemed secure—an attendant until midnight, sturdy gates, and security cameras—but all of a sudden she pictured thieves prying off tires, breaking the window, and rifling through the glove compartment. Police cruising through the garage, shining a flashlight onto each license plate, in search of the stolen van.

If he wasn't already en route, Boss Yeung soon would come after them. He'd have the help of his friend Uncle Lo, a man of vast resources, to hunt them down. And wouldn't Daisy's frantic parents search for their runaway daughter?

The baby kicked, her head down, in ready position, impatient to squeeze herself into the world. Daisy flipped her pillow, in search of a cool spot, and her hair whipped into Scarlett's mouth. Scarlett gagged. She couldn't stand the proximity with a near-stranger, not now, not night after night until their delivery. She sat up. Enough! Daisy tugged on the sheet and Scarlett tugged back so hard that the teenager was left exposed.

She expected Daisy to snap at her. Scarlett wanted to fight, to shout, to vent all that roiled within her, steam howling out of a tea-kettle.

Instead, Daisy clutched her pillow. "I've never shared a bed." She stroked the edge of the pillow as she would a lover's arm. She and her boyfriend probably never had a chance to spend the night together, spooning. Daisy didn't realize that you might share the same bed, but dream different dreams. A man who held you in his arms might at that very instant be plotting how to part you from your child.

Scarlett had known none of that when she'd started her weekend driving lessons with Boss Yeung. They traveled in an hour what once would have taken a week to walk, days by donkey cart. She studied maps—taking in the highways from Harbin to Hong Kong, Shanghai to Kunming—that crossed China like lines on a crone's palm. She'd never felt more self-contained, self-sufficient than in the car with him on the weekends, stopping and going as they pleased, the climate, music, direction, and speed at their fingertips.

A couple of weeks later, they became lovers on a visit to a local tourist attraction, century-old towering brick homes. For decades, men from this county had been going abroad to find work. Only the luckiest had returned with gold heavy in their pockets, and with it they commissioned the domed roofs and terraces they'd seen abroad.

Boss Yeung had noted the intricate pattern on the tile floor, red and black eight-pointed stars. "Imported. From Italy." He had an eye for quality and refinement, and he'd judged her valuable, too.

They were alone on the top floor. As she ran her fingers along slits in the walls, he came up from behind. "To take aim on the enemy below," he said, his arm brushing against her. She exhaled, and leaned back slightly toward him. The air thickening between them, they clutched each other in the sticky heat. They left for the nearest love motel, one they'd passed a few kilometers away. Their room had been tricked out in purple velvet, with a karaoke system bristling with as many knobs as a starship. Parched with desire, she drank deeply of all his textures: his soft lips, his prickly stubble, and the smoothness at the back of his neck, where his years hadn't yet reached.

He never acknowledged their age gap and neither did she: the silver hairs in his crotch, the creak in his neck, the menus he squinted at before handing to her to read, her ease in squatting down to retrieve something he'd dropped. He'd lived out his youth, settled, and started his business before she'd been born. The years that had shaped him most were years she would never know. The age difference had been part of the attraction: she made him feel young, and he made her feel young, too. As old as she felt, he was older, and for a time, she found him wiser.

She failed the written test for her license three times. Everyone said the questions were confusing and that you had to bribe the examiner to pass.

She didn't need a license, Boss Yeung had said.

"What if there's an emergency?" she'd asked. "What if—what if something happens and you can't drive?"

He had grimaced. He didn't like contemplating any future that debilitated him. The next day, he had presented her with a recording he'd made of the exam, reading aloud questions and the answers. She listened through her headphones every day, while she slept, his voice becoming dear to her.

She never wanted to hear that voice again. She threw the rumpled sheet back over Daisy and herself, but their feet poked out of the tangle. The teenager tottered up—now what?—and yanked the sheet off the bed. Before Scarlett could protest, Daisy snapped the sheet up and let it float down, a calming sight in the half-light from the street. The heat of their bodies dissipated and when the sheet settled upon her, Scarlett felt tidy and smooth.

"My mother used to make the bed over me," Daisy said.

Scarlett suppressed the silly urge to ask Daisy to float the sheet over her again, even though she craved the feeling of a sheet falling over her like snow. She was drifting off when she awoke with a start. Daisy was turned toward her, her expression guilty.

"You touched my face," Scarlett grumbled.

"It was an accident."

"Don't touch me again!"

"You were breathing so loudly. I thought—if you turned away—it wouldn't be so loud."

Scarlett couldn't help but laugh. Daisy shrank back. Scarlett knew why the teenager had touched her because she'd done the same to Boss Yeung, many times when he was starting to snore. The sound was maddening! Scarlett rolled over, drawing the sheet over her shoulders. A siren went by and down the hallway, the communal toilet flushed, and the tidal pull of sleep drew them under.

The tasseled lamp was hers for the taking. The stack of cookbooks, the cracked radio, and wooden chair, too, if Scarlett wanted. All were heaped on a corner at the edge of Chinatown. The selection was best at the end of the month, Old Wu explained, when people moved out of their apartments, leaving couches, computer monitors, microwaves, and dumbbells in their wake. If you knew when and where to go, you could find treasures daily.

They were on their way to the Pearl Pavilion, a banquet hall that welcomed skimming, side deals, and other loose interpretations of the rules. Old Wu suggested they sell the van to the manager in the lull between lunch and dinner. Every hour in the parking garage racked up more fees and every hour, Mama Fang and Boss Yeung were drawing closer. Daisy was at the library, searching online for William.

"Can't we come back for this?" Scarlett didn't want to show up to the negotiations carrying a lamp like an itinerant peddler.

"It'll be gone," Old Wu said. You had to be prepared, willing to snatch something up no matter where you were going. You wouldn't have a second chance. Blink, hesitate, and the treasure would disappear into the hands of the decisive.

At Perfume Bay, she had been coddled, her every minute, her every bite and breath scheduled and monitored. The shock of all the choices before her now felt like plunging through ice. She tucked the lamp under her arm and followed Old Wu, who crowed about his top finds: outside of a luxury mattress store, he'd once discovered crumpled twenties, eighty dollars total. After testing out mattresses, a rich shopper must have been so relaxed that the bills tumbled out of his pocket! Another time, Old Wu spied a baggie full of green leaves, oily and densely packed, pungent as a skunk—*da ma*! Marijuana. He didn't have much use for it, but he made sure it didn't fall into the hands of a child or an addict. He smiled slyly. He'd given it to his neighbor Joe Ng, the one who'd gotten into a fight at Portsmouth Square. For all his boasting talk, Joe lived with his mother at Evergreen Gardens, and the rascal benefited from *da ma*'s relaxing medicinal qualities.

Only the poorest and most desperate in China picked through trash, grannies searching for glass bottles and aluminum cans to redeem. Wearing thick gloves, sticky with spilled juice, they batted aside wasps to fill clanking burlap bags. At the parks, some of them hovered nearby, taking the empty can from your hand. If the pampered wives of Perfume Bay had seen Scarlett carrying the lamp, they would have jeered at her. But if those women were forced to fend for themselves, they would have given up within the hour.

Old Wu took the lamp from her. After retiring from the restaurant trade, he'd turned scavenging into an art, transforming the streets of San Francisco into a shopping spree. You had to see possibilities where others did not, he told her. Maybe you never imagined yourself with a chrome stool, topped with a red leather cushion, but you understood how it might fit into your apartment or your neighbor's. You couldn't be greedy. Just as you were to leave a few grains of rice at the bottom of your bowl to seed your next meal, you shouldn't rake the sidewalk clean.

They skirted the edge of Chinatown, quicker than fighting the crowds on Stockton Street, and passed a narrow house, trimmed in gold and purple, where toys were arrayed on the front steps beside a sign, FREE! Wooden puzzles with missing pieces, nested cups, a plastic pail and shovels, and a green-striped caterpillar. She'd seen that caterpillar—many, in fact—at the toy factory where she used to work, before she'd taken the job at Boss Yeung's.

The caterpillar seemed brand-new, straight out of the box, soft and cuddly, not a thread frayed, the colors bright after its long journey: rolled off the assembly line, packed onto a cargo ship, offloaded onto a truck, and driven to a store here. Not a trace left of the factory's harsh chemical reek of plastic and rubber, the dizzying paint fumes, the stink of the industrious. Maybe she knew one of the women whose hands had touched this caterpillar, stuffed in the fluffy fibers, attached the shiny eyes, and sewed the body closed. Did Scarlett process her paperwork, or eat with her in the factory canteen?

She tucked the caterpillar under her arm—her daughter's first toy. Long before she'd known she would come to America, her touch had rippled across the ocean. The goods had been designated export-quality, unavailable for sale within China—too expensive, too fine for locals—but she had never considered the endpoint. She *had* often puzzled over the exact purpose of the items they manufactured. Did the strange objects—green plastic bowler hats, necklaces of bunny-shaped beads—fill a pressing need or create one by coming into existence? This house must bulge with plenty, shelves, bins, and boxes overflowing with toys.

Back in Chinatown, they slipped through an alley on cobblestones slick with garbage, and passed a market where turtles and frogs flopped in plastic buckets. The bubbling tanks sounded like beakers boiling over in a mad scientist's lab. They were a block away from the Pearl Pavilion. According to Old Wu, legions of tourists ordered neon-orange chicken and heaps of fried rice during the day. At night, at its banquets, the restaurant served shark's fin soup, chewy slices of abalone, and hand-pulled noodles.

He asked a busboy where they could find Manager Kwok. In the back, in his office. A dirty dish cart sat by the kitchen, piled with scraps grander than any feast Scarlett's village had ever celebrated. Fistfuls of rice, beef, bell peppers, and bean curd sat untouched. Hunger dug at her. As a child, she'd eaten meat only once a year, and this much wasted food made her want to cram the leftovers into a take-out box so she and Daisy could feed themselves for days.

Manager Kwok, slouching in a baggy pin-striped suit, looked up from his paperwork and smiled. "*Sifu!* You're too late for lunch, but we can find something in the kitchen."

Old Wu had explained to Scarlett why the manager owed him. Years ago, he'd worked as a busboy at a restaurant where Old Wu, the cook, kept the staff well fed. "I didn't come for the food—I came for you," Old Wu said.

"Don't believe everything you hear," Manager Kwok told Scarlett. He had the uneasy swagger of a man in charge in practice though not in name, at the whim of an absent master. She'd heard the rumors: the owners of the Pearl Pavilion lived in Hong Kong and used the restaurant to wash dirty money clean. Manager Kwok's mildewy office, cramped and dim compared to the immense, brightly lit dining room, had fake wood paneling and a stained swamp-green carpet. A cigar humidor and a model of a motorcycle, with swooping fenders and bulbous tires, perched on top of a liquor cabinet. Old Wu shifted the lamp from one arm to the other.

"You lift that off the back of a truck?" Manager Kwok asked. Old Wu set the lamp onto the floor and pulled out a chair for Scarlett, who awkwardly cradled the caterpillar in what remained of her lap. In the toy's midsection, bells tinkled.

"You want to book a red egg and ginger party?" he asked, referring to the meal that celebrated a baby's survival and marked his first hundred days.

Boss Yeung must have something grand in mind: a banquet in Hong Kong in a hall that overlooked the harbor, with Italian marble, floor-to-ceiling windows, abundant gold leaf and crystal chandeliers. The baby dressed in silk satin prince's robes, tiger hat and tiger shoes to ward off evil, cradled in Boss Yeung's arms and no one else's.

"We can do any menu you want. Roast pig? Roast duck? We're using the recipe that *Sifu* taught us! How many? Ten tables, we'll get you a discount." He nodded at Old Wu. "In addition to the discount we reserve for our friends."

"Don't you need a second delivery van? I have a bargain," Old Wu said.

Scarlett bristled. For all his kindness, she'd had enough of other people speaking on her behalf. In business matters, she knew better than him. Hadn't she cut costs at Boss Yeung's factory?

Manager Kwok leaned back in his chair, the leather squeaking under him. He tented his fingers together, his nails buffed to a shine, the pinky on his right hand kept long as a talon. "I don't have the budget for it." The cost of food had gone up and banquet bookings had gone down.

"The engine's powerful, very powerful," Old Wu said.

The manager checked his phone.

"Built like a tank. Hit by another car, won't get a scratch. The other car will crumple."

The manager laughed politely. He didn't look up from the cracked screen of his phone.

"I'll try the Jade Dragon," Old Wu said. "But I wanted to give you the first chance."

The seat dug into the back of Scarlett's thighs. Old Wu had told her the manager wasn't above serving stolen liquor at banquets, and she had to appeal to his greed. "The van's old, probably older than the one you have."

Manager Kwok studied her. "That's not much of a sales pitch."

"It's reliable and roomy. Sell the one you have and buy mine. An easy profit." She'd let him realize that he could pocket the difference.

"No profit comes easy." But he rubbed his chin, considering.

# Chapter 5

The stylist snipped at Scarlett's hair, the shears rasping. Scarlett was grateful she wasn't chatty. She glanced into the mirrors and saw Daisy in the chair beside her, her eyes closed. She must be as exhausted as Scarlett felt. To disguise themselves, they were lopping off their hair. They might have saved a few bucks by doing it themselves, but Scarlett didn't want to end up looking like a lobotomy patient.

Besides, if they'd stayed a minute longer in their apartment, they might have gone mad. Evergreen Gardens was permeated with the smell of many bodies and many years, the steady accumulation of sweat, steamed rice, and sesame oil. Their tiny apartment held a double mattress left by the last tenant, and milk crates stacked high, packed with their diapers, wipes, clothes, and other baby supplies. Their stockpiling reminded her that she would never travel light again. Each day, Old Wu had dropped off another find: portable cribs and umbrella strollers like new. Even with his help, the money she'd taken from Mama Fang and received from the sale of the van would dwindle quickly.

He'd confirmed that the big and busy hospital in San Francisco accepted patients in an emergency without insurance and with every kind of malady. Together, they'd practiced the route and peeked into the hospital: red brick with wrought-iron window frames and a few cracked panes, the complex resembled a haunted house, but inside the hallways were clean, the equipment modern, and the staff seemed calm and efficient.

Without Old Wu, they wouldn't have gotten settled. She was grateful for his attentions, which must have gone far beyond his usual efforts, but maybe none of his other neighbors had ever needed as much help. Others at Evergreen Gardens seemed to have noticed his sweetness toward her; a few times, they'd come in together from the street, and the aunties standing in the hallway had fallen silent, probably gossiping about them.

Scarlett's due date was fast approaching, which added urgency to her days. If she and Daisy didn't cover their tracks, they'd get caught, putting an end to all they wanted for their babies. That morning, in the middle of their apartment, water had gushed from between Scarlett's legs, spattering the floor. She'd been certain she was going into labor until she realized she'd pissed herself—another humiliation that her body wanted to squeeze in before delivery.

The salon was thick with the smell of hair spray, chemical solutions, and burned hair. The scissors poked Scarlett's scalp and she yelped, jerking away. The stylist didn't apologize and resumed cutting. Scarlett had pointed out what she wanted in a dog-eared magazine, but how many times had she walked into such salons, requesting a trim but leaving with a bob, asking for a body wave and getting a dowdy perm? Chinese stylists—here or back home—had minds of their own.

"Not too short," Scarlett reminded her.

"You don't want the baby pulling on it," the stylist said.

Scarlett studied the wet hair piling up on the floor, hair that Boss Yeung used to run his fingers through, hair that had grown long in their months together. That was all behind her now. She'd begun thinking about the future. Not only next month, but next year, the next two years and longer still. She wouldn't return to China, which she might have known from the moment her flight descended over Los Angeles.

To stay in America, Scarlett would have to find a job and fix her papers. Only then would she be safe from Boss Yeung, who must have detectives fanning out after her. She didn't have enough money to hire an immigration consultant. But if they found Daisy's boy-friend, his family could help Scarlett pay for a lawyer.

At Boss Yeung's factory, the men had expected even the most se-nior women on staff to serve tea and defer to them in meetings. All around China, princelings, the pampered children of high Party of-ficials, prospered, drawing upon connections that Scarlett lacked. And Scarlett, born in the countryside, didn't have the papers that made her eligible for public schools and hospitals in China's cities, and neither would her daughter, who would be born overseas. If she and Boss Yeung had remained together, he could have paid the fine, giving their child a mainland residency permit. Without him and his support, her daughter could only attend the worst schools, dim, crumbling, and poorly run. The other students would jeer at her, the bastard daughter of a single mother, second-class in every way.

In America, without these limits, Scarlett and her daughter could attempt so much more.

She no longer feared he'd disown the girl she carried. Now she was certain that he would steal the baby out of spite, if Scarlett couldn't get her papers in time. The Americans would side with him. That boy from Cuba, whose mother drowned trying to bring him here—he'd been sent back to his father. The pregnancy had changed Boss Yeung as much as it had changed her, or maybe she'd never known him. All the qualities that drew her to him, all the qualities she'd thought they shared, she now questioned. Clever or duplicitous? Determined or single-minded? Clear-eyed or cruel?

He used to awe her, when he made his rounds at the factory, his stride long, his gaze sharp, when he addressed the battalions of workers in their jumpsuits and caps lined up in front of the gates. How powerful he'd seemed. He'd done this, made this, was in charge of all these people. The women in their hairnets straighten-ing as they passed, murmuring, *"Lao ban, lao ban."* The boss, the boss.

Much of her life in the city had been ephemeral: new streets paved and blocks demolished overnight, and the neighbors revolv-ing through her apartment building. Strange as it sounded, the business that Boss Yeung built up had seemed a monument for the ages. He'd been solid, steady like no other man had been in her life: not the father she didn't remember, not those she dated who soon left her after discovering she would never put their interests ahead of hers.

When she was with him, she pondered places, possibilities she might never have noticed. She'd been intent as a mole on her goals—and as blind to the world above where she burrowed. With him, she'd raised her head. She studied his habits and how he ran the factory; she took his advice on dealing with her landlord. After he turned controlling, she told herself that no one had ever cared enough to make such demands upon her, and that he valued her as no one else did. She'd come to realize he must have deemed her worthless but for her womb. The prospect of an heir had made him as ruthless as one of those legendary emperors who waged wars, emptied royal treasuries, and swallowed crane eggs and tortoise soup for a chance at immortality.

Scarlett shifted uncomfortably in the stylist's chair, her tailbone sore. She could taste the prenatal vitamin pill she'd swallowed an hour ago, their last chance to plump up their babies, to give them mighty lungs, bright eyes, and sleek skin, and their last chance to muster their own strength for the delivery ahead.

Daisy squealed, staring into the mirror at the pixie cut that complemented the delicacy of her features. "I love it—but will William recognize me?"

This afternoon, she was going to stake out the computer science department at Cal, the university her boyfriend attended. His email and social media accounts had been deleted, and if not for Daisy's bulging belly, it would have seemed to Scarlett that he might never have existed. Someday, he might make himself known. For now, he'd retreated from the world. Still, Scarlett understood Daisy's insistence that they find the father of her child so he could attend their son's birth.

"*You'll* recognize *him*," Scarlett said. "We don't want anyone recognizing us."

Daisy ran her fingers through her hair. "My head feels so much lighter." She started talking about the night she had met him, when he'd been bargaining in his broken Chinese at a market in Taipei.

He offered the equivalent of twenty U.S. dollars for a knickknack worth two dollars. "I want two," he said.

The knickknack seller gave him far less change than what he was owed.

"You're getting played," Daisy informed him. "Don't cheat him," she told the vendor.

"*Na liang kuai na dai zhe qu.*" Mind your business. "*Gun dan.*" Get lost.

"*Buyaolian,*" Daisy shot back. Shameless.

"You like getting cheated?" Daisy asked him. He was holding two carved turtles, tiny in his hand. Vendors found American-born Chinese the most gullible of all foreigners, with their fat wallets, ignorance of local customs, and their misplaced trust in their brethren.

"She needs it more than me," he said.

Daisy had looked where he was looking, at a little girl paging through a book underneath the stall. She brushed past him. She hated him for making her see Taiwan through his eyes, every cripple, every beggar. Though she hurried through the market, he caught up to her.

"I wasn't insulting you," he said. "You seem like someone who stops something bad from happening."

Daisy now repeated his comment with pride. He'd described exactly the woman Daisy wanted to be, and he'd been the first to see that possibility in her.

No wonder she'd fallen for him.

Daisy had already told her what happened next: over the winter, her boyfriend had returned to Taipei to visit his ailing grandmother. A month later, Daisy discovered she was pregnant. Some girls found special doctors online who made the problem go away, but she didn't want to decide alone.

She'd messaged him, called him, but he'd never answered. Busy with school—or another girl? She never said she was pregnant, only that she needed to talk to him. When she finally wrote to him with the news, he had called her immediately and proposed over the scratchy video. He gnawed at his fingernails as if he might chew off his hand. Before he could wire her money for a plane ticket, a gust had plastered her shirt against her belly, revealing her secret to her family. After taking away her phone and laptop, cutting off contact with him, her parents shipped her to Perfume Bay. Even though Daisy was a U.S. citizen, she hadn't lived in America long enough to pass on automatic citizenship to a child born outside its borders.

Her boyfriend could have passed on his U.S. citizenship, if he'd claimed paternity. But her parents told him that she'd terminated the pregnancy.

As controlling, as vindictive as Scarlett's mother had sometimes been, she never lied.

Daisy never had a chance to tell him what happened, not after her parents had grounded her at home, and not while she'd been held prisoner at Perfume Bay, where Mama Fang denied her access to laptops and phones.

Scarlett didn't have the heart to tell her that the boy must be relieved to be free of this burden. He wasn't ready to raise a child, and neither was Daisy, but he should still know the truth.

Scarlett staggered up the hill. She felt a hand at the small of her back—Daisy's, supporting her. Hummingbird heart in her throat, Scarlett checked the map. They'd been traveling for more than two hours, by foot, by bus, and by BART to get to the university, now a few blocks away. Though she didn't want Daisy to make the trek from Chinatown alone, she wasn't going to be much help.

As a group of students approached, Scarlett searched their faces. Like a bodyguard, she had taken to checking crowds, as if hunting for assassins and escape routes. Until she and her daughter had their papers, she could never be at ease. She noticed that Daisy's belly rendered her invisible to the students; the men didn't seem to find her attractive, and the women didn't compare themselves to her. Watching them walk past, Daisy couldn't hide her hunger to join them. The hulking engineering building came into view. Perched on the hillside, covered in mottled green tile, it resembled one of those drawings that skew with the perspective, all arches, arcades, and sloping lines. Inside, Daisy hung flyers on bulletin boards—the characters for Little Dumpling, her nickname for her boyfriend—in huge print, like a wanted poster, asking him to call in a matter related to the McDonald's pie à la mode. He would understand the code words.

At the McDonald's in Taipei, William had always ordered an apple pie—fried, not baked—and vanilla ice cream—dairy, not chemical frozen yogurt—both unavailable in the United States after a push to turn menus healthy. He prided himself as a traveler, not a tourist. *Tourists* sought out McDonald's for its clean bathrooms and precision-cut French fries, for the whiff of Wichita in Moscow or Johannesburg, for the global might of an empire where the sun never set on Ronald McDonald. A *traveler* ordered like a local, he said, choosing the regional specialties on the menu, corn soup and fried chicken in Taiwan and the shrimp burger in Japan—items that signified you were an insider with a discerning palate, who could find gold even at a fast-food restaurant.

*Erbaiwu*, half a brain! Why not order from a street vendor, Scarlett wondered, for a fraction of the price? And try as he might, William would never be native. Only someone with the privileges of an American would so readily try to give up those privileges.

Although Daisy shared stories bit by bit about her life, Scarlett didn't reciprocate. She couldn't, not with someone less than half her age who—despite her pregnancy—seemed so unripened. Scarlett had long since fallen from the tree.

William was a year older than Daisy, but sometimes it felt like she'd gone off to college, not him, she said. She was the firstborn and he was the baby of his family. *Ma bao,* a mama's jewel, whose mother dictated his friends, education, career, and his wife. Although they were both ABC, his family had stayed while hers had returned to Taiwan. Both felt something missing in their lives, something they suspected they would only find across the ocean. He'd looked east, in search of a land where he wouldn't feel out of place, wouldn't be taunted as meek and nerdy. He watched anime and trained in martial arts from an herbalist–calligrapher–kung fu master. To impress her, he'd bust out backflips on their outings, in the park and on the sidewalk.

Unlike her boyfriend, Daisy faced west, listening to indie rock bands and browsing travel guides for cities she had yet to visit: Los

Angeles, New York, San Francisco. She might be staking too much on this boy, who sounded compassionate yet *tianzhen*, naïve. Keeping the baby must have been the first major decision of their lives, and they were both so young that taking responsibility must have seemed like an achievement.

Maybe the loss of Daisy and of his baby had shaken him. Maybe he'd never been enrolled at Cal, and little of anything he told Daisy had been the truth. Had he wanted to impress her with his stories? Scarlett's time with Boss Yeung—their nights together, their trips, his promises—had been a lie, too.

Daisy's love hadn't been complicated, compromised by marriage, by age, by class—all the differences that led Boss Yeung to betray Scarlett. Maybe he felt he'd done her a favor, offered a helping hand to a peasant by trying to buy her off. Scarlett would yank him down with her before she let him believe he was pulling her up again.

The night she'd conceived, Boss Yeung had lingered inside her, and they'd been cozy as nesting dolls, cozy as she'd never been. He kissed her shoulder. "I—" he said. He didn't continue. He'd waited until they couldn't make eye contact to attempt a confession he couldn't force out in the end. Did he love her or was he going to leave her? He'd started to withdraw and she had settled against him, a few seconds that had determined their end.

She and Daisy peered into classrooms and lounges where students scribbled into notebooks and pecked on their laptops. Back in the hallway, Daisy stroked her hand on the high dome of her belly, a fortune-teller reading her crystal ball. "I'll catch up."

To make a life with her boyfriend, she would have to graduate from high school, pass the entrance exams, and apply to Cal. If she found him, if she got in, his parents could look after the baby while they both attended school. If, if, if. Unlike Scarlett, Daisy wasn't worrying about their basic survival—a privilege the teenager had from birth, a privilege she wasn't even aware of having.

Daisy hung a flyer beside a bright yellow leaflet with perforated tabs. She tore one off, explaining it listed an information session for financial aid and scholarships.

"Can't your parents pay?" Scarlett asked.

"My parents!" Daisy couldn't hide her scorn. She could never trust them again. She'd been sent to Perfume Bay not only to give her son citizenship, but also to conceal her pregnancy. Her father had been appointed to a high government post, and he didn't want the scandal public. If she returned to Taiwan, her parents would send her to boarding school, keeping her apart from William, and she would become a stranger to her baby. They would adopt her son and expect her to refer to him as her brother.

If she refused, they'd find a way to take him and then disown her, she said. They'd lie to the authorities just like they'd lied to William and his family, and lie to her son, turning him against her.

She couldn't depend on her younger sister for help. She had been the one to spot Daisy's bump and gleefully inform their parents; her sister had always resented Daisy for telling her what to do. She resented Daisy's U.S. citizenship and its bright prospects, and she'd resent Daisy's son, too, pinching and taunting him in secret.

"They failed me," Daisy said. "I won't let them fail my baby."

She stroked her belly, her fierce expression softening. She stopped a student in a striped button-down with rolled-up sleeves and asked in Mandarin, "Do you know William Wan?"

He clutched the strap of his backpack, slung over his shoulder, and replied hesitantly in the same dialect. "Excuse me?"

Scarlett was relieved. She'd taken English classes off and on for years, nights and weekends, methods that ranged from yelling vocabulary at the top of her lungs to falling asleep listening to cassette tapes. After she met Boss Yeung and her diligence wavered, much of her English had faded into static. If Daisy had switched into English, Scarlett would have been left in the dark.

"William Wan. He's Chinese. About your height," Daisy said.

He laughed. "That describes most of us."

She narrowed her eyes. "You can't tell the difference between us?" She and Scarlett were about the same height. She had a point, but Scarlett wanted to pull her aside and advise her that the biting tone did her no favors. Then again, with her spirit, Daisy swayed men as Scarlett never could.

"Do you have a picture? Maybe I'd recognize him," he asked.

"He has a mole under his right eye. His hair is short and spiky."

He eyed Daisy's belly and asked for a flyer. "If I meet someone by that name, I'll give this to him."

After he left, Daisy sagged, feisty when granted an opponent, lost without one. In the lobby of the building, they discovered that the flyers had been torn down. She poked her head into the nearest office. The receptionist glared at Daisy, they argued, and as the woman reached for the phone, Daisy slunk out.

"Flyers need a stamp from the Student Affairs Office—no exceptions," Daisy fumed to Scarlett.

They stopped in the restroom, where their reflections startled Scarlett. She was still getting used to her shaggy bob streaked auburn. She sat on the toilet and sighed, resting her swollen feet squeezed into cheap canvas sneakers. She studied the graffiti scrawled on the bathroom door, the phone numbers and names and words whose letters she could identify and sound out but whose meaning she couldn't decipher. Short of standing in the school plaza with a sandwich board and a bullhorn, Daisy couldn't get a message to her boyfriend. Unless—the graffiti. Here she could add her plea to a captive audience. In block letters, at eye level, where dozens of students would see it each day. No—not here—not in the women's bathroom. The men's. Above the urinals and in the stalls.

A slim chance, but the only chance Daisy might have to get past the school's censors. In the men's room across the hall, they shouted *hello, hello* before pushing open the door—empty. While Scarlett stood guard, Daisy left her mark with a Sharpie that squeaked on the metal and tile, her desperation beating out little staccato thumps.

Daisy burst through the door with a kung fu kick. She was beaming. Petty vandalism revived her as no prenatal vitamin ever could. Beautiful and fiery as she must have been the night she met her boyfriend. She raised her leg again, poised to kick in every door in the hallway, thunderbolts thrown by a goddess giving birth to the world.

# Chapter 6

Boss Yeung was jet-lagged, blinking in the hazy Southern California sunshine that felt like a violation. The sky should have been dark, he should have been asleep on the other side of the world, and Scarlett should have been resting at Perfume Bay in the final days of her pregnancy.

He'd landed that morning at LAX, on a nonstop from Hong Kong. Perfume Bay's website had listed this outdoor Chinese mall as a local attraction for its guests. Scarlett might have shopped here regularly, visiting its sprawling supermarket, boutiques pumping Canto-pop, and restaurants wafting cumin and garlic. A month ago, she could have stopped here for supplies before leaving town, or maybe she'd holed up nearby. He wanted to retrace her steps.

He entered a boba tea shop on the upper level, an outpost of a Hong Kong chain, and at the counter, he ordered jasmine bubble tea with a fat pink straw and the chewy tapioca balls that Scarlett loved.

"I'm looking for . . ." Boss Yeung trailed off.

"Do you want to add whipped cream?" the clerk asked. "Chocolate syrup?"

Further confirmation he'd ordered a kiddie drink, an undignified choice for a man about to turn sixty. How to explain, where to begin with the clerk? The photo from her personnel file at the factory was so blurred you couldn't make out her features, and he had no record of their affair, no proof that they were linked in any way but for the ultrasound that the technician printed at twenty weeks. A feat of technology greater than the moon landing, a blurry image of the son he'd always wanted.

Ultrasounds hadn't existed during his wife's three pregnancies, all mysteries until delivery. Nine months spent predicting, puzzling over the baby's health and sex. Carrying low or high, the mother's predilection for sour or sweet, the mother's age and the lunar month of conception, all factored into their calculations. Three times, his wife gave birth to a girl, with a mounting sense of inevitability and defeat.

A relentlessly catchy tune came out of the loudspeakers, the one he'd been hearing in television commercials and thumping from shops in Hong Kong. The refrain was inane and in English, "I love you hot." He would forbid his daughters from playing this song at home.

"What is that?" he asked.

"*Bao Wu,*" the clerk said. The Guardian. "He's from San Francisco," the clerk added, as if to explain the odd name.

Boss Yeung knew the type: born in America, but idolized in Asia. When his eldest daughter had been a teenager, she had adored a floppy-haired heartthrob by way of Los Angeles.

A new version seemed to appear every year.

Back outside, at the first sip, he regretted ordering the bubble tea, which had a cloying sweetness that tasted counterfeit. There must be something in the air, something in the water in Hong Kong that couldn't be replicated here. Nausea gripped him, a side effect of his medication, and he tried not to heave. Swaying on his feet, he pressed the sweating plastic cup to his forehead to cool down. He pictured Scarlett dead, their son and heir born early, born sick, hooked to tubes, or the tiny body unclaimed in the morgue. His every secret, stifled fear was surfacing at once, every worry that had driven him to America on this impossible mission.

A half hour later, he studied the house at the top of the hill. Yellow police tape slashed across the front door, and in the alley, garbage cans stacked high with trash and recycling, tins of cooking oil, balled-up diapers, and flattened cardboard boxes of infant formula and baby wipes. Authorities must have shut down Perfume Bay, something Mama Fang neglected to mention in their conversations in the month since Scarlett's disappearance.

He wouldn't call her, not yet, not before he investigated. The diapers had been fermenting like thousand-year-old eggs, and he covered his nose to ward off the ammonia stench. The backyard's weed-choked, yellowing grass, patches of dirt, and concrete patio had the charm of a prison camp, nothing like the photos from the website that featured a pond under a willow tree, a view of snow-capped mountains, and a young mother serenely cradling her plump son. With scant due diligence, he'd entrusted Scarlett and their child to this sham operation. In how many other ways had Mama Fang's promises fallen short?

Finding the sliding door locked, he crept along the house until he found an open window. He tried to pop off the screen, coated in grime, the dust thick as moss. He could have left then, but after envisioning a clue, a sheet of paper that would lead to Scarlett, he picked up a plastic lawn chair and swung it over his head, grunting with satisfaction when it tore through the screen. He pushed the chair under the window and climbed into a bedroom. The impact when he dropped to his feet jolted through his spine. He'd thickened about the waist, stiffened about the knees, no longer a naughty tree-climbing rascal, but he'd landed on his feet. Not many his age, not many in his condition could.

Later this fall, he would complete what the ancients had deemed a full span of life, and the cycle would start over. Boss Yeung had outlived his father, his grandfather, possibly every male in the long line of ancestors that led to him. Against his protests, his eldest daughter, Viann, was planning a lavish celebration in Hong Kong, with longevity peach cakes gilded in 24-karat gold flakes. To celebrate him, but also to present herself as both the filial daughter and a deal-maker on the rise. The Harvard grad had been scheming with Uncle Lo, who had six more years to go before reaching this stage in life. An uncle not by blood or marriage, but by long association. Neither understood that Boss Yeung wasn't eager to publicize his age and give off the impression that he was close to retiring, no longer in possession of the fire that lit the ambitions of his youth.

He searched Perfume Bay room by room. The guests had left in a hurry, casting aside tracksuits, slippers, and sanitary pads thick as bricks. The mess had the feel of a helter-skelter evacuation from the unexpected approach of bombers on the horizon. Dusty footprints tromped across the carpet, traces of a man's heavy boot. Police? The services at Perfume Bay were legal. Maybe Mama Fang hadn't paid her taxes, maybe she'd been running a secret side business. He recoiled from a giant pair of tan underpants, but then reflexively noted the quality cotton spandex fabric and the double-layer crotch—this assessment second nature to him, after years of manufacturing clothes, electronics, and consumer goods.

Back in his childhood, his mother used to drop coins into monks' metal alms bowls, a clattering display of her devotion. Ever practical, she piled oranges on the family's ancestral shrine in the living room, lit votives at the local Catholic church, and festooned musky marigolds at the Hindu temple. Whatever god or gods ruled the universe, she'd ensured their favor for her family.

Boss Yeung didn't believe in any kind of luck except the kind you made. He'd rebuilt the fortune his father had squandered at the horse track and on a string of mistresses. At his death, his father left debts and a shortbread recipe that his grandfather, a houseboy, had learned from the British. Armed with that paltry inheritance, Boss Yeung searched for a source of cheap, high quality butter— with the taste of pasture and sky—and when he combined it with rice flour, icing sugar, and cornstarch, the biscuits were simultaneously light and rich, crisp and melting. He spent extra on sturdier, glossier plaid tins customers coveted as gifts and used as kitchen storage, landed orders with the most fashionable department stores, and charged four times as much as his competitors to make the biscuits a luxury. With his success, he expanded with new factories, with new lines of business: plastic flowers so lifelike a honeybee might sniff them and mobile phones affordable enough for an *amah* to call home to the Philippines every week.

He retrieved a baby's sock curled on the floor, as big as his thumb. He'd forgotten how tiny, how helpless newborns could be. Shortly after the birth of their first child, his wife had fallen ill. Though he could have left Viann with the *amah*, he soothed her like no one else could, rocking her until she fell asleep against his chest. If she started to wake, he'd take a deep breath, to let her know he was still there.

As infants, his daughters all seemed to have a strong resemblance to their father—him in miniature, crowned with thick tufts of hair. With each passing year, though, the girls became more his wife's, dressed, fed, and schooled as she wished. Each time he returned from his business trips to his factories, clients, and suppliers after months on the road or on-site, he felt more and more like an interloper. His daughters became strangers and his wife stranger still, and he had only Uncle Lo to confide in.

They were both outsiders in Hong Kong, born into unpromising circumstances, tolerated but never accepted by those born rich, those who had been attending the same private schools and respectable social clubs since the time their grandfathers and great-grandfathers achieved the monopolies in palm oil, in shipping, in shrimp paste and oyster sauce from which their families' wealth sprung.

A lifetime ago, Boss Yeung became an ally of Uncle Lo after tipping him off about a rival publisher inflating its circulation.

"It's not fit for fish-wrap!" Uncle Lo had said, and bought him a snifter of brandy. Uncle Lo drank two shots to every one of his and told stories ten times as wild. He'd escaped China by clinging to an inner tube and swimming to Hong Kong. He'd sold candy aboard trains, jumped onto the tracks to save a little boy, the son of a publisher who gave him a job in the newsroom. He'd once climbed barefoot into a python's cage, and had punched out a conniving upstart in the boardroom. He seemed to have dirt on everyone in Hong Kong.

From the beginning, Boss Yeung had known he couldn't keep up, but around Uncle Lo, no venture seemed too daring, and in the decades since, both men had prospered.

\* \* \*

Boss Yeung rubbed his face with both hands, fighting the urge to take a nap on one of the many beds at Perfume Bay. Not long before he'd met Scarlett, doctors had diagnosed him with a chronic blood disease, its course unpredictable. A patient might live two months, two years, or two decades more. The doctors had asked about his family history, if he'd inherited the illness from his mother, father, or a grandparent. Impossible, he said. Exposure to chemicals at his factories—it must have been that. His bloodline wasn't tainted. If his ancestors had cursed him, then he'd cursed his children. He told no one, not his wife or his daughters or Uncle Lo. He didn't want their pity or their fear, or the prayers of the Celestial Goddess, who had extracted a fortune from his wife. Besides, a cure might be found before he experienced his first symptoms.

The illness had unleashed something in him, sent him chasing after new business and chasing after a clerk in his factory. Scarlett's compact, sturdy strength stirred him, and so too her youth, the thick locks that she shed onto his pillow, hair without end that he could have woven into a rope to climb down from a tower. They spent most nights together at his apartment on the factory grounds. Her pregnancy seemed a good omen, for what dying man could create life? When the ultrasound revealed a son, it seemed his fortunes had turned. Although he had dismissed the religion and rituals of his mother and his wife as superstition, he now began grasping for signs and omens. For certainty.

Because no greater certainty existed than the rights, privileges, and protections of every U.S. citizen, he sent Scarlett to Perfume Bay. Uncle Lo had promised she would have VIP status.

They had arrived early for her flight. While at the airport café, he marveled at the size of her belly. Her pregnancy had filled her out, softening her sharp angles and her sharp temper, and after a series of fights, she'd begun eating the traditional diet he wanted for her and the baby. He already missed her body, tucked next to him in his bed, and her calm navigation on their weekend drives. She studied maps for days, weeks in preparation, and had an unerring sense of direction, like a bird that migrates to another hemisphere and finds its way back.

She thought they should postpone her trip to Perfume Bay. He'd been waking up drenched in sweat, and she wanted him to see a doctor. "Don't talk nonsense," he'd said.

The departures hall had echoed with chatter and the clack and whine of suitcases as passengers sprinted toward the security gate. The new terminal was all curves and skylights, the latest foray by foreign architects who came to China to build projects at a speed and scope like nowhere else. A dizzying futuristic white reflected in polished stone floors, cold and barren as the moon. If he told her about the illness ticking within, she wouldn't leave him. First he'd have to admit to her—therefore to himself—that he might sicken, might die. Chimes sounded, followed by an airport announcement. He couldn't make out the words over the hiss of the steamer on the espresso machine.

As Scarlett walked toward the counter to get a refill of hot water, a *tai tai* with huge sunglasses tried to flag her down, asking for sugar. Scarlett was dressed in black, just like the attendant behind the counter, but so were a few other travelers in the café. The *tai tai*—a haughty Chinese housewife with a diamond ring big as a gumball—had sized up Scarlett as part of the servant class.

Scarlett shook her head. The *tai tai* sighed in irritation and offered her a crumpled yuan note. Taking in the scene, Boss Yeung rose, ready to intervene in case Scarlett lost her temper and cursed out the *tai tai*. He waited as Scarlett returned with a glass sugar dispenser, and without saying a word, started pouring into the *tai tai*'s cup. Even after the *tai tai* said, "Enough—enough!" Scarlett kept pouring, finally emptying the dispenser all over the table. The *tai tai* opened her mouth, as if to protest, but the sight of Scarlett's fury seemed to silence her.

"Would you like anything else?" Scarlett asked.

Boss Yeung pulled her away while the *tai tai* fled, knocking over a suitcase in her haste. Scarlett would send herself into labor, getting worked up like that! She was unrepentant, angry that he'd interrupted her revenge against the *tai tai*, who must represent every wealthy woman who had snubbed her, and maybe served as a stand-in for his wife. She could have been angry that he was sending her away. He'd come to believe if they'd left things differently that day, if he'd told her how much she meant to him, all their later troubles might never have followed.

He found no sign of her at Perfume Bay. None of her clothes, not her honey-scented body lotion that she rubbed on her belly to prevent stretch marks. Without Scarlett, he'd been robbed of his senses, found himself in a world without color, light, sound, taste, or touch. After Scarlett left, orders had fallen, credit tightened, and a worker on the assembly line killed herself by jumping off the roof of the dormitory. A teenager, a girl far from home, someone's daughter, someone's sister, crushed by the seven-day workweeks and fifteen-hour days. To prevent copycat suicides, the plant manager put a new lock on the door to the roof, gave raises, and hired a monk to purge the factory of evil spirits.

Working, working, always working to make up his losses, Boss Yeung turned gaunt as a candle flame. Weary, the simplest tasks accomplished only through monumental effort. Even his walks around the factory floor seemed to take twice as long. He vowed never to be careless again, not in business, not with this pregnancy, and so for an additional fee, Mama Fang had provided daily reports about Scarlett.

Maybe Mama Fang had exaggerated and lied, just as she'd exaggerated and lied about the accommodations. According to her, Scarlett had stopped eating and Mama Fang forced her to drink cans of chocolate-flavored nutritional supplements. And she'd broken another guest's finger, while fighting over the remote control; the medical costs had been added to the fees Boss Yeung had to pay.

Scarlett must have suffocated here, the air stale and hot with the scent of bitter herbs and vinegar. He couldn't remember if he or Mama Fang had suggested that he take custody of their son. With her kind, her wishes dissolved into yours, and she anticipated what you needed before you knew yourself. If she'd been an entrepreneur in China, Mama Fang would have built an empire that rivaled Uncle Lo's, one of those self-made billionaire queens who trafficked in commercial real estate, medicinal ointments from Tibet, and recycled cardboard boxes.

The night he'd authorized Mama Fang to pay off Scarlett, the night Scarlett had escaped, he'd come down with a high fever. He'd woken in sheets soaked in sweat, and all but crawled to his driver to take him home to Hong Kong. The rash on his calves had returned, a constellation of tiny red spots. Doctors confirmed his illness had turned aggressive and recommended a bone marrow transplant. A sibling or a child provided the best chance of a match. Boss Yeung had outlasted his younger brother and sister. His daughters, then. In the old tales, filial children cut out a chunk of their own flesh to feed starving parents, enslaved themselves to pay for funerals, and sat shirtless all night to draw mosquitoes away from their sleeping mother and father.

In the dining room, before the cook served the meal, he gathered their cheek swabs. To search their family's past and predict future health, he told them, but secretly, he'd get their bone marrow typed. At least one had to match.

His wife had been away on a high-level, high-priced pilgrimage in the mountains with the Celestial Goddess. None of them knew about the baby. If they rejected the boy, Boss Yeung would cut off their allowances, disown them, and divorce his wife. Would they mourn their father when he died? Only out of obligation, not out of love, except for Viann.

Viann had opened her mouth, much like when she was a child and he would pop in a melon seed or haw flake. He swabbed up and down, applying firm pressure. Of all his daughters, she was the most likely to suspect an ulterior motive.

He dropped the swab into the collection tube and snapped on the top. "Maybe we're descended from emperors," Viann said.

Daughter No. 2 had gagged on the swab and tears sprang into her eyes. She didn't want to know what genes she carried for disease and the years she might have left before the onset of symptoms. "It's like reading the date on your gravestone."

"Nothing's set in stone," Viann said. "Nothing defines you, not even your mistakes."

A jab at No. 2, who was banned from several of Hong Kong's finest department stores after pilfering luxury goods, avoiding jail time only after Viann intervened by cutting a promotional deal with the buyers.

Daughter No. 3 had dropped out of university to become an assistant to the Celestial Goddess. Her breath stank of wet dog, despite her strict vegetarian diet. After Boss Yeung swabbed her, she announced she'd live to 127. "A prime prime."

"You might," Viann said. "What's the use of a long life, without meat or fish or drink? You must feel 127 already!"

No one matched. His two youngest shared half of Boss Yeung's markers, and Viann, none at all, a consequence of fate and of genetics. He'd wanted a match between him and Viann, he admitted only then. Of his children, she was most like him, in her shrewdness and ambition.

She had once asked why he and Uncle Lo had never gone into business together. He had dismissed the idea with such vehemence that she must understand that their camaraderie might not bear the open acknowledgment of Uncle Lo's superior financial acumen.

Uncle Lo had arranged an appointment with a highly regarded specialist and launched a bone marrow drive, getting himself, his wife, and his children all typed, but the tycoon's greatest gift had been his suggestion: a cure might be found in the baby that Scarlett carried, in the stem cells circulating through the umbilical cord. The men were in the steam room of Hong Kong's most exclusive private club, with a years-long waiting list you joined in the hopes your children, yet-to-be-conceived, might someday terrorize their *amah* at the pool while you perfected your tennis stroke, relaxed over dim sum with a real estate magnate, or bet huge sums at each golf hole.

Around Uncle Lo, Boss Yeung felt chosen, marveling at how their friendship brought adventure to what would have been an otherwise predictable existence. And what did Uncle Lo find in him? A friend who could be counted on—for drinks until dawn, for secrets of any size—who was grateful for the attentions, but not overly, obsequiously so. Uncle Lo had enough of those.

"Your own blood is the most powerful medicine." Uncle Lo leaned back, exposing the birthmark splashed on his chest.

"Then let's join our blood." Boss Yeung inhaled a cloud of steam and coughed. He'd always wanted their eldest children to marry.

Uncle Lo had resisted. "If our children are old enough to get married, then it means we're getting old."

The excuse wounded Boss Yeung. Why would his friend reject the idea of uniting their bloodlines—because he thought Boss Yeung's was tainted? The future of that bloodline was slipping away, along with the chance of a cure. He entered the kitchen. Sometimes when Boss Yeung called Mama Fang, he'd heard the clank of pots and pans, and so her office must be nearby. Thirsty, he searched for a glass, but the cabinets were bare. Cupping his hands under the faucet, he slurped tap water with a mineral tang and walked into the ransacked office, with an upended leather desk chair, a dead plant, and filing cabinets. He sought files about the guests, jotted notes with details only he might understand were significant to Scarlett. He yanked out drawers—empty. Receipts scattered on the floor, including one for Lum Femcare, which sounded like a medical clinic. The slip listed an address on Foothill Boulevard, where he'd exited the freeway for Perfume Bay. He'd go there next.

The private investigator hadn't found Scarlett, but he'd worked for a paycheck, not out of duty or love. A search of her mobile phone, left behind at Perfume Bay, turned up a listing for her mother, but the calls went straight to voicemail. Nothing on her Internet browser or work emails led to her village, either, and no one in the factory had heard from her. Scarlett's apartment held few photos: a man with his daughter on his shoulders; a laughing woman on a carousel; and a blond man with a cleft in his chin, rugged as a mountaineer. Not friends or family but strangers, printed on the slips of paper that had come with the frames. A discovery that kneed Boss Yeung in the gut—how alone she'd been in the world.

The trail petered out in California, too, even though the runaway teenager had been the strongest lead. The boyfriend's parents had been shocked to learn the baby they believed aborted remained gestating and did not allow his detective to interview their son. "Who's to say it's his?" they asked. The detective was still trying to track him down separately.

In the last bedroom, Boss Yeung found a square outline in the rug, matted down from a heavy load. From a massage chair, like the one he'd requested for Scarlett? A flash of blue caught his eye, a slip of paper sticking out from underneath the closet door. The blue of the Pacific, on the California page, which she must have torn out of the atlas he'd given her. He smoothed out the paper, worn soft as cotton after being folded and unfolded many times. She didn't have many belongings, in a life where she never had belonged anywhere for long.

Scarlett would have stared at the map until the freeways were imprinted in her memory, a web of veins. The parallel lines of the 5 and the 99 and the 1 and 101, the ladder rungs of the 80 and the 10 and the 60, crossing the immense state. She'd torn it out in preparation for this trip. Even before leaving China, she might have suspected he would betray her and brought the map to plan her escape routes. He heard footsteps outside. Mama Fang! When he swung open the front door, two police officers stared him down.

Short and stocky as a gingerbread cookie, the officer wore aviator sunglasses, masking her expression. Her brawny partner stood behind her. Though she'd identified herself, Boss Yeung hadn't caught her name. Neighbors must have reported an intruder. Stonily, she asked him to step outside and for his identification. That much he gathered, as he cursed himself for his limited English: he read some, understood less, and spoke almost none at all.

She wasn't much older than Viann, and the stiffness in her manner made her seem a recent graduate of the academy, eager to prove herself yet already assuming, already resenting those who questioned her authority.

Sunlight winked off her badge, and her poly-blend pants had a knife-edge crease, with no stains or loose threads. She'd left the engine running on the patrol car, its radio crackling with a garbled shaman's chant. Her partner headed around the corner to the backyard, where he would presumably find the busted window screen.

"How much?" he asked. In China, he had settled such matters by paying the fine on the spot. He hadn't withdrawn much from the airport ATM, sixty dollars minus what he paid for lunch, and he hoped it would be enough.

Her mouth hardened, and she repeated her request for identification. The dry heat was making him light-headed. He reached for his passport, in a travel pouch tucked into his waistband. The officer ordered him to keep his hands up and she patted him down. Yesterday, he'd been a chief executive, used to deferential and preferential treatment, but here he was nothing.

The officer's belt bristled with a walkie-talkie, a nightstick, keys, and a gun—a gun. Police in China didn't carry guns. They didn't have to, but Americans were violent, and so too their police. Patches of sweat began blooming under his arms and on his back, and his bowels went hot and loose as a bowl of ramen.

She found nothing on Boss Yeung, and neither did he. His identification had gone missing, along with his wallet and mobile phone. He pointed at his car, mimed pulling open the glove box, hoping she'd understand. She nodded and followed him. He got into the car. Maybe he'd left everything under his seat, tucked in the sun visor, or under the rental paperwork? No. He popped open the glove compartment and out spilled amber bottles of his medication, which he'd stowed for safekeeping after taking a dose in the mall parking lot.

He was drowning in the car's toxic fumes of hot plastic and air freshener. He'd paid for his boba tea, and then—he must have left his wallet in the shop, or dropped it in the parking lot. The officer scrutinized his bloodshot eyes, his nervous hands, his rumpled clothes, and his scarecrow frame—that of a junkie, of a thief in search of his next high.

After he climbed out of the car, she asked if he had—had what? He didn't understand the word, until she said, "doctor." She must want the prescription. He didn't have one on him. She made the motion of opening the car door, with a look that seemed to be asking for permission. If he resisted, he'd seem guilty. He nodded, and she motioned for him to sit on the curb.

She held each pill bottle up to the light: the pale blue painkillers, white and canary-yellow pills to boost his blood counts and keep the disease at bay, taken three times a day, once before bed, on an empty stomach, or with food, each dose a bitter reminder he'd become an invalid. Chinese medicine, too. Prescribed by an herbalist, the tiny black balls smelled like burning autumn leaves and in the eyes of this American, it must have seemed like dark magic.

He felt naked, her scrutiny intrusive as a finger jammed down his throat. The officer frowned and checked to make sure he remained sitting. He noticed the black metal bars on the rear windows of the squad car parked behind his. She'd arrest him, detain him, and tie him up in legal proceedings, wasting time that he didn't have. He couldn't try bribing her again, not with his wallet gone. Then he remembered the change he'd stuffed into his back pocket. The bills, damp as tofu skin and stained by the touch of many hands, filled him with as much jubilation as if he'd won the lottery.

"I help," he said. The officer ignored him, or perhaps she didn't hear over the crackle of the walkie-talkie. He waited until a woman walking her poodle passed. Officials who campaigned most loudly against corruption had the blackest hands, and the officer wouldn't want witnesses. He stood and rapped on the trunk, trying to get her attention.

She spun around, and he flashed the bills at her, his hand quick as a blackjack dealer's. She thrust her face into his and barked something at him. She sounded angry, and he wondered if he'd sunk himself deeper into trouble. He sat down on the curb, watching to see what she would do next. Returning to the car, the officer picked up a bottle with a loose cap and pills cascaded with a clatter onto the seat, onto the floor mat, and likely every one of the car's crevices. She bent over, scooping up pills.

If he'd been thinking clearly, he wouldn't have slipped around the corner. He wouldn't have crossed the intersection and flagged down the bus. But then, the fleetness of his step wouldn't have returned, either, nor the speed and strength he thought he had lost forever.

Until he mentioned Mama Fang, the Chinese receptionist remained tight-lipped, and wouldn't confirm Scarlett had visited the clinic.

"She's a client of Perfume Bay," Boss Yeung said. "You saw her about a month ago."

The receptionist's expression darkened like a thunderhead.

"She's a client of Mama Fang."

"Mama Fang," she muttered, and he suspected the proprietor of Perfume Bay had left the clinic with a large bill. "You're in touch with her?" Her nails, long red talons, tapped her desk with indignation. "Ask her!"

"She told me to come here. Before we meet this afternoon."

Mama Fang had said no such thing, but the doctors of Lum Femcare must be interested in finding her. "Please," he said. "I'm the father. I can pay any remaining charges."

He was the only man in the waiting room, and he could feel the patients staring at him. They, too, were all Chinese. Shifting uncomfortably, their ample bottoms spilling out of their seats, their breasts swelling into udders, and their inquisitive faces round and gleaming. No matter how much the women had wanted their children, each at some point must have cursed the man who'd done this to them, the father who wouldn't suffer the aches of pregnancy and the agony of labor.

The receptionist exhaled, and Boss Yeung wondered if the financial hit had threatened her job, if the clinic might close. He told her he could put the doctor in touch with an investor at Perfume Bay, who could take care of the rest of the bill.

After she left her desk, he studied photos of the babies tacked onto the walls. Round cheeks, chubby fists, little faces in cozy knit hats, and wearing embroidered silk tunics from their red egg parties. Jealousy stabbed through Boss Yeung's chest. These mothers had always been certain of their children's whereabouts, memorized the curve of their noses, every mole, the shape of their big toes. Boss Yeung could only guess at his son's. His son! What traits would his son inherit from him: The same long fingers? His bowlegged walk? The set of his mouth, or the intense focus that he was starting to understand might drive others away?

Until now Boss Yeung hadn't understood why she'd fled. After escaping the police this afternoon, he grasped how fear and anger fueled your first steps, and how defiance kept you going.

The longer she remained on the run, the harsher the punishment Uncle Lo would try to exact. He'd made the hunt his, compelled to intervene because he'd been the one to refer her to Perfume Bay. Married to a daughter of Communist royalty, he had the backing of the Party to go after his enemies: a supplier who cheated him was imprisoned and died a month before his release. A rival lost his factory to eminent domain, after the government rerouted the subway through his neighborhood. Uncle Lo wanted Scarlett jailed, somewhere she could think upon her crimes, and with each passing day, Boss Yeung wavered.

The receptionist returned to her desk and began typing, her fingernails clacking on the keyboard. A patient interrupted. "I've been waiting for an hour!" Her skin was blotchy as rotting strawberries, and her body seethed like an overgrown garden.

The receptionist glanced at her. "The doctor will see you soon." She pulled out a file.

"I'm going to pee on the floor," the patient warned, and the receptionist waved her in. A moment later, the patient shouted she needed toilet paper.

Sighing, the receptionist got up, leaving the paperwork that held the secrets of his baby's health, his growth and progress, secrets that might shed light on Scarlett's state of mind and hint at her whereabouts. Secrets to finding his cure. Reaching over the counter, he snatched the file and might have escaped for the second time that day, but for the mother squeezing her double stroller through the door—twins, two girls with lace headbands and dumpling cheeks. The mother apologized, flustered.

He tried to ease the stroller through. The wheels caught on the doorjamb, the toys hanging off the stroller's handle rattled crazily, and the newborn on the right gasped, a held breath that sucked the air out of the waiting room, stopping time yet also carrying the inevitability of a cresting wave: the piercing howl that would follow.

Those cries—that need. The mother popped a pacifier into one newborn's mouth, which she spat out. He yanked the stroller again, to no avail, and the mother picked up her daughter, shushing as the other twin wailed, thrashing her head back. She'd give herself whiplash.

He dropped the file and opened his arms, and the desperate mother thrust the baby at him so she could tend to the other one. He crossed his arms, clasping the baby against his chest, as her head fell back, tiny and bird-bone light. He supported her neck, and with his other hand, cradled her bottom. The overhead light trans-fixed her, and he turned to give her a better view over his shoulder. Viann had loved lights, too. The baby smelled like fragility, like talcum powder and diaper cream.

The receptionist returned and retrieved the file from the floor. Although he braced himself for her scolding, she told him the doctor could see him now. He handed the baby back to her mother, the quivering heat fading quickly, too quickly, from his chest.

At her desk, Dr. Lum was younger than he expected, perhaps ten years out of medical school. Stanford, he noticed with approval. Her hands were scrubbed clean, the nails squared-off, and she emanated the scent of antibacterial soap, of probing efficiency. In addition to her diplomas, the wall behind her featured posters of Mickey Mouse and a papa bear tucking his baby into a cradle. He didn't bother with pleasantries. He needed a bone marrow transplant, he said, and his daughters didn't match. Unexpectedly, his eyes welled with tears he'd never allowed himself.

"Children usually aren't matches," Dr. Lum said. "You need at least six of the eight markers, and children typically have half from each parent."

He explained that daughters No. 2 and No. 3 had four of his eight markers, and Viann, none at all.

"None?" Dr. Lum asked. "That's impossible."

"My doctor's a VIP."

"None?"

"None."

"Then she's not your daughter."

He must have contaminated the sample, or a technician must have mixed up Viann's swabs in the lab. He'd have to get her tested again. Yet his doctor in Hong Kong had seemed so agitated. Hesitating, unlike his usual brusque manner. Suppose—suppose the test had been accurate. What if his doctor wanted to spare a terminal patient the news that he'd been a cuckold almost three decades ago?

Dr. Lum didn't know him and didn't care about preserving long-held illusions. He swallowed, his tongue unbearably thick and disgusting. For months after giving birth to Viann, his wife had stayed in bed and wept, pushing the baby girl away. That distance always remained between mother and daughter. A coolness, born out of jealousy and resentment, he'd always believed, as his wife's beauty faded and Viann's blossomed.

Boss Yeung spread his hands in his lap, long fingers that he and Viann shared. Dr. Lum flipped open the chart and told him that the baby was healthy, with a strong heartbeat and developing normally.

Did his wife consider each subsequent daughter a punishment for her affair? Her guilt might have driven her into the plump arms of the Celestial Goddess. If he wasn't Viann's father, then who? Did his wife have a fling with an old classmate, or an instructor at the club? She'd briefly taken tennis lessons. A friend's husband? His thoughts were like feathers in a storm, whirling out of his grasp. He tried to remember her friends, from the days before the Celestial Goddess.

A friend—of his? He had no friends, no friends but Uncle Lo. Uncle Lo, who'd resisted pairing his son with Viann. Uncle Lo, who had twelve acknowledged children. Uncle Lo, who'd always taken an interest in Viann, arranging pop stars to visit her birthday parties and an internship at his flagship magazine. He struggled to catch his breath. Uncle Lo had his pick of women and never would have betrayed him. He couldn't recall a single moment of suppressed ardor passing between his wife and his friend. It had seemed she considered Uncle Lo an irritation, fuming when he kept Boss Yeung out until dawn.

Early in their marriage, she had been loyal as a dove, and thrifty, too, careful to make use of every scrap of food and to tailor their clothes to remake them like new. In those days, he'd been ignorant of the mechanics of sex and had bought a manual, as if she were a radio to take apart and put back together. A geometry lesson of angles, an engineering feat of completed circuits, with little of the tenderness, passion, and spontaneity she must have craved. The years sped by. Even after she began worshipping the Celestial Goddess, he'd been faithful to her. Until his diagnosis. Until he met Scarlett.

Viann had the intelligence and drive that her sisters lacked, that he'd thought she must have inherited from him, from her father. From Uncle Lo? He felt as though everything he'd taken for granted had failed him, as if gravity had disappeared, as if air had turned into water. The room blurred around him and faintly, he heard Dr. Lum asking if he was okay. He found himself on the floor, staring up at her. In her grip he felt as a newborn must, drowsing against a parent. Oh, Viann. She might never have been his to give up.

The walk took longer than expected, and when he arrived at the outdoor mall, the sky had turned apocalyptic, the murky air slashed by streaks of rust and orange. Despite the heat, he was shivering and in a cold sweat after missing a dose of medication. He sat on the edge of the chlorinated water fountain, its blue tiles covered in hundreds of coins, shimmering like the scales of a fish. So many wishes—for his son, for himself. For Viann.

He had to get to the boba tea shop on the second floor, where he'd ask if the staff had found his wallet. He lurched to his feet. At the top of the escalator he teetered, then fell. Each tumble, a blow that split mountains and hatched new gods. As he filled with the light of an exploding star, ten thousand bronze bells tolled.

# Chapter 7

Scarlett's labor pains began on a sunny afternoon. She gasped, dropping her spoon into the porridge she'd been dishing up in the communal kitchen. She held on to the counter, her back aching and her belly cramping. She'd been feeling twinges since yesterday, but now her body seized up like never before.

Daisy dropped a tin of tea and rushed to her side. "What is it—is it . . . ?"

Scarlett nodded, and Daisy shrieked with excitement. On the run, then in hiding, she would at last pass through to the other side. Her daughter, her daughter. As the tightness eased, Scarlett insisted on keeping to their plan: they'd take the number 10 bus to the hospital instead of calling an expensive cab. If they arrived too soon in her labor, the emergency room might turn them away. She and Daisy slurped down the porridge, uncertain when they would eat next, grabbed a bag with snacks, toiletries, and a change of clothes for herself and the baby, before catching a bus that rattled through the Chinatown tunnel and down the hill, past the glittering boutiques, the fortress of a courthouse, and along broad boulevards flanked by warehouses. The air scented with bodies packed tight, French fries and cigarettes.

Aside from scavenging expeditions within a few blocks of Chinatown, much of San Francisco remained a mystery to Scarlett. The trip took nearly an hour, delayed by double-parked cars, tourists fumbling for change, and shouting matches between the bull-necked driver and a pair of teenage girls in neon miniskirts. Scarlett panted, her legs spread out over two seats. When a teenage boy in sagging jeans tried to sit next to her, Daisy shooed him away. Slipping off his ear-buds, he noticed Scarlett bent over, gripping onto the seat handle, and muttered—according to Daisy's translation—"Damn! Somebody call this lady an ambulance."

With each bump and jounce, Scarlett prayed her water wouldn't break. Her belly held floods that would sweep over mountains and rise to the heavens. The passenger window was tinted, scratched with thin white lines that crisscrossed Scarlett's faint reflection. For the first time, she could see Ma's face in hers, in the skin stretched tight around her eyes and in the cords in her neck. At this age, Ma had raised a daughter old enough to leave home.

Scarlett had last seen her during the Spring Festival. She'd planned to stay for a week, but left after two days in the wake of their endless arguments. She'd been pregnant, though she didn't know it. Exhausted, from the twenty-hour ride in the packed train car. Lonely, because she'd parted from Boss Yeung.

Hundreds of millions of migrant workers returned to their villages for their annual visit. The factories shut down, and the trains jammed for days with fathers, mothers, sons, and daughters bearing gifts to make amends for their long absences. Westerners marked the arrival of spring when the weather fitfully began to warm, while the Chinese looked toward spring and its renewal from the depths of winter. In preparation, she and Boss Yeung had gone shopping beforehand. He'd suggested a puffy blue jacket, a hot water heater, rubber boots, and fleece blankets zipped in a plastic case, and offered to pay. She got everything, but paid for it herself, shouldering the load into two large duffels.

He told her to ship it ahead.

"You can't arrive empty-handed," she had said. She eyed the tin of peanut candies he'd bought for his family—a favorite of his eldest daughter. He would be spending the holidays with them all in Hong Kong. "Not even you."

Early in the morning on the first day of the Spring Festival, she climbed the hill behind her village, where the mobile phone signal was the strongest. Tradition dictated you were to live this day as you would all year, with a new haircut, a new set of clothes, new shoes, cleared debts, and feasts with family. She stamped her feet, trying to stay warm, her body grown used to the mild winters of the south. The scent of burning straw hung in the air, tinged with manure. Somewhere in the village, pigs snuffled. A little girl in pigtails, her breath steaming in the cold, watched Scarlett from the doorway until a harsh voice summoned her back inside. She called Boss Yeung. If he answered, then he loved her. She pictured him in a kitchen, reading the newspaper, the morning light falling across his face. His thick hair unruly and mussed from sleep. His family in bed, away from him, somewhere, anywhere she didn't have to imagine.

He didn't pick up.

She trudged back home, where she broke several rules that shriveled the new year's bounty of good fortune. She sliced an apple (no cutting) and knocked over her teacup, which shattered on the damp floor (no breaking). She had pushed shards into the corner to start a trash heap (no sweeping, to avoid clearing out the year's new luck).

Ma had never remarried, for no one wanted a widow with a vinegar disposition. She jerked the splintered broom out of Scarlett's hands. "Clumsy!" she had shouted, thereby breaking another new year's day rule: no arguing. Unmarried, childless, Scarlett was no more than a teenager to Ma. And Scarlett couldn't help reacting like one.

Ma had yet to enjoy any of the good luck she worked so hard to preserve. "You never listen," Ma said. "If you listened, you wouldn't be running around like a ghost."

A hungry ghost with no home and no family, forever roaming and restless. Condemnation, even though Ma didn't know about the affair with Boss Yeung. Condemnation for all the choices that kept Scarlett alone. Her self-sufficiency, her greatest strength and her greatest fault.

"You'll die and no one will remember you," Ma said.

Condemnation over the men she'd dated, whom she'd rejected as too ugly, too childish, too short, too lazy, lacking in a sizeable apartment or goals. Condemnation for the life that refuted her mother's in every way. Ma's lack of a grandchild must have felt like a curse from all the women whose pregnancies she had ended.

Squatting, Ma had scooped up the remaining shards, nicking her fingers, blood dripping down her hands. Scarlett offered her a clean rag, which she batted away. Wordlessly, they piled the shards into the corner. Ma had been the last surviving child, out of six brothers and sisters lost to disease, to accident, to revolution. An orphan, a widow, who'd lost her only son and her husband in the same year. No one left to share her memories of childhood, no one else to confirm whom she'd been before she took a job at the clinic. No wonder Ma held on to the rituals that promised fortune and abundance, rituals that Scarlett would now have to decide if she wanted to pass on to her daughter.

The bus rumbled through the wide intersection. They had to be getting close to the hospital. Another contraction hit and Scarlett clenched her hands until the pain passed. She could reach out to her cousin Dongfeng online, the one who'd opened a hair salon in Hefei, the provincial capital. Her cousin spent all her free time online, plastering social media with her every sigh, with her every pose. She could get a message to the village and to Ma. Eventually, but not now, while Boss Yeung was hunting her down. Not now, when Ma would have to wait years to meet her grandchild.

The bus stopped a block from the hospital. The path through the grounds wound past flowerbeds, a patchy lawn, and a concrete fountain dry except for a dribbling rust stain. A legless man and a fat woman, both in hospital gowns, sat in wheelchairs, their tawny weathered faces turned up to the sun.

Scarlett's skin was sticky with dried sweat and her fingers grimy from clutching the bus's handrail. She wanted a shower—better, a bath. She wobbled and Daisy caught her. She closed her eyes and took a deep breath, trying to gather herself together, before they staggered the last few meters to the entrance. In the lobby, Daisy filled out the paperwork. Her hands, holding the cup of ice water to Scarlett's cracked lips. Her hands, changing the channels on the television, adjusting the bed and fluffing the pillows. The delivery room was dingy with jaundiced-yellow paint and scuffed linoleum floors. The scent of blood, vomit, sickness, and decay hovered beneath the cloying sweetness of disinfectant, like bubble gum and vinegar.

Hours passed. Scarlett was grateful for Daisy's company, hard as it was to admit she needed help from anyone, hard as it was to groan in front of her. Though they'd been sharing the same bed for weeks, though they'd stopped averting their eyes when they changed their clothes, labor laid Scarlett bare. To Daisy, everyone more than a couple of years older must seem unfathomably ancient, unfathomably *far*, in another galaxy light-years away. Yet the teenager didn't flee or faint. She seemed to be taking a forensic approach to this preview of her own upcoming ordeal.

If Scarlett had remained at Perfume Bay, Mama Fang would have held vigil at her bedside. No wonder she'd encouraged her clients to schedule C-sections, less than an hour of her time, and not half a day or more of labor. Boss Yeung hadn't planned to witness their child draw a first breath, and Scarlett felt no guilt for disappearing and depriving him of their daughter's birth. Every day she remained hidden served as a reminder of the limits of his power. Still, she missed his hand holding hers, his bargaining tactics—he would have demanded that the doctors and nurses keep Scarlett and their child foremost in their attention at all times.

Like their child, Scarlett and Boss Yeung were born under the sign of the enigmatic snake, said to be intelligent but reserved, acting according to their own judgment. There were twelve animals in all, rotating in a cycle, returning to your sign when you were twelve years old, twenty-four, thirty-six, forty-eight, and so on. Each return brought turbulence, requiring caution to avoid the year's dangers—a superstition that Scarlett had never paid much attention to until now.

Daisy flipped the television to a talent show, where a man in blond dreadlocks to his waist strummed an acoustic guitar and sang what sounded like a lullaby. She sighed, and said she and her boyfriend had once performed this pop song at KTV, one of those karaoke clubs with private rooms that charged by the hour, where customers snacked on expensive fruit plates, sipped imported liquor, and nuzzled their beloveds under a disco ball.

Daisy rubbed her fist in the small of her back. There wasn't much padding on the hospital chair. Judging by the girl's wistful expression, Scarlett guessed karaoke might have been the first time the couple had been alone in a room, maybe even the first time they'd kissed.

The Indian anesthesiologist arrived and instructed Scarlett to sit up. Her gown flapped open, and she shivered as he swabbed her back. He returned a few minutes later to inject her with the epidural, the needle long and stout enough for knitting. She felt no pinch, only pressure against her skin, which had gone numb and rubbery.

Soon, very soon, she'd meet her daughter. Another contraction swept through her and Scarlett grunted, her body in the grip of a giant's fist. She thought of her mother, her grandmother, all the mothers in the maternity wing. She felt a sense of connection rare in her life—to all mothers, to the universe itself—that she suspected would not last after her labor ended. Odder still, she felt a bond with cats, dogs, all animals that pushed forth their young between their legs. Though she held the traditional Chinese notion that animals were meant for work and for consumption, she was now acting sentimental as an American.

Were the drugs turning her woozy? Daisy read aloud from a brochure she'd picked up at registration: how to make a cord-blood donation to a public bank. Scarlett had first learned about cord blood at Perfume Bay, the spoonfuls left in the umbilical cord that held potential cures for cancer, leukemia, spinal cord injuries, and more. Lady Yu had signed up, Countess Tien, too, for the service that would ship and store the stem cells for a family's private use.

"How much?" Scarlett asked. The pain was gone, but not the sensation, the same immense pressure that turns coal into diamonds. She settled against the pillows.

"Free," Daisy said. "And anonymous." She flipped over the brochure and showed Scarlett the logo, a cartoon of three infant heads in shades of pink, yellow, and brown, topped with wisps of hair, the petals of a flower. The donation could go to anyone who matched. In China, the government harvested organs from executed prisoners, but in America, a donor apparently had to give permission. As valuable as the liver, heart, or cornea might be, here they ended up in the trash, cremated or buried, without the individual's consent.

"Why not?" Daisy asked. Scarlett agreed. If the potential cures provided a few more days or months of life for a stranger, the donation—more than her birth on American soil—should secure her daughter's right to live here.

Scarlett closed her eyes, bearing down, and with one last exhausted push, her daughter emerged, wailing. She felt turned inside out, run over, smeared flat. She'd lost almost all awareness of her surroundings in the final moments of delivery. Bombs could have gone off and she wouldn't have looked up. She struggled to sit up, dazed by the bright lights, the commotion of the darting nurses and the beeping monitors. She'd done it, somehow she'd done it. Never in her life had she been at such peace, resting in the stillness of the eye of a hurricane. Joy bloomed in her chest. She reached out her arms, straining with the last of her strength, as the nurses wiped off the smears of blood on the baby and laid her against Scarlett's chest. So tiny, so perfect, her skin warm and soft as kitten's fur. She stroked the sweet curve of the baby's ears and marveled at the tiny chips of her fingernails. The nurses slid a knit cap onto the baby's head and placed a receiving blanket over her.

Scarlett craned her neck, trying to get a better view, and gently pushed back the cap, which had fallen over her daughter's eyes. The baby's mouth gaped, taking in her first breaths of air, and she was looking back at Scarlett. Probably, she was just as spent and shell-shocked by the ordeal; after months spent in the warm dark, she'd been pushed and squeezed into a whole new world of light, sound, and smells. It seemed just as unreal to Scarlett that her companion of all these months—the most difficult months of her life—was now outside of her.

She had the smushed features of a newborn, those flattened ears and that squashed nose, and it seemed too soon to tell whom she would take after. And Scarlett still hadn't come up with a name. Everything she'd tried before giving birth had been too slippery or too clunky, but now one popped into her head: Liberty. Liberty Chen, three flowing syllables paired with an emphatic surname.

She looked up at Daisy, who was watching them. She didn't fully understand Daisy's expression of awe and disbelief until three weeks later, after she witnessed the birth of Daisy's son, a slimy creature surfacing from the muck, with a thatch of dark hair and a high-pitched mewl.

Scarlett snipped the leathery umbilical cord, tougher than she expected. Daisy had done the same for her, a shared ritual that linked them for life. The nurses weighed him, flicked the soles of his feet, cleaned off the blood and waxy, creamy coating, and nestled him against Daisy's chest.

"Those eyes," Scarlett said. Black and shiny as watermelon seeds.

"Like Daddy's." Daisy kissed the top of his head. She hadn't found her boyfriend, and Scarlett imagined that her longing for him would only intensify with a newborn. Daisy hummed a lullaby, the song she and William had sung at karaoke.

The doctor massaged Daisy's belly, telling her to push, and with a gush of blood, the placenta slithered out, attached to the other end of the umbilical cord. Scarlett hadn't seen her own, and she couldn't stop staring at it—larger and more substantial than she expected. After the nurses dumped the placenta into a plastic bin, she returned to Daisy's side.

The striped receiving blanket slipped off her son's shoulder, and Scarlett tucked it back around him. He whimpered and from her bassinet, Liberty joined in with cries of her own. The nurse in charge had been flummoxed when Scarlett arrived at the delivery ward with her own newborn, and might have sent her away but for Daisy's youth. The nurse didn't want a teenager laboring alone, but had warned if Liberty caused too much of a commotion, she'd have to leave. Scarlett had nursed her on and off throughout the night and in the final stretch of labor, Liberty had napped in a sling tucked against her chest.

Now Liberty howled, as if she knew that she would no longer be the sole focus of their attention. For weeks, Scarlett had tended to her baby as Daisy tended to Scarlett, propping her up with pillows and bringing her cups of tea and bowls of soup while she recovered from giving birth.

They had already suffered the sleep deprivation of new parenthood. With a second newborn, their sleep would shatter again and again.

The nurse glowered, and Scarlett carried her daughter into the hallway, down the elevator, and into the courtyard. A change in surroundings, a change of temperature sometimes calmed her, and Liberty quieted, gazing up at the peeling gray bark of the sycamore trees.

In the set of her mouth, didn't she resemble Boss Yeung?—which shouldn't have been a surprise yet it astonished Scarlett all the same. Such a burden, inheritance. When family gathered on holidays, the claims on their children invariably began. Your nose, shaped like your mother's. Your long earlobes, like your grandfather's. Traits, features, and habits from legions of ancestors, shuffled in each new generation. The body died, but blood lived on. Nothing had belonged to Scarlett alone until she left the village.

Liberty was sturdier than she looked, but Scarlett still found herself holding her breath around her. She wanted to believe Boss Yeung didn't know where or how to find them, but every time she left Evergreen Gardens she felt jumpy as a soldier crossing enemy lines. She didn't know who might be setting their sights upon babies of a certain age, who might be watching now. She glanced up uneasily at the windows that ringed the courtyard and went back inside.

At Evergreen Gardens, busybody grannies dropped off vats of gelatinous pig knuckle stew, bland mashed adzuki beans, and black silky chicken soup. A multitude of Mama Fangs insisted on their rules and rituals to protect the newest mothers among them.

Even though the October heat wave had transformed the building into a sauna, Granny Wang, leaning on her cane, slurred at them for not bundling themselves up, and Widow Mok warned them to avoid fans and open windows, tips to restore balance in a mother's body. A draft that seeped into your bones would never leave you. Scarlett guessed that the tradition must have begun long ago to ward off infections in women weakened after delivery.

"I was once as tall as you," Granny Wang told Scarlett.

"I was once as quick as you," Widow Mok told Daisy.

Both old women had given in to the temptation of cooling themselves sometime in the month after giving birth, a moment that remained vivid in their memories: Widow Mok had leaned into a breeze, and Granny Wang had scrubbed her arms and face with a cool washcloth. After that, they were never the same again, they warned.

One afternoon, just after Scarlett and Daisy had gotten the babies down, they collapsed onto the mattress, ready for a nap of their own.

Someone knocked at the door. "Don't answer," Scarlett said.

"They'll just keep knocking." Daisy cracked the door open and Auntie Ng forced her to take a sloshing pot of soup.

"You should be in bed," Auntie Ng chided. If Daisy had had more energy, she might have explained that she'd been trying to do just that. And if new mothers were supposed to remain tucked away inside, why did the ladies keep coming? She didn't yet realize aunties specialized in contradictory advice. No matter how much you obeyed, they could still find reasons to scold you.

Daisy put the soup beside the two tureens they had yet to finish. They lived a primitive, feral existence, knuckles to the ground, incapable of speech for the most part. Unwashed and unkempt as vengeful ghosts, they stewed in the air fetid with the smell of spit-up, the overstuffed diaper pail, and their half-eaten meals filmed with grease. The conditions would have disgusted Boss Yeung, and would have been reason enough to assume custody of his child. Ma would have said they'd lost their senses. Not one, but two unwed mothers living in squalor together? They'd brought it upon themselves.

Daisy balled up a diaper and tossed it onto the top of the heap.

"It's going to spill," Scarlett said.

"I took it out last time."

Scarlett wanted to start another heap, another and another until one of them gave in and took out the trash. Poor Old Wu! The stench—not to mention the wailing—must be coming through the walls to his room next door. He'd brought them bales of blankets that remained stacked against the walls. It might have been her imagination, but all of Evergreen Gardens moved sluggishly, irritably these days, kept up nights by two infants, and maybe they were finding their revenge in the guise of the endless soups.

Daisy sat down on the mattress, wincing. Her breasts had turned huge and lumpy, her nipples bloody, and when her son awoke from his nap, his cries were desperate. She squeezed her breast as she might an udder, so hard that she left bruises and pimples broke out. The milk dripping into his mouth set him off—*more, more.* She couldn't force any out, any more than she could have commanded herself to fly. He was an alarming shade of red, dark as a pig's liver. She'd named him after his father, but called him Didi, or "little brother" to Scarlett's daughter. She couldn't hide her envy of Scarlett, whose daughter heartily nursed, her jaws pumping like a piranha's, her throat quivering with each swallow.

Liberty. A name Scarlett had picked because of its meaning and its chiming syllables, bright as bells. She couldn't predict or control what her daughter inherited from her and from Boss Yeung, but she could teach her to define the world by its possibilities and not its limitations, something she hadn't learned until she left home.

Becoming a mother made Scarlett reconsider her own childhood. The day she had picked her English name, she'd spent hours on the assignment. Nothing from the textbook, nothing too common and boring for her. Nothing too fantastic, not like her scrawny classmate who claimed Cinderella, though there was little hope she would ever transform into a princess. A boy had picked Fish, translated from his name in Chinese, while another picked Lonely, because it sounded like his name, Long Li. Pointless. Why use Chinese to speak English? Something would get lost in translation. Your Chinese self should remain a given, your inheritance, while your English identity could be entirely different. An identity in which you might take risks. In the last of the daylight, she'd been practicing her new signature, the swooping curves of the tall *S* and the double *t* like grass, in letters no bigger than a grain of rice, to fit more onto the page. Her workbook had to last through the school year. Under her breath, she repeated the name over and over: the hard scrape of the first syllable, and the softness of the second.

Ma had nagged her to gather greens for dinner. She always interrupted when Scarlett seemed too intent on her studies, but complained her daughter was lazy, a stupid egg, if she had less than perfect marks. After she returned with dirt deep under her fingernails, she discovered Ma studying her signature. "What's this?"

The Cultural Revolution had ended her mother's schooling, and even processing the forms at the clinic tested the limits of her education. She neither understood nor read any English.

"My English name. Red, like the flag. It's patriotic," Scarlett said.

"What's wrong with your name?"

"I need an English name for English class."

"You are Chinese. You are in China."

Not forever, Scarlett had realized then. This name might be hers for years, might fit the life she hoped would take her from the village. To the city, to the moon, away, away, away.

"It's a name foreigners can remember and pronounce." Scarlett rinsed her hands in a plastic basin and dried them on a rag.

"When will you meet a foreigner?" Ma tossed the workbook aside and chopped a long white radish.

"Before you will."

Ma grew up a few kilometers away, this valley the whole of her world. She'd never left the county. "I've eaten more salt than you've eaten rice," she snapped, claiming the authority from years of experience that Scarlett could never match.

In her fury, Ma thrust the workbook into the stove, but didn't stop Scarlett from pulling it out, singed and smoking. Scarlett threw it to the ground and stomped out the embers. The edges charred black, the floating ash choking and stinging, punishment Scarlett bore in silence. And later still, Ma would spoil dinner, leaving the radish half-raw and bitter and boiling the greens until soggy. Later, Ma would pick another fight, chasing Scarlett with a broom, their shouts spilling into the lane.

Scarlett didn't know how fully she would someday assume her chosen name. Jumping from factory to factory, walking away from her clothes, her jobs, her friends, her hairstyle, her history at each turn and never looking back. Through all those years, through all those changes, she kept only her name, a name that now gave rise to Liberty's.

Scarlett tried to help Daisy nurse—adjusting her shoulders, getting another pillow to prop up the baby—but she couldn't teach something that she'd never actually learned. Her success came not from prior knowledge or study, but out of luck, luck that Daisy had had in abundance until now.

Daisy bowed her head, her body trembling with silent sobs while her son's crying slackened into hiccups. Scarlett slid over a bowl of stew, forced a spoon into Daisy's hand, and took Didi into the crook of her arm. He flopped against her bare chest, his eyes closed, his lips chapped and puckered.

Though she couldn't show Daisy, she could show him. She hesitated. Was nursing another woman's son odd, apt to make Daisy jealous, serve as a reminder of her failure? Was the act old-fashioned, backward, transforming her into a wet nurse, a servant to Daisy? Her son rooted his head against Scarlett, his mouth millimeters from her nipple, his hunger undeniable. Daisy slurped down the stew and tipped the bowl, draining the broth.

"I can—do you want me to?" Scarlett asked. It wasn't her decision or Daisy's. Didi fell upon her and suckled, his mouth at an awkward angle, holding the tip of her nipple until she settled him onto her. Plenty pulsed within her. Daisy set down the bowl, yawning until she noticed her son was nursing. She snatched him away. Scarlett yelped and milk spurted from her breast, spattering her arm and torso. Didi wailed.

"Did you ever give blood?" Daisy asked.

Scarlett jerked her head, no. Why did it matter? She curled over, trying to stem the pain caused by Didi unlatching abruptly.

"Did you ever sell it? Your plasma." Daisy jiggled her son, which made him cry harder. Liberty woke and answered his hungry sobs with her own. Scarlett gritted her teeth and picked up her daughter and nursed her on the other side.

Daisy must think Scarlett was tainted, one of those peasants who peddled their plasma, the leftover blood pooled with other donors and pumped back into their veins polluted with HIV.

Scarlett had never sold herself, but Daisy, Mama Fang, and Boss Yeung kept assuming that she had and would. She dug her fingernails into the palms of her hands, a curse caught in her throat. She shouldn't turn on Daisy, who was as lost and terrified and exhausted as she was. Stiffly, she told Daisy that Old Wu would buy formula, the expense added to what she owed.

As soon as they could, Scarlett and Daisy made the trip to City Hall to pick up the birth certificates. The aunties warned them against going outside, which would upset their energy balance, causing aches they would suffer now and in their old age, but Scarlett couldn't wait any longer. She needed legal proof that Liberty belonged to her and that Liberty belonged in America.

City Hall's gilded dome was elegant and imposing. At the security check-in, the bored guards searched their bag, pushing aside the spare diapers, wipes, extra onesies, changing pad, burp cloths, powdered formula, and bottle—more belongings on this short trip than she'd had with her when she'd escaped her village as a teenager. She had to protect her daughter against the calamity found everywhere these days: in the boiling pot that might splash on Liberty's tender skin, the gutter into which she might tumble, booby traps springing from each unguarded moment.

As they walked away from the metal detector, their footsteps echoed on the marble. She'd never been inside a building as grand as a palace, and she felt as if she were seeking an audience with a king. The sense of power was forbidding but also reassuring: whatever decree, whatever papers were issued here carried the weight of a nation.

Inside the windowless room lit by sickly fluorescent bulbs, Daisy helped her fill out the forms. Scarlett left the space for the father's name blank, and slid the money order across the counter to pay for the birth certificates, each shaded pink and blue like a sunrise, printed on paper heavy with legitimacy. No matter what happened, even if authorities forced them out, her daughter had a claim to America. As limited as her opportunities might be in China, Liberty could someday make her way back here.

Outside, Daisy asked Scarlett to snap a photo of her and Didi, one of dozens taken each day, she explained, to provide her boyfriend with a record of every moment he missed: bath-time, the grunt and strain of a bowel movement, peekaboo with a blankie. At least she wasn't a teenager who took endless selfies, but when it came to her son, nothing was too incidental.

A woman walking by offered to take a photo of all four of them. Neither baby looked at the camera, Daisy squinted from the sun, and Scarlett was openmouthed, mid-sentence, yet it felt like their first chance to celebrate since they'd emerged from birth.

"I— Thank you," Daisy said.

The woman had already walked away. She must be thanking me, Scarlett thought. For what?

"If it wasn't for you, I'd still be trapped at Perfume Bay."

"You would have found another way," Scarlett said.

"And gotten caught each time. You, though." Daisy's eyes held something that Scarlett didn't expect: gratitude, maybe even admiration. It wasn't easy for Daisy to ask for help. It wasn't easy for Scarlett, either, but their circumstances had been overwhelming.

Pigeons pecked and flapped at their feet.

"You fought Lady Yu!" Daisy said. "You don't let anyone bully you."

"But I did." Until now, she'd never alluded to Boss Yeung or why she'd fled Perfume Bay. Admitting it, she felt a rush of shame and then a curious relief to reveal what she'd walled up. She was thankful that Daisy had the courtesy not to ask anything more.

They stored the certificates in a biscuit tin along with their passports and savings, protection against the roaches and rats that skittered in their apartment at night. Scarlett snapped the tin shut and Daisy placed her hands on the lid, too, their fingers almost but not quite touching. Scarlett felt as newlyweds or explorers must, headed into the unknown, these possessions their only certainty, their pledge of a future together.

# Chapter 8

For more than a week, no one realized Boss Yeung had gone missing. His factory managers assumed he was in Hong Kong, and his family believed him at the factory in China. At the hospital in Los Angeles, he was incoherent and anonymous, lacking identification or a cellphone. He remembered none of it: not his fall on the escalator nor the trip in the ambulance, where he'd called out for his daughter. Viann. Viann. Viann. The reptilian part of his brain, in charge of breathing, body temperature, and balance, had also known what else was necessary for his survival.

When his senses returned, and the hospital notified his family, Viann was on the next flight out. En route, she contacted her friends from business school—at Harvard, she'd run with a crowd of international elites, the children of diplomats and industrialists—and asked for the best doctors, the best hospitals in the country after learning about his illness. The privileged upbringing Boss Yeung had provided for her—unlike his in every way—was paying off.

She'd cornered doctors and nurses, demanding their attention. To curry their favor, she had platters of fruit skewers delivered to the break room and remembered the names of the staff and their interests—all of which kept Boss Yeung in their thoughts. He turned his veins over to the nurses, who flooded him with painkillers, steroids, and anti-inflammatories, and plumped him up with pints of blood, as if he were a vampire. When they flushed the IV line with saline, he grew accustomed to the rotten orange peel taste in his mouth before the rush of morphine followed, the tingling heaviness of his limbs and a detachment from the world that Buddhists spent a lifetime trying to perfect. Holding still, he watched as technicians performed endless scans of his gut and his heart: the scrolling moonscape, the wiggle of the aortic valve, the blue and red of blood pumping in and out. The universe he held within, of which he knew almost nothing, just as little as he knew of the universe outside of him.

Viann told him the treatment options she'd analyzed on a spreadsheet: New York, Minnesota, and Houston had top cancer hospitals. For Boss Yeung, the choices seemed unbearably far from the last sighting of Scarlett. By now, she must have given birth to their son—their son! By now, she could be anywhere, but he sensed she was in California. Scarlett had asked if there was a maternity center in San Francisco. She'd always wanted to stroll across the Golden Gate and turn her face into the wind at the edge of the continent. He told Viann he didn't want to travel far, and pushed for San Francisco. "For a hospital as high tech as Silicon Valley."

She got him into a clinical trial there, at a hospital where her classmate's uncle was a world-class oncologist, a regular Op-Ed contributor to *The New York Times*, a wiry marathoner with soft hands and bright blue eyes. She borrowed a friend's condo in a luxury high-rise in downtown San Francisco that had the look of a cruise ship tilted onto its propeller. Aside from trips to the hospital on the hill, they never left the apartment, with its sweeping view of the emerald bay streaked with whitecaps and dotted with sailboats.

When he suggested they visit Chinatown, Viann dismissed the food as fit only for tourists, greasy and cheap. The residents were low-class, peasants spitting and squatting on the sidewalk. She hired a Chinese chef to prepare broths and porridges, dull and nourishing, and forced him to drink chalky chocolate protein shakes, thick as mucus. During his treatment, banquet dishes would have tasted mealy and metallic in any case. His eyes, his nose, and his mouth were always parched.

When the burly nurse swabbed his hip and prepared the needle for the bone marrow biopsy, Viann took his hand for the first time in decades. His scabbed and swollen, hers cool and smooth. The gesture intimate, almost obscene. He jerked his hand away. Surrounded by the infirm and the elderly, she'd get sick. "Get out of here," he said.

"Hold still," the nurse said, and Viann took his hand again. Before he could protest, the nurse plunged in the needle. He gasped and involuntarily squeezed her hand, tight. She didn't flinch.

The nurse exclaimed, and Viann translated. "You have hard bones. Hard as an Olympian." Viann added her own aside: "A hard head, too."

His sixtieth birthday came and went, another day hooked up to the drip-drip of drugs at the imperceptible speed at which stalactites formed. Drowsing in the recliner, his head aching when Viann presented him with the longevity peach cakes. He gagged on the first bite, the red bean paste repellent, overly sweet and sticky as glue.

With his condition stabilized, they made plans to return to Hong Kong. The day before their flight, he urged her to go sightseeing, to take a walk along the beach or go shopping.

She resisted. "I've seen it before. Nothing here that I can't get in Hong Kong."

He no longer could send her away with a roll of bills and orders to spend it. He'd never replaced his wallet or credit cards, and was entirely dependent on her, which hadn't mattered until now. He didn't even have a key to the condo.

She cleared his bowl of porridge sprinkled with peanuts and scallions. He'd taken only a few bites. "Aren't you hungry?"

Boss Yeung feared she would try to spoon-feed him. "Go, go."

She set down the bowl, grabbed her phone, and dialed. She was calling back Uncle Lo; he'd left a message yesterday. She would often put him on speakerphone and Boss Yeung always begged off from joining the conversation, claiming he was too tired, too nauseous.

Should he let their long association be destroyed by a hunch? His suspicions about his wife's infidelity—and Uncle Lo's—receded but hadn't disappeared, deferred only until he was again of sound mind and body. If confronted, Uncle Lo would lie, both to protect their friendship and to prevent his empire from becoming further divided among his many heirs. Uncle Lo would do anything for Viann, anything except acknowledge her as his. He was going to send a driver to the airport to pick them up in Hong Kong, he said, and arranged for a police escort to avoid traffic. Boss Yeung twitched. The sound of his oldest and dearest friend's voice had become grating as a donkey's bray. Every time Viann laughed, his insides twisted.

"I'm bringing dumplings—five dozen," Uncle Lo said. From their favorite late-night spot.

A long pause, and Boss Yeung knew he was supposed to make a joke, something about his gluttony. "And what will *you* have?"

"Can you get a list of the ingredients?" Viann asked. She'd never allow the dumplings to pass through his lips. Resentment surged through him. If she took control of Yeung Holdings, she'd disregard his wishes. He regretted sending her to business school. She wanted to do away with haggling and handshakes, and bring in modern management practices. Maybe he'd held too much of the company in his head, but at work he felt necessary as he never did at home.

"No pork," she said. "Not unless it's organic. Can you have her make a special batch with bitter melon and lily bulbs? To clear the heat from his system."

With a start, he realized she was treating him just as he'd treated Scarlett, and he understood now how much she must have chafed under his thumb. Being pregnant wasn't like being sick, not exactly, but both conditions offered up your body for public discussion and put you at the mercy of people who thought they knew what was best for you. Everything turned upside down: daughter reborn as his mother, and him acting like a father to Scarlett. But he didn't want to be coddled, and neither did Scarlett. He wished he'd listened—listened as he now wanted Viann to listen. More than that: he wished he'd known what she'd wanted.

"The dumpling lady won't give up her recipe," Uncle Lo said. "Not even to her son."

Son. Sons.

"Doesn't your son like dumplings? Bring him along," Boss Yeung said. "He'd like to see Viann, wouldn't he?"

She smiled tightly. Uncle Lo's eldest son was affable and soft-spoken, bland as tofu, taking on the color and flavor of any seasoning.

"I'll worry, until you're settled," Boss Yeung told her.

"A pretty girl needs a pretty boy," Uncle Lo said.

"How about Teddy?" Boss Yeung asked. Uncle Lo's younger brother, recently divorced. Stoop-shouldered, stunted from growing up in Uncle Lo's shadow. All the younger Lo men were dull, perhaps as a matter of survival.

"You don't want ugly grandchildren!" Uncle Lo said.

"I may never see my grandchildren," Boss Yeung said.

What started off as rhetoric cut Boss Yeung with the truth of it. The end might come soon, with so much he would never see, never touch or taste. Never hold.

"They've been asking about you at the club," Uncle Lo said. "The steam will make you feel like new."

To sit in hot, wet quarters with Uncle Lo seemed a chamber of hell, akin to the pit where demons ripped out the tongues of gossips, snipped off the fingers of adulterers, and crushed those who abandoned their children.

"It's too much," Viann said. Too much for Boss Yeung's fragile immune system.

"I'll clear out the sauna for us." Boss Yeung shuffled off without replying. Uncle Lo must sense that Boss Yeung wanted nothing to do with him.

In the bathroom, his piss dribbled out. He was bald, his body swollen on steroids, his skin dark and tough in patches. Viann would forget he'd ever been whole and healthy, at a safe remove where he could remain high in her estimation. She'd forget the days when he lifted her up to see into the fish tanks in restaurants. When he used to carry her into the house after she'd fallen asleep in the car, and she'd tuck her head into the crook of his neck. When she was still an only child, and he had no doubts about her paternity.

One afternoon, after drinks with Uncle Lo, he'd lurched into the nursery and discovered Viann with a pair of scissors. She might have been four. "What are you doing?" he asked.

She'd snipped out dozens of flowers printed on her cotton blanket, the blades still swishing and clicking in her chubby hand. "I'm picking flowers for my dolls."

He took the scissors from her. "Where did you get these?"

From the top of the dresser, where her mother left a pair. Viann had pulled out each drawer, like a flight of stairs and climbed up. Her foot had plunged through the bottom of one, and all the drawers were cockeyed in their tracks.

Uncle Lo chuckled. "Clever!"

His presence had spared her punishment, turning Boss Yeung playful and proud at this proof of her intelligence and determination. Now, every time Uncle Lo had intervened on Viann's behalf seemed cause for suspicion.

Viann knocked. Uncle Lo had finished what he'd had to say to her, and now wanted to talk to him, she said. He wasn't going to get to avoid talking to him. He took the phone from her, turned off the speaker, and pointedly closed the door in her face. She remained in the hallway, eavesdropping, casting shadows that crept under the crack.

Uncle Lo told him the detective had uncovered murky surveillance video at a gas station north of Los Angeles, a shot trained on the tail end of a white van that resembled the one that had gone missing from Perfume Bay. His knees shaky, Boss Yeung shut the toilet lid and sat down.

The front of the van was out of the frame and the vehicle blocked the view of the driver getting in and out, but in the video, the runaway teenager had circled the vehicle, carrying a squeegee. Scarlett did not turn up in the footage from inside the convenience store, and the clerk didn't remember serving a pair of pregnant Chinese women. But the hospital security cameras—which had shown Scarlett driving off—and this video, taken the day after their disappearance, seemed to suggest that Scarlett and the girl had escaped together in the van, and not separately in the chaos of that evening.

The detective was looking for more footage along the I-5, and planned to put the boyfriend's parents under surveillance, tap their phone line, and go through their trash to see if they were harboring the fugitive mothers and their newborns.

"She'll turn up, with her hand out," Uncle Lo said. "Her kind always does."

"She's a stubborn one."

"Nothing that a *laojiao* can't cure."

Uncle Lo had to be joking. At this kind of labor camp, Scarlett would be forced to make shoes or cheap electronics, getting "re-educated"—brainwashed or worse.

If Scarlett had gotten this close to San Francisco, she would have stayed. Of all the cities in America, she'd mentioned San Francisco the most. She might still be here, and Boss Yeung had to find her. When he returned to the living room, Viann was rinsing his bowl.

"You should go out. Before it gets too late," he said.

"You can't be left alone." She spoke so softly he wasn't sure if the words were intended for him.

"Don't talk nonsense," he said. "The doctors cleared me to travel."

She looked past him. "What if you fell?"

"I'll nap. I can't fall far in bed."

"What if there was a fire?" she asked.

He wasn't a toddler who would play with matches.

"What if you left the apartment?" She locked eyes with him, and he understood she had questions that she couldn't yet bring herself to ask: Why had he left Hong Kong without telling anyone? Why had he been in Los Angeles? Business, he could have said, but the look she gave challenged him not to lie.

"My trip, I came because . . . because I was looking for my son."

Viann stared at him.

"For your brother."

Her nostrils pinched as if he'd turned into a rotting fish. "My brother?"

"I . . ." He faltered. She must know that factory bosses had mistresses, even if he'd been faithful until Scarlett. Every man cheated if presented with temptation and opportunity, in need of softness and warmth along with the sex.

"Who?"

"Someone from the factory."

Scarlett's low laugh, her love of maps, her lively intelligence— Viann wouldn't want to hear any of it. She held herself so still he knew that she was on the verge of exploding.

She sneered. "The factory?" She must picture an assembly-line worker, a teenager in tight jeans. "What a bargain."

"It's not— She's not—"

She slammed the bowl onto the marble floor, a mess of shards and spattered porridge, shouldered her purse, and left without another word. In the silence that followed, he wondered if he'd confessed with exactly that outcome in mind.


Eyes watering, he took another bite of the fried chicken laced with peppercorns from Sichuan that numbed his mouth like Novocain. Sick of his invalid's diet, he'd ordered a tableful of dishes at the basement restaurant in Chinatown, packed with a Chinese-only clientele who ordered from handwritten menus on strips of pink paper pasted on the walls.

His first chance to feel alive and his last chance on this trip to visit Chinatown and resume his search for Scarlett. Though he didn't know if she'd ended up here, he had to try the neighborhood where newcomers from their country landed. He'd have to persuade her to give their son his birthright. Not in America, but in Hong Kong, where the boy would be steeped in the family's legacy. Scarlett would remain his mother, with important duties yet to be defined. She couldn't deny how much more Boss Yeung could provide for their son and for her.

Sated, he sipped his tea and paid for lunch from what he'd stolen out of Viann's suitcase—money that was technically his, from her monthly allowance, two hundred dollars tucked into a shirt pocket. He crumpled the napkin in his lap. Viann. He'd hurt the one person who loved him, and for what—for the sake of a baby he didn't know. He'd never forget the sorrow in her face. She must know the significance of a male heir: a future in which she would run Yeung Holdings only until her brother was old enough to take the reins.

Twenty-five years or so of her life given to the company, only to end up as a footnote in the family history.

In his final years, his father had been a drunk. On his deathbed, he'd begged Boss Yeung to redeem the family's name. A man's job. He himself never had to speak as a father to a son, never had to teach a boy how to become a man. Boss Yeung had learned not to emulate: not to gamble, not to spend extravagantly.

What would he tell his own son, if he had the opportunity? To honor your parents, carry on the family line, to build upon the foundation he'd laid down. To rise early, and be neither envious nor fawning. He couldn't remember giving any advice to his daughters, though Viann had absorbed these lessons on her own.

He walked through Chinatown, but couldn't go for long without sitting down again. The block lengthened with each shuffling step, and when a granny elbowed him to get by, he felt as if he might break apart on the sidewalk. Every woman with a baby caught his eye. Coming up too close, staring for too long at the babies, he must have seemed like a kidnapper. One mother clasped her arms around her baby and glared at him, and another veered around him and sped up, the toys rattling on her stroller like wind chimes in a storm.

Out of breath, he braced himself against a lamppost. His doubts about Viann's paternity made him more desperate to find his son, born from his blood. His son starting life, just as Boss Yeung was leaving his. At funerals, weren't children a comfort to the living? Their plump bodies and new skin, the features and mannerisms passed down and passed on from the departed. His son, his infant son, dressed in a coarse mourning tunic, a squiggle of black cloth pinned to his chest, peering into the coffin where Boss Yeung would recline in three layers of silk finery, his face waxy with makeup. His son's stubby fingers reaching for him. It could be the only touch to ever pass between them.

His head spun. Needing to rest again, he stumbled into a dim sum palace where a hostess shouted into a microphone, calling for customers. The restaurant was alive with chatter and the festive clink of chopsticks against porcelain, two floors of diners, tables of ten, three generations of snoozing babies and kids on iPods, parents and grandparents slurping. Families, all.

He ignored the twinge in his back, strained by walking, he told himself—not the flu, not the pain that had heralded his last relapse. He tried to slump onto the last chair in the waiting area but a granny in a walker beat him to it. Her granddaughter flanked her, glowering at him like a guardian foo dog statue. He leaned against the silver wallpaper, sticky with grease. Even if he hadn't fallen ill, even if he hadn't taken a mistress, he hadn't had a noisy family meal in years. On his rare dinners home, a few days out of every three months, he choked down his wife's bland vegetarian cuisine while checking his phone before retreating to his study. On his last trip to Hong Kong, Viann had talked about a new project she'd initiated at the shortbread factory: installing insulation, double-paned windows, compact fluorescent lighting, and solar panels on the roof. Some days, Yeung Holdings was selling back energy to the power company.

Her ingenuity should have pleased him. Instead, he'd rewarded her with a condescending smile, and told her they'd use it for the red envelopes of lucky money given to children during the Spring Festival. Symbolic and inconsequential. He'd treated her badly, then and now. Had she returned to the condo and discovered him missing? He hadn't left a note and wasn't carrying a cellphone. Or was she riding aimlessly in a cab, shaking with rage, unable to face him and unwilling to go elsewhere? Crying, calling Uncle Lo. If she only knew how Uncle Lo might have rejected her long ago. Boss Yeung's stomach cramped and he clenched to keep from shitting himself. He was a practical man, not cerebral, not a scholar or a poet, but he hated how he'd become a slave to his bodily functions. The line to the bathroom snaked down the hallway, full of sharp-eyed, sharp-elbowed, hard-hearted matrons who wouldn't let him cut. His bowels settled. He'd hurry back to the throne of a toilet at the condo, a fancy Japanese model that could do everything except pull his pants back up and wipe his nose.

Air, he needed air. Gasping, he stumbled outside, drawing in deep breaths. He studied the apartments above the shops, no doubt hovels with peeling lead paint and mold billowing across the ceilings. Heat crept up his neck. He'd wronged Scarlett, but she still shouldn't have fled.

In his compromised state, a cough from a wheezing old man, a sneeze from a waitress fighting the flu, any and all errant germs could bring him down, and by the time he hailed a cab to the condo, his body blazed.

He awoke in the hospital, his lips cracked and throat scorched. Viann was curled beside him, her head against his chest. She mumbled and when he brushed his hand along her back, her breathing slowed and evened. The scent of sleep, of her greasy hair and a trace of her citrus perfume. A few minutes later, she stirred awake. He didn't move, letting her climb off the bed and compose herself.

She must think him a hopeless case. In and out of the hospital, for now, for a while, for the rest of his miserable, truncated life. When he opened his eyes, Viann was standing by the bed. She'd tied back her hair and smoothed out her blouse. She was far too thin, her head a sunflower on the stalk of her body.

He cleared his throat. "Did you get any sleep?"

She nodded; her eyes were hollow and haunted. He shifted, and his flimsy hospital gown slipped off his shoulder. She recoiled. His swollen body must disgust her. Most anyone would flinch from the first sight of their parent's wrecked body. He straightened out his gown, and she bowed her head and apologized. He asked her to raise the bed, then for water that he sipped from the cup she held to his mouth. He tried not to dribble, but his lips felt slack. She blotted his mouth with a napkin, and the briskness of the gesture reminded him of someone—of Uncle Lo. The wide set of her eyes was just like his friend's, too. He'd been studying her surreptitiously, but until this moment, he'd denied the resemblance, told himself she'd inherited this quality from his father, or that trait from his grandmother. He couldn't pretend any longer.

Uncle Lo would never submit to a paternity test, but during the bone marrow drive he'd spearheaded, hadn't he gotten his entire family typed, in the ultimate show of their commitment? Boss Yeung could compare that test to Viann's, the columns of dots, letters, and numbers serving as a crude approximation of the paternity test. Shared markers, shared blood. Not definite, but evidence enough to determine whether to take the next step: steal Uncle Lo's DNA. The nick of blood on a razor tossed into the trash at the club. A stray hair plucked off his suit jacket. The saliva left on a glass of cognac, over drinks between two old friends.

# Chapter 9

**Mama Fang** paused before the empty storefront, where dust inside glittered in a beam of sunlight. The counter could go there, by that pile of papers, and the desks back there, by the heap of metal fixtures. This location had good feng shui—though perhaps not so favorable after all, because the last business here had presumably failed. Yet the Chinese supermarket and the bank drew a steady stream of traffic to the strip mall, and most important, it was located down the street from the top-ranked middle school in Cupertino. She jotted down the phone number of the real estate agent listed in the window. On the drive here, she'd passed a shopping mall packed with cars between light poles adorned with banners of pumpkins and autumn leaves.

Soon after Scarlett and Daisy went missing from Perfume Bay, her neighbors had complained to police about the frequent turnover of pregnant women—a brothel in reverse—and the stink from the industrial-sized trash cans overflowing with diapers.

During the predawn raid, the sound of heavy pounding reverberated through the house, the front door shook, and then the men in black uniforms and helmets burst in. Babies cried without end. The guests had to submit to hours-long interrogations. Within the week, Perfume Bay had been condemned as structurally unsound, the regrettable outcome of an unlicensed contractor and unpermitted renovations. Mama Fang had to refund her guests, in addition to covering their meals and hotel stays until they returned home to China and Hong Kong. Uncle Lo had lost his entire investment, but even worse, he'd lost face to all the clients he'd referred to Perfume Bay.

As soon as she could, Mama Fang moved north to Cupertino, a Chinese enclave in the heart of Silicon Valley, where no one would know her, a sprawling city of low-slung ranch houses and office parks surrounded by rolling hills. She had settled in quickly, for Chinatowns the world over shared markets selling live fish and dusty imported foods, cultural centers with the familiar clack of mahjong tiles and the whine of the opera, all attempts to remake, remember, and reclaim.

It wasn't the first time she'd started over. Back in Hong Kong, she'd opened a series of businesses that expanded in scope and ambition, but with the handover to China looming in 1997, she joined the many who left. The wealthiest immigrated to Canada, the United States, and Australia, while Mama Fang arrived in Panama after sinking her savings into a residency permit she could afford. She'd heard the little curve of a country was a back door to the United States, and she married a retired American serviceman who wanted a nurse on the cheap. Medicine wasn't too hard to learn with a bit of practice, and Mama Fang was a quick study. She'd changed his bedpans, administered an IV, and fetched him the beer he drank most hours of most days, its sourness leaking from his pores. She'd divorced him soon after her green card arrived.

With the money from her settlement, she'd bought a plane ticket and rented a cheap room fifteen minutes down the freeway from the Tuscan-style mansions with three-car garages popular with Chinese who were settling in the hills east of Los Angeles. After embarking upon several ventures, she'd eventually written Uncle Lo with her business proposal for Perfume Bay.

She had to give up the expansion she'd been planning: a private villa or two in the backyard of Perfume Bay; tours of Stanford and Harvard, the future alma mater of these American-born children, tacked onto the beginning or end of the trips; and even surrogates. You could get a baby with U.S. citizenship, without going through the indignities of pregnancy, and without traveling abroad—services that many of her clients would have eagerly added after spending tens of thousands of dollars on fertility treatments and sex selection, rounds of acupuncture, and offerings to Guanyin, the Goddess of Mercy.

She had to set her ambitions elsewhere now, but she'd always had more ideas than lifetimes.

Mama Fang returned to her car, and as she strapped herself in, her mobile phone rang—Uncle Lo.

"Any news?" he asked.

News about Daisy and Scarlett. If his detectives couldn't find them, how could she? Although she'd learned never to look back, she hoped they were safe, clean, dry, and well-fed, or living on the streets after their money ran out. Or if they were dead. They'd been spotted heading north, and Mama Fang sometimes wondered if they might have taken shelter in Cupertino, too, if she might come upon them at any minute. By now, they both would have delivered their babies.

Each day Scarlett remained on the run, each day she survived without Boss Yeung, she triumphed over him and men like him. Scarlett would never know how closely Mama Fang's convictions echoed her own.

"How's Boss Yeung?" Mama Fang had despised him—he'd all but wanted her to track the frequency and quantity of Scarlett's bowel movements. She blamed him more than herself for Scarlett's disappearance.

A long pause. "It's hard to know. He's still in the hospital. His condition changes from moment to moment." He exhaled, and she pictured him blowing out cigarette smoke. "Just find her."

"The newspaper," Mama Fang said. "Advertise in the classifieds of your newspaper, in all the Chinese newspapers. Offer a reward."

Uncle Lo couldn't hide his scorn. "You think they're telling people their names? Why not hire a skywriter?"

"Offer *her* a reward," Mama Fang said. "So much she can't refuse."

Silence, not the click of a hang-up. Her heart lurched. "Money makes the mare go," she added. A proverb, of the kind he used to teach her, long ago in Hong Kong. "Even a nag like Scarlett."

He didn't laugh, gave no salty grunt of appreciation. "She won't go anywhere after we find her."

Taking Scarlett's child from her seemed punishment enough, but Uncle Lo appeared to have harsher retribution in mind. "Call me if you hear something," he barked, and hung up.

She studied the phone, willing it to flash with an incoming call—Scarlett's. The phone remained silent. Mama Fang couldn't allow herself such foolish thinking. Even if Scarlett had the number, she wouldn't have called for help. Scarlett would find her way, just like Mama Fang always had. A car honked, and the driver motioned with his hands, checking if Mama Fang was going to pull out. She shook her head.

She might never find Scarlett, but she could still return to the good graces of Uncle Lo. Her ideas intrigued him—always had, and always would, so long as he profited from them. She'd been planning to call the real estate agent after the weekend, but now found herself dialing the number. The name was Chinese. Would the agent be taking the weekend off, or like so many immigrant Chinese, did she work every day except during the Spring Festival?

The agent answered on the first ring.

# Chapter 10

**When her daughter** cried without end, Scarlett strapped her onto her chest and walked ceaselessly, like a soldier on Chairman Mao's Long March. Past the bubbling tanks where catfish bobbed and gaped, the markets pungent with bitter greens and oranges, past the stores selling hell money and incense to honor the dead. Liberty would fall asleep within a few minutes, soothed by the heat of her mother's body, the swaying steps, and the steady beat of her heart.

She and Daisy never walked together, granting each other a reprieve from their joint captivity. They were guarded and solitary women; their passage into motherhood felt as if they themselves had been wrenched through a birth canal once more.

One night, after Didi had been clingy and fussy for hours, Scarlett offered to watch him while Daisy showered. His bowels let loose and she changed him. Taping down the flap, she remembered to tuck his penis in, to keep him from peeing up his shirt. She wondered if she would have been a different mother to a son. If she would have tussled with him like he was a puppy, or expected him to carry her on his back when she was old. As she rubbed his belly, he kicked her in the nose, so hard she saw stars.

Daisy returned, humming the lullaby she'd sung with her boyfriend. The sound sweet as a lark's, but repetition turned the tune into the whine of a dentist's drill and drove Scarlett out of the apartment.

In the hallway, Old Wu tried to stop her. *"Guniang!"* Young maiden. He showed a certain gallantry—or a certain obstinacy—by using the title when Scarlett was clearly anything but. A nickname just for her, and she suspected that he might be developing a crush on her.

The other residents at Evergreen Gardens called her Big Sister, while Daisy was known as Little Sister.

"It's dark. You might get lost." Old Wu eyed her swelling nose.

"I can find my way back."

"It's not safe."

She reminded him they had walked home from dinner last week. The restaurant had picked up his tab, and he'd insisted on paying for her and Daisy.

"With me," he said.

As if he'd protected them! She didn't need his coddling or anyone else's. She'd lived in cities where muggers on mopeds tore earrings out of your earlobes and snatched the sunglasses off your face.

"I'll just go around the block a few times," she told him. She ventured past the shuttered storefronts, along humming cable car tracks, and into a neighborhood north of Chinatown. Nothing here worth scavenging, the sidewalks picked over by this time of night. Nothing else would fit in their apartment, which was crammed to the ceiling. Her stomach growled. She and Daisy had been thinning their rice porridge until it was almost translucent, flavored with a few drops of soy sauce, and hadn't eaten meat in weeks. The flesh on her stomach sagged, so stretched out she could lose a fist in herself, but her ribs and her hips jutted out as they hadn't since she was a girl, the year that drought left the earth cracked as a turtle's shell. Though her milk still flowed, nursing left Scarlett ravenous and often she bit the inside of her cheek to quell her pangs. As frugally as they lived, they were almost out of money, and in two weeks, by the first of December, they would have to pay rent, six hundred dollars. Unfortunately, Daisy seemed no closer to finding the father of her child than when they'd first arrived, no closer to providing the shelter and financial support she'd promised them both. No one had responded to the graffiti scrawled in the campus bathroom.

They couldn't sell the other passports stolen from Perfume Bay. No one wanted a Chinese passport, except a North Korean trying to sneak across the border, or a terrorist on a watch list. At least they'd had the satisfaction, as they ripped apart the passports, of the trouble they must have caused Mama Fang.

Footsteps came up from behind her, and Scarlett wheeled around, her arms tightening around Liberty. Only a granny, hurrying home. Every time she lulled herself into forgetting Boss Yeung, a stranger's glance lingered, or a shadow crossed her path, reminding her of the rough hands that could wrench Liberty from her arms. She was never more than a few steps away from her daughter, but very soon, she and Daisy would have to trade off babysitting between shifts. If they could find work. Daisy had never held a job, never spent any money but her parents'—and now Scarlett's. Without papers, Scarlett could land only the worst positions, where you cleaned and scraped and dug and kneeled six days a week, where bosses cursed you, groped you, and held back your wages.

She stroked Liberty's head, her wispy hair now grown into a fringe. What if she returned after work to find the apartment ransacked, her daughter whisked off, policemen waiting to clap on handcuffs for kidnapping? Boss Yeung wasn't the only threat. After her visa expired, authorities could pick her up at any time. Forever at risk, forever on guard.

Under the marquees of the strip clubs, the lights were bright as day. Bars spilled out drunken men, red-faced as the god of war, and women in tiny dresses flaunted legs muscled as a weight lifter's. In China, they would have been mocked for having legs lumpy and ugly as a white radish. The customers lined up at a cart for bacon-wrapped hot dogs topped with grilled onions and peppers. The vendor, with his tawny skin and a tilt to his eyes, resembled the Uighurs, the tribesmen in China's far west, but he talked in round sounds that she guessed might be Spanish. Noticing her watching, he smiled and nodded at her.

Not much choice compared to the scores of hawkers in Chinese cities who sold every kind of food on a stick, from the air, land, and sea: skewers of roast quail, barbecued squid trailing tender tentacles, and glistening jewels of crab apples. She'd strolled and snacked at night markets since she was a teenager eager to spend her first factory pay. She missed the frenetic bass blaring from stalls, salt and smoke and meat, bubbling cauldrons of oil, aisles packed shoulder to shoulder, people lit with excitement, staying up late after lying low during the heat of the day, compelled to browse all night, never looking back at the stalls they'd passed because something better was ahead.

The vendor tapped his tongs against the grill to entice her. She looked away. She could almost taste the hot dog, the skin snapping under her teeth, the crunch of green peppers and onions. Down the block, a car service arrived and a customer who had taken a couple of bites of her hot dog tossed the rest into the trash. A gym-toned blonde, she probably would have regretted finishing it. The hot dog rested on a folded newspaper, still steaming, fresh off the grill. Scarlett's fingers twitched. She hadn't eaten since this morning, and she was dizzy with hunger. No one was watching, and she wouldn't have to reach very far inside the garbage can. No. As she took a deep shuddering breath, Liberty stirred against her, and Scarlett walked back home.


Two months after giving birth, Scarlett still felt off-kilter. Sweat dripped between her swollen breasts, pooled in her armpits, and trickled down her back.

Manager Kwok eyed her but said nothing. Pockmarked with a boxer's nose, he resembled Jackie Chan, but had none of the actor's boyish charm. She'd sold Manager Kwok the van, which she'd seen headed out on deliveries, a reliable ride that he appreciated enough to grant her an interview. She wasn't willowy or young enough to be hostess in a tight *qi pao*, but she could take her place among the sullen legion of cart ladies squawking out their specialties, shrimp dumplings, egg tarts, or pork buns. She'd arrived in mid-afternoon, following the lunch shift that left the restaurant wrecked: rice ground into the carpet, tables piled high with dirty plastic dishes, the air thick with the scent of grease, soy sauce, and sesame oil. China-town was always hiring new arrivals: restaurants in search of girls to pass out flyers, a garment factory seeking seamstresses, and a foot massage parlor searching for therapists, establishments that wouldn't ask for work authorization papers or any papers at all and kept double accounting books.

She folded her arms against her chest, and then let them drop to her sides. Her arms felt empty without Liberty, whom she'd left bawling at the apartment to get to the interview on time. At the door, she'd lingered, and Daisy had urged her to go. It was the first time either of them had cared for both babies for more than a few minutes. Millions were being made in San Francisco, at tech com-panies that rivaled the biggest ones in China, but Scarlett found no gold in the streets of Chinatown. She could start at the lowest rung of jobs, wash dishes at a restaurant, clean an office and try to climb up, though this time she wasn't a teenager, this time she couldn't consume herself in industrious self-improvement.

Because her baby was three weeks older, Scarlett felt she should look for work first. They both lacked high school degrees, but Daisy—with her perfect English and her talent in science and math—might be able to find a higher-paying job. Tutoring? Daisy seemed to lack the patience for students who couldn't keep up. Salesclerk? She wouldn't cave in to demanding customers at a bou-tique or coffee shop. Daisy never talked about what jobs she wanted. To admit she needed a job would be to admit that she wasn't about to find her boyfriend. Pining for him had shrunk Daisy's world and stolen her ingenuity, and Scarlett couldn't allow her to wallow much longer.

Hugging herself, she realized she was wearing her wraparound shirt inside out, the seams striping the sleeves. She tugged on the cuffs, hoping Manager Kwok wouldn't notice. The job was hers to lose. She asked about the model motorcycle on the liquor cabinet. "You ride?"

No, he said brusquely. "Not anymore."

Maybe he'd given it up, following an accident, or his wife forced him to quit after they started a family.

"Have you eaten here?" he asked.

"Many times! Your soup dumplings are the best I've had."

He frowned. "We don't serve soup dumplings."

She once could have talked her way into the job within minutes, but her thoughts had become perpetually fogged. "The pork buns."

Manager Kwok nodded. "My favorite, too." His phone pinged and as he checked his screen, she wondered if Daisy had calmed Liberty or if she'd been crying unabated for the last hour.

"What hours are you available to work?" Manager Kwok asked.

"Whatever's available."

"When can you start?"

"Tomorrow." Her throat was parched, and she fell into a fit of coughing. "How busy does it get?"

"Nine hundred people," Manager Kwok said. "On a slow day."

"*Waah!*" She'd coax him with compliments. "How many employees?"

The figure he named seemed too low, every shift teetering into disaster, every shift ending in unpaid overtime.

Her expression must have betrayed her misgivings. Manager Kwok abruptly told her that someone had just accepted the position, but that he'd keep her name on file.

Scarlett clenched her hands, digging her nails into her palms. She shouldn't have asked so many questions. Rejected: not because of her red-rimmed eyes or her hunched posture, but because she wasn't as naïve as he wanted. She thanked him and shakily stood up. She felt a breeze and discovered her shirt had slipped open, exposing her milk-swollen breasts and her flabby belly covered in stretch marks. Manager Kwok stared at her not with lust, not with disgust, but with a humiliating pity that she fled.


At daybreak, Scarlett joined the line that snaked around metal barriers and down the block in the neighborhood that stank like a vast squat toilet. Those in front had been waiting since midnight. A week before Thanksgiving, a church was handing out frozen turkeys, hard and gleaming as the decapitated head of a marble statue. She inched forward as disco dance hits soared from outdoor speakers.

She brushed her arm against her chest. She winced. Usually she nursed every three hours, and now her breasts were tender, full and tight. She shivered under two layers of sweaters, blowing on her numb hands. She'd come first to hold a place in line among the Chinese, grannies in puffy jackets and bulky hand-knit scarves, teenagers with hoods flipped up and tightened around their faces, and uncles leaning on their canes. Other kinds of people, too: a towering transvestite in a crop top, oblivious to the cold, and a plump, ruddy-cheeked woman wearing at least five layers of skirts, as if she might break out in a can-can, and a man with a ginger-colored bushy beard. She'd never taken a handout, and if she'd gotten the job at the Pearl Pavilion, she wouldn't have come. Her hunger now outmatched her pride.

An hour later, the straps cut into her hands, wrenching her shoulder as she carried the sack bulging with canned corn, fruit cocktail, a bag of spongy rolls, pasta sauce, and a frozen turkey, plus free tickets for a science exhibit in San Francisco. The clanking load whacked her hips. It was mid-morning, and Daisy hadn't shown up with the babies. Waiting in line for charity must have seemed a poor substitute for finding her boyfriend by Thanksgiving. Maybe she'd decided it was too cold to go outside, or she didn't want to leave the apartment. Useless. Lazy.

Harsh words, but they were entering their hardest times yet. On the corner, people jostled around a sedan with the trunk up, crowded with giveaway sacks. A man was handing out money in exchange for the groceries. Just as quickly, people returned to the church giveaway line. Scarlett stopped a Chinese granny with a child's plastic flower barrette in her stringy hair, and learned sacks with turkeys sold for five dollars, and chickens for three dollars.

"What's he doing?" she asked. The granny ignored her and pushed past with the determination of a woman who would have trampled children to get on a lifeboat. A scarecrow of a man hurried by. She guessed he'd used the money to buy liquor, drugs, whatever he wanted most, and not on a meal that would remind him of what he no longer shared with his family.

Even if the food had been remotely appetizing, the buyer obviously didn't intend to eat it. He'd sell it for double what he paid here, maybe to a restaurant, or by walking door-to-door. He wore an expensive puffy coat, warm enough for Siberia, and sleek leather gloves, protection against the brisk wind. The sales seemed illegal, or at least against the wishes of the donors.

Scarlett admired the buyer and his disregard of tradition, of etiquette and expectation, the kind of attitude that drove Boss Yeung to build his factories in China and compelled Mama Fang to scheme at Perfume Bay. Irrepressible ambition had spurred Scarlett to leave home, and was just what she needed to provide for her daughter.

Not long before she turned sixteen, she'd been struck with dread that she was bound to repeat her mother's life, lacking in adventure, luxury, and love. She wanted to extend her world beyond the reach of her fingertips, and factories were hiring, if you were strong enough and could brave the journey hundreds of kilometers south, to the land of rice eaters, bandits, and barbarians.

Factories shut down during the two weeks of the Spring Festival, and after the holidays, workers switched jobs and scores of newcomers took their places. It was the best time of year to get hired. By the light of the full moon, she had slipped out of the bed she shared with her mother. She dug up the clay jar buried in the floor and stole their savings, a fistful of soiled bills and grimy coins. Ma wouldn't have any expenses for a while; with one less mouth to feed, their stores would last longer and soon the spring vegetables would be ready to harvest. By the time Ma needed money, Scarlett would have sent back everything she'd taken, times ten.

She had hesitated at the doorway. The bed was warm with sleep, the embers glowing in the stove, and their ramshackle home almost cozy. Ma's sleeping face was open and vulnerable. Snoring softly, Ma stirred, her arms reaching for the space Scarlett had vacated. She had groaned and Scarlett held still until Ma's breath deepened again. Ma had called the migrant workers unfilial. She kneeled and rested her head beside her mother for a few breaths, which amounted to the closest physical affection that had ever passed between them. Scarlett drew the comforter over her mother's shoulders and left. She walked all night to the provincial capital, following signs and tracks to the train station.

To stay awake, she'd sung quietly to herself, revolutionary songs celebrating heroes who could stop a gun with their chests, hold a bomb in their hands, and stand in a fire without moving. The Party taught her the lowliest could make the country great, but the factories promised independence and a future different from the one handed down to her. She rode for three days, dozing in a smoky, packed train on a wooden bench beneath a bare lightbulb, harsh as an interrogation chamber. She had ignored passengers who spit watermelon seeds and chicken bones onto the floor and played raucous card games. As the train moved south, more and more teenage passengers boarded, also in search of work. The air was thick with sweat and possibility. Upon arrival, she bought a fake identity card with the last of her money. You weren't allowed to work in the factory until you were sixteen, a month away, a month Scarlett couldn't wait. She'd started on the assembly line of a shoe factory, living in a dormitory, twelve girls to a room, in a village made vertical, suffocating in summer and freezing in winter. Her pay was docked if she talked back to her supervisor, if she fell behind production goals, and her schedule—to shit, to shower, to work, and to eat—was timed to the minute.

She quit that factory and joined another girl whose friend promised a job with good wages. When they arrived at the squat concrete building, however, an oily man locked them into a room on the second floor. Scarlett had climbed out of the window and dropped into a trash bin to escape, while that girl remained behind, afraid to jump and unwilling to believe she had been tricked. Scarlett no longer remembered her name, only that she'd been pretty, apple-cheeked, and nervously tossed her head like a mare.

How easily Scarlett also could have been lost. No one in this world understood the journey she'd taken, the threats and disappointments she'd overcome, and how thin the line between survival and failure. Exaggerating, lying her way into a clerk's job, and later still into human resources and sales while taking classes in English and negotiating skills. During those years, she'd taught herself how to accumulate seconds in which she might breathe. In which she might dream but also scheme.

At Boss Yeung's factory, she'd worked with college graduates who were younger and softer. She had never questioned her place alongside them because of her work experience, her knowledge applied and theirs theoretical. She'd known her strengths then, and she had to remember now to act with confidence and daring.

After selling her first bag, she lined up for another turkey, rubbing the grubby five-dollar bill between her fingers, as if by sorcery she might conjure a stack of money. She savored the yeasty aroma of ink and the greenback's distinctive feel of wealth and durability. Like Boss Yeung, she could make something cheaply and mark it up. Like Mama Fang, she could sell her services to customers willing to pay a premium. She reached the front of the line. Although she worried volunteers might turn her away for taking part in the scam, the enthusiastic young woman handed Scarlett a sack and wished her a happy Thanksgiving.

If she hurried and sold this bag, too, she could get back in line for a third time. When she returned to the corner, however, the buyer had driven off. Though the five dollars in her pocket and the giveaway sack she carried were a windfall, her disappointment tasted sour as vinegar, as if she'd been denied a bonus she'd been working toward all year.

Her stomach growling, she swallowed a clot of saliva to quell her hunger. Across the street, a steam cleaner roared down the sidewalk, its rotating brushes spitting out a harsh chemical detergent that fouled the gutter. The sack grew heavier as she climbed uphill. Her calves ached, and when she reached Chinatown, she'd gone weak in the knees. Her senses assaulted by the chirp of fake crickets for sale, the red paper lanterns strung over the street—year-round, not only during festivals—to attract the tourists who shot photos of pagodas that housed discount gift shops instead of gods. The Chinese penned up in this neighborhood were a curiosity, like the tigers in the zoo that she and Boss Yeung had visited.

That day, Scarlett had pictured him as a father. Not to their child—she wasn't pregnant then—but to his three daughters. A little girl in pigtails, bouncing with excitement by the cage, had dropped her skewer of raw meat, and twice he'd picked it back up for her. Scarlett's heart had thrummed at the gentleness she didn't expect to see in him—akin to discovering he could play the piano or speak Russian. A hidden talent, a hidden history of a life much bigger than what she knew of him.

A life she would never know. And he had never known her, not if he believed she would give up her child. All those months together, they had been strangers. If she couldn't trust her judgment of him, how could she trust any of her decisions?

Not that he was a model father. His youngest daughter had dropped out of university, the middle was regularly arrested for shoplifting, and his eldest, Viann, was the only daughter he mentioned by name, polished, clever, and ambitious, a leader in the making, the kind of daughter a modern man wanted to raise but not to marry. His favorite, until he learned that Scarlett was having a son.

He would have said his desire for an heir was ancient and noble, not subject to the trends that dictated the lives of Lady Yu and Countess Tien. He wouldn't treat his son like an accessory. He would have claimed he was nothing like Scarlett's neighbors in the village who placed two daughters for adoption before their son arrived.

She walked past a music shop blasting that silly refrain: "I love you hot." Classic Canto-pop, swelling, sentimental, orchestral, sung by stars formed from the same injection-molded plastic. She spotted Daisy across the street, carrying not one but two sacks of groceries, knotted on the handle of the rickety stroller where her darling, her daughter waved her fist. Daisy had strapped her son onto her back, where Didi peered out. She must have won the sympathies of a volunteer who decided that Daisy, with two infants, had double the need. Scarlett had to work twice as a hard to attain the riches given to Daisy. She wasn't competing with Daisy, yet she felt outwitted and flat-footed.

Two grannies called out, "Twins!"

Scarlett fought back her annoyance. She wanted Liberty's resemblance to her to be unmistakable, for the world to acknowledge that her daughter could never belong to anyone else.

At a bubbling tank of turtles, Daisy turned the stroller to give Liberty a closer look. She squatted down, pointing something out. Scarlett squirmed. She never thought to stop; her daughter usually rode in the sling, head tucked out of sight. If you remained in Chinatown too long, the narrow alleys and tiny rooms could dwarf you, like those miniature trees in a pot. None of them had ridden a cable car, visited the Pacific, or strolled along the streets with mansions outside of Chinatown. "Daisy, Daisy!" she shouted. If she got past thinking about money, there was so much to see, so much they could do for almost free.

Daisy didn't seem to hear her and walked on. Scarlett ran after them, trying to catch Didi's attention, hoping he might squeal in recognition. The sack slipped out of her hand and groceries spilled onto the sidewalk. Scarlett kneeled down, scooping up the dented cans. The sidewalk was gritty, the cement draining what heat she had left in her. Her body felt heavy and awkward, and when she tottered back up, she discovered that Daisy had disappeared.

The smell hit her, a greasy finger beckoning her to a take-out counter of a café. Hypnotized, she handed over the five-dollar bill in exchange for a quarter of a duck the clerk whacked apart, his cleaver flashing like a master swordsman's. In the steamy shop, blood rushed to her cheeks. Before she was out the door, Scarlett was cramming the fatty flesh and crispy skin into her mouth, savoring the taste of wildness, of wings beating in flight.

It was said the cunning traded their way up, a flea for a dog, a dog for a hen, a hen for the hand of the village beauty. Scarlett had a different prize in mind: her rent. Full for the first time in months, she could think clearly. Her landlord was rumored to be going into debt to pay for his daughter's wedding, and she had to come up with something he wanted as much as her rent.

She cut through an alley jammed with trash bags, its cobbles slick and stinking, and returned to Evergreen Gardens where she knocked on the door of Granny Wang's. After recovering from her stroke, she spent her days unraveling old sweaters and knitting with the recycled yarn. She'd made orange hats for the babies. Stooped, Granny Wang wafted the sharp scent of Tiger Balm ointment. Housebound for the most part, except when she bought her groceries and visited her doctors. Though she now had a permanent limp, Granny Wang could elbow through the tightest crowds for a market bargain. In her palms, she rotated metal balls to keep her hands dexterous, with the delicate sound of a temple gong summoning worshippers to prayer. She stared into the giveaway bag so intently that Scarlett could tell Granny Wang wanted one. Because Daisy had procured two bags of groceries, Scarlett would gamble with her own.

"Shameful, I can't, I can't." Granny Wang politely refused even as she was reaching for the sack that Scarlett held up to her. She followed Scarlett's gaze to the dusty plum liquor on top of her bunk bed. A few weeks ago, Scarlett had seen the bottle while bringing her scavenged wool sweaters, and Granny Wang now offered it to her. "Rub it on baby's gums, when she's teething."

The bottle filled her with a sense of possibility: the sound of its sloshing like splashes at the beach, the scent of time and refinement, everything she wanted for her daughter. Back in the apartment, the cold damp extinguished her excitement. In the chill of late autumn, they had to string their laundry overhead instead of hanging it outside the window, turning the air humid and making the ceiling feel low as a coffin. Daisy was playing with the babies on the double mattress that she and Scarlett shared. Scarlett squeezed around the portable cribs, the stacks of diapers, baby clothes, and crates converted into storage. Her breasts were close to bursting, of her and yet apart from her, a time bomb tick-tick-ticking away the minutes she'd been apart from her daughter.

Daisy gave her a crumbly roll that Scarlett wolfed down. "Where's your bag?" Daisy eyed the bottle of plum wine. She sniffed the air, as if to check whether Scarlett's breath had the sour tang of alcohol. Scarlett hoped she couldn't smell the duck she'd eaten. She should have explained, but didn't want Daisy pitying her if she failed in her quest. She swaddled the bottle and tucked it into a crate for safekeeping until she could figure out her next trade. "How did you get two bags?"

"I asked if there were any extra," Daisy said. Her blitheness irritated Scarlett and steeled her resolve to keep her plans a secret awhile longer. Petty, perverse, but she didn't want Daisy to interfere. Daisy might top her and trade away the items in her giveaway bags for a new car or a trip to Europe.

Scarlett sank onto the bed and pulled aside her cotton bra. She nursed Liberty, the electric tug of milk flowing through her breast. Her daughter, her eyes closed, throat pulsing with each gulp, awed her. No one had ever needed her like that. Motherhood had cracked her open, left her raw and vulnerable as a crab without its shell. She yawned, her eyes sandy with exhaustion after what felt like centuries of overtime shifts. As a teenager, she had routinely worked seventy-hour weeks, until her hands curled and her back bent into assembly line position in bed. Women her age weren't meant to have babies. Her mother had been just out of her teens when she'd given birth to Scarlett, and as a widow, had been young and strong enough to till the family plot by herself.

Scarlett brushed crumbs off her daughter. No longer a scrawny newborn with an alien's scaly skin, she'd come to resemble Boss Yeung. No one feature, but her single-minded focus that shut all else out unmistakably made her his daughter. The puzzled squiggle between her eyes that caused Scarlett to gasp. At times Boss Yeung seemed to be accusing her, via Liberty's face, asking why she kept them apart.

At the airport, the day Scarlett had left him, he'd been so weary. When the *tai tai* had insulted her, insulted him by treating her like a serving girl, he'd rebuked Scarlett as if she were a child, and their age gap never seemed as great as then. Had his vitality returned, or had it been the beginning of a long decline?

She burped her daughter, pleased by her heft, that flesh, that bone, that blood nourished by her alone. A certain hunger flickered across Daisy's face. Her milk had dried up, and she never spoke of wanting to nurse. She must wish she could. She didn't take easily to failure. "I thought you couldn't drink if you nursed," Daisy said, glancing toward the plum wine.

"It's not for me." Scarlett set Liberty on her belly, rocking her gently, willing her to roll over onto her back. Boss Yeung had doubted her ability as a mother, and Liberty thriving served as a rebuke.

She could have told him the heir he pined for was no heir at all. For eons, men around the world—peasants and emperors alike—

had also yearned for a son. At his factory, several women were in management, more than Scarlett had seen elsewhere, and Boss Yeung seemed to value hard work and good ideas above gender—so long as you weren't related to him.

Liberty fussed, frustrated that she couldn't turn over.

"Have you tried putting her on her side?" Daisy asked.

"The bed's too soft." She pressed her fingers against Liberty's torso and hip. The baby's face twisted in alarm and she threw up, her vomit the gooey white of viper's venom, warm and wet. Scarlett wiped her off with a clean rag, and Liberty squealed in protest. The blankets were spattered with sour milk, the stench of a cowshed. In the bathroom down the hall she rinsed off the rag, and when she returned, blotted on the blanket where Liberty kicked in the air. She couldn't wash the blanket in the sink, and dreaded dragging it to the Laundromat.

Daisy's son rolled over, from his belly to his back, on a foam play-mat adorned with the alphabet. He'd been turning over for a few days. "You're lucky you can put Liberty down and she'll be where you left her." Her boast, intended or not, grated on Scarlett.

"The two babies—how was it?" Scarlett asked.

"I couldn't have managed, not without Little Fox," Daisy said. Their neighbor, who had been unlucky in love, once engaged to a man who had run off to escape gambling debts. She had an extravagant interest in the babies, who must have represented the dreams she'd put on hold. Little Fox had helped Daisy carry them down the stairs.

"When they both can get around—" Daisy shook her head. Scarlett pictured the babies grown into toddlers, tottering, running in opposite directions, into traffic, into danger.

"There are leashes," Scarlett said.

The suggestion seemed to offend Daisy. "They wouldn't need a leash at William's."

His parents' house. Daisy's usual big talk about the big house, big yard, and big meals they would have after reuniting with her boy-friend, when his family took them in. "It's a five bedroom," Daisy said.

"Find him then," Scarlett said bluntly.

Daisy had to stop thinking that her boyfriend would save her. Since the night she'd run away from Perfume Bay, she'd been saving herself—and she couldn't give up now. Because Daisy had broken off ties with her parents, because she wasn't in school, William had swelled in importance. Although Scarlett cared enough for the teenager to wish that she could devote more time to her, Liberty consumed her. She had nothing left, not for herself, not for Daisy.

"We should hire someone who can. A detective." Daisy leaned back on her heels.

You couldn't trust a person who dug through garbage and tailed vehicles for a living. Snoops sold information to the highest bidder, and Scarlett didn't want Boss Yeung or Daisy's parents coming after them.

Until now, Daisy had never asked for anything, and kept track of what she owed Scarlett in a small notebook. With each passing day, it seemed unlikely that she'd find William and repay her share. After the babies arrived, the savings had dwindled faster, and Scarlett couldn't waste money on outlandish schemes.

"Little Fox recommended a good one on Clay Street, expensive but worth it." Daisy offered her son a rattle. "He found her man."

"After he'd died! Little Fox is a little fool." Scarlett balled up the rag. "What did you tell her?"

What gossip would Little Fox let slip in Chinatown, what details would bring Boss Yeung to their doorstep?

Daisy fiddled with the edge of the blanket. "Nothing."

"What did you tell her?"

"Nothing!" Daisy said. "*She* brought it up. That one doesn't stop, once she gets started."

Scarlett nodded.

"The detective doesn't have to know everything. All I need is what's left"—she looked at the biscuit tin that held their savings—"William will pay the rest later."

"Paying later won't pay for now." She strapped on Liberty, took the money from the tin, grabbed the plum wine, and left.

# Chapter 11

Scarlett knocked on Widow Mok's door. Fat as a grub, her neighbor had once been a famed Chinese opera singer, performing screeching ballads, with mincing steps, a jingling headdress, and snowy face paint. And despite her title, she hadn't lost her husband. She'd been the mistress of a Chinatown leader who had kept her in style, and it was said all she had left of her former riches were her fabulous gowns. Nowadays, she wore satin sweat suits and remained vain about her tiny feet, shod in silk slippers embroidered with peonies, the only part of her wardrobe into which she could still fit.

Scarlett proposed trading plum wine for a *qi pao* that now wouldn't have contained one of Widow Mok's arms, a tunic dress that seemed modest until you noticed the tightness of the bodice and the slits up the sides designed to reveal flashes of leg. Scarlett had never owned one—nor had the occasion to wear one herself.

"For that?" Widow Mok sniffed. "My dresses were made by the finest tailor in Shanghai."

"And this by the finest herbalist." Scarlett unscrewed the bottle of plum wine, which released the fragrance of blossoms set afire. Liberty, strapped to her chest, started to shift, and Scarlett rocked from side to side to keep her asleep. She'd taken the baby with her to gain the sympathies of those she haggled with, but Widow Mok seemed unmoved.

"Plum wine helps with digestion, to fortify your *qi*." Which could help Widow Mok lose weight, Scarlett didn't need to add. She poured two cups, toasting to her health and longevity. The sip burned, and something unfurled in her and the widow, too, like a bright red silk banner rippling in the wind.

Widow Mok's eyes glittered. "Is Daisy getting married?"

Only Daisy would fit into the *qi pao*. Only Daisy seemed worthy of a man's attention. Scarlett's skin prickled. She was no beauty and had never staked her ambitions or her future on her appearance, but she'd also never looked so haggard. She resembled a lank-haired, hollow-eyed ghost from the old tales, those who lured travelers to their death. If Boss Yeung could see her now, he'd recoil. During her pregnancy, the shape-shifting, however humiliating, however uncomfortable, had sustained the baby. Now the wreck of her body lacked any nobility, and she felt like an old sow before the slaughter.

The *qi pao* stank of mothballs, the scent of not letting go, the last reminder of Widow Mok's youth. Glamour, grace, and desire. The dress lacked its top frog closure, only its frayed threads left behind, as if it had exploded under high pressure the final time Widow Mok tried it on. Yet it also had nearly invisible stitches, the sort that blinded a dedicated tailor, and embroidery so fine it seemed painted on with an eyelash. A quality unavailable in Chinatown, unavailable most anywhere except the imperial court, and Scarlett knew just who would want such a dress. The landlord's daughter wasn't the only one getting married. Little Fox was also engaged, though her groom remained in Guangzhou, unable to get his fiancé visa or afford the plane ticket. Their wedding had been postponed three times. Her last fiancé, the one who'd jilted her, the one who'd later died in a car accident, not only ran out on her, but left her with a worthless engagement ring. When she tried to sell it, she discovered the diamond was a fake. For this marriage, Little Fox would surely want a fine dress.

She didn't have the money for one. If she did, she wouldn't have been living at Evergreen Gardens, and she would have spent her savings on getting her fiancé here. Little Fox welcomed her into the apartment. Though she lacked cash, she still might have something of value she could trade. Looking around, Scarlett noticed a man's suit—its heavy fabric matte and tasteful, its understated cut digni-fied as a banker—protected in a dry cleaner's clear plastic bag. She could make an even better trade with the suit. Fit for a wedding, it must have belonged to Little Fox's first fiancé.

Little Fox had a narrow face and delicate chin, and might have seemed sly but for her broad smile that rendered her feelings trans-parent. Her eyes grew wide when Scarlett showed her the dress. Little Fox held it against herself, stroking the silk. She must have been imagining herself in the arms of her husband-to-be at her wedding banquet.

"It's yours," Scarlett said. "Trade me that old suit."

Little Fox wanted Fiancé No. 2 to wear it to their wedding, she said. "I can't. I already promised it to him."

"A dress like this, you can't get for such a bargain." Scarlett was sweating, the baby radiating heat like a car engine against her chest. "Bad luck. Start off new. Listen—why do you think your man can't get here?"

Little Fox asked, "A ghost?" She bought lottery tickets every week, paid for blessings at the temple, and lit incense daily.

"Whose ghost?" Scarlett asked.

"Of my first fiancé!" Little Fox buried her face in her hands.

Scarlett must have hit upon her deepest fear. Just as Scarlett felt the relief of pulling off another trade, Liberty grunted with the red-faced exertions that heralded a bowel movement. A disgusting but now familiar warmth seeped in the sling against Scarlett's chest. Parenthood plunged you in more shit and piss than raising pigs. Little Fox slipped on the dress, transforming her into a princess that no man ever could have abandoned. She smoothed her hands on the silk and sucked in her soft belly. If she lost a few kilos, the dress would fit perfectly, as if she'd been poured in.

Liberty squirmed, trying to escape the sling. The stinking diaper would end the negotiations if Scarlett didn't hurry. Scarlett zipped up the *qi pao*, which glimmered over Little Fox's curves. She turned

Little Fox toward the hand mirror nailed to the wall—too high up and too small to reflect the stain on the hip. "Grow old and white-haired together," Scarlett told her. "A good match of a hundred years."

Traditional wedding congratulations that Little Fox must have longed to hear. She handed over the suit. Her fiancé—her dead fiancé—had excellent if expensive tastes. She beamed, confident in the new fiancé she had fallen in love with online, confident as Scarlett never had been and never would be. Scarlett hurried away, her eyes stinging, thinking about Boss Yeung.

On a trip to an island off Zhuhai, they'd splashed on the beach and feasted on prawns, pink and plump, sucking garlicky sauce off their fingers. He served her the parts of the crab with the most succulent, easiest-to-reach meat. Afterward, he skipped stones, and she clapped her hands with a girlish delight she had never allowed herself. She didn't know how to swim, but she followed him into the water. She clung to him, breathing into his ear as he breast-stroked through the waves. She kicked her legs along at the surface. Here she gave in to weakness, to vulnerability. His back muscles rippled beneath her, as if he were the great sea turtle Ao who held up the sky.

One time he'd swum so far with her on his back that the crescent of sand disappeared and only the sapphire sea surrounded them. The depths dropping down, down, down. After a wave splashed into her face, she sputtered. Boss Yeung told her to close her eyes. To shut out her fears. His movements, steady and sure, told her he wouldn't fail her.

If he'd been slow to reassure her, in her panic she might have strangled him and dug her knees into his back, drowning them both to stay afloat for a few seconds longer. But he had calmly kicked back toward shore, the sound of his breath the only sound left in the world.

She yearned for him now, for his attentions, light and circling, her back arching to meet him. His weight on her—in her. His lips at her neck, his hands at her rib cage, their bodies sweaty. The air heavy with the scent of their lovemaking, the salt of the ocean, and the green of a bamboo grove.

Never again. Heading back to her apartment, Scarlett passed by the communal kitchen, where Old Wu called out, *"Guniang!"*

*"Sifu!"* she replied. She would change Liberty's diaper, then come back to check out the preparations for a communal dinner. Auntie Ng had commandeered a legion of volunteers, and frozen turkeys crowded the counter, uniform and menacing as a fleet of alien spacecraft taking over earth. Three bobbed in the plugged-up sink beside a stove where a pot of boiling water steamed up the kitchen.

She startled at the sound of glass shattering. Old Wu had dropped a jar of pasta sauce that spattered red like a crime scene, and Auntie Ng threw him out. He followed Scarlett to her apartment, saying, "She insisted, but she'll never want my help again." After cooking for decades in Chinatown restaurants, he could have prepared a feast, but these days, he spent as little time as possible in the kitchen, eating for free in the many places where he'd trained waiters-turned-cooks.

Although she stepped back, hoping he couldn't smell the dirty diaper, he reached for Liberty's head peeping out of the sling. He stroked her head, and the baby rewarded him with a toothless smile.

"I'll be right back," she said.

"Hold on." He emerged with a pair of silver-sequined shoes for Scarlett. The soles were scuffed, but he knew a cobbler who could do the repairs, for a good price. "Fit for a princess!"

Scarlett held the shoes in the palm of her hands, exotic birds about to take flight. "I wish I had an occasion."

"We'll find one," he said.

Was he trying to ask her out for a date? In the last week, he'd brought her a discarded flower arrangement and a glass bead necklace. He studied the suit she carried. "Seems like you have one already?"

Liberty wasn't crying; maybe the diaper could wait a minute longer. Scarlett hurriedly asked if he knew anyone who needed a suit, who might be willing to trade. Not the butcher, not the orderly, not the bus driver. "The only men I know wear uniforms, not suits," he said. "What kind of buyer are you looking for?"

Wasn't there a youth organizer who lived upstairs? Maybe he needed a suit, she said, when he met with government officials.

"When you ask for money, you need to look poor—not rich!" He cocked his head at Liberty, who copied him. "A suit like this, you might find only once in a lifetime."

He didn't need a suit, but she couldn't allow him to protect her. She could never return his affections, and she didn't want to mislead him as Boss Yeung had misled her.

He touched the sleeve. "What are you asking for it?"

"Two sows, a goat, and a dozen hens," she said lightly, and she excused herself.

Back at the apartment, Scarlett discovered that Daisy and her son had gone out. Usually, if one woman left the room, the other sprawled out with her baby, like one of those capsules dropped into water that expands to fifty times its size. No chatter, no breath, no presence, just you and your baby.

Daisy's side of the clothesline was empty. No—no. Quicksand pulled at Scarlett and she stumbled to the biscuit tin where she found the birth certificates, and in the corner, Daisy's belongings, folded and stacked, and Didi's favorite rattle, a ball within a ball. She hadn't packed up and left. Maybe the walls had pressed in on her, and she had to get out to breathe.

Scarlett shuddered. She fingered the savings that she'd taken the precaution of tucking into her pocket. At Daisy's age, she would have left without question if anyone had put her down the way Scarlett had. The long days would grow longer without another pair of eyes, another pair of hands to help her. She'd known all along, but the full force of it hit her now: if and when Scarlett found a job, what would become of Liberty without Daisy to babysit and without Didi, the playmate she'd known almost since birth? On her own, Daisy might call her parents within the week, maybe within the day, and without her, Scarlett couldn't last much longer in San Francisco. But anyone she sought for help—her mother, Boss Yeung, Mama Fang—would attempt to part her and her daughter.

She smoothed the birth certificates flat. That day, after they'd returned from City Hall, they made a silent promise to their children and to each other, but their future together suddenly seemed in jeopardy.

Liberty bawled. Scarlett hadn't changed her diaper in time and now it had blown out. Scarlett rinsed her off in the shower, Liberty's screams echoing off the tile; changed her into another outfit, which she fought, thrashing; and scrubbed the shit-stained baby sling while Liberty rode her hip. Her squawks bouncing off the tile made a din louder than a henhouse under siege.

Soon after Scarlett finished cleaning up, Daisy returned to the apartment. She didn't say where she'd been. Her face was flushed, her hair windblown. She must have wandered Chinatown or might well have climbed up onto the roof to howl.

When Didi fussed, Daisy started building a tower out of bags of rolls, boxes of stuffing, and cans of fruit cocktail to entertain him. It tumbled over, cans rolled in every direction, and Daisy drove the heels of her palms into her eyes, at the end of her patience.

When Scarlett touched her shoulder, she whirled around and grabbed the suit's pant leg. "What's this? If we don't have money for a detective, we don't have money for this."

Scarlett might have told her but for Daisy's ungrateful tone. She'd been living off of Scarlett for months, and she shouldn't be questioning her. They tugged on the suit, the seams straining, until it flew out of Scarlett's hands and knocked over a bottle, splashing formula all over. Scarlett blotted the snail's trail with a wet wipe, darkening the stain. The smell of wet, oily wool rose up in the stuffy room, the smell of winter and brisk mornings.

Daisy reached for the suit. "Let me. There has to be someone—"

She'd lived with *ayis* all her life, and knew only how to issue orders.

"You make messes. I clean them up." Scarlett had become a scold like Ma and for the first time, she understood why she'd enraged her mother, who yelled because she felt old and because her flailing arms and shouts might cover up her fear. Because Daisy, willful and impulsive, reminded Scarlett of all her own failures since.

★ ★ ★

In the hallway, Scarlett fanned the wet spot on the suit, blowing on it while trying to lull Liberty back to sleep. She tucked the sling over the baby's head and paced. Joe Ng bolted out of the apartment he shared with his mother, his jeans sagging so low he tripped on the hem. Auntie Ng stood in the doorway, the fight gone out of her. They'd been arguing ever since he spent savings earmarked for his tuition on a used motorcycle he restored to showroom perfection. Auntie Ng wanted Joe to finish school, to land a desk job in the glass towers where she toiled, cleaning offices in the Financial District.

Scarlett followed her back into the apartment. How better to imagine her son in the life she wanted for him than with a new suit? With this suit, he could interview tomorrow or next week, start off in Chinatown at a real estate office or insurance agency.

"The suit will inspire him," Scarlett said.

Auntie Ng's face, wrinkled with worry, resembled a paper sack crumpled and smoothed out. "The only thing that inspires him is the motorcycle." He parked it on the sidewalk in front of Evergreen Gardens. The apartment was chilly, the window open to air out the stink of polishing cream and motor oil in bottles stacked against the wall.

"Get rid of the motorcycle," she said, in a flash of inspiration— the most uneven trade yet, and Scarlett wasn't sure if Auntie Ng would risk the wrath of her son. Auntie Ng sighed, glancing at Liberty, as if longing for the days when she alone satisfied her son's needs.

"I have to check on the turkey."

"He can never repay what he owes you," Scarlett said.

Auntie Ng brushed her fingers on top of the combination television and DVD player. "Take this."

To an outside observer, the exchange would seem reasonable, with a slight edge in Scarlett's favor. She'd find many takers for electronics. Or would she? Old Wu had scavenged a slender silver stereo that he'd found in the street, and few would want a television boxy as a fish tank. Auntie Ng's son probably planned to replace it.

"We don't have room," Scarlett said. She laid the suit on the bottom bunk. Auntie Ng placed her son's jeans and shirt against the suit. Too big, but he'd fit.

"He'll grow into the suit." Scarlett tugged the keys out of her hands. "Or you can get Tailor Hu to hem it."

Auntie Ng touched the lapel. "It's a serious color. For serious business." She turned the television on, a cartoon. "Your kids can learn English, by watching." Just as Scarlett had invoked Auntie Ng's son, so too would Auntie Ng appeal to maternal guilt. She was shrewder than Scarlett had supposed.

"It's only a matter of time until he gets in an accident," Scarlett said.

"He says he's careful." Auntie Ng stroked the suit again.

"He can't stop a driver who doesn't see him from running him over."

Auntie Ng rubbed her temple. "I should ask him."

"Missy wouldn't like it, if he sold it," Scarlett said. His girlfriend, who wore bright lipstick and denim miniskirts that showed off her thighs when she straddled the motorcycle. "With a job like that, he'd never have time for her. *Zaogao*." How unfortunate.

She left before Auntie Ng changed her mind, and headed to the Pearl Pavilion. She'd sworn never to return after she'd inadvertently humiliated herself in front of Manager Kwok during her interview, but the restaurant hosted banquets for Chinatown's rich and powerful—including, Scarlett knew, the wedding reception of her landlord's daughter.

She knocked on his door. He was sitting at his desk, paging through a stack of paperwork. The model motorcycle, its curves freshly polished, sat on top of the liquor cabinet.

"You again," he said. He was courteous enough not to bring up what happened at their last meeting. She mentioned Old Wu, how he'd escaped kitchen duty back at Evergreen Gardens by dropping the jar of pasta sauce.

Manager Kwok grinned. "He learned that from me! It worked a couple times, until he realized what I was doing and kept me on the worst duties."

She'd coax him into reminiscing. "What kind?"

"Peeling and chopping hundreds of onions. Shredding a mountain of cabbage. Oh! And the slush bucket."

"Slush bucket?"

"Where you pour grease, leftover drinks, any liquid. It's heavy, it's smelly, and you have to dump it at the very end of the shift, when all you want to do is fall into bed." He laughed. "I learned my lesson."

"You can't get anything past Old Wu, can you?" Scarlett asked.

"I've stopped trying."

She had him affectionately recalling those days, proud of what he'd survived and what he'd become. His mood grew expansive, open to the possibilities that Scarlett wanted to offer him. "You need a motorcycle?" she asked.

"You're a door-to-door dealership!" he said. "Not today."

"For deliveries. For places the van can't go," she said. "It's free to take a look. Go for a test drive."

Manager Kwok followed her up the street to Evergreen Gardens, where the motorcycle crouched like a tiger ready to spring. Its chrome trim gleaming mirror-bright, cared for unlike anything else on this shabby block. He circled the motorcycle, his hands twitching with the desire to touch. He kicked the tires, pointed out nonexistent dents and scratches, and she knew he wanted it but didn't have the money himself. She proposed a trade. The motorcycle, for six hundred dollars off her landlord's wedding banquet bill.

"The next couple months must be so busy, with the holidays. Thanksgiving. Christmas. Spring Festival." A hint he could pad the ledger of other banquets to make up the difference. His boss would never notice. He reached for the keys, asking for a test drive, and she knew he'd been sold.

After Manager Kwok and her landlord had agreed on the new price, and after her landlord waived next month's rent, dusk had fallen. Scarlett had to excuse herself and nurse Liberty in the restroom of the Pearl Pavilion. She perched on the toilet of the handicapped stall, her shoulders hunched and knees drawn up, trying not to fall in, not to drop Liberty, not to smell the stench of piss and disinfectant.

She'd neglected her daughter in the morning, and then dragged her around all afternoon. Liberty's cheeks were red from the cold, and snot crusted under her nose. Boss Yeung had called her an unfit mother, and she had already fallen short in so many ways. Though she'd paid off the rent for now, the month would speed by, and she'd be back where she started, climbing up only to fall backward like a crab trying to escape a basket. She would never be able to save up enough to fix her papers or to repay the hospital.

Even though the labor and delivery had been free, she wanted to reimburse the U.S. government. She'd given back the savings she'd stolen from Ma, times ten, and someday she'd drop off payment at the hospital's billing counter. She didn't want her own daughter to start off in America as a beggar. On the contrary, Liberty had made a priceless gift—cord blood—that flowed through her body, Scarlett's, and someday, or maybe already, a stranger's.

Daisy tracked them down outside the Pearl Pavilion. This time of the day lengthened, its span geologically slow, those long hours to go before sleep. Daisy tucked her son into a sling so that Scarlett could put her daughter into the stroller. The teenager had known Scarlett would be tired from carrying her baby around all afternoon, and it was a relief to free her aching back and shoulders. Daisy handed her a roll slathered with plum sauce, which was surprisingly tasty. Scarlett gave half back to her. An apology, or the start of one.

They cut through Portsmouth Square, empty but for a small group of followers of the Celestial Goddess practicing their poses. A video played on a laptop with an oversized screen, in which the Celestial Goddess appeared barefoot, perched on embroidered gold cushions while devotees flocked around her. She had an eerie wandering left eye that seemed to gaze into another dimension, and plump hands that she waved before her, as if conducting an orchestra—as if she were conducting you. Her warm, cajoling manner drew you in until—unless?—you realized her words didn't make any sense. Scarlett moved closer to the screen, and so did Daisy. If Boss Yeung's wife was among them, she wouldn't have known. She'd never seen any pictures of her, but the followers—of one

mind, of one heart, of one future—all seemed to resemble one another, with vacant eyes and vacant smiles. Mostly Chinese, although
the camera occasionally panned onto a stray German or random
American whose presence displayed the global reach of the Celestial Goddess. Scarlett suspected they had been hired; a foreigner
demonstrated your sophistication and appeal, whether in a temple
or a boardroom.

Daisy turned back toward the followers, intently studying them,
as if trying to decode a secret message in their poses. A woman
tried to hand them a flyer. Scarlett recognized her, their ringleader,
the one they called Sister Fan.

"You're out here every day," Daisy said. She shushed Didi, who
was squirming, tucked against her chest. "Why?"

"Everything the Celestial Goddess has done for me, I want for
you." Sister Fan was as genial as an electroshock patient.

"For *me*?" Daisy asked.

The devotees were spaced out, but Scarlett didn't like Daisy teasing them by feigning interest.

"For everyone," Sister Fan said.

"Everyone?" Daisy looked around Portsmouth Square. "There's
no one here."

Scarlett pushed the stroller to lead them away. Daisy shouldn't
humiliate someone incapable of defending herself.

"They come, they go, they know where to find me," Sister Fan
said.

"How do you keep going?" Daisy's voice broke, and Scarlett
abruptly understood what the teenager wanted to learn: how not to
lose hope. She must feel like she was doggy paddling across the
ocean, keeping her head above water but unable to get any closer to
the father of her child.

A view from above might ease Daisy's despair, reminding her of
the world beyond the present moment. Scarlett tugged her toward
a grim gray slab studded with porthole windows looming on the
east side of Portsmouth Square, the tallest building in Chinatown.
She led Daisy into the elevator, which groaned and creaked to the
top floor that housed a restaurant, a rival of the Pearl Pavilion. They

couldn't afford a meal or a snack, but Scarlett crossed the moss-green carpet with speed and purpose, pushing the stroller like an icebreaking ship. If you squinted in the dim bar, you might glimpse the glamour otherwise overpowered by the sweet reek of many years of spilled drinks.

By the floor-to-ceiling windows, they pressed their fingers against the cold glass, which was reinforced with chicken wire and streaked with grime. San Francisco as they'd never seen it, high above the rooftops. Daisy went silent, awed. She loosened the sling and turned Didi toward the windows. He reached out his chubby fingers, yearning to touch and to fly.

The waiter asked if they'd like a table, but they ignored him. Scarlett picked up her daughter, showing her the view as day slid into night. A spotlight flooded over the blunt nozzle of a tower perched on the hill, and moments later, the double spires of a church lit up. Liberty giggled. When bridge cables started to glow, she craned her neck at Scarlett, as if amazed and utterly convinced her mother had performed a miracle of lights.

In the kitchen, the turkeys had been hacked in half to fit in the oven, and glazed in honey and vinegar, the crispy skin glittering. The spaghetti was boiled, then stir-fried with the canned vegetables into an enormous pan of chow mein; canned fruit cocktail was ladled upon luminous almond jelly, and the tomato sauce was thinned into a hot and sour soup.

Blankets were spread across the hallway, like a picnic under the harvest moon for the Mid-Autumn Festival. Old Wu made a nest for the babies with a fluffy comforter, and Scarlett leaned against the wall and slid down into it. She might fall asleep sitting here, lulled by the warmth of the kitchen and the chatter of her neighbors.

Despite the labors of Auntie Ng and her assistants, the turkey was dry and tasteless. Chinese didn't usually eat turkey. Big as a peacock, ornamental rather than edible, and mythical as a phoenix, the bird was found nowhere in the villages or in the markets, nowhere in song or memory in her country. The Chinese preferred roast ducks hung in shop windows, the skin lacquered brown, the plump birds dripping grease into metal pans. Every part but the quack consumed: slices of the mahogany skin and the bones boiled into a broth. Her mouth watered. Puffy buns held juicy dark meat so savory you wished you could catch the ducks flying in formation high in the sky.

Neighbors brought out their jarred condiments to add flavor to the turkey: red chili, mouth-numbing peppercorn, black bean, plum, and soy sauces. Scarlett spread plum sauce on an American roll, layered dark meat and sprinkled chopped scallions, and served it to Daisy.

Delicious, Daisy proclaimed. "It's like a Chinese slider." Scarlett understood the word only because she'd eaten miniature hamburgers, a snack at a fancy hotel bar with Boss Yeung. The sliders had annoyed him. A scam, he said, to replace beef with bun, yet she'd understood their appeal. Nothing tasted as good as the first bite, your teeth sinking into perfection for you and you alone. Nothing signified your wealth and refinement more than dining on toy-sized food. The American way: nothing to linger or labor over, instant gratification gone in an instant.

Soon Scarlett was making enough for everyone.

"It's good, but I prefer *mantou*." Old Wu took another bite. "American bread is so sweet. So dry. It's soaking up all my saliva."

Joe Ng stormed into the hallway, yelling that his motorcycle had been stolen. His mother pulled him into their apartment, where the fighting continued. The door opened and the suit flew out, trailing empty arms and legs, hit the wall and slid down. He and his mother emerged, glowering at Scarlett. "Cheat! Cheat!" he said.

"She's a snake," Auntie Ng hissed.

"You could convince a chicken to fly into the pot," Scarlett retorted. "You're no fool."

"Where is it?" Joe Ng shouted.

"Ask Manager Kwok."

Scarlett knew he couldn't get the motorcycle back, not unless he wanted to face the wrath of Manager Kwok's gangster cronies. A vein pulsed on his forehead until Old Wu handed him a plate of food, and he grudgingly began to stuff himself. Someone else ran out for a batch of steamed buns from the bakery around the corner, and Scarlett assembled more sliders. Even better, everyone agreed.

Good enough to serve at the Pearl Pavilion, Old Wu said. "Sure to sell out."

A joke, yet Scarlett pictured a shiny cart, the steamer tray of buns and the roasted meat, basted in a honey-sweet glaze, for five dollars per sandwich—not in Chinatown, but a few blocks away, in the neighboring nightlife district. *Chinese slider,* tastier and more unusual than the bacon-wrapped hot dogs Scarlett had seen for sale. She'd scavenge frozen giveaway turkeys no one wanted in Chinatown, and she'd soon sell enough sliders to pay for future rent. Small enough for drunks streaming out of clubs to gobble in a few bites while catching their ride, cheap enough to encourage gluttony, to fill their American hunger, a hunger like nowhere else in the world, born from abundance and prosperity.

# Chapter 12

**Scarlett knocked** on Old Wu's door. The floorboards inside creaked, and he stifled a cough. He was avoiding her. She knew his routine. He usually slept in and then strolled to a bakery for a bun and a cup of tea, played mahjong at his social hall, ate lunch, napped, joined card games in Portsmouth Square, and visited surrounding neighborhoods to scavenge.

It was past ten, and he must be hungry for breakfast. With the frozen turkeys culled from the church handout and Old Wu's help, she'd assembled dozens of her rendition of *hanbaobao,* the Chinese word for hamburgers. By her third night, she'd known she had a hit. To support her family and Daisy's, she needed his introduction to suppliers, his advice on how to cook quickly and efficiently at volume, his tantalizing recipes, all the knowledge he'd accumulated in his decades in Chinatown's restaurants.

Daisy was listlessly paging through an SAT prep book. Progress, however small, a sign that she was reclaiming what she'd put on hold. The first time Daisy changed a diaper or offered a bottle to her son, she'd done so with trepidation and curiosity that gave way to satisfaction when she figured out how. But now, these tasks had settled into thankless repetition, with no relief in sight, and her sorrow was deepening. She could not yet accept what Scarlett had long suspected: William didn't want to be found, and Daisy would have to forge a life without him.

Scarlett had to get her out of the apartment before she fell into a state of hibernation from which she might never rise. She shifted Liberty on her hip and knocked again. No answer. She cleared her throat and could hear Old Wu's labored breathing on the other side of the door. "I'm in trouble," she said.

The door swung open and Old Wu peered at her in alarm. "Liberty—is she okay?" He doted upon the baby who now cooed, offering him a wide, toothless grin.

"I need your help," Scarlett said. "Can you train me, *Sifu*?"

He didn't return her smile. For once, he wasn't teasing. "I've been asking around. An electronics factory is hiring."

"The *hanbaobao* sold out every night," Scarlett said.

"That's no life for you," he said roughly. His voice was scratchy, thick with mucus. "That life—she'll never see you. You don't want that life."

"You did."

He coughed and spat into a rag. "I left that a long time ago." He opened his door. His room was tidy, small as Scarlett's, though his held a leather armchair patched with duct tape. He'd lived here for decades, so long that the room seemed an extension of him. The faded brown windowsill matched the color of his cheeks, and his scent of mothballs and tea was strongest here. He gave her a look, a warning. If she didn't hold on to her daughter, she could end up alone like him.

"Trying to run your own business, it's too risky," he said.

"On a good night, I'd take in more than I would in a week in the factory." In China, she'd lacked the *guanxi* to start her own business and to grease the palms of local authorities, Party officials, and vendors. She didn't want a job comparable to the one at Boss Yeung's factory—she wanted better, and she believed she had that chance now.

"On a bad night, you'd make nothing," he said. "I've seen a lot of people who wanted what you want. They failed."

"All of them?"

"Take a factory job for a while. Then you can decide."

She didn't have a while. Her visa would expire toward the end of January and fixing her papers would cost thousands of dollars—if they could be fixed at all. She might not make enough selling *han-baobao* to pay for an immigration consultant, but she most certainly wouldn't at a factory. She wanted to avoid a green-card marriage and the years-long ruse it entailed. Old Wu might agree to marry her, but he cared for her far too much. And she cared far too much for him. More than a few times, she'd been aware he was staring at her. Auntie Ng's jealousy told Scarlett that his attentions were unusual. If he attempted to woo her, she didn't relish the thought of turning him away.

"You can take pieces home, to work on at night," Old Wu said. "Or I could put in a good word with Manager Kwok."

The Pearl Pavilion. "He didn't hire me the first time."

"If you worked there, then you'd see what it's like to run a restaurant."

The more he attempted to dissuade her, the more stubborn she became. "I'll ask Granny Wang."

He snorted. He wasn't impressed by their neighbor's cooking.

"Show me," she said. "Everyone says your buns are so light they could float to heaven. That your roast pork could make a monk give up his vows."

"They don't know. Just talk."

Liberty squirmed, restless. She wanted the ground. On her belly, she'd raise her head, sleek as the Sphinx. On her back, she'd kick her legs, pedaling an invisible bicycle. The thrum of life, pulsing, twitching, that vibrated through Scarlett, too.

He sighed.

"Let me try to run my own business," Scarlett said.

"I never did." He looked away. He might regret the family he never had, the restaurant he never opened, but he'd resigned himself to his circumstances. Liberty squealed, heavy in her arms.


The flayed beige skin, ghoulish grins, and flexed muscles red and raw as sirloin didn't disturb Scarlett—the eyes of the corpses did. Each and every one had Chinese eyes: undeniable in the man running, the lovers embracing, and the woman bending to touch her toes. In the man seated at a chessboard, the top of his skull popped off to reveal the wrinkles and folds of his brain.

Old Wu had turned her away. Later that day, trying to raise Daisy's low spirits, Scarlett had insisted they visit the exhibition hall a few hilly blocks east of Chinatown and redeem the free tickets from the church donation sack. Daisy's interest in science had begun in her father's engineering lab, a vast playground where she'd roamed. After one of his promotions, he put an end to the visits. It set a bad example to his employees to bring her, he told her. A distraction could lead to accidents, to loss of face.

Daisy studied the display's thick web of blood vessels crossing a woman's face.

Scarlett pointed at the sign. "What's it say?"

"The human body has almost ninety-seven thousand kilometers of blood vessels," Daisy said.

Scarlett flushed, blood tingling, circulating and circulating in her veins. She wasn't squeamish, but she'd seen enough of the exhibit to know that she preferred her insides to remain a mystery. She pushed up the shade on the stroller to shield Liberty, who cooed and batted at the rubbery giraffe dangling from the handle. Her liveliness made the preserved corpses all around them more horrendous.

Daisy might have inherited her father's scientific mind, or maybe he'd bred it into her. Without looking at Scarlett, she recounted how he'd questioned her aptitude and appetite for research, and told her to pursue a practical degree like accounting, a job without long hours on nights and weekends.

No, Daisy told him. She'd narrowed her major down to chemistry or physics.

"Marry a smart man," he'd said. "You'll have smart children."

"He thought he was complimenting me," she said bitterly. Soon after, she'd met William, who doubted her in nothing.

Scarlett had never known her own father, had never suffered his rejection. Daisy's heart must have broken, and was breaking still. Scarlett sniffed but detected neither the whiff of rotting flesh nor chemical preservatives, only the industrial scent of the freshly shampooed carpets. On a pedestal under a spotlight, a corpse played a saxophone. He had the stocky build of a peasant and Scarlett doubted if in life he'd come close to playing jazz.

Daisy rushed down the aisle ahead of her, ignoring the exhibit, which may have upset her. Or maybe the science she'd memorized in middle school bored her now. A trip here wouldn't rouse her out of her depression. How then? Scarlett could give her money to sign up for college entrance exams, even if she then had to defer her admission for a year or two. The uncertainty that mired Daisy mired her, too. Scarlett didn't know how long it would take to establish the *hanbaobao* business, if and when she could fix her papers, if Boss Yeung would find her before then.

Something compelled Daisy enough to halt a security guard and question him. He offered the official explanation to her questions: the bodies had been donated.

"From China?" Scarlett asked.

"He didn't know," Daisy said.

Impossible, they agreed. In China, no one donated their bodies to science. If you were rich you had a grand funeral, were laid out in a copper casket, all accompanied by chanting monks, clouds of incense, three layers of silk funeral garb, new shoes never worn, and a pearl in your fist to light your way into the next world. Even if you were cremated, your descendants burned paper houses, luxury cars, mobile phones, and stacks of hell money to ensure your enjoyment in the afterlife.

"But their faces. Anyone can see they're Chinese," Scarlett said.

"I asked, 'Did the hospital get permission from the families?'" Daisy said. "He said, 'Maybe the hospital didn't know how to find their families.'"

"Everyone's?" Scarlett asked. Scores of bodies were on display.

"They must be prisoners," Daisy said. "I asked, 'Are these bodies from prison? For what kind of crimes?'"

The guard was looking around uneasily, as if searching for the exit.

"He told me, 'Maybe they deserved it.'"

Deserved it? Their offenses could have been fabricated. In China, if you crossed the powerful, you met your doom.

And Scarlett had crossed Boss Yeung. She shuddered, hit by a sudden vision of herself flayed and on display, forever lost to Liberty. On their way in, they'd ignored a clump of demonstrators, followers of the Celestial Goddess. They'd carried signs that complained of body snatching and persecution.

As they exited, the protestors pressed around them, shouting that the Chinese government sold organs from executed prisoners, and now their bodies, too. Scarlett shuddered and steadied herself on the stroller, gripping so hard that her fingernails dug into her palms.

That would be the worst punishment, to be posed like a naked mannequin in a traveling exhibit.


Although Scarlett had only stepped away for a moment to check on Liberty, the common kitchen filled with smoke and would have set off the fire alarm if Evergreen Gardens had possessed such amenities. She grabbed the handle of the pot and immediately let go, the hot metal branding her palm. She was trying to make plum sauce for the sliders. The pot clanged against the stove and tumbled onto the buckling linoleum. Her hand throbbed and she ran it under cold water in the sink. Palm sugar burned fast, hot and sticky until it charred. She was trying to reconstruct Old Wu's recipe for plum sauce. She cursed herself for not watching him more closely when he'd helped her prepare sliders. It was now the day before Thanksgiving, and so far he had refused to give up his secrets. Ma wasn't much of a cook, and neither was Scarlett, having long survived on meals from the factory canteen or street vendors and noodle shops.

While Liberty napped, Daisy was out with her son, likely at the library. The exhibit had stirred her, and she'd been reading whatever she could find about the bodies. In one city, protestors threw blankets over them and hurled paint at the signs. In another, the health department had shut down the exhibit after the bodies started oozing a clear liquid. Daisy had spoken in such detail, such excitement about the chemical process of preserving the bodies that Scarlett expected to find the girl pickling a luckless frog purchased from the wet market. Ghoulish, but at least her new obsession kept Daisy's mind off her boyfriend. She seemed on her way to finding herself again, or at least on her way to trying.

Scarlett used the hem of her shirt to lift the pot and douse it in the sink, sending up clouds of noxious, foul-smelling steam. Auntie Ng arrived, carrying pink shopping bags bulging with bitter melon and dried goji berries. She had an upcoming blood test and was cramming as she might for a final exam, determined to live to 120. "It stinks in here!" She looked into the sink. "What's this?"

"It's soaking," Scarlett said.

"It's your kitchen?" Auntie Ng snapped. Living here led to daily competition. The moment you heard the communal toilet flush or the shower turn off, the moment your neighbor left the kitchen, you raced to take your turn. You had to hurry, and when you finished, you packed up every bit of your presence. If you treated public spaces as your own, you faced the wrath of your neighbors. Auntie Ng coughed and rushed to the window, which was stuck closed.

"I'll—I'll get a fan." Scarlett flexed her burned hand, pain stabbing through her palm.

Auntie Ng stomped away, her footsteps pounding on the stairs to the kitchen on the next floor. After she'd traded away her son's motorcycle, his girlfriend had left him. Auntie Ng should have been grateful, but still she scowled at Scarlett. She suspected that the woman had a more than neighborly interest in Old Wu. His friendship with Scarlett annoyed the women in Evergreen Gardens who considered him a community asset.

With the heel of her burned hand, she braced the pot against the side of the sink and used a butter knife to scrape off the char, which clung like a space-age epoxy. She was about to tap the mess scented like a crematorium into the garbage can when she realized how she could persuade Old Wu to help her. She removed the foil she'd tented on top of a roasting pan on the counter. She hacked off the leathery end of the pork roast she'd overcooked that morning, jammed it into a crumbly stale bun that smelled like wet newspaper, and heaped on the char. She rummaged through the fridge and pulled out old jars of strawberry jam and red chilies that she smeared onto the bun. She knocked on Old Wu's door and presented the *hanbaobao* to him.

He wrinkled his nose at the stench while she explained that she'd perfected the recipe. He studied her, as if waiting for her to admit that she was playing a joke, but she thrust the plate at him again, keeping her expression eager and proud.

He didn't want to hurt her feelings. The bun crumbled in his hand, but he couldn't bring himself to take a bite. "I'm full."

"I'll save it for you," Scarlett said. "It tastes better on the second day, after you reheat it and the flavors combine."

Old Wu winced, likely picturing the stale, soggy mess that would reappear the following day, but he did not—as she hoped he would—volunteer to help her.

"I followed your recipe," she said.

"Mine?" he asked.

"Watching you was like going to cooking school," Scarlett said. "I've been calling you my *Sifu*. And people have been calling me your student."

Old Wu looked aghast. He didn't want her ruining his reputation with inedible, possibly toxic food. After Liberty began wailing next door, he announced the three of them would go on a walk.

Their first stop was a wet market with bubbling vats of fish, customers elbow-to-elbow at the meat counter, and overflowing produce bins rolled onto the sidewalk. "You'll find vegetables you can't get anywhere else," Old Wu said. He inspected a pile of bitter greens, checking for wilted leaves and held up jade-green scallions to her nose. "Avoid anything that's yellowing and wilted, or soggy."

She repeated after him, her eyes closed, taking in the sharp green scent, and added the bundle to her shopping cart. Old Wu peered into the meat case. "No good."

"The bones are good for soup," the butcher said.

"Not even dogs would want these!" Old Wu exclaimed.

The butcher scowled. She and Old Wu set off in search of spices. He was teaching her how to prepare tantalizing sauces with the bite of ginger, the tang of vinegar, and the sparkle of star anise that made bottled ones taste like American ketchup in comparison, fit only for children.

The aisles were so narrow that they had to turn sideways. He put an arm around her waist to guide her past a towering stack of cartons. His hand lingered. His introductions to Manager Kwok, his offer to buy the bartered suit, and his invitations to meals could have been expressions of friendship, or reflected his hopes for more. Was he restraining himself because he sensed she wasn't interested? Whatever the exact nature of his feelings, he didn't hide his pleasure in her company.

When a woman swept by in heels and a gray pantsuit, her hair a helmet of permed curls, he placed a protective hand on Liberty's back. Madame Tom, he told Scarlett. She'd worked in Chinatown for decades, with the elderly, for the arts, in affordable housing, before becoming the assistant to the dean at the community college's Chinatown campus. She was married to the president of the neighborhood's second-most-important association, the kind that newcomers joined to find a lead on a job or an apartment to rent. When you settled down and started a family, you applied for a scholarship for your children and, later, made arrangements to be buried in their cemeteries.

Madame Tom pursed her lips, and seemed annoyed to be running a lunchtime errand that she found far beneath her. Old Wu said hello, and she nodded curtly and turned away. He explained to Scarlett she'd tried to recruit him to teach a cooking class, and he'd refused. He'd made an exception only for Scarlett.

Someone brushed against her, a man with hunched shoulders, his hair gray and close-cropped, his scent metallic and earthy. Boss Yeung—he'd found her. Her knees buckled. He'd grip her wrists and demand his heir. He must have detectives with him, who'd push down Old Wu and frog-march her into a waiting sedan. Then she realized this man was too short, with a large mole in his eyebrow, and a gopher's receding chin. Old Wu glared at the man—"Watch yourself!"—steadied her and led her away.

# Chapter 13

Scarlett diced scallions into strands uniform as tooth-picks. After a couple of weeks of strong sales, she'd expanded from premade sandwiches sold from a chafing dish to a steam cart she'd started renting. Now she could make *hanbaobao* to order, though the drunkest customers weren't choosy. She could have served them stale buns and overcooked meat to sop up the alcohol pulsing through their veins. But some demanded their own specials: buns stuffed with scallions, sauce, and no meat for vegetarians; double meat at double the price for carnivores; romaine lettuce leaves for those who ate no bread.

She used to fear her customers would go elsewhere if they had to wait too long. Wasn't this city populated by impatient tech million-aires on paper and in the making? Instead she discovered that lines prompted passersby to ask what they could get. Let in on the secret, people were eager to join a line that made them feel like an insider.

Christmas was coming and she couldn't tell if sales would go up among merrymakers sick of holiday ham and turkey, or if she'd lose business because people stayed home. She slid the scallions into a plastic container and snapped the lid shut. Sometimes she lost her-self in tasks, buying the ingredients, preparing the *hanbaobao*, and packing it for transport, before all at once longing for Liberty—an ache in her chest and a hollowness in her arms. Missing her at this very moment, though she was sleeping close by. Her squeak and giggle. Her fresh warm head. The kitchen bristled with dangers— knives, stove, and oven—but she wished she could have strapped on Liberty to bring with her, as her mother had strapped her on to work in the fields. That had surprised Scarlett, how much she'd been thinking about Ma. Their circumstances couldn't have been more different: Scarlett in the city, not the countryside, in America, not China. And their circumstances more alike: she and Ma both raising daughters without the fathers of their children.

Scarlett took out the plastic mixing bowl. She'd make the buns next, stir together flour, yeast, and water, and let it rise, swelling like a frog's throat. Punch it down, roll it into a log, and cut off sections to steam in bundles neat as swaddled babies.

Last night, she seasoned five kilos of pork shoulder with handfuls of salt, sugar, and pepper, and stashed it in the fridge. This morning, she started the first batch in the oven, roasting it on low. She pulled out the pork to spoon the drippings over it. In the next hour, she would shred the pork and start the next batch in the oven. Before the markets closed, she'd pick up more pork to season overnight. Each hour ordered by the checklist of tasks.

Daisy's days were shapeless, and any routine she might have attempted was subject to the whim of twin tyrants. Later this afternoon, she could take them to the park, although the weather was getting chilly, or the library, though she'd once been kicked out when Didi wouldn't stop crying. As winter set in, Daisy would be trapped inside Evergreen Gardens.

Just as Scarlett set aside the dough, Liberty began crying. She'd left the door to their apartment cracked open so she could hear her. She wiped her sticky hands on a rag and rushed back to the apartment, but when she tried to nurse her, Liberty turned her head away. Scarlett had been nursing at bedtime, at night, and upon wake-up, attempting to make up for their hours apart during the day. Now it was her daughter's turn to reject her. Scarlett bounced up and down as if her knees were on springs. It was raining, and Scarlett couldn't strap her on and go for a walk, not while the pork shoulder roasted in the oven, and not with the kitchen a disaster, spills and splashes and dishes piled in the sink that would enrage their neighbors even more.

The Ngs had been making trouble for Scarlett. Auntie Ng had nagged her son to register at the community center, but classes were full for the semester that would begin in January.

"You shouldn't have waited!" she'd shouted from inside their apartment.

"You shouldn't have given away my motorcycle!"

"I was tricked. I'm an old, stupid woman," Auntie Ng wailed, her words aimed not at her son but at her neighbors at Evergreen Gardens. If it weren't for Old Wu, they would have run her out.

Scarlett shushed into Liberty's ear, to no avail. Daisy burst into the apartment. She was drenched, her jacket sopping and zipped over her son. A tuft of his hair poked out above her collar.

Scarlett grabbed a towel, but Daisy waved her off. "Come on. Quickly, before it stops. You have to see this."

She didn't move, and Daisy tugged on her elbow. "Hurry. It's the first rainstorm since they were born. Liberty will love it."

"You'll catch cold."

"It's warmer than the showers here."

"Don't talk nonsense." She jiggled Liberty.

"It won't hurt. It's only water. And the change of scene—it'll help."

Liberty's wailing forced Scarlett into motion and after they'd clattered down the stairs to the door, a humid breeze wafted in, lush and inviting. She joined Daisy on the sidewalk. Daisy unzipped her jacket and her son peeped out his head like a turtle, blinking in wonder. The streets were slick and the air free of car exhaust, the scent wet and fresh as the breeze coming off a river.

Liberty stopped crying, staring at the drops falling from the sky. Her rosebud lips parted, her hands reaching up like Didi's. Her astonishment became Scarlett's, too. So much to experience in a universe that was rapidly expanding. Her curiosity—at the blurry whirl of the ceiling fan, at the glitter of a mirror, at the cool drops sprinkling on her face—made the world new.

Scarlett opened her mouth, letting drops fall in. She'd never been thirstier and water had never tasted sweeter. From her school days, she dimly remembered the water cycle, the muddy river beside her village, drawn into the clouds, liquid to steam to ice before falling back to earth. The drops she tasted might have begun in that same river, frozen crystals riding on the jet stream, now melting and falling and washing her clean.

"Careful," Daisy said. "You don't know what's flying by."

"You caught something." She poked Daisy's hair.

Daisy yelped, touching her bangs. When her hand came away empty, not covered in bird poop, she realized Scarlett had been teasing.

"It's good luck," Daisy said. "When a bird spreads its droppings on you."

"Good luck for the person standing next to you!"

Daisy snapped a photo of Scarlett and her daughter. Scarlett rubbed Didi's cheeks, jowly as a baron's. *"Bao bei."* Darling. He had an easy giggle, set off when Scarlett tickled his belly. His lips were rosy as a doll's and the neighbors said his long lashes were wasted on a boy.

Pedestrians ran by, shielding themselves with newspapers or jackets draped over their heads, or stood in clusters under awnings, waiting out the storm. Anyone watching Scarlett and Daisy would have thought that they were insane, women in peril, fleeing fire or fists to take refuge in the rain. Scarlett kissed the top of her daughter's head, sweet with shampoo, the downy hairs tickling her face.

Didi craned his neck, swiveling his head to observe everyone going by.

"He watches everything," Scarlett said. "Like a Secret Service agent."

"Not Secret Service," Daisy said. "He will be the one they are guarding." A president-in-the-making. She ruffled her son's wispy hair. As his head grew, Didi had gained the unfortunate receding hairline and flyaway tufts of a clown. "Next month, he's a hundred."

A hundred days. Scarlett hadn't been keeping track, but since her daughter was slightly older than Didi, that must be coming up for her, too. Liberty didn't care, didn't know one day from the next. Scarlett couldn't record her daughter's every development, but a now-familiar guilt twisted in her gut for failing Liberty. Her own mother had never celebrated Scarlett's birthday. None of the children in the village did and even now, it didn't carry much significance for her. But because a hundred days mattered to Daisy, it mattered to Scarlett. She couldn't help resenting Daisy, whose family could have paid for a dozen parties in honor of their grandchild.

"I heard I'm supposed to shave his head," Daisy said. Drops glistened in her hair.

"Who told you that? Auntie Ng? Granny Wang?" Scarlett asked. The rain was starting to slacken. Liberty cooed, demanding her mother turn the sky's spigot back on.

"It will make his hair grow in," Daisy said.

"First he'll be bald as an egg!"

Daisy stroked his head. "Maybe that's why. So your baby will look like a red egg."

To celebrate their baby's first hundred days, parents served red eggs for luck and unity, pickled ginger, and other delicacies. She and Daisy didn't have money to pay for celebrations, nor anyone to invite except for Old Wu. She'd never attended one—she didn't know any parents in Dongguan wealthy enough to keep their children with them in the city. Their babies remained in the village, under the care of their grandparents.

Her expression wistful, Daisy mentioned the embroidered silks and tiger shoes she and then her sister had worn in pictures, shoes that their mother kept in a teak chest in her bedroom. Having a child made you consider your own upbringing. Daisy didn't remember much of the festivities that honored her younger cousins: gifts and a roast pig.

How could Scarlett and Daisy keep a tradition alive if they'd forgotten most of it, or if it was foreign to them, too? And why look back? You had to let go of the past and its demands on the future. Daisy was hardly a traditional maiden, plucking at her zither under a willow tree, her feet bound, love letters hidden in her sleeves, or a filial daughter serving her father tea and bowing before her mother.

An auntie pushed past, the wheels of her shopping cart squeaking, loaded with pink plastic bags. The pork. The pork! *Aiya!* Scarlett raced upstairs, deposited Liberty into her crib, rushed to the kitchen and pulled the pan from the oven. The ends of the shoulder were overcooked, tough as leather, but fat had bathed the rest, the glistening meat tender and shredding under her fork. She exhaled, relieved she hadn't ruined it, and shredded the rest.

When Daisy arrived, she gave her a taste of the pork. Daisy swallowed, murmuring in enjoyment, and sucked her teeth. "It needs salt."

Scarlett grabbed the fork out of Daisy's hand. "That's how I've made it every time."

"The saltier it is, the more drinks you could sell."

"I don't sell drinks." She scrubbed the fork in the sink.

"You could. Get them cheap, sell for twice as much. Don't your customers ask?"

"They're hungry," Scarlett said. "Not thirsty. They've had enough to drink." A gust spattered rain against the window. "If they come out tonight."

"I can help you. I mean, I can work the cart."

Scarlett stared at her, first surprised—then territorial. "No."

"You shouldn't have to do it all yourself."

"I have a system."

"It's my turn," Daisy said quietly but firmly.

Now she understood. Daisy didn't want to be stuck in the apartment, not when the world had beckoned to her this afternoon. Scarlett came home with stories about odd customers, the strange sights—the male belly dancers or the man who bought out her night's supply, paying from a wad of hundred-dollar bills; the redhead who spoke Mandarin. Daisy wanted to see for herself. Scarlett knew a pretty girl might sell more *hanbaobao*. But the *hanbaobao* had been Scarlett's idea, Scarlett's creation, and she wasn't ready to share. "Not tonight."

"Tomorrow?"

Scarlett said nothing.

"She cries when you leave," Daisy said.

Liberty. Scarlett flushed. As if she had any choice! As if she preferred her customers to Liberty.

At times she did. To move freely without little hands, a ravenous mouth, attached to her. To complete a task without interruption. To end the night with success, sold out. She tossed the squeeze bottle at Daisy, who fumbled and caught it.

"Fill it," Scarlett said.

Daisy tugged on the top, and then tried to unscrew it. "How?"

Scarlett reached into the refrigerator for the second pan of pork shoulder, the metal cool against the burn on her palm. She slammed the pan onto the counter. The forks jumped and clattered onto the floor. Daisy flinched.

"Make this." She slid the pan toward Daisy, the metal hissing against the counter.

"How— For how long?" Daisy looked at the oven with trepidation, as if the door were the jaws of a lion about to swallow her whole.

"You don't know how. You don't know a thing."

Scarlett winced under the garbage bag, a makeshift poncho. Rain was falling, and at sundown, the temperature was dropping. She hoped that the lure of Friday night would bring out customers. But those who braved the rain rushed past her cart and into waiting vehicles. She rubbed her forearms, trying to warm up. The hem of her pants was soaked from the gutter, and her feet were wet and numb, but she couldn't go home until she sold enough to pay for tomorrow's ingredients. She checked under the lid, the billowing steam a slap to her face. She stirred the roast pork turning dry and stringy. She wanted to curl up on the buns, pile them under her head and tuck them under her neck. They'd go stale after tonight, hours of labor, cups of flour wasted.

"Han-bao-bao! Han-bao-bao!" she chanted as a group of men passed—white, Indian, and Chinese—clad in polar fleece jackets. They ignored her. When she called out, "Free sample!" the tallest one halted. She'd never offered samples—she'd never had to—but she split a bun in half and made him one, radiating steam. Her fingers tingled from the heat. He gobbled it down and wiped his fingers on his jeans. "Thanks." He loped to the car where his friends were calling for him.

She balled her hands into fists. She wanted to fling a bun at the back window. She should have let Daisy run the cart tonight; she never would have wanted to try again. A moment later, she felt small as a gnat. Daisy's talk of a red egg party had reminded Scarlett of all that her daughter lacked. All that Scarlett couldn't provide. The lightning strike of rage—she'd learned that from Ma, or maybe she'd inherited it. Either way, she knew she hadn't escaped. When Scarlett was at her most frayed, Ma settled like a mask over her face.

Her mother had been forged by the Cultural Revolution, when people had to go for the throat or else get ripped to shreds. The Party forced them to act in a manner they privately reviled. Ma might have wished she'd never taken a job at the clinic, but she'd resigned herself to cracking down on other families, in order to provide for her own.

As cold and discouraged as Scarlett felt tonight, she knew she had more choices than Ma ever did. *"Han-bao-bao! Han-bao-bao!"* she chanted, three falling notes that enticed no one.

Boss Yeung would have said she couldn't provide for her child, but he'd also had forays into failure—miracle socks that needed no washing, indestructible mobile phones heavy as bricks—that he kept in a glass case in his office, a reminder of the mistakes that had shaped his success.

She blinked. Her life with him had ended. He would steal Liberty out of her arms if he had the chance. Rain fell harder, and she edged under the green awning of a pizza parlor where a waterfall gushed. She'd always maintained a respectful distance from the entrance of bars and restaurants, parked in between or by the intersection, but the gutters were full, flooded with murky water and trash, the storm drains backing up. The pizza parlor was empty, too, the owner glumly leaning across the counter on his hairy forearms. A row of pizzas slick with grease sat under heat lamps.

She heard a voice calling from down the street. *"Hau Hanbao-bao!"* Shrimp Boy cried.

Queen of the Hanbaobao. A crony of Manager Kwok's, he was known for his schemes, both illegal (collecting protection money) and borderline (reselling goods of possibly stolen origins). He also had a reputation for violence, though tonight—damp from dashing from awning to awning—he seemed less intimidating. His girlfriend was at his side, too young to be out so late. Her phone rang, that song Scarlett had been hearing in Chinatown, with the refrain in English, "I love you hot."

Shrimp Boy glared at his girlfriend and she silenced her phone. Despite the chill, he'd unbuttoned his shirt halfway to his navel and Scarlett glimpsed the tattoo etched on his chest, the tail of a dragon or a curving sword. He had a thin scar above his right eye—from a knife fight?—and his bulbous nose would someday become purple with drink.

"Slow night?" His voice was low, scratched by cigarettes. His hands were soft, unpricked, unburned, unworked. He folded a twenty-dollar bill into her hand. "Take care of yourself."

He must think himself benevolent. His girlfriend fidgeted, impatient, and they disappeared into a bar just as a pair of giggly white women emerged, wobbly in their high heels. Under short coats, their legs were bare to the elements. This time, Scarlett thrust samples at them. They swallowed, and out of sympathy or out of hunger, they split an order, taking dainty bites, trying to not smudge their lipstick.

A pack of men was headed down the street. If she could detain the women, they would attract the men, persuade them to line up and treat themselves to a snack. With street food, crowds generated more crowds.

Scarlett tried to hand them another bun. "Fresh, hot."

While the women declined her offer, the men got in line and she sold five orders. If she sold five more, she'd have enough to buy meat tomorrow. If she steamed the buns, they might revive enough to last another night, slathered in the sauce. From the corner of her eye, she felt someone watching her, and when she turned, she glimpsed a man ducking into a bar.

"Are you ever in the Mission?" a customer asked. She shook her head. "You should come to the Mission." After hearing the question several times recently, she'd gathered it was a neighborhood in San Francisco, but too far to walk to from Chinatown. Even on nights with slow sales, at least talking to customers improved her comprehension of English and of the city.

She searched down the block for potential customers. When she turned around, she stood face-to-face with the irate owner of the pizza shop who must have noticed that she'd intruded on his sidewalk. Scowling, he pointed down the street and told her to go away—now. She quickly assembled a *hanbaobao* for him, which only irritated him more. "You got a permit for that?"

Permit. The police. Scarlett took off with the cart, her heart pounding, and slipped in a puddle at the end of the block. She landed hard on her knees, the breath knocked out of her and the cart slid out of her grasp—no, no, no—into traffic. Cars veered and honked, brakes squealed and miraculously the cart survived two lanes of traffic only to hit the curb and tip over with a clang and a crash, spilling its load. The white buns bright against the dark street, like toadstools against a muddy hillside.

An hour later, Scarlett unlocked the door and heard frantic rustling. Inside the apartment, she discovered Daisy lurching toward the CD player, emanating an otherworldly music, new and strange to Scarlett, echoing harps and plinking strings. Daisy leaned back on her heels, a guilty expression on her face. Was this how she passed the hours alone with the children? Those minutes that added to infinity but were never long enough to complete a thought, a conversation, or a cup of tea. The babies were asleep in their portable cribs, Didi's fists above his head, Liberty's flung apart as if she were singing an aria.

She'd never witnessed Daisy getting them down at the same time and she'd never asked how. Now she felt queasy with guilt.

"Sold out?" Daisy asked.

Scarlett wasn't ready to discuss the evening's disasters: the total loss of *hanbaobao*, the dented cart, and the temporary banishment from that stretch of North Beach. "What's this?" She glanced at the CD whirling in the stereo.

"Found it," Daisy said quickly.

"In the rain?" Scarlett hadn't seen anything to scavenge on her walk home. "Where?"

Daisy didn't answer. The space heater whirred beside her. She stretched up her arm and swung her head, repeating the gesture three times. It almost looked like an imitation of a Celestial Goddess pose, itself a rip-off of traditional *tai qi* exercises. Her teachings had caught on because of their familiarity, a mash-up of Buddhism, astrology, and wishful thinking.

Scarlett tore off the garbage bag and sat on the bed, tugging at the wet shoes and socks that clung to her skin. Her toes were wrinkly and pale as earthworms. She'd scraped her stomach and her knees in the fall, and her right hip would have a big bruise.

She slipped out of her clothes, toweled off, and changed into her pajamas. Old Wu snored through the walls, the sound ragged and wet. She leaned into the portable crib and touched Liberty's head, half-hoping that she might stir awake and she'd have to pick her up. Soon enough, Liberty would cry for her and Scarlett could take her to bed. Daisy gave her a mug of hot water from their portable tea-kettle. Scarlett warmed her hands, closing her eyes, letting the steam bathe her face. She sipped, her insides thawing. Scarlett didn't want her peddling *hanbaobao*, but Daisy would stifle in the apartment with no company other than their neighbor Little Fox. Her fiancé had finally arrived from China. The wedding was scheduled for this month, and Little Fox's daily prayers now concerned her desire for imminent conception. Scarlett could help Daisy find some other preoccupation: a set of science textbooks or tickets to the planetarium or the zoo. Not much, but she had nothing else to give her.

Daisy had so much of her life ahead of her, all those years in which Scarlett had preferred the uncertainty of the city to the stability of the village, solitude to companionship, responsible to no one but herself. Giving birth had changed all that.

Daisy repeated the stretch, her body supple in ways Scarlett no longer felt. She could have been a typical high school student studying for her final exams but for the baby in the crib.

Scarlett climbed under the covers. Couldn't Daisy turn off the light? *Mei you limao*, no respect, no consideration for her elders.

The teenager wore a thick pair of wool socks, and her sweater looked new, too, cream cable knit with navy blue piping at the V-neck, her size, the sleeves not yet frayed, the knit not yet pilled. Cans of formula stacked in the corner, though Scarlett couldn't remember the last time they'd replenished it. Another community giveaway? No one at Evergreen Gardens had mentioned it. Stolen from a market? Laden down with babies, Daisy couldn't move with stealth, or maybe the commotion of two squirming infants provided the perfect cover. Or were they gifts from a new suitor? Daisy, lonely, might have fallen under the spell of the next man who could rescue her. Scarlett yawned, too tired to consider the matter further, and when the music faded away, so did she.

# Chapter 14

After settling into his couch, Boss Yeung passed the cigar under his nose, inhaling the aroma, and cut off the ends with a V-shaped incision. Both men puffed as Uncle Lo passed his gold-plated lighter beneath the cigars, rotating the flame. Boss Yeung drew the smoke into his mouth, the end of the cigar glowing red, his head swimming. He hadn't had anything stronger than smog in his system in months and the chemo had changed his sense of taste, turning the cigar foul as leaves moldering under a wet log.

Upon their return to Hong Kong, he'd instructed Viann to tell the family about Scarlett and the baby. No one had mentioned it again. If his wife had shown any resentment toward him, he would have lashed out, asked how long she'd carried on with Uncle Lo, but she remained translucent and fragile as dried wax, overwhelmed by earthly matters, utterly out of touch. Any confession would have been as nonsensical as everything else that came out of her mouth. At least she'd never become one of those wives who flashed their phones finished in gold, who elbowed people aside when they shopped in Europe and screamed at salesclerks to ring up armfuls of designer purses. He wasn't going to confront her. He needed evidence that Uncle Lo couldn't deny, proof born of bodily fluids.

Uncle Lo leaned his head back and exhaled a cloud of twilight-blue smoke. Boss Yeung coughed.

"Easy now." Uncle Lo set his cigar on the edge of the crystal ashtray.

"Don't let me stop you," Boss Yeung said.

"You never did."

Viann was checking out an experimental treatment in Shanghai in case he relapsed. Last week, his wife had summoned the Celestial Goddess, who chanted over him and called upon the stars to heal him. Her portrait hung in their living room, an oversized oil painting with gaseous planets ringing her head. Though her primary residence was in Taipei, the Celestial Goddess frequently traveled to Hong Kong; both places had certain protections that the mainland lacked, but who knew for how much longer? His wife's spiritual and financial devotion to the Celestial Goddess might someday hurt his prospects over the border in mainland China, but he had never ordered her to give up what had become her reason for existence—not even after he suspected she'd turned him into a cuckold.

Boss Yeung puffed on the cigar and asked if Scarlett, most likely running low on funds, had tried to get in touch with Mama Fang, if she'd been desperate enough to attempt to make a deal.

Uncle Lo frowned. "No." Despite his wealth, despite his power, he'd been outsmarted by a peasant. "We'll find her."

There was a spot waiting for her at a prison in Tibet, he said. His friend at the ministry had arranged it. A sky-high place where you were kept in solitary so long you lost your words, where eye contact with a guard brought a shot to the head. The collapse of Perfume Bay had humiliated Uncle Lo, but it wasn't all Scarlett's fault, Boss Yeung had to concede. It was also Mama Fang's, and to be honest, also his own.

"Don't waste your favors on her," Boss Yeung said. "Cost of business."

He had to choose his words with care. If he sounded too imploring, too concerned about Scarlett, Uncle Lo would disregard his wishes as that of a sick man. "Call it a write-off."

When his young *amah* tried to clear the ashtray from the coffee table, Boss Yeung shot out his arm to block her. "We're not done yet."

Frightened, she plunked down the ashtray and Uncle Lo's cigar tumbled off. She was young, dark, and new, and might have spent every day barefoot in rice paddies out in the provinces in the Philippines before getting shipped to Hong Kong. She peeked at the portrait of the Celestial Goddess, as if trying to draw strength and calm. In her short time here, the *amah* had already been indoctrinated by Boss Yeung's wife, but he couldn't tell if she truly believed or if she gave off that impression to remain employed.

As she scurried into the kitchen, Uncle Lo reached for his cigar, his eyes lingering on her shapely bottom. He'd always had a taste for mud, for sturdy women with bodies built for labor.

"We can get more cigars," Uncle Lo said, and brought up his upcoming visit to the Bay Area. After making a significant donation to Stanford, he'd demand that doctors at the university's medical center look into Boss Yeung's case. They would go there together, he insisted.

"It's too much," Boss Yeung said.

"It's nothing. You—Viann—" Uncle Lo cleared his throat, unable to go on.

He understood what Uncle Lo could not say: for Viann's sake, he would do everything in his power to save Boss Yeung. "After I'm gone—"

Uncle Lo set down his cigar. "You're not—"

No matter your wealth, you couldn't outrun mortality. "When I'm gone, look after her. Promise me you'll look after her." Boss Yeung's voice went hoarse. "She's good, very good." *Gwaai,* Cantonese for the concept of good wrapped up in obedience.

He was close to weeping, his natural reserve dissolving. Uncle Lo put a hand on his shoulder, the weight heavy and reassuring. They would have slipped apart, gone back to their smoldering cigars if he hadn't also patted Boss Yeung's back—hard. They weren't hugging—men of their generation didn't hug their wives or their children, much less their friends—and because they couldn't hug, any form of physical contact had to involve pushing and shoving. When he tried to pull away, Boss Yeung wouldn't let him.

A game they'd played for years: Boss Yeung holding back Uncle Lo trying to get past him in the hallway; Uncle Lo blocking him from getting to the dinner table. A playful show of force that would explode into aggression, arm wrestling and flinging each other into walls. To push and to struggle with all their might as they never could at their desks. Boss Yeung punched Uncle Lo's kidney, a blow against the possible betrayal, a blow against the illness brewing within him.

Their bodies strained against each other, their elbows and hips knocking cushions off the couch. Uncle Lo bumped into a wooden sculpture perched on the end table, which clattered against the marble floor. They pulled apart, flushed, panting, set free. They could have been thirty-five again, taking on the world. Decades away from sickness, decades away from doubt.

At the front door, they parted with an ease Boss Yeung knew they might never share again. The next time they met, he would know if Uncle Lo had deceived him. In the living room, he discovered the ashtray had been emptied by the overzealous young *amah*. No—no. He lurched into the kitchen and dumped the trash onto the floor, on his knees and pawing through eggshells, soggy vegetable peelings, and bloody meat scraps. Blood seeping onto the cigars would contaminate the DNA samples. His hands were slimy, and he heaved at the smell of garbage. His insides felt eviscerated, carved out. The cigars weren't there. He dropped onto all fours, the world at a tilt. Did the cigars go down the sink, get flushed down the toilet? He heard footsteps, and the *amah* sniffling. He slowly climbed to his feet, pulled himself up by the counter. His hands shook under the strain.

"The ashtray?" he asked.

From behind her back, the *amah* brought forward a plastic baggie of the cigars, extinguished and preserved like lab specimens. He washed his hands and opened the bag. He inhaled tobacco, the scent of ash and burning leaves, as if the odor alone might prove Viann's paternity.

Looking at her shoes, the *amah* admitted she'd saved them for her father. She thought he'd like to try them. Filial daughter, her shoulders hunched in misery. Homesick, did she flock to Victoria Park on Sundays, joining hundreds of other *amahs* who picnicked, flirted, and daydreamed after sending home most of their earnings?

Her family must have saved for years to send her to Hong Kong. How much tuition for her siblings, how much medicine for her grandparents had been staked on her salary?

Under her breath, she was chanting a prayer that his wife must have taught her: "Make peace, you are love, you are beautiful." Stealing was one of the gravest crimes an *amah* could commit against her master. She sniffled, hiccupping. She must know Boss Yeung would fire her.

He sent her away, not forever, only to the post office, with instructions to ship the remaining cigars home to her father, a cedar box brimming with Cuba's finest, festooned with red bands, with a scent dark and smoky as a midnight bonfire. Her family would sell off the cigars one by one to pay for emergencies—a miracle the *amah* would forever credit to the Celestial Goddess.

# Chapter 15

The Churro Lady stared Scarlett down, and Scarlett stared back.

After getting chased out by the pizzeria owner last night, Scarlett tried a new neighborhood. In between deliveries, the Pearl Pavilion's van had dropped her off on Mission Street, outside of a row of fancy bars and restaurants with chic interiors: concrete floors, exposed brick walls, and steel beams across their ceilings. She hadn't expected the broad boulevard, the orange and red murals, and the stubby palm trees, nothing like the narrow alleys of Chinatown. The neighborhoods could have been in different hemispheres, though the crowds were as young as in North Beach. Here they rode up on bikes sleek as greyhounds, the men in plaid and hooded sweatshirts and candy-colored suede sneakers, right pant legs rolled up; the women in cardigans over print dresses over leggings, their shoulders topped with bright elaborate scarves. They seemed especially intent on indulging after the rains had kept them inside yesterday. More than enough customers on a Saturday night for every cart and food truck pumping out the smell of grease and salt, of excess and indulgence.

At this pace, she'd sell out within two hours. She could have peddled double or triple the *hanbaobao* she'd brought. She'd outgrown the communal kitchens at Evergreen Gardens and had cut a deal with the manager of the Pearl Pavilion for use of the kitchen and rides with her cart hitched to the van. Manager Kwok hadn't charged her anything for tonight's trip and wouldn't much in the future, she suspected. After all their dealings, she'd entered his trusted circle of associates whom he could count on for underground forms of commerce.

A group of men with oversized beards and aggressive sideburns challenged one another to buy from every cart and food truck in the vicinity. They snapped photos of the *hanbaobao* and of themselves, grinning and gobbling, the joy of showing off on social media greater than the eating itself. They licked the grease off their fingers, swiped their screens, and uploaded the images before heading into a bar with a neon martini in the window. The clack of the pool balls spilled onto the street, where the sticky sweet scent of marijuana smoke drifted by.

A pair of leathery women who looked like they could scale a cliff with their bare hands placed their order. They snuggled against each other in the chill. In China, such women were known as *lala*, and in the cities, underground bars and nightclubs catered to their kind.

Just before Scarlett left China, same-sex marriages had been in the news after getting legalized in the United States. She'd seen pictures of men kissing men, women kissing women, waving rainbow flags outside the Supreme Court. A close-up of two pale, hairy hands with two gold bands. Another American curiosity like gun violence or the morbidly obese.

Though both carts were busy, the Churro Lady seemed affronted that Scarlett had breached her territory. When Scarlett's line waxed while hers waned, she pushed her cart within a few meters, and via hand gestures and English as broken as Scarlett's, she ordered her to leave.

"Do you have a permit?" Scarlett asked coolly.

The Churro Lady scowled. She was built like a teakettle and though the cinnamon and sugar wafting from her stand were delectable, she looked as bitter as her churros were sweet. Her eyes were beady and suspicious, her feet flat and wide, stuffed into dirty pink house slippers. A large family descended upon her, buying some of the churros that curled in the glass case under a heat lamp.

As soon as the rush dissipated, she returned to glaring at Scarlett, whose line never flagged. The Churro Lady fired up her burners and fried squirts of pale dough that hissed and bubbled in the golden oil, her hands nimble. To sweeten the Churro Lady's temper, Scarlett would buy a batch to share with Daisy. Churros had spread to China, popping up throughout the night market. Boss Yeung called churros an overpriced version of *you tiao,* those greasy sticks of fried dough dipped into soymilk at breakfast.

Scarlett recognized the redhead approaching her cart—Casey. San Francisco was a teacup of a city, and she'd served Casey a couple of times in North Beach. She spoke a few phrases in Mandarin, with a surprisingly clear accent. Maybe she'd backpacked around China, seeing more tourist attractions and natural wonders than Scarlett ever would. She handed her the *hanbaobao.*

"*Xie xie,*" Casey said. Thank you.

"*Bu ke qi,*" Scarlett replied. Casey spooned a heavy dollop of chili sauce, and she sighed with contentment at her first bite even though her eyes started to water. A man behind her blurted his order and Casey headed down the street.

The *hanbaobao* cart faced a photo studio, the shop window crowded with portraits in golden frames: dusky women in ball gowns and feather boas, a toddler in a white tuxedo, a Chinese beauty queen in a gold *qi pao* with a sash and tiara, a student with a mortarboard tilted on his Afro, and a baby girl in a cloud of pink tulle fluffy as cotton candy. To Scarlett, the portraits seemed not only an act of celebration, but of defiance, too. Although their circumstances may have been humble, those portrayed deserved the finery and posterity worthy of royalty. A yearning most of her *hanbaobao* customers, with their abundant selfies, would never understand.

A man with a mop of dark curls paused at the Churro Lady's cart before getting in line at Scarlett's. The Churro Lady stomped toward Scarlett and knocked over a stack of her paper napkins, which tumbled into the wind. Scarlett chased after the napkins and when she returned, the Churro Lady was squirting plum sauce into the gutter, the bottle wheezing, sauce splatting against the concrete.

Some customers backed away, while others were too engrossed

in conversation or playing with their phones to notice. Scarlett shouted at her to stop. The Churro Lady's wild eyes didn't seem malicious so much as deranged. She tossed the bottle aside and grabbed the jar of chili sauce, as if to hurl it, when Daisy caught her wrist. She hadn't nagged Scarlett again about coming out tonight, but she must have followed her from Chinatown.

Daisy forced the Churro Lady's arm down and retrieved the jar. She was yelling something in Spanish, the trilingual benefits of an education at an international private school in Taipei. The Churro Lady retreated to her cart, glowering, and angrily stirred her wire basket into the bubbling oil, flicking drops that hissed and steamed in the chill. The crowd scattered out of the cross fire.

The children. "Where are they?" Scarlett shouted.

With Little Fox and her fiancé, Daisy said. She had defended the cart, backed Scarlett as no one else ever had, but she shouldn't have left Didi and Liberty in the care of their neighbor, who wouldn't notice if the babies were choking—unless it was on her phone that never left her hand. *Sagua,* a silly, melon-headed fool. And her fiancé was so lazy he would starve to death if food wasn't regularly placed within his reach.

"Old Wu could do better," Scarlett said. His cough had grown steadily worse, violent enough to crack a rib. Though he slathered Tiger Balm onto his chest, his eyes had sunk into deep pits, and his jokes had turned into labored squawks. "Widow Mok. Auntie Ng. Anyone else at Evergreen Gardens."

"They wanted practice."

Scarlett straightened the lids on the cart. "They can practice on their own children."

"The babies are asleep."

"If they wake up, they don't know Little Fox. She doesn't know them."

"They see Little Fox every day," Daisy said. "They see her more than you."

That stung—Daisy always returned to how Scarlett was failing her daughter. "At least I see them more than William does."

Daisy gasped. They'd both gone too far, though neither would apologize, not for telling the truth. If the argument continued, it might have been the end of them, but the Churro Lady had called in reinforcements: one reedy man with a pompadour and heavy-framed glasses like a secret superhero, the other burly with a shaved head and a thick gold chain. Her sons? Despite the differences in size and style, they shared a resemblance in the set of their eyes and nose, pinched too closely together. They were arguing with her, the pompadour trying to push the cart away from Scarlett's, only to have the Churro Lady slap his hands to stop him. She rubbed the arm that Daisy had grabbed, her face twisted in pain, perhaps feigned, one of many complaints she'd made over the years that her sons never could learn to ignore.

The men approached and seized Scarlett's cart, rocking it back and forth, so it wobbled on its wheels. Their expressions were oddly apologetic, not menacing. They might be trying to scare her, get her to leave on her own so that they could persuade their mother to go home. Scarlett clutched the handle, struggling to keep the cart upright. If the cart crashed a second time, it might have to be scrapped. The sons weren't throwing punches or kicks at Scarlett, but what if they turned violent? Daisy grabbed the steam tray covers, clanging them together like cymbals. A call for help, a call to action, turning heads across the street and the length of the block. Scarlett shouted at her. She didn't want to draw more attention, or worse, for the police to show up. She could get detained, arrested for the stolen van, for kidnapping. Who knew what Mama Fang had reported to authorities?

Daisy whipped out her phone to snap photos, and bystanders did the same. Casey, the redheaded customer, had returned and stood at the front of the pack. The flashes firing from the phones dazed the sons. Everyone's footage was no doubt blurry and confusing, but recording felt urgent and necessary. The sons covered their faces with their hands, vampires warding off light until the bald one took out his own phone and sheepishly started snapping pictures of the crowd. Soon he and his brother slunk away from the *hanbaobao* cart, the fight gone out of them.

"I'll call the driver," Scarlett said.

Daisy pointed her chin at the Churro Lady. "If we leave now, we'll never be able to come back here. She'll think she chased you out of this corner—out of this entire neighborhood."

They could work together, Scarlett said. They could promote each other's snacks, savory and sweet, dinner and dessert. "Tell her."

"I don't speak Spanish," Daisy said.

"But—"

"I can curse, that's all."

Casey asked, "Are you okay?" She slipped a ten-dollar bill into the tip jar. The kindness nearly overwhelmed Scarlett as Casey dropped another bill into the Churro Lady's jar.

Most of the crowd had wandered off after the fight, but a half-dozen people were lining up at Scarlett's cart. When she turned to ask Daisy for help making change, the teenager had disappeared without saying goodbye. Though she'd wanted her gone, wanted her looking after the babies, perversely now, she felt abandoned, lonelier than if Daisy had never come looking for her. Her throat tight, she finished making the order with triple meat for a white man with a handlebar mustache and knit cap. The Churro Lady's sons were arguing with her. Were they going to launch another attack, rough up Scarlett this time to satisfy their matriarch?

Daisy returned, swinging a plastic bag from the drugstore on her arm. She pulled out a purple can of hairspray big as a nightstick and a cheap plastic lighter. Her eyes gleamed with the same mischief that had driven her to sneak out of Perfume Bay, crash the van into the neighbor's mailbox, and kick open bathroom doors at the engineering building. Scarlett didn't try to stop her now. Daisy was a survivor, wily and driven and untamed, qualities that Scarlett had once shared, and hoped she still did.

Daisy flicked her thumbnail on the lighter, which click-clicked and caught fire, dark blue at the base of the flame, the bright white light of a star. The customers cheered. In China, people would have stampeded away from such lunacy, but Americans loved a circus. Scarlett watched as Daisy locked eyes with the Churro Lady. With a sweet blast of hairspray and a flick of a lighter, she shot fireballs into the air, dragon's breath, a warning, a dare.

# Chapter 16

Scarlett rode the elevator to the third floor, the corridor lined with signs for insurance agencies, accountants, and notaries. Green and red lights flashed on a fake Christmas tree at the end of the hallway. The immigration lawyer's laminated wood door was unmarked but for a faded gold banner inscribed with old Spring Festival fortunes: MAY MONEY BE PLENTIFUL and BRINGING WEALTH AND PROSPERITY.

It was said Lawyer Loo could find every loophole through which an immigrant might squeeze, and turn black to white before a judge. She fingered the two hundred dollars in her pocket, grimy fives, tens, and ones—the sum total of their savings. She suspected the lawyer's fees would be steep, but doubted that his clients—the waitresses, dishwashers, nannies, and busboys of Chinatown—had much, either. Maybe she could leave a deposit today and pay in installments. Or she'd have to borrow money from someone at even steeper terms.

She'd timed her walk to coincide with Liberty's midday nap, bundling her coat around them against the winter wind. She held the lapels together, since the jacket could no longer fit over the sling and Liberty's growing body. Back at Evergreen Gardens, Daisy watched over the pork roasting in the oven while her son jiggled and cooed in a bouncer, another gift scavenged by Old Wu.

Inside the office she discovered two men sitting knee to knee on both sides of a desk. The room reeked of stale tea, greasy takeout, and musty old files piled high, of clients who must be pleading, howling for help. Scarlett nearly backed away.

"Fatty Pan, get her a chair!" the older man barked. He must be Lawyer Loo.

The reedy young man cleared a stack of newspapers, dumping it onto the floor beside another teetering pile, and Scarlett perched at the edge of the chair. Liberty shifted in the sling, gurgling, which startled both men.

"There's a baby in there!" Fatty Pan pushed his glasses up the bridge of his nose. "You're . . ." He trailed off, embarrassed he'd stated the obvious.

"Born here?" Lawyer Loo asked.

She nodded. She liked that he already was assembling her case. Having a U.S. citizen as a child could be a mark in her favor. She explained that she'd arrived on a tourist visa that was expiring next month, but didn't mention Perfume Bay, Mama Fang, or Boss Yeung—the less said, the better. She'd arrived legally, not like those Chinese who paid snakeheads, or smugglers, to bring them into America. The most desperate hiked through the deserts in Mexico, or hid in coffins or under the floorboards of boats, shipped in like any other made-in-China cargo.

"Can you get me a green card?" Scarlett asked.

No, Lawyer Loo said without hesitation.

She sagged in her seat. He was supposed to work miracles and yet he'd given up within five minutes.

"Not at first. We can change your status." He snapped his fingers, and Fatty Pan fetched a thick black binder. Scarlett recoiled from the photos of Chinese badly beaten, black eyes, bruised lips, their mouths and noses crusty with blood.

"What happened?" Scarlett said.

"These are all victims of the Chinese government," he said. "Asylum seekers."

"I don't have pictures like this."

"You don't need to." Fatty Pan pulled up photos on his laptop. The same photos that were in the album but different somehow.

Scarlett blinked, her eyes watering. The faces had been changed, different people artfully transformed. Fatty Pan might be dim-witted, but he had his talents. Her nostrils twitched. She smelled his lunch on his breath—all over him—as if he'd been dipped into duck grease and hung in a shop window.

Lawyer Loo laughed. "He gets chased by dogs in the street." He explained that his assistant lived above Tommy To's, the most famed barbecue shop in Chinatown, and the scent of smoky grease had pervaded every part of him. Fatty Pan hunched his shoulders in misery.

"You Christian?" the lawyer asked.

Scarlett shook her head.

"Doesn't matter," he muttered.

"Won't the government want proof?" she asked.

Lawyer Loo dug through his drawer and showed her a receipt. For his services? No—proof of attendance at a local church. "In return for a modest monthly donation, we have a blank book."

He seemed to enjoy explaining the process, but it also served as his sales pitch. She, like the other supplicants in this dingy office, didn't care about the details so long as he guaranteed legal resi-dence. But showing the lengths to which he worked on behalf of his clients would justify the high price of his services.

"Everyone's a Christian? Won't the government get suspicious?" Scarlett asked.

He nodded at Fatty Pan, who rested his hands in his lap, thumb to forefinger, closed his eyes, and bowed his head. Perhaps her question wasn't unusual, perhaps it prompted the next part of the presentation. "The Celestial Goddess," Lawyer Loo said. Beijing had banned the group.

"I'll get pictures of you in Portsmouth Square," Fatty Pan said.

"No pictures."

"Not to worry!" Lawyer Loo said. "Some clients, they can't re-member what they ate yesterday. The photos help them remember the sequence. But you—you seem like someone who can tell a story."

He recited the details she'd have to memorize if she claimed Christianity as her cause: late-night prayer meetings, the knock at the door, the government thugs tearing apart the Bible and slamming her to the floor. "That's not too hard to remember," he assured her.

When Scarlett had arrived in America, the bored immigration official at the airport had flipped through her passport, but an asylum application would undergo far more scrutiny.

"Americans think the Communists are barbaric," Lawyer Loo said. "If your story confirms that, they believe anything you say."

"I want to do things the legal way," she said.

"You came here to make a better life for yourself. For your baby," he said. "You worked so hard to get here, you should be able to stay."

Lawyer Loo couldn't have been more wrong about the circumstances that brought her to America: getting accidentally pregnant and caving in to her lover's demands. Still, she'd worked hard to remain here, and in the attorney's eyes—if not the law's—that must count, too.

"You have to petition within a year of arriving," he said. If approved, she could start working, and after a year she could apply for permanent residency.

"Are there other stories?" Scarlett asked. A story she could believe, a story that could stir her emotions during the green-card interview.

"For a woman, your age, usually forced abortion or a forced sterilization after your first child," Fatty Pan piped up. "Usually." He eyed Liberty. As Scarlett caressed her baby's head, she remembered the other mother, the one who'd fled.

On a spring night, Scarlett had woken up alone in the bed. She might have been eight or nine years old. She'd heard low voices outside, Ma and the headman and others she didn't recognize. Scarlett had followed the group of five, crossing a swollen river to a nearby village where they stopped in front of a house whose straw thatch had the look of mangy fur. They burst in without knocking. The men shouted and cursed—whomever they wanted to surprise must have escaped.

Scarlett heard panting up ahead, and she'd spotted a pregnant woman waddling around the corner, wincing with each step. All winter, she must have been hiding her pregnancy under layers of heavy clothes. Scarlett's shout curdled in her mouth. She'd been proud of Ma, proud of the work that served the country and kept her out of the fields, unlike the other mothers. Yet maybe she should lead Ma astray. Or she could run alongside the woman, put an arm around her waist to ease her load. She had wanted the woman to escape. But if Ma found out—Scarlett never should have followed her here. She should go back home and hide under the covers.

The woman backed into a chicken coop by accident, setting off squawking hens. The group ran out of the house, chasing down the noise, and caught sight of her. Running as well as she could, the woman reached the river and waded in up to her waist. Her feet slipped on the rocks, her arms outstretched for balance, as the current battered her body. Two men ran over the bridge to the other side, blocking her escape.

She'd wept, begging, pleading that her mother-in-law would beat her until she had a son. "I know it's a son, a son." She howled, a sound that tore the world apart, a sound that Scarlett couldn't escape even with her hands pressed over her ears, a sound that she knew she would never forget. Until that day, she'd thought the women deserved their punishments, but maybe Ma and her job were at fault?

Then Scarlett saw her mother's face, lit with grief and regret, and realized Ma might agree. Couldn't she let the woman run away and lose the paperwork? Ma had locked eyes with Scarlett, silently telling her it was too late and she had to finish what had been set in motion. No one moved until Ma squared her shoulders, waded in, and dragged the woman away.

How broken the woman had been afterward, shambling, her hair matted, with no son and no hope of ever having one, at the mercy of the stone-hearted doctors who would abort her baby and then sterilize her.

Woozy, Scarlett gripped the arms of the office chair. She felt herself dissolving, blurring, fading. Soon she'd have to nurse, her breasts full with milk. Milk that the other mother must have had to squeeze out. Scarlett steadied herself, and everything rushed forth as she told the men the story: Ma's work at the clinic and what happened to the woman. She'd killed herself by swallowing a bottle of pesticide. Her body convulsed so hard she'd bitten off her tongue, it was said. She'd never gotten over the loss of her son, no matter how much she might have loved her first child, her daughter who would leave her, someday marry and belong to another family.

Scarlett had been at school when she heard. She stabbed her pencil into the palm of her hand, driving the tip deep into her flesh, to keep from screaming. That day, she'd vowed she would never become like Ma.

The men's eyes widened. For all the stories they'd concocted, the real one electrified them. She'd never told anyone. Not Boss Yeung. Not Daisy. Despicable—she and Ma both. Scarlett should have warned the woman and should have led her to safety. Her skin started to itch and her hair felt unbearably greasy. She longed to stand under a hot shower, rinse it, rinse herself down the drain.

There was a backlog, Lawyer Loo said, but he could move up her case if she paid her deposit today. He acted as if he'd won the lottery. Taking her on must have seemed easy money. "Ten thousand dollars, with a one-thousand-dollar deposit."

A thousand dollars! Even if she started doubling, tripling her batches of *hanbaobao*, she would have to work for months to save up. But she possessed something far more valuable: the truth. Detail after detail that had the power to shock, unlike the lawyer's rote, repeated tales. If he waived the deposit, she'd spill more stories of the villagers that Ma had punished, and tell him every detail the government wanted lost.

"You can get those stories from the Internet," Fatty Pan said.

"You think the government isn't taking them down? No one else has the ones I can tell you."

"If I give you a discount, everyone will ask for one," Lawyer Loo said.

"No one else will know. And no one else has stories, not like mine. It's not a discount. It's a trade." She'd bartered her rent money, and now she'd barter her way into his services.

"Talk doesn't cook rice," Lawyer Loo said.

"Lawyer Tam will want to meet with me," she said. A competitor.

The Party had trained its people well. To survive, you had to lie, cheat, and steal.

"No one could save her," Scarlett said. The woman who ran into the river. "But her story could save someone else."

The next morning, she stirred a pot of porridge, preparing Old Wu's breakfast. Slow strokes, to keep the grains creamy, not mushy, sweet and not burned. She sliced a thousand-year-old egg to reveal the yolk, soft and dark green, and the whites transformed into brown jelly, the smell fierce and savory, a treat to whet his appetite.

She knocked on Old Wu's door. No answer. Another knock. The door was unlocked and inside she discovered him sprawled on top of his sheet. His head tilted back, his mouth slack, and his hands curled at his sides. She dropped the bowl, which shattered and spattered, but did not wake him. Stepping over the shards toward his bed, she clapped a hand to his forehead, and felt him burning with fever. After wrapping him in coarse brown blankets, she grabbed his wallet, and carried him into the hallway, where Auntie Ng gaped, pulling her ragged bathrobe around her.

"Get the door!" Scarlett shouted. Widow Mok poked her head into the hallway, rubbing the sleep out of her eyes. She didn't want to miss the commotion.

Auntie Ng ran ahead and Scarlett lurched down the stairs. She tightened her grip on his frail body, the heat coming off him like an iron. Outside, wind whipped through the alleys, scattering trash in the gutter. With each step, Old Wu seemed to grow lighter, not heavier in her arms, and she clasped him tighter, to keep him from floating away like a balloon, until he was just a dot in the sky.

She almost missed the flyer taped to a light pole. A photo of her by the *hanbaobao* cart, her hair wet and stringy, next to another picture of a blurry rat, warning that she ground up rodents for her sandwiches. The accusatory tone straight out of the Cultural Revolution, all but calling her a capitalist running dog, a paper tiger. Old Wu moaned. She didn't have a free hand to yank down the flyer.

Who would go to such trouble? The Churro Lady? She couldn't

have hung them so soon, and neither of their customers were found in Chinatown. It had to be someone who wanted to ruin her reputation among her neighbors. The owner of the pizza parlor? She doubted he could write in Chinese.

Joe Ng. The other night in North Beach, hadn't she felt eyes upon her? Maybe he'd been meeting Shrimp Boy and his girlfriend at the bar, noticed Scarlett, and snapped a photo, seeking revenge. The flyer was probably plastered around Chinatown, and any detective nosing around might spot it.

She shifted Old Wu's weight in her arms, her muscles starting to burn. A man offered to take Old Wu by the feet, and together they staggered to the hospital. In the emergency room, Scarlett lowered Old Wu across three chairs. She'd never been in this Chinatown hospital, which was too small to have a maternity ward. She tugged the blanket over his toenails, dark and thick as tortoiseshell. He was never dressed in anything less than trousers, a newsboy cap, a button-down shirt, and a sweater vest, and his bare feet seemed indecent.

She filled out the paperwork with his address, name, and age—ten years older than she had guessed. It shamed her, how little she knew about him, neither his inherited maladies nor his dreams.

For more than a century and a half, people had been leaving the Pearl River Delta to work on railroads in the Americas and to open shops and restaurants all over the world.

His parents would have borrowed to pay for his passage to San Francisco, resting their hopes on a child. Upon arrival, he once told her, he'd been detained on Angel Island, grim barracks in the bay—a prison, like Alcatraz. They'd been kept lower than rats. Held for months, answering questions over and over again about the layout of the homes in their villages, the number of steps to their houses, and about their neighbors, if certain women had bound or natural feet. Answers he'd practiced and memorized on his journey here. Officials had been trying to catch them in a lie, to see if his story matched up with the man who was pretending to be his father. For almost as long as Chinese had tried to enter America, America had beaten them back. Like many old Chinatown bachelors, he never married. U.S. laws had once barred most Chinese women from immigrating; families weren't supposed to take root here.

She put her face in her hands, which were sore from gripping Old Wu. Until getting pregnant, she'd rarely been sick, had never visited a doctor and had never spent the night in a hospital. She'd existed in the vast middle of life for years and might have for many more. But the night she drove Lady Yu to the hospital changed her. For the first time, she'd understood how thin the line was between birth and death. Her world now held her daughter bursting, blooming, Old Wu shriveling, and her own body stiffening with age. She was going to die, as would her mother, Boss Yeung, her daughter, Daisy and her son. She'd always known that, but until now, she'd never felt such desolation. Barreling headlong into the future, she'd never much considered her end or anyone else's.

Old Wu's wallet was worn, the leather cracked and white at the edges, tucked into his back pocket for years. It was heavier than she expected, and inside she discovered his mailbox key and a wad of hundred-dollar bills. Her mouth went dry. She glanced at Old Wu slumped beside her. In the corner, a woman fussed with her elderly mother in a wheelchair, and in another, a man flipped through a newspaper. No one was watching her. She opened the wallet in her lap and surreptitiously counted the bills: two thousand dollars! Maybe he didn't trust banks and carried around his savings. Maybe he was on his way to wire money to family still living in China.

She should take the money and hide it under her mattress. Or—or—she could borrow it for supplies. Lawyer Loo had taken her two hundred dollars and waived the rest of the deposit, but soon she'd have to pay off his sizeable fees. Old Wu would want her to have the money. He might have intended to give it to her. She snapped the wallet shut. She'd never been a thief—aside from the train fare she'd taken from her mother years ago, which she'd repaid—and well, aside from the van she'd driven off from Perfume Bay.

Still, she couldn't steal from Old Wu. And yet, didn't Liberty come first? Old Wu would understand. No—he would need his savings in the weeks ahead to cover whatever treatments his Medicare wouldn't. But he might have more. He was exceedingly frugal; he could be one of those millionaires who amassed their fortunes pennies at a time. He wheezed beside her. He'd never know who'd taken his wallet. If Scarlett denied it, claimed the wallet had been empty when she found it, he might accuse another neighbor. He might say nothing, blaming himself for keeping so much cash around.

Old Wu snorted but didn't open his eyes. If she followed this line of reasoning to its end, she'd soon start robbing banks in the name of Liberty. She held the wallet between her thumb and forefinger, as if it were radioactive waste. She'd take it back to Evergreen Gardens and put it somewhere out of her reach. A gurney arrived and orderlies whisked Old Wu into triage where the nurse checked his temperature and his blood pressure, and promised that the doctor would see him soon.

Five minutes, ten minutes passed, and they moved into an examination room, which had a long curtain instead of a door. Old Wu was tiny and withered against the pillows, and Scarlett had the oddest sensation that he just needed to be dipped into water—like a dried mushroom—and he would plump up, fully formed and refreshed. Each time someone walked by, Scarlett rose from her seat. She listened to his breathing, labored against the hiss and beep of machines and monitors.

She hoped he wouldn't have to stay overnight. Checking the clock, she thought of the babies, who had to be awake by now. Of those posters, flapping around Chinatown, maybe in surrounding neighborhoods, too, that she'd have to tear down. She felt antsy until she spotted a tub of petroleum jelly that she rubbed into Old Wu's hands, his skin growing supple and his nails shiny. She could show her greatest kindness only when he would not remember, when he could not respond. That was the cruelty of his affliction, and of hers. What if she'd relented and married him for a green card? She pictured them spooning in his bed, her arms around him, his body light as a sack of rice hulls. Their hands together were silky, gliding as if underwater, touching but never grasping, hands on the verge of slipping apart. She circled her fingers around his wrist and his hand twitched in hers.

★  ★  ★

Scarlett tucked the last *hanbaobao* onto the tray, one of a dozen that she'd wrapped in tinfoil to carry down the hill and around the corner, to the local branch of the community college. Classes were over for the semester, but the administrative offices were still open. There, she studied the stern portrait of the dean, whose eyes eerily seemed to follow her, and took the elevator up to the offices.

Scarlett and Daisy had pulled down the flyers, but Joe Ng would put them back up as long as he remained idle and angry. The *hanbaobao* were a bribe, not for the dean, but for her assistant, Madame Tom, who might be able to get the troublemaker off the wait list and into classes next semester. Not the accounting courses that Auntie Ng wanted him to attend, but ones for the mechanics program that would keep him knuckle-deep in grease and gears. Only then would he stop loudly complaining in the hallways of Evergreen Gardens about his lost motorcycle, and his vendetta against Scarlett would end.

As Madame Tom clicked on her screen, Scarlett noticed that she was playing mahjong on her computer. She glanced at the clock. She'd timed her arrival to just before lunch, and Madame Tom must be bored—and hungry. "May I help you?" she asked, in a tone that implied she'd rather not.

"Delivery," Scarlett replied.

Madame Tom waved her back toward the door. "Our holiday party was last week."

Scarlett set the tray on the counter. "It's for you." She tugged open the tinfoil, and fragrant steam rose off the *hanbaobao*. She faltered, thinking of Old Wu. This morning, she'd brought a few to the hospital, but the scent didn't stir him awake.

Madame Tom wet her lips.

"Courtesy of the Pearl Pavilion," Scarlett said. The name and its legacy in Chinatown would carry weight. "For your long service."

Madame Tom didn't take the tray, but she didn't push it away. She seemed the type who ate only when seated at a table, with a napkin in her lap, letting no bite mar her lipstick, no crumbs fall in her lap. She exuded the power of a queen in her little kingdom, her place ordained by the heavens.

"People say you keep this place running," Scarlett said.

"I support the dean in whatever she needs."

"If I may, would you consider a request from the public?" Scarlett asked. Her tone obsequious, as if she were bowing her forehead to the ground. She told Madame Tom about Joe Ng, a filial son, a neighborhood boy trying to support his widowed mother, if only he could get into the college's mechanics program.

Madame Tom pushed the tray of *hanbaobabo* back toward her. "You think *this* will buy me off?" She pointed at tins of tea, crates of tangerines, and boxes of cakes. "People have been bringing me gifts all day—all week! I take what I want, and give the rest to my dogs."

"Lucky dogs," Scarlett said, her tone still fawning. "Luckier than a lot of the people coming to see you."

Madame Tom studied her. "Why should he get to jump the line?"

"He's very talented," Scarlett said. "He knows so much already, just from what he taught himself. He can fix anything, take it apart, put it back together. But to get a job, he needs a certificate."

"Anything?" Madame Tom asked. "What about my stereo? The CD player skips."

Anything, Scarlett said. If Madame Tom got him off the wait list, he'd come by her home to fix it. If she wasn't satisfied, she could kick him out of the class.

Next Saturday, Madame Tom said, and asked her to deliver more *hanbaobao*. "Five trays," she said. "We're having a party for my son. Back for the holidays."


Old Wu woke up, asking for Scarlett and a bowl of beef noodle soup. She found him propped against his pillows. Color had returned to his cheeks, flushing their dull yellow with a hint of pink. "I'd enjoy being here more if I wasn't sick," he said. "Hot tea whenever you want."

The television flashed above him, the sound off. She handed him a greasy sack of sesame balls, still warm, and promised him noodles later. She'd considered bringing Liberty, but didn't want her catching anything from the hospital. She handed him a letter, airmail from China, Old Wu's name and address written in spidery English. The rest of his mail had been junk.

"Aren't you going to read it?" she asked.

"It's from my mother."

"Your mother?" She had to be ancient. Scarlett thought of her own mother, who must be expecting her for the Spring Festival next month. She'd never missed one. The holiday would come and go, and Ma might fear that Scarlett had fallen ill, had an accident, or died. Would Ma try calling her? Her number would be reassigned to someone else, months after Scarlett stopped paying the bill. She wanted Ma to think she'd abandoned her. She preferred Ma's resentment to her mourning.

"She's ninety," Old Wu said.

Ninety! "Is she sick?"

"She'll outlive us all," Old Wu said. "I know what it says, same as she's been sending every month for the last six months. 'Come back. Come back and find a wife before I die.' She asks every few years. I never went, and she won't stop asking."

Scarlett wondered if his mother had been ailing and wanted to see her son settled. He gave her a hollow smile. He was a lifelong bachelor. An imported wife would crowd his tiny room, toss his street finds, and make demands on his time. He came and went as he pleased, took a midnight stroll if he couldn't fall asleep, ate when and where he wanted, devouring sesame candies for breakfast if so inclined. More recently, he may also have disobeyed his mother out of the hope—no matter how infinitesimal—that Scarlett might fall for him. Crossing the ocean and making a life for himself in America must have once seemed impossible, too.

His every scavenged gift, his solicitous attentions had been a kind of courtship, she had come to see. After Boss Yeung, she didn't think any man would love her again—that any man had ever loved her. She couldn't offer Old Wu the warmth of her breath on his cheek, and the get-well present she'd prepared for him fell so far short of what he wanted that it now seemed an insult. She tried to hide the sign behind her back, but he caught sight of it, a vinyl banner with a menu featuring OLD WU'S PLUM SAUCE.

"My customers ask me for the recipe, all the time," Scarlett said. "One man wanted to bottle it, sell it in stores."

He looked out the window. "I learned it from Cook Liao, and he learned it from someone else."

"It changes under every hand," she said. "You can also taste every hand that's come before it."

His sauce, his achievement, his immortality? An honor, but not one he had wanted.

Nurse Ding checked his vital signs. Old Wu seemed a favorite with the staff. An aide entered every few minutes to fill his pitcher of water or plump his pillows.

"We're glad to send him home before Christmas! Such a lucky man to have such a daughter," Nurse Ding said.

"I'm lucky to have such a father," Scarlett said.

Old Wu kept his eyes fixed on the television, but his mouth twitched with an embarrassment and disappointment that he could not hide. He must know she never had and never would see him as a lover. He was decent and generous, but he must think she trusted him only because he possessed no threat of sex, no threat as a man. The four decades between them were a distance too far for romance to cross.

# Chapter 17

**Yellow police tape** crossed Lawyer Loo's door. Scarlett had been scheduled to finish telling him the stories, sessions that left her shaken each time, left her struggling to get up from the lone visitor's chair. Though Liberty couldn't understand what she was saying, she wanted to cover her daughter's ears to protect her from the fate of these unfortunate women. She would never tell Liberty that Ma had terminated so many pregnancies, and that Ma might have been forced to end Scarlett's, too. She cocked her head at the door and heard nothing, but she didn't dare knock in case police lingered inside. She could try an office down the hallway to see if they knew what was going on, but authorities might return at any moment, with questions for Scarlett on matters she would rather not discuss.

She knocked lightly on one door, then another. No answer. The hallway had gone silent, no phones ringing, no hum of a printer or clatter of drawers or conversation. The air had the heaviness that follows in the wake of violence, like the times that Ma smashed a pot or kicked over a table. Liberty whimpered, and Scarlett shushed her, swaying and rocking, willing her to be quiet. Her mouth twisted in despair. Though Liberty was three months old, at times she was as indecipherable as she'd been on the day she was born. Scarlett hoped she wasn't on the cusp of a tantrum. She could spend hours trying every possible measure to calm Liberty—nursing, shushing, a long walk, a trip to the Laundromat to pace in front of the dryers because of their sometimes soothing sound—or a combination thereof that she blindly, desperately applied, like throwing knives at a bull's-eye in the dark.

As Liberty's whimpers turned to wails, Scarlett bolted to the stairwell, where she sat on a concrete step and tried to nurse her, hoping no one would stumble upon them. Liberty's cries echoed as if there were dozens of her. Maybe she needed a change of scenery. Straightening her shirt, Scarlett eased the baby back into her sling and ran two steps at a time to the floor below, where the offices were open for business. She rushed into a travel agency, where posters advertised bus trips to Los Angeles and an upcoming concert in Macau starring the Guardian.

The travel agent looked up from her computer screen. Over Liberty's screams, Scarlett asked if she knew what had happened upstairs, if the police had come by. She had to repeat the question, but the woman kept her focus on Liberty.

"Is she wet? Maybe she's hungry?" the woman asked.

"Lawyer Loo, where is he?"

Upon hearing his name, the travel agent wrinkled her nose in distaste or in fear, as if the lawyer's troubles—and Scarlett's—might contaminate her.

"You know him?" Scarlett asked.

The phone rang as Liberty's cries reached a frantic pitch. "Can you—?" the travel agent asked, pointing at the door. Scarlett paced back and forth along the hallway. She squeezed Liberty tightly, so tightly Scarlett knew her hug hadn't come from a place of comfort, but from the selfish desire to shut her daughter up. Letting go, she dropped her arms to her sides. She wanted to scream like Liberty, to rattle the earth to its core. Lawyer Loo had taken her money and added her name and address to his file cabinet. In preparation for their meeting, he might have even set her file on his desk, where the police would find it. And then the police would find her.

The hairs on the back of her neck prickled. His assistant had scrawled notes on a yellow legal pad. Could she get in trouble for aiding their schemes? For supplying their invented stories about the followers of Jesus and the Celestial Goddess, about the victims of the one-child policy? She had to beg the building manager to let her in and get back the notes. Flexing her right foot in its puffy white sneaker, she considered kicking in the door. She pulled out a lighter, the one Daisy had used in her battle against the Churro Lady, which could set off the sprinklers and drown the paperwork. She blinked. Nothing would get her deported faster than tampering with a police investigation. Exhaling, she tried to compose herself. Old Wu might have known what to do, but days after getting out of the hospital, his pneumonia cured by antibiotics and Auntie Ng's herbal brews, he'd bought a last-minute ticket to China. He'd been gone since last week, on a flight that left Christmas Day.

His abrupt departure had troubled her. She wished they could have celebrated the holiday together, but when the nurse assumed they were father and daughter, he must have understood Scarlett would never see him any other way. Faced with the prospect of his death, he'd apparently begun to rethink his bachelor's life. She guessed that a trip to his village would salve his wounded pride and restore his dignity. Some women would view him as eligible, even if Scarlett did not.

She tried another office, where a notary from upstairs had witnessed everything: the police frog-marching Lawyer Loo from the building, and box after box of files wheeled out. Scarlett's gut twisted. Her files. The police might be combing through them now, but she couldn't flee Chinatown. After buying supplies, she had only a couple hundred left in their biscuit tin, and she had to finish making tonight's *hanbaobao*.

"It was only a matter of time," the notary said. "I warned him."

She wondered how many times this man had repeated this story, if he'd witnessed the arrest and was embellishing with each retelling. She asked if he'd taken any photos, and he whipped out his phone and thumbed through a blurry set shot from above, through the dusty window. Lawyer Loo being escorted out to the police car, his head down and his body slumped, utterly defeated.

"What about his assistant?" Scarlett asked.

"His assistant?"

"Fatty Pan. I never saw them apart." She had to find him. He'd know the status of her case.

The notary sputtered, but knew nothing more. Fatty Pan must have eluded the police, lucky for once in his life. If he hadn't skipped out of Chinatown, he would soon. With his skills, he could create a new identity, and start his own business modeled after the one where he'd long apprenticed. A new title, a new life, a chance to start over. He might be terrified, wherever he was, but she envied him this moment, a moment that must have struck like a bell, vibrating through him.

For more than an hour, Scarlett searched for Fatty Pan. Her daughter squirmed against her chest with increasing impatience. She walked briskly, purposefully, head held high as if she had nothing to hide, though if she'd spotted the police, she might have crumpled. She was about to return to Evergreen Gardens when the scent of roast duck hit her with the force of a slap, dark and gamey as sweat socks and leather. In her panic, she'd forgotten that the lawyer's assistant lived above Tommy To's, the hole-in-the-wall famed for its barbecue. There were only six apartments, three on each floor, and she rang every doorbell until someone buzzed her in. Liberty squirmed against her, and she'd soon descend into howls if Scarlett didn't get her back home and out of the sling.

The smell of roasting meat fogged the building; if Scarlett had dragged her fingernail along the smudged walls, years of grease might have peeled off like wax. Trudging upstairs, she found an open door to a studio apartment, where a soap opera blasted on the television. When the granny inside looked up from the screen, she seemed unperturbed by a surprise visitor. Scarlett asked if she knew Fatty Pan.

"I've lived here fifteen years," the granny said. "Never heard of him."

"Who's the landlord? How could I find him?"

"I don't know what you're talking about." The granny turned back to the television.

Scarlett knocked on the other doors. No one answered. In a month, her visa would expire. She was the only non-citizen in their household, the only one to blame if authorities split them up: she'd get deported and Liberty sent to Boss Yeung, because he'd surely find her after Scarlett had been detained. Daisy, a minor, would get shipped back to her parents, who'd declare her an unfit mother and keep her from Didi.

Scarlett had never sought Daisy's advice on how to fix her papers. And yet, she depended on Daisy for much else, just as Daisy depended on her, together on the run, together in hiding. She should have brought Daisy along to Lawyer Loo's offices. She told herself she didn't want Daisy and her son mixed up in such matters, but she'd also been too proud to ask for help. She wanted to bang her forehead against the door. She never should have trusted Lawyer Loo and his easy promises. *Huogai,* her fault.

Turning to leave, she discovered Fatty Pan in the hallway, a towel wrapped around his waist, his hair slicked back, returning from the communal shower. He froze and ran to his room, fumbling with the key on a strap around his neck. He tried to slam the door on her. With Liberty in the sling, Scarlett was top-heavy, clumsy and slow. She managed to yank his towel with the tips of her fingers. He held on to it. Clinging to his towel, she forced her way into his apartment. It was sparsely furnished, a monk's cell in contrast to the mess of Lawyer Loo's office: a neatly made twin bed, a single bowl, cup, and pair of chopsticks, and three identical shirts and pants hanging on a metal rod jammed across the window.

"Can . . . can you . . . can you look away?" he stammered. "I have to get dressed."

"So you can hit me from behind?" she asked.

He was about as imposing as a mouse, but she didn't know what he would do if cornered. She stroked Liberty's head. If she'd had time, if she'd thought it through, she wouldn't have confronted him with the baby. Fatty Pan turned his back to her, pulling up his pants underneath his towel and buttoning his shirt.

"Why are you still here?" Scarlett said.

He sighed. "My mother." She lived next door.

The granny who'd denied his existence. She suffered dementia,

he said. Last year, he'd tried to move her into his apartment building, but she'd run back, drawn to the memory of her room, these
stairs, the movement embedded in her muscles, the familiarity
keeping her upright. As soon as he could, he'd moved in here. This
morning, he'd taken her to a doctor's appointment, and that had
saved him.

"But now—" she said.

"I don't know." His mother's government check was coming in
the mail today or tomorrow, he said. They'd cash it, and then he'd
decide if they should stay or go.

Though Lawyer Loo charged exorbitant rates, Scarlett guessed
that only a fraction went to his assistant.

He and his mother didn't have enough to travel very far or for
very long, he said. He'd have to barricade the door wherever they
stayed to keep her from running away.

"Should I go?" Scarlett said.

"You? Why would the police want anything to do with you?"

"The paperwork Lawyer Loo filed—won't I get in trouble?"

"If they go after anyone, it will be clients with cases in progress.
But he didn't file a thing for you—not for most people who came
through in the last year."

Lawyer Loo had committed a double crime: defrauding the government and defrauding his customers.

The stink of the grease intensified, and Scarlett's head swam.
"Everyone said he was the best in Chinatown." She retched, and
might have fallen if Fatty Pan hadn't sat her on his bed. The sling
was tight, choking her, and she had to get it off. She tore at the
straps and Liberty tumbled on the bed, elated to be free.

"People hear what they want to hear," Fatty Pan said. "And he
figured they'd be too scared to complain. He'd always say there was
a backlog, that the papers were coming."

"Why?" Scarlett asked. "Why did you let him trick me?"

"He—we—didn't start off that way," Fatty Pan said. "We offered
people hope. More hope than anyone else. So many were coming
for help, he got behind and he never caught up. Then he realized he
didn't have to do anything but take their money."

"Why take my stories?"

Fatty Pan looked away. "He's trying to bring over a friend."

"Can I get back my money?" She picked up Liberty, who thrashed in her arms with the might of a salmon swimming upstream, and shoved her back into the sling. He gave Scarlett such a look of pity that she wanted to slap him. When he offered her a twenty-dollar bill, she took his wallet. With resignation and remorse, he let it go. She emptied it and left.

# Chapter 18

The drip of dozens of IV bags sounded like the patter of rain, a steady beat over the scratch of pencils at Little Genius. The teenagers bent over their worksheets didn't gossip, didn't text, and didn't fidget while hooked to the silvery lines with the ghostly look of jellyfish trailing their tentacles.

The motion detector chimed over the front door, and as Mama Fang rushed from the classroom and into the reception area, she found a woman impatiently tapping her credit card against the counter. Classes were full, Mama Fang announced. "But I can add you to the wait list." She knew what the mother would ask next: how long? "One year." One year in which her child would fall further behind, one year in which rivals would vault ahead with the miracle study aid that Mama Fang had introduced to Silicon Valley almost three months ago. One single year that would determine the entire fate of her child: which university, which profession, which spouse, and thus which grandchildren. One year without the amino acids, vitamins, and minerals supplied through the IV that enabled the students at Little Genius to study longer and harder, to ward off and recover from colds, to sharpen their eyes and to brighten their skin.

"Call me if there's a cancellation," the mother said. A command, not a question, not the plea that other prospective clients made on behalf of their children.

"I'll add your name." Mama Fang ran her finger down the long wait list.

The mother studied the length of the list, the mock letters of acceptance to Yale, Stanford, Harvard, and MIT on the wall, and the flattering lighting and glossy dark-wood trim that marked Little Genius as a place of high standards. "I'll pay the deposit now."

Mama Fang closed her book. "No need." She handed the mother a business card, using both hands, as if she were passing a delicate cup of oolong tea. Polite, but a send-off all the same.

The mother drew herself up. *"Xiao Jie"*—Little Miss—"when will your boss be in?"

*Xiao Jie*, as if Mama Fang were pushing a cart at a dim sum restaurant, as if she weren't at least twenty years older than this woman, as if she were still the household help sleeping in a room off the kitchen in Hong Kong. Mama Fang nodded, her expression proud and disdainful, to indicate that she was in fact the owner. The customer's imperious reserve crumpled after realizing she'd treated the proprietor so dismissively.

"I can pay the full amount now," she said, thrusting forward her credit card while extolling her son, his obedience and his brilliance.

Mama Fang did not move, did not say a word, and the mother offered twice, then three times the class fee to move her son higher on the wait list—as Mama Fang had known she would. Like every parent who'd signed up their hapless child for Little Genius, with the desperation of refugees fighting to get out of the country.

For an additional fee, you could move the world.

"There's an opening this afternoon only," Mama Fang said. "Maybe next week." If she crammed the desks together, she could squeeze in another row of students. "We offer priority enrollment, if you pay six months in advance. And unlimited access to green antioxidant boosts."

"Is it organic? What discount for two kids?" Even affluent clients haggled to feel as if they'd come out ahead. As VIPs, they'd boast to their friends and family and bring in more customers.

Leaning over the counter, Mama Fang lowered her voice. "There's a special cash price."

By the time the mother left—left and returned from a trip to the bank to withdraw funds—Mama Fang had pocketed four thousand dollars, and it wasn't yet noon.

In China, patients demanded IV drips of antibiotics and fluids, not willing to wait to heal on their own from colds or the flu. If they felt run-down, they stopped by clinics for instant health and vitality, an idea that was spreading in the United States. First in Chinese neighborhoods, and now among Americans, Hollywood stars and the rich who wanted hangover cures.

Mama Fang's inspired new idea had been to offer services to students worn out by the competitive grind they'd faced since their parents began comparing their first steps and their first words to those of their peers. Parents who spent without restraint so their proxies, their children, could get ahead.

After putting away the cashier's check from the pleading mother, Mama Fang washed her hands under a cloud of antibacterial soap harsh enough to wear enamel off a pan. Her skin had chapped, cracked as if she were once again scrubbing household laundry. A necessary precaution, to prevent her students from developing sepsis, the bacterial infection from IV lines; it started off like the flu—fever, aches, chills, fatigue, malaise—but soon shut down the body.

In her pocket, her mobile phone buzzed. She dried off her hands and strode to her office, hoping Uncle Lo was calling her back. For weeks, he'd been ignoring her calls. With the Spring Festival approaching, maybe he was giving her a chance to clear old debts.

A click, and then a chipper woman asked, "How would you like to lower your mortgage rates?" Mama Fang hung up on the telemarketer. She rolled her shoulders, sore as if she'd been beaten by hammers. She was fifty-six, and had never felt her age as keenly. She must be coming down with something; the children here were like sewer rats carrying diseases. She began every day with a treatment, many nights, too, if she needed a burst of glucose.

Forty years ago, before he became Uncle Lo, he'd been Young Master and she was the *amah*. The Lo family hadn't been rich, but rich enough to keep a cook-maid, and rich compared to the Fangs, refugees from China. In the early 1970s, cheap maids from Indonesia and the Philippines were starting to arrive in Hong Kong, like a great twittering flock swept off-course in a typhoon. Mrs. Lo, who believed Chinese were more hardworking, devoted, and virtuous, continued to hire local *amahs* like Mama Fang.

Mama Fang had a heavy hand with the soy sauce, was sloppy with the wash, and left streaks on the window glass, but Mrs. Lo marveled at the market bill—half of what she used to pay! Mama Fang had known that saving her mistress money would redeem her failings in the household arts.

The Los' *amahs* in the past must have been cozy with certain meat and vegetable stalls, getting a kickback, but Mama Fang passed the savings on to her employer. After Mrs. Lo bragged about her thrifty maid to her friends, Mama Fang told her about bargains offered by other vendors—those in partnership with the stalls where she shopped. By driving additional sales, Mama Fang negotiated deeper discounts.

She gathered information through gossip and observation, and made connections others did not. By providing favors, she put everyone in debt to her—the market vendors, the shop owners, Mrs. Lo and her friends—and she enjoyed that, too. Mama Fang became greater than the toil of her hands alone.

No one had expected much from a girl like her. Her mother had died in childbirth, and from early on, Mama Fang had taken care of herself and her father. Even then, she'd been known as Mama Fang because of the children she minded while their parents toiled. She hitched them onto her back, knotted rags into dolls, and braided strings around their wrists. Each time, they grew up and left her.

Soon after she started working for the Lo family, Young Master set off firecrackers underneath the stools of a noodle shop because he'd spied the owner using cooking oil skimmed out of the gutter. He had fancied himself a bandit-hero, defending the people. The downtrodden remained exotic to Young Master, who hadn't yet learned to ignore the lives of servants outside of their duties. To probe too deeply meant uncovering circumstances that might disrupt smooth household operations.

At fourteen, he was two years younger than Mama Fang, and like her, he was an only child. Although Mrs. Lo might have wanted more children, giving birth must have hollowed her out. In the laundry, which revealed the household's every bodily secret, Mama Fang found no evidence Mrs. Lo bled each month. At least she had survived delivery, unlike Mama Fang's mother. The yearning for her mother never left Mama Fang, though the shape of that want changed over the years. As a child, she longed for hands to plait her hair and for arms to wrap around her in the dark. As a teenager, she wished for her mother's advice on her new curves and the attentions they drew from men. Her body felt like a stranger's—was it becoming like her mother's?

Mama Fang couldn't imagine her mother at sixteen, one year from meeting the man she would marry and three years from dying in childbirth. Even if she could have traveled back in time, for a chance to pass her mother in the street, she wouldn't have warned her. She wouldn't have stopped her death, because it led to Mama Fang's life. It might seem heartless, but she valued her own existence more, and she would never lose herself to any person, to any man or child. She had to watch out for herself. No one else had, or ever would. She did not know then that this vow would harden her. If you only looked out for cheats and con artists, you only found cheats and con artists. You became one yourself.

That afternoon, the mother who'd struck a deal with Mama Fang returned with her eight-year-old son. He twitched in his mother's lap, ignoring the educational cartoon playing on a computer tablet. He couldn't take his eyes off the IV needle.

"You want to see it?" When Mama Fang showed him the coiled tubing, the boy stared as if it were a cobra about to strike. Inserting the IV properly was akin to making an entrance onstage, demonstrating that Mama Fang was a skilled professional. As he stroked the plastic with his finger, his shoulders relaxed, and in his eyes, the tubing turned harmless and silly. "See how it's hooked to Big Brother and Big Sister?" she asked, pointing out the other students. He nodded with hesitation, and then pride, to be counted among them.

She took the boy's arm, gently massaging the flesh to make the veins stand out. A little darling, with the vitality of a tadpole.

Her hands felt weaker than usual. She hooked the IV fluid onto the rack, careful not to puncture the bag hanging above the boy; flushed the line, driving the bubbles out; and tied on the tourniquet. She told the boy to flex, pumping her own arm to demonstrate. She grunted with a bodybuilder's might, which often made first-time students laugh. Not this one. The boy shivered under the swipe of alcohol, the chill raising goose pimples, and whined from the swipe of numbing cream.

"This will hurt, just a little. A tiny pinch." Mama Fang tugged at the thin skin on the boy's forearm, taut with tendons and blue veins. Children wanted honesty, in appearance, if not actuality. Her heart was racing. When she tried to take a deep breath, she realized she was panting. She'd had too many cups of tea this morning. Her hands trembled so much she almost dropped the needle. Steady—steady.

Here—no there—twice she stuck the boy with the needle. His mother protested.

"Keep him still," Mama Fang ordered sharply. She poked through a vein, blood pooling under the skin into a thundercloud of a bruise.

"The toxins are getting flushed out." Mama Fang removed the needle. The boy thrashed and his mother whispered into his ear—a threat or an endearment, or both, Mama Fang couldn't tell, but he was in danger of hurling himself to the floor. Maybe she shouldn't accept students his age.

"Count backward from one hundred," Mama Fang said, kind but firm, and the boy went still long enough for her to insert the needle. She applied light pressure to the incision and screwed the tubing into place. She reached for the transparent dressing on the tray. As she pulled it out of the wrapper, it folded in on itself, sticking together. *Aiya!* In the supply closet, she found an unopened dressing that had dropped to the floor. She squatted, wincing. Her joints had gone stiff during the latest cold snap. After securing the line, she popped off the tourniquet. "Good boy."

Now that she'd figured out how to deal with kids this young, she'd recalculate her financial projections, shaving off the months and years it would take to earn back the trust of Uncle Lo. She'd first learned how to an insert an IV on her ex-husband, for his medications, and with practice, it was coming back to her now. Mama Fang set a sesame candy and a worksheet before him. The boy tugged on his ear with his free hand. He smelled like chewing gum and rubber erasers, and she had to stop herself from stroking his soft ears, which stuck out like a fox's.

She'd read somewhere that amputees feel pain in their lost limbs, how their brains retain a memory of it, how nerve endings send signals that trick them. She understood how their pain never left them, like the ache she carried for her son she'd given up, whose weight remained heavy in her empty arms.

At Perfume Bay, she'd been surrounded by newborns who mewled and slept, abstract and unformed, and had never felt much for them or their pampered mothers who didn't appreciate their good fortune. However, among these children at Little Genius, who'd developed into people, with their own desires and habits, she yearned for her lost son—for a family—as she hadn't yearned in years.

When Young Master had asked questions about her life, Mama Fang exaggerated and invented. She wanted to impress and entertain him, and telling lies was easier than recounting the lonely squalor of their flat, of her father slumped in a chair. She claimed she was the eldest of five children, with a blind sister who memorized hundreds of songs, another talented at sewing and the youngest at making dumplings, and a clever brother who strummed a pipa he'd made from tin cans.

Young Master was a head shorter, with cheeks smooth of stubble, and at least ten kilos lighter, a sapling to her sturdy trunk of a body. He had yet to grow into his hawk's nose, into his oversized hands and feet and caterpillar eyebrows, the imposing features he would possess as Uncle Lo.

On her afternoon off, she answered the door and discovered he'd followed her home. He glanced around the stuffy flat in search of her stories: her hunched granny who told fortunes and her father who raised fierce fighting crickets. The crowded, colorful life Mama Fang had longed for, which Young Master had wanted, too. She wasn't family to him—she'd known at every moment that he could get her fired—but she'd wanted him to trust her. To look up to her as the children she'd cared for once did.

He turned and ran. The next week, he crumbled biscuits in his bed, swished his shoes through the gutter and tracked prints across the living room. He hid a spring roll under the cabinet, which stank like the dead and attracted swarms of ants. She shouldn't have deceived him. She wanted to tell him she'd never known someone like him to be so interested in someone like her. She was sorry, she needed his mercy, and she needed this job.

When his parents went out to dinner, she heard a crash and discovered a stinking mess of soy sauce, ink, fermented black beans, and shards of glass on the floor of his room. He sat on the bed, his expression defiant. She suspected his revenge would turn elaborate, blame heaped upon her, unless she stopped him now. She pinned him to his bed. His mouth parted, his breath held, and hers caught in her throat. Oh—his eyes. She'd never seen the flecks of black. His body, not scrawny but sinewy. His scent carried traces of his day: the sun on his skin, smoky mischief with his friends, and milk custard on his breath. She slid off him, their crotches grinding against each other.

Over the next few weeks, they occupied themselves with straining and stroking, above and then under their clothes. Their bodies fit together as if designed for no other purpose, his hands cupping her breasts, her nose nestled in the curve of his neck. His eyelids fluttered, pale as moth's wings. Their shirts came off, revealing a spilled chili sauce of a birthmark high on his chest. She'd never seen it. She touched it, thick and rough as a scab, and he flinched. He guided her fingers under his waistband. It was smoother and hotter there than she expected, like a feverish forehead.

He slid into her, and his helpless gasp embarrassed them both. She shuddered against her will, releasing all that had been tightly held within her. A moan slipped out that she couldn't swallow back and everything scattered like newspapers in the wind.

Their time alone disappeared after Mrs. Lo broke her leg, slipping on the slick marble floor of the bank. For months, she never left the flat, asking Mama Fang to fetch this, fix that, to massage her bony shoulders and rub her calloused feet. Every time Young Master tried to touch her again, she found a task that brought her to Mrs. Lo. She'd come to her senses and wouldn't risk her job again.

Mama Fang missed the signs, when she heaved into the sink, nauseated by the tang of fermented tofu. When her midsection thickened, she blamed the rich meals she cooked for the Lo family. She let out the waistband of her pants and the seams on the tunic of her uniform. Smells turned intense, as if she'd developed a bloodhound's tracking skills, and the metallic scent of shrimp made her gag. Sometimes she suffered indigestion, and felt bubbles of gas gurgling through her guts. She wasn't keeping track of her periods, which had always been light and spotty.

If only her mother had been alive. Her mother would have known the cause, and could have told her. Young Master didn't notice, either. Just when she thought he had forgotten, forgiven her, her panties went missing. She had to wash her only pair every night, and it never dried completely, damp and clinging like a popped blister.

When the cramps arrived, her back aching as if squeezed by iron pinchers, she denied the pain until it drove her to her knees. Mrs. Lo rushed her to the hospital, where—to everyone's great shock—Mama Fang gave birth to a son. The nurse had pressed him to her breast, and she pushed him away, this creature her body had violently expelled, the waxy tadpole splotched with a red birthmark. Like the one on Young Master's chest.

Upon waking, she discovered Mrs. Lo intent on the newborn in the bassinet, her face lit with wonder. Mrs. Lo wanted to touch him, hold him, with a surging need that Mama Fang lacked. If she hadn't been delirious, if her disgust toward the baby weren't so overwhelming, she might have held back the confession that would end her employment. She had no maternal instinct, but was dimly aware of how much Mrs. Lo hungered for this child.

She blurted, "He's yours. Your grandson."

What Mama Fang had done to Young Master—what he'd done to her—now seemed impossible, strange and faraway as a half-remembered dream. Anger roiled across Mrs. Lo's face. The threat every *amah* brought into a home: she might seduce, might steal, might stab you in the night. Liar, Mrs. Lo said, and left.

The ceiling pressed in like the lid of a coffin, and from far away, a baby wailed. Whose? Sometime later, Mrs. Lo returned with her husband. Though they couldn't be sure this baby was Young Master's, they would raise him as their own and in return, they'd give Mama Fang a year's salary.

Months after giving birth, Mama Fang understood that some new mothers felt nothing at first, that fierce adoration developed over days and weeks. She might have come to love her son. At that moment, she had only wanted him gone. She took the money and dragged her ruined body back home. Her father must have known she'd suffered, but he didn't question her or the money.

Sometimes she would forget about her son, for a few minutes or a few hours, and then all at once she would remember. She'd spot a newborn, or she'd meet someone else with the surname Lo. She avoided the neighborhood where they lived, but as his first birthday approached, she could resist no longer. She stood across the street, searching the balcony for a glimpse of her son, when the doorman called out to her. "You're too late."

Too late? Her son? She couldn't breathe, couldn't move. She might shatter at the slightest vibration.

The Lo family had left Hong Kong, he told her. For where, he didn't know.

Probably, they wanted to conceal the baby's origins, she understood. Around the corner, out of sight from the doorman, she wept. The pain and regret of losing her son would never leave her.

She had discovered Uncle Lo on a list of richest men in Asia. In their decades apart, Young Master had been building his empire as

Uncle Lo, a public honorific befitting his age and stature. His title's sense of familiarity and authority were also menacing, as if he ruled over your affairs without your consent or knowledge.

He'd embroidered his biography with details drawn from the stories she used to tell him long ago. He wanted to be known as a self-made man, not one who grew up with a servant and meat at meals every other day. Anyone who suspected the truth stayed silent. He had a fearsome reputation, a man you didn't cross if you wanted your business, your family, and your name to survive. His retaliation was calculating and caustic: an enemy's socialite wife was cropped out of photos of all the charity events published in his magazines. An investigative report exposed the toxic practices of a dishonest supplier, landing him in jail.

Uncle Lo had twelve acknowledged children among his mistresses and wives, each son and daughter reflecting his enduring strength and virility. Mama Fang had been his first lover, the first among the beautiful, the rich, the powerful women, the first to bear him a child, and the one he would never forget. She wrote to him about Perfume Bay, a plan she couldn't pull off without additional capital, without introductions to wealthy Chinese.

He rang her a month later, his voice deeper than she remembered, probably scorched by cigarettes. "What's your plan to grow? When will I get a return on my investment?"

She had groped for the light on her nightstand, stumbling in her answers until he asked, "What makes your business different from your competitors'? Not only the ones today, but the ones you've never heard of, the ones that don't yet exist?"

"The difference is me," she'd said. "No one knows what people want like I do."

He came to rely on her for advice other people couldn't offer him: crude, centered between the legs, and aimed at the knees. During a newspaper war in Hong Kong, Mama Fang had told him that girls in tight shirts should hawk his tabloids to commuters. "No one will pass up a smile from a pretty girl."

He never mentioned their son, who was in charge of his satellite television operations and was identified in the press as his younger brother. The closest Uncle Lo got to the subject was complaining about the equestrian expenses for his niece—in reality, the grand-daughter descended from him and Mama Fang.

His niece and her brother were both too soft, Uncle Lo said. Hadn't learned to struggle and fight back from an early age. "Not like you," he said. In all his years, he might never have found another woman he respected as much. In all her years, she'd never found another man who listened to her as closely.

Rarely sick, with the iron constitution of a child who's survived every communicable disease, she had decades ahead of her—even if lately, she'd been feeling run-down. She'd become obsessed with her final days, like the women from the ancient tales who spent their savings to build their coffins. She'd die old and alone, no one to bury her, to remember her, to honor her. Alone again at the upcoming Spring Festival, when even the humblest visited their families and honored their elders.

Had her grandchildren inherited any of her features or her habits? As long as she was alive, she might have a chance to see for herself. In about a month, he was headed to Stanford to make a major donation, a bid for posterity that would also guarantee admissions for his grandchildren. She'd read an announcement about the gift in his newspaper. Uncle Lo could allow her to watch them from afar.

The front door chimed. She hurried to the reception counter, added the customer to the wait list, and promised to contact him when Little Genius expanded its hours. Her body ached. As soon as the last student left, she'd treat herself with an infusion. As the sole instructor, as the sole owner, Mama Fang didn't have to share her profits, no longer had to nag a staff—her gossiping nurses at Perfume Bay, her crotchety cook, her fender-bender-prone driver. But some days—on a day like today—she wished for help. For Scarlett, who wasn't the typical mistress.

She'd spotted a business opportunity when Countess Tien boasted about the classes in pinyin, English, music, and brain training for her three-year-old daughter back in Shanghai.

"Are the classes full?" Scarlett had asked.

"Everyone from her preschool," Countess Tien said.

"If everyone's taking the same classes, no one gets ahead."

Countess Tien had opened her mouth but nothing came out, her expression bovine, struck by the unpleasant truth.

"Start earlier," Scarlett said. "Start now, with your baby. Mama Fang must know someone."

Together, she and Mama Fang could have prospered at Perfume Bay. She should have given up her baby, accepted her reward, and become not only a business partner, but the daughter Mama Fang never had. But they were not alike in the end. Scarlett lacked Mama Fang's courage. Her stony heart.

A girl in pigtails raised her hand. Done! Mama Fang brought her another worksheet. When she noticed a boy dozing, she clapped her hands by his ear. *"Lan dan!"* she spat. Lazy. Coddling American parents would call Little Genius a form of child abuse, and then clamor to learn the techniques. Her own education had been sporadic, but many Chinese schooled their children as if for the imperial examination. For more than a millennium, a young man in China might turn the fortunes of his family by passing the exam and becoming a bureaucrat, ensuring his parents, his wife, his children, dogs, cats, and even his chickens flew to heaven. The exam system had been abolished, but the pressure to perform in China was no less great. Greater, in fact, since most families had only one child.

The parents who migrated to America struggled in a language and culture not their own, and even the most prosperous had to endure snubs, slurs, and worse. Yet they persisted for their children, who would have every opportunity denied their struggling parents. For the poor, children doubled as their only retirement fund. For the well-off, their children were still a kind of currency, in the rivalry among one's friends and colleagues, and in the lifetime tally of success.

What pressure on these narrow shoulders! The most miserable students must wish the solution in the IV bags could send them off to sleep forever. Though their schools were closed for winter break, these children still had to report here. Some would be holding out for the reprieve of the Spring Festival, when Little Genius would be shuttered for the day, though they'd remain trapped with their extended families and their questions about grades, college applications, majors, and internships. There were as many daughters as sons enrolled at Little Genius, which seemed more a measure of pragmatism than progress. In this new era, girls would also have to support themselves and their parents one day.

She locked the front door to keep people from coming in while she finished the day's paperwork. As she turned off the lights in reception, her stomach roiled, and she rushed to the bathroom and retched into the sink. Her mouth tasted bitter as a rotten lemon, and her eyes were bloodshot, the skin beneath puffy and dark. Stumbling back out, she tapped her forearm, a hollow yet decisive sound, searching for a vein. The infusions offered her calm, forcing her to sit still and close her eyes. She bypassed her stomach, just as she cut out all intermediaries in business and in life. But she couldn't find a place to insert a line. She'd opened herself up too many times, and the veins had collapsed, like a heroin addict's.

She'd try again in a few minutes, prospect the back of her hand, which resembled a mountain range crossed by rivers of blue veins. When had her hands become so old? Though the IV drips hadn't staved off this irritating new illness, Mama Fang felt certain that the treatment would speed her recovery. Her body burned with a fever she could no longer ignore.

While waiting, she logged into her bank account to take another look at the monthly deduction she'd noticed last night, a charge that had slipped her attention. Fifteen dollars, for the emergency mobile phone stored in the glove box of the van Scarlett had stolen from Perfume Bay.

She rubbed her eyes, her vision hazy. She wanted to check the phone statement, but she couldn't remember the provider. The logo was blue, or had it been orange? GoNo—GoKnow—GoNow. On-line, she noticed a single repeated area code in the long list of charges: 415. San Francisco, about an hour north. She dialed the number that appeared the most, and when the call picked up, she heard a whoosh of motion and a rattling engine she'd know any-where. Her van. "On my way back," the voice on the other end said. It sounded like he hadn't looked at who was calling and had assumed someone—his employer? his girlfriend?—was checking on him.

"Where to?" The words clogged in her throat, hard to speak, hard to think.

"The Pearl Pavilion. Back in five minutes."

The name sounded like a restaurant. Scarlett may have sold the phone off or tossed it in the trash on her way out of town, but it was still a clue no one else had. If Mama Fang found her, she could persuade Scarlett to come back and turn over the baby. Only then would Uncle Lo forgive Mama Fang. Too late for Mama Fang to know her son, but she might see her grandchildren.

Twilight had fallen, her office at Little Genius suddenly so dim she couldn't make out her hands. Her computer screen turned into a faint, distant blur. She gasped for breath. Where were her keys? Mama Fang didn't like driving in the dark, not on the freeway, the lights dazzling and distracting, and the curves abrupt and lethal. She doubled over, panting, her stomach cramping. She was going to soil herself. She couldn't rise from her chair. How long had she been feeling sick? She'd been off-kilter for days, but had attributed it to age, to work, to weather. She'd been so busy, but now she forced herself to go over her symptoms one by one. A fever . . . fast, shallow breath . . . a rapid pulse . . . abdominal pain. Any single malady she could ignore, but together they signaled something that might kill her. She'd been careful, washing her hands again and again to protect her students from developing septic shock. But she must have slipped up one of the many times she'd started a line on herself.

Too late, she realized the IV had been the cause, not the cure, of her present condition. Sepsis was seeping through her, decaying from the inside, and if she closed her eyes she might never open them again. Fumbling with her phone, she dialed the only one who might save her.

# Chapter 19

Scarlett pulled out damp bunches of scallions, handfuls of plums, ginger, and garlic from the walk-in cooler, and listened to the kitchen gossip: since New Year's Day, a customer had lingered at every meal at the Pearl Pavilion, drinking pot after pot of tea.

The waitress complained that she wanted to close out his bill so she could go on break. The cook promised he'd prepare a special dish for the man's dinner. "So many chilies, he'll have trouble sitting down tomorrow."

For two days in a row, this customer had eaten alone and tipped cheaply, rounding up to the nearest dollar.

"His eyes don't blink!" The waitress shuddered. "Like a lizard."

"I know where he'd like to flick his tongue." Smirking, the cook leaned on the counter. Jowly, with bulging eyes and a wide mouth, he had the look of a toad king. The waitress squealed in protest.

"If they're not sleeping together, they soon will be," Scarlett murmured to Manager Kwok. He laughed. He'd stopped in to check supplies in the pantry. Each afternoon, she left him a plate of *han-baobao*. He'd set aside space for her in the walk-in, and he didn't charge rent for using the kitchen or the van. He'd never tried to grope her in the walk-in cooler or flirt in any way. Perhaps because she crackled like a downed wire—*don't touch,* and perhaps because he respected her entrepreneurial spirit, unlike his attitude toward his workers, whom he clearly considered lazy and witless without his guidance. If he didn't have a wife and teenage sons stashed south of San Francisco, she might have asked him to marry her. He seemed game for an off-the-books business proposition. Manager Kwok could suggest other candidates, but men who would marry for financial gain had to be unsavory. Shrimp Boy? She didn't want her legal status hitched to his arrest record. She couldn't imagine living with any man, even Old Wu, for two years, as a condition of marrying for a green card. He was still in China. Since the raid, a pall had settled over Chinatown. Its permanent residents and U.S. citizens didn't appreciate authorities riffling through the neighborhood's private matters, and they had loathed media reports that portrayed Chinatown as less than upstanding.

Lawyer Loo remained in jail for asylum fraud, held without bail because authorities believed he would flee to China, given the chance. Fatty Pan had turned himself in, and it was rumored that he'd spilled the lawyer's secrets in exchange for immunity. Though she'd avoided the policemen's snare, Scarlett didn't have much in savings. She didn't know how or if she could fix her papers before her visa expired, and she felt hollow, helpless each time she considered her future.

But she had to get through each day. She fell into the rhythm of her preparations: chopping, stirring, pouring. As the cook dished up fried rice for the staff meal, she heard a commotion in the alley. Scuffling, the slam of a door, the thump of metal, and a pair of busboys dragged a man into the kitchen. They'd caught him inside the delivery van, they shouted.

The van she'd stolen from Perfume Bay. She dropped the knife and dove into the walk-in cooler, stumbling through the tangle of thick plastic curtains. Heart pounding, she left the door cracked open so she could see a sliver of the kitchen. The man was stocky, in a blue nylon jacket and slacks that gave him the look of a stadium security guard. Those unblinking eyes—was he the troublesome customer the waitresses despised? She strained to hear what he was saying.

He wasn't stealing the van, he said. He wanted to buy it.

"Tell that to the police!" the cook said, and barked at the busboy to fetch Manager Kwok.

Though the stranger's interest could have been commercial, she suspected he was a private detective. Why else would he care about a junky old van? He might have been nosing around the Pearl Pavilion for days. And how did he track her here? Scarlett never ventured into the dining room and didn't work in the kitchen during meal service. Boss Yeung or Mama Fang might have guessed, or maybe they'd found an informant. Snooping in the alley, the detective must have discovered the van, back from the repair shop today.

Her breath steamed in the cold air, illuminated by a single dim bulb. She flicked off the lights. She should have darted into the pantry, hunkered under sacks of rice flour, hidden behind a wall of canned water chestnuts and bags of dried shrimp. She had to get to Liberty. To protect her, to cover her with her body as she might against a collapsing roof.

When Manager Kwok entered the kitchen, the detective insisted that he was scouting for a Hong Kong movie studio. For a comedy, and the hero of the film was a surfer who lived in his van. He'd been looking for months, and filming was about to start. "That van, you can see every kilometer on it. It's more than a van—it's a supporting character."

Her fingers were going numb, her body livid with goose pimples. Couldn't Manager Kwok tell the man was lying?

"Who's in it? Anybody I'd know?" Manager Kwok asked, his curiosity piqued.

"I'll come back with a cashier's check in an hour." The detective's tone was silky, though he might never have dealt with anyone who drove as hard a bargain as Manager Kwok.

"You haven't taken it for a test drive!"

"I can pay up to ten thousand dollars."

More than four times what Manager Kwok had paid Scarlett. He snorted. "You'll run off, thief."

"Come with me," the detective said. "Hand me the keys and the bill of sale, and I'll drive it away today."

The paperwork. No such documentation existed; the man must be trying to confirm the van had been stolen. He might have been searching it for clues that linked it to Mama Fang and to Scarlett and her baby.

"It's not for sale," Manager Kwok said, his tone impassive.

"Everything has a price," the detective said. "And you know a good deal when you see it." Scarlett glimpsed their legs. They were standing by three cases of cognac, probably stolen, that Shrimp Boy had delivered earlier that day. A coincidence, or was the detective implying he knew all about the illicit dealings at the Pearl Pavilion?

He ushered Manager Kwok off to the side, closer to the walk-in. She shrank back behind a rolling rack. "You know your way around. A place like this, you see hundreds of people a day." His tone turned conspiratorial. "You see things. You ever come across a woman named Scarlett Chen? Pregnant or with a baby? She might be with a teenager, Daisy Yuan?"

Her heart moved with the frantic wing beats of a bird caught in a trap. He sounded like he was about to bribe Manager Kwok for information. What a blessing that the manager didn't know her by that name—no one in Chinatown did except for Daisy—but he must suspect it was her. Although she never told him what brought her to Chinatown, he might have guessed that a pregnant single woman did not have a charmed past.

"You got a picture?" Manager Kwok asked

The detective showed him something on his phone.

"A sketch?" Manager Kwok asked in disbelief. It wouldn't show the change to her hairstyle. If the detective had only a rough idea of what she looked like and didn't know what name she went by in her new life, she might be able to maintain her cover—but only if Manager Kwok kept her secret.

The men coughed and then she smelled it, too: the plum sauce simmering at the stove, now burning in a thick black cloud. Shouting, shuffling, then the clatter of a lid to suffocate the fire, and the scrape of the pot pushed off the gas burner. They stood with their backs to her. If only Manager Kwok would lead him out of the kitchen, she could try to slip out the exit.

Manager Kwok berated the cook, who protested that the mess wasn't his, it was—

She had to stop him from mentioning her to the detective, who would be very interested in a newcomer to this kitchen. She slid an empty tray off a rolling rack, making it clatter onto the floor.

"What's that?" the detective asked.

Though the noise had distracted the men, she'd also drawn their attention to the walk-in. Stupid, stupid. Her fingers scrambled on her phone. Scrolling down her log, to when she'd called Manager Kwok a few days ago to arrange for a pickup of the *hanbaobao* cart. She hit the button. The sound of a text pinging on his phone might draw the private investigator's attention away from the walk-in. Her fingers had gone stiff from the cold. Typing as quickly as she could, she told him she was hiding in the walk-in and begged him to get the stranger out of the kitchen. The text didn't go through— no signal, the walls too thick. Her palms went slick with sweat and the phone nearly slipped out of her hand. No escape, no way out.

She hid behind the rack as Manager Kwok peered inside the walk-in and spotted her. She stared back, her eyes pleading.

A second set of footsteps approached—probably the detective, who would peek over Manager Kwok's shoulder or force his way into the walk-in. She closed her eyes, holding still, trying to shrink herself.

"Someone in there?" the detective asked.

Manager Kwok whirled around. His body filled the doorway, blocking the detective. "Who are you working for?" he roared. "The Golden Dragon? Hunan Gardens?"

"A producer. From Hong Kong."

"You trying to steal our recipes? You with the health department?"

No, no, the detective protested.

"If you wanted the van, why did you snoop around the alley? You a spy—or a thief?"

The detective backed off. "Let's speak in your office."

Manager Kwok called out to the cook. "It's a mess in here! Everything's about to fall. Get your kitchen in order." Then he slammed the walk-in's door.

* * *

Daisy and the babies weren't at the apartment, or at the library. Scarlett doubled back to Portsmouth Square and searched the playground. School had let out, flooding the sidewalks with students wearing oversized backpacks, clutching the hands of their grandparents, gawky teenagers in tracksuits, and tourists, beefy men in baseball caps and flushed women in cable car sweatshirts and fanny packs, stopping every few meters on the sidewalk to check the tourist map and snap photos of the curved eaves, undergarments hanging to dry in the windows, and other foreign attractions.

Daisy couldn't have gone far, and Scarlett wanted to get all four of them off the streets before Manager Kwok finished his meeting with the detective. She had an hour at most. She was on edge, ready to duck into a shop if she spotted him, and kept turning to check if he was tailing her. She hurried past the jewelry shop, the glittering display case with buttery gold necklaces catching her eye, and past a boba tea shop thumping with techno music.

She rounded the corner and discovered Daisy cross-legged on a tarp, relaxed, chatting, and sharing snacks with the disciples of the Celestial Goddess. The babies napped in a nest of blankets in a nearby patch of shade. Scarlett pulled Daisy to her feet while the women around her clucked. She scooped up Liberty, who screwed up her mouth in protest before settling into Scarlett's arms, reaching her tiny hand to graze her mother's chin. Scarlett exhaled. Her daughter was safe—for now.

Daisy glanced at her son. "Didi's sleeping."

"Now."

"I'm not finished eating." Daisy reached down for her plate and took another bite.

"Come," the woman said. Sister Fan, the local group's leader. She gestured at the unappetizing platter of beige meat substitutes. "There's plenty."

Scarlett remembered the CD of tinkly music, the new clothes, the baby formula, the exercises and poses—gifts from the followers of the Celestial Goddess? Daisy fetched her son, who stirred awake but kept his eyes squeezed so tightly shut they looked gouged into his face.

"You don't believe this nonsense," Scarlett said.

"They're the only ones protesting the science exhibit," Daisy ventured. "Remember those corpses from China?"

She had forgotten her boyfriend and thrown in her lot with fools. "This isn't your fight," Scarlett said. Daisy must have been hungering for a cause and a community. Scarlett couldn't help thinking that their life had been simpler when Daisy had been miserable and fixated on finding her boyfriend.

In the park, children shrieked in the swings, a group of men squatted around a card game, and a pair of grannies chatted on the bench. No detective could be seen, not yet, but maybe he'd already been by, asking questions and offering a reward.

"You think anyone cares what these women think?" Scarlett asked. Pedestrians all around them gave the believers a wide berth. Sister Fan rose to her feet from the blanket and walked toward them.

"I'm writing the complaint on their behalf," Daisy said. All those hours at the library. "The city will shut it down."

"And if they don't?"

"We will." Daisy had the same defiant expression as the night she'd shot off fireballs at the Churro Lady. What if she was plotting to do the same at the exhibit? It was all flash and smoke, but authorities wouldn't know that. They'd arrest her and Scarlett, too, and take away their children. Muddle-headed girl! Scarlett wanted to slap her, to feel the purifying sting of skin on bone against skin on bone.

The devotees of the Celestial Goddess might not know what Daisy had in mind. Scarlett had to get her away before the teenager's willfulness and aptitude for chemistry and their zealotry combusted.

Scarlett tugged on Daisy's arm. "Let's go home."

Daisy's expression hardened, obstinate as a donkey's. She didn't accept orders, not from her parents, not from Scarlett.

Sister Fan stood beside them. "You live together?" Her eyes were appraising. "Your babies seem close in age—very close." The back of Scarlett's neck prickled. She didn't like Sister Fan hovering, questioning.

She kept searching Portsmouth Square for the detective. She

wanted to curl her body around Liberty, curl up and disappear. She rubbed her daughter's back, comforted by the sound and the feel of cotton swishing under her fingertips.

"We'll finish the letter. Then I'll go," Daisy said.

Forever talking back! For once, couldn't the teenager stop fighting? Couldn't she listen? They'd been raising their children together long enough for her to know that Scarlett must have an emergency. "You're talking nonsense."

"You can't tell me what to do," Daisy snapped.

Scarlett had to end any future contact between Daisy and this group.

"Too bad about Lawyer Loo," Scarlett said, turning to Sister Fan. She was calculating that the devotees of the Celestial Goddess had been meeting with the immigration consultant, too. Maybe not for a kickback like the church, but to count the ballooning number of asylum cases as proof of the Communist Party's evil. "I wonder if there's a reward. For helping the police," Scarlett said.

Sister Fan looked away, uneasy. The police must have questioned her about her involvement with Lawyer Loo, and it seemed she did not want to undergo another interrogation.

"You are brave, very brave, to call attention to yourself," Scarlett told Sister Fan. "Most people want nothing to do with the police. They don't want to get blacklisted."

Daisy interrupted. "This is America. Not China."

That emboldened Sister Fan, reminded her that she was the local emissary of the Celestial Goddess. "We're the largest gathering outside of Asia," Sister Fan said. "The vibrations are strong here."

Ridiculous. Scarlett caught Daisy's eye, but the teenager still wasn't leaving. "Maybe you can cure her," Scarlett told Sister Fan. "She's a slippery one. She once attacked an old woman with fireballs."

She took no pleasure in insulting Daisy, but the teenager didn't understand the danger they were in.

Daisy reddened. "She's lying!" She turned toward Scarlett. "I—I was defending you."

Sister Fan was already backing away. She didn't know who to believe, but she didn't want to get caught in the cross fire of their grievances. A child's shrill scream pierced the air. A little girl in pig-tails, getting chased on the playground, desperate to outstrip her pursuers. A ball thumped, a band of teenagers dribbling their way through Portsmouth Square. A bus groaned down the hill. Scarlett sagged, the adrenaline that fueled her flight—and fight—gone out of her. In a hush, she said, "There's a detective."

"A detective? You hired one?"

Scarlett shook her head.

"William did?"

As soon as Scarlett said yes, she regretted it, but nothing else would hustle Daisy through Chinatown. Excitement and apprehension rippled over the teenager's face. All of a sudden self-conscious, she ran her hand over her hair and straightened her rumpled sweater. She must think he was waiting for them at Evergreen Gardens, and the next five minutes were probably the longest in Daisy's life. They pushed past aunties jostling for bargains, and a pack of teenage girls, the tips of their hair dyed blond, giggling and huddled around a phone. They were watching a video, singing the chorus of that silly song together, "I Love You Hot." There seemed no end of people on the sidewalk, as if she and Daisy were struggling up a down escalator.

Didi was inconsolable, his mouth a dark black circle of misery, gasping, hiccupping to catch his breath. He kept turning his head away from the bottle, away from the pacifier that Daisy offered him. Always quick to laugh and quick to cry, he was sensitive as a seismograph to the emotional tremors around him.

Liberty studied him with curiosity and concern.

"Look, look!" Scarlett pointed at a bike messenger laboring up the hill. Bicycles fascinated him, the wheels turning round and round, but the sight didn't soothe him now.

Outside the front door of their apartment, Daisy took a deep breath and smoothed her son's hair. She didn't ask why William hadn't come along to Portsmouth Square; maybe she thought Scarlett had wanted to give her a few minutes to prepare herself. All these months, she'd been whiplashed between hope and despair, losing sight of who she was and what she wanted besides him. Scarlett ached for her. This bright beautiful comet of a girl brought to a standstill over a boy who most likely didn't deserve her. She'd begun to move past that struggle and now Scarlett had pulled her back in. She almost blurted the truth, but Daisy pushed ahead. Her hands shook, unable to get the key into the lock. Scarlett took it from her and opened the door.

Daisy rushed in and peered around the empty apartment in confusion, as if expecting him to pop out from under the bed or behind the front door. "Where is he?"

"You weren't leaving," Scarlett explained, and told her what had happened at the Pearl Pavilion.

Daisy froze. Was she going to hurl the baby bottle she was holding, toss shoes, books, everything within her reach? She sank to the ground, her chest heaving, her son shrieking in her arms. A mother and a teenager, too, a girl who yearned for the boy who completed her. Scarlett wanted to tuck her into their softest blanket with the babies, envelop Daisy in their sweet scent of shampoo and talcum, and turn the radio on low. She squatted beside Daisy, not daring to touch her. "I didn't know what else to do."

Daisy ignored her. Standing back up, she stalked the narrow path between the cribs and the window. She swiveled her hips into a figure eight, a trick they'd learned calmed Didi. As if a switch had been flipped, he went quiet. Scarlett couldn't tell if the calm was only momentary, if Daisy would shout at her, if she'd flee back to Portsmouth Square.

Daisy looked upward, her thoughts turning and turning until she arrived at a solution. You could see it, how the bolts and pins of her thinking slid into place, how figuring out a problem calmed her. She excelled at taking tests and would coolly extinguish a fire in the lab while others fled.

"Get Manager Kwok to say he bought the van from you." She offered Didi his pacifier again and this time he accepted it, his eyes heavy.

"Shouldn't he say he's never seen me?"

"If he denies it, the detective will hang around Chinatown. Manager Kwok can say you were going to Seattle."

The detective would spend weeks chasing down the false lead. Daisy's face lit up with another burst of inspiration. "And—that you were in the company of a man. A young guy, someone that Manager Kwok had never seen before, who spoke with a Fujianese accent. And that his hands were all over you."

It would throw off the investigator. Daisy had surprised her again.

Scarlett pawed around the toys and handed Liberty a rattle, then picked up her phone. She didn't know if Manager Kwok had betrayed her, kept the van and taken the detective's reward money. If he was now leading the detective to Evergreen Gardens. She hated putting herself at someone's mercy, but Liberty was depending on her now—Daisy and Didi, too. She texted him and within a minute, he called.

"He's gone," he said.

"Gone? Did he leave his number?"

Manager Kwok snorted. "He left in a hurry."

"Was he— Did he get hurt?"

In the silence that followed, she guessed that the detective had been scared off, probably dispatched with threats or a beating by Shrimp Boy. The detective had brought it upon himself, waving around cash, acting as if he could buy his way into Chinatown's secrets. Manager Kwok's pride had been at stake.

But he had also done it for her. He viewed himself as a guardian of the neighborhood. She pictured him in his office, in his wingback chair, a glass of cognac before him. The starburst of wrinkles around his eyes that deepened when he was tired.

"There was a man," Scarlett said, her anger, her hurt at Boss Yeung's betrayal, no less than the night Mama Fang tried to bribe her.

"There always is," Manager Kwok said gently.

Until Chinatown, Scarlett had never felt herself accepted, not in her village, not at any factory or apartment. She'd come to San Francisco to recede into anonymity. If you let down your guard, thieves and swindlers preyed upon you. Boss Yeung had tried to steal her child, and she'd lost much of her savings—and nearly her freedom—to Lawyer Loo.

But if you let down your guard, others might, too. After she'd taken Old Wu to the hospital, the ladies at Evergreen Gardens dropped off food, tins of biscuits, plates of noodles from a double batch they'd made for dinner. After she'd come to know Manager Kwok, he'd sheltered her. And—Daisy. After the intensity of their early days, they had to be apart more often than together. It surprised Scarlett, how much she missed Daisy each day—her sharp tongue, her sharp wit, and her capable hands.

She felt bound to this place and to these people. To the gusts off the bay that swirled dead leaves into a cyclone, mesmerizing Liberty. To the scent of the meltingly soft egg tarts from the corner bakery that Didi would eat by the fistful if allowed. The groan of the cars laboring up Chinatown's steep hills. To the early morning sunlight, golden on the eaves and against Liberty's cheek. The sweet naps and happy squeals in the apartment, the babies tugging toys back and forth, in a family that fit no definition but their own.

Scarlett tightened the blanket around herself and the babies, bundled up and tented in her lap against the winds whipping along Ocean Beach. Every few meters, the orange-red of bonfires flickered like beacons on the second weekend of the new year. In the distance, a group was beating drums and chanting. The ritual felt ancient, people banding together for warmth and courage on a cold winter night. Closer by, a woman in a puffy jacket and wool cap twirled a bucket of fire on a metal chain, mesmerizing loops and spirals that hurled in the air. The chain rattled, the medieval sound of a knight's clanking armor. How powerful the woman must have felt, swinging the wide arcs of fire to ward off enemies, dragons, and all else that lay beyond in the dark. Her friends whooped and cheered, and sipped surreptitiously from flasks to avoid getting hassled by the police. The ends of their joints glowed like fireflies.

Earlier that day, Daisy had made the arrangements with the driver of the Pearl Pavilion van. He'd be back in an hour with Scarlett's cart. Tonight would be a busy one, as it had been during the holidays, but before Scarlett went to work, Daisy had wanted to celebrate.

Last week, after Scarlett had fallen ill with a cold, Daisy had delivered the *hanbaobao* trays for yet another one of Madame Tom's parties. She lived in a spacious apartment with her husband up the hill from Chinatown, with gleaming hardwood floors, crown molding like the piping on a cake, and a huge bay window overlooking the city. Her salary at the community college couldn't have been much, but like many Chinese, Madame Tom might have bought real estate early and often with her husband. In a city surrounded by water on three sides, the Chinese knew no better investment.

Daisy had been carrying in the last two trays of *hanbaobao* when a man in a gray suit, with the blond swoop of hair and cleft in his chin of an old movie idol, offered to help. She was leading him into the kitchen when Madame Tom swooped in to scold her. "Lazy girl!"

Daisy gathered that he was a man of some importance, maybe from the college or the city government. Madame Tom offered him a *hanbaobao*. "You must try one. I don't know what you call it— sliders?—except Chinese." She asked him about the mayor and his wife.

The mayor? If Scarlett had made the delivery, she would have left as quickly as she could. She lacked permits to prepare food, to work, and soon even a legal visa. But Daisy had seized upon the encounter as an opportunity. After Madame Tom left to greet another guest, Daisy cornered the man, telling him about the problems at the cadaver exhibit. The devotees of the Celestial Goddess had been protesting, she said, seeking a public official whose support they would return many times more. He listened attentively and took down her phone number, out of politeness or as a means to escape her. After eating a few *hanbaobao*, however, he must have felt inclined to help. Within days, the city's health department had started conducting an investigation into the exhibit, which shut down for the time being. It was all over the news.

With that settled, Daisy would no doubt find another cause this year. As much as Scarlett tried to sway her, the girl had an iron will. Scarlett had been thinking about the night she herself had left home. Ma might have known. She was a fitful sleeper, and in retrospect, quiet as Scarlett had been in slipping out of the house, it seemed unlikely Ma hadn't woken up. She might have pretended to sleep, might have chosen to let Scarlett go, a daughter who wasn't like the others in the village, a daughter Ma had decided to let make her own way in the world.

She now understood why Ma had taken the job at the clinic. A young widow in the countryside had dim prospects; her daughter, even dimmer, and Ma had to support them, no matter how horrendous her duties. Scarlett had no doubt that Liberty might someday judge her harshly for her decisions, as harshly as she'd judged Ma.

Digging out supplies from her backpack, Daisy told Scarlett to stay turned around. Scarlett hugged the babies, each one tucked into the crook of an arm. They held flashlights. Liberty shook hers like a rattle, while Didi waved his. On their own, each would have been frightened of the dark but together, they had the comfort and confidence of twins. She hoped that Didi would always have Liberty's back, and Liberty would always have his. Underneath the blanket, the air was warm and moist, cozy in contrast to the cold, coarse sand around them.

Out in the darkness, the Pacific pounded. At the edge of the world, you couldn't help but think about what brought you here and what—and who—you had to let go. A year ago, she was pregnant but didn't know it yet. A year ago, she and Boss Yeung had been at their happiest. She'd harbored a dream of someday visiting America and standing on this side of the ocean, gazing toward China.

A year ago, Daisy's life had also been about to change. A year ago, she'd been thinking about her homework assignments and how much she missed her boyfriend, wondering when she would see him next. Neither she nor Scarlett had known they were about to step through a threshold into motherhood, opening their eyes and their hearts in ways they couldn't foresee. It was a riddle Scarlett still hadn't solved: how small her life had become, parenthood confining as a swaddle, everything a blur except for a few meters around her, and yet how infinite, how intense the universe now seemed.

Her papers. Her papers, her papers, her papers were never far from her thoughts; she'd have to figure how—if—she could get them fixed, or if she'd lost her last chance to Lawyer Loo, and would have to prepare for a life even further underground. She heard the click of a lighter and Daisy cursing softly as it went out. She tried again and when she told Scarlett to turn around, she was greeted by a bonfire, its light warm against her cheeks. She scooted around on her bottom, keeping the blanket tented around the babies. Daisy squatted beside her, her hands stinking of jellied gasoline. Her eyes were bright, reflecting a rainbow of flames.

Later, Scarlett would learn the ruby color sprang from hand sanitizer mixed with a road flare, the rust from bleaching powder, the yellow from salt, and the emerald green from disinfectant. But at this moment, she marveled at the fire dancing on the sand, the heady stink sending them reeling against each other, their gasps and giggles echoing into the night.

# Chapter 20

**The taxi driver** refused to go any farther. He didn't want to damage the undercarriage of his car on the grooves worn deep into the dirt road that led to the village. Boss Yeung would have to walk the rest of the way. He asked the scrawny driver to wait. To get here from the airport, they'd had to ask for directions several times, and the driver said he wanted to return to familiar territory before sunset, which was in less than an hour. A five-hour flight north of Hong Kong, at this time of year the sky in this part of the country went dark by mid-afternoon.

"I'll need a ride back to the airport hotel," Boss Yeung said. The driver, looking mournful, climbed onto the hood and lit a cigarette.

Boss Yeung shuffled past stubbled fields, toward the wisps of smoke drifting from the cooking fires of Scarlett's childhood village.

After the factory hired a new worker, the other ladies had mentioned the search for Scarlett and the name sounded familiar to the girl, a friend of her cousin. A call confirmed that the cousin and Scarlett had worked together at a shoe factory years ago.

Scarlett hailed from Five Dragons—the cousin was certain, because she'd briefly dated a boy from that village. Sometimes, Scarlett seemed a figment of his imagination, an embodiment of his feverish desires for youth, for immortality. In other moments, it felt like she was in the next room, and he only had to call out her name and she would come through the door, carrying their son.

He had never visited Anhui province, said to be so poor a family of eight had to share a pair of pants. His factory hired many teenagers from here, but Boss Yeung hadn't pondered the circumstances that prompted their migration from this heartland of wheat and noodles, wide open plains, so different than the lush rice paddies of the south. The farther north you went, the heartier and cruder the people. In this regard, Boss Yeung hoped that his son had taken after Scarlett. When he got off the plane in Hefei, the provincial capital, he'd noticed the local men had towered over him. It was said that northerners were sincere and honest, tending toward stupidity, while southerners were clever and skilled, tending toward duplicity. Nonsense, or maybe not. The land of your birth shaped you, even if later, like Scarlett, you led your life in opposition to it.

He doubted he'd find her, but perhaps she'd gotten a message to her mother, letting her know that she was in America and that she'd given birth. Maybe she'd sent a photo in advance of the Spring Festival. A photo! At last he might glimpse his son. He passed under a village gate with blue-tiled eaves, upon which five rusty wire dragons perched. A flock of black-and-white magpies burst out of a stand of poplars along the river. He kicked aside chickens and slogged past gray brick homes splotched with fading whitewash. Somewhere in the village, pigs snuffled, settling down for the night. A little girl, her breath steaming in the cold, watched him from a doorway. Was she somehow related to Scarlett, a cousin, a daughter of a cousin? He searched for a family resemblance, Scarlett's pointed chin and her thick chevron of eyebrows. The girl waved at him, and he waved back. She had a charming, gap-toothed smile. A scratchy voice called from inside and the girl retreated into the house, shutting a weathered wooden door.

He wondered if Scarlett took after her mother, if he would encounter a vision of how she might age, a version of his lover that he most likely would not live to see. She never talked about her mother, but he assumed she was a peasant who spent her life in the fields, back bent, exposed to the wind and the sun that would turn her skin to leather. Would he recognize her?

He'd start here, where he could tell people were home. A granny opened the door, her teeth nubby and brown. He offered greetings and she replied in an accent so thick and guttural it seemed a miracle that Scarlett had ever shed it. When he asked about her, the woman seemed puzzled. He wasn't sure when Scarlett started going by her English name, if she'd adopted it only after she worked in the factories or sometime later. The granny disappeared inside and returned with a steaming mug of hot water. He pretended to sip—the water must carry a dozen kinds of contamination and sickness—and she asked if he'd eaten.

"Do rest with us awhile," she said. Poor, but more hospitable than he would have been if she'd arrived at his front gate in Hong Kong.

The next home was abandoned, the front door missing, with a collapsed roof and crumbling mud-brick walls. Its occupants probably now lived in a city. No one answered at the next home, though he heard pots clanking. The sun was fast slipping toward the line of hills on the horizon, and if he didn't hurry, the driver would leave without him. He could try coming back tomorrow, yet this close to picking up the trail to Scarlett, he couldn't bear to stop now.

Another knock, another garbled conversation. An elderly man with hands gnarled as a gingerroot, his odor stale, dried sweat and black tea. The man didn't recognize Scarlett's name, the city where she worked, or the name and type of factory Boss Yeung ran. The gnarled man followed him. This unexpected visit would provide weeks of gossip. At the next house, the villager conferred with a granny carrying a baby on her hip. His son? No—this child was too big, already in pants split in the rear for potty training.

A stout neighbor approached, unexpectedly taking Boss Yeung's hand in hers. He almost jerked away in surprise. Her hands were warm, the pressure reassuring, telling him she would help him. More shouts, and soon a dozen people were following him—the very old and the very young—as if he were leading a parade. Boss Yeung felt ridiculous, but the attention could draw out Scarlett's mother from her home.

Ten minutes later, he'd completed his circuit of Five Dragons, whose total area and population were a fraction of any one of his factories. In a country of 1.3 billion, there could have been another Scarlett Chen, the same age and from this province, too. The new factory girl's memories could have faded, and she might have mixed up the name. He seethed, cursing her for leading him astray. Cursing Mama Fang, Uncle Lo, and his own failing body. He'd never find her.

Then he noticed a sour-faced woman carrying a bucket of water. She planted her feet wide outside a home he'd assumed had been abandoned, its roof missing many tiles, the front walls massed with dead weeds. The woman shouted at the gathered crowd and the gnarled man timidly replied with something that Boss Yeung couldn't make out. He huddled close behind Boss Yeung, as if taking cover.

When Boss Yeung mentioned Scarlett's name, the woman's scowl flickered. She and Scarlett held themselves the same way, the same determined set to their shoulders. She must wonder what business brought him here, if he were a policeman or government official.

"Who's Scarlett?" she asked, her accent heavy but comprehensible.

He held up his mobile phone and asked her to bring out hers, pointing at his and then at her. She retreated into the house. Peeking inside, he spied soot-blackened ceilings, and against the wall, a stack of fleece blankets, still zipped in their plastic case. The same ones that Scarlett had bought last year while shopping with him. Blankets that Scarlett brought every year, which Ma must have stubbornly set aside, a form of protest against her daughter for never moving back home.

Ma emerged with the phone. It seemed she wouldn't admit to knowing Scarlett, not until she determined his purpose here. He helped her turn on the phone. It was almost dead—she probably never charged or used it—and the service was spotty. He called the number Scarlett had listed as her mother's. The phone rang. Startled, she fumbled with it, as if it were a grenade about to go off. Confirmation that she was Scarlett's mother, that Scarlett had grown up in this hovel, in this speck of a village. He couldn't find her in the present—only in the past. She had walked these lanes, run through these fields, gulped in the air that he now breathed. He wanted to swallow it all and let this place circulate in his veins.

He hung up. "How is she?" he asked. Sounds carried farther here; a whisper could wing across Five Dragons without competing with honking cars, whining buses, or the shouts of hawkers. He leaned in closer to Ma so the neighbors couldn't hear him, close enough to see her wiry catfish mustache. "How's your grandson?"

She gaped. Scarlett must have sunk like a stone from her life, too. "What's she done now?"

"He was born in September."

She pursed her lips, and must be calculating whether Scarlett had been pregnant when she'd last seen her.

"In America."

Her eyes widened again, though only for an instant. "Impossible. The women in my family, their firstborns are always girls. Me. My mother. My grandmother."

"It's a coincidence."

"It's a curse." She folded her arms across her chest. "You saw him yourself, checked between his legs?"

Was she trying to throw him off? Maybe Scarlett had called and Ma was trying to protect her. The neighbors were murmuring, pressing closer to hear, and he held out his arms to keep them back. A little boy poked up under his armpit, curious. He wore so many layers it looked difficult for him to bend his arms or legs. Boss Yeung shooed him away, gently as he could, and asked to see Ma's phone, a clunky silver model. If he searched the logs, he might uncover a number from the United States.

"If she owes you money—" Ma said.

He offered her the red envelope of cash for the upcoming Spring Festival. She didn't take it, nor did she turn over the phone. "I'm just trying to help."

He reached for the phone, but she tucked it behind her back. She studied him intently. She must suspect that he was her daughter's lover and the father of her child, and find him wanting. If only he could tell her that he didn't have mottled skin, puffy cheeks, and a stooped back when Scarlett met him.

"She must have called," he said.

She narrowed her eyes—his words sounding like an act of provocation—and she dropped the phone into the bucket of water, where it buzzed and crackled. *"Waaah!" "Aiya!"* the crowd shouted. He plunged his hand into the bucket, wiping the phone against his pant leg. He blew on it, trying to dry it, and would have given mouth-to-mouth if it could resuscitate the phone. The screen had gone dark, but he pocketed it anyway.

"She's fierce as you," Boss Yeung said.

Ma snorted, but he detected a hint of a smile. He shivered in the chill, his dress shoes damp with mud. To the villagers, he must have seemed out of place as a rooster strutting in a skyscraper. He could have sent an assistant or called on the authorities to intervene, but he'd made the journey himself. For too long, he'd relied on others who failed. For too long, he hadn't understood her. Now he was ailing, and might never recover. Would Scarlett's mother count that for or against him in her appraisal?

"If I find her, is there anything you want me to tell her?" His tone was low and humble.

Ma went back inside and returned with a notebook, its pale blue cover singed at the edges, like a pirate's treasure map. She tugged the red envelope out of his hand, in exchange for the notebook. He flipped through it, through yellowed pages of tiny characters and wobbly block printing of Scarlett's name in English. Her hands had smoothed these pages, and he could barely keep himself from rubbing it against his cheek, sniffing for a trace of her.

Ma's face twisted with the grief she might never allow herself, over the loss of Scarlett and her grandchild she didn't know, over any suffering Scarlett had endured alone. Nothing lasted for long in the village, paper especially, nibbled by insects, consumed by mold, shredded into nests by mice, or fed into the fire. Preserving this notebook must have required a monumental effort by Ma. All these years, she had saved it for a future that never arrived. A notebook he suspected that Ma herself couldn't read.

Getting sick didn't turn you into a saint; Boss Yeung—and his father—were proof of that. But he saw the world as he never had in the past. The prospect of death coming closer made you consider your life, what you wanted in what remained. And he had to get that notebook to Scarlett and their son.

The taxi driver honked his horn. The first stars were appearing, the sky the deep purple of eggplant shading into black. Boss Yeung hurried, gripping the notebook to his chest, like a kite that might carry him high and away.

# Chapter 21

The newlyweds kissed, and Scarlett prepared for the rush of *hanbaobao* orders that would follow on a bright winter afternoon in San Francisco. She was catering her first wedding, and if she shined today, more contracts might follow, steady work with a guaranteed take.

This ceremony wasn't in a banquet hall, but a backyard; it boasted not a tiered cake, but a cupcake tower. Not a twelve-course banquet, but a potluck of steaming enchiladas, pasta salads, chili, and the *hanbaobao* cart on the damp lawn. Most surprising of all, it featured not a bride and groom, but a bride and bride, which Scarlett hadn't realized until she arrived at their purple bungalow in a neighborhood of hilly, narrow streets.

The crowd on the concrete patio parted before the *lala* newlyweds, the two women stopping for photos, hugs, and kisses under soap bubbles glittering with rainbows. White paper lanterns danced on the wind above the centerpieces on the long picnic tables, silver pails of rosemary, sage, and lavender.

Casey, the redhead with the mermaid tattoo on her arm, had hired Scarlett. A regular customer, she always left sizeable tips and practiced her *ni hao* and *xie xie* in serviceable Mandarin. Today she wore a short white dress edged in lace and white knee-high boots, and her amber hair in two braids. Her wife wore a tight *qi pao*, red satin embroidered with phoenixes. With her short black hair marcelled into waves and carmine lips, the wife resembled a Shanghai sophisticate from a vintage advertisement.

That too had been a surprise, the Chinese bride. She and Scarlett were the only Chinese at the reception, the bride entirely absent of family, who could have been abroad and unable to get visas, or maybe had refused to attend. The guests gobbled down their *hanbaobao* and got back in line, asking for another, crazy for the sauce's sweetness with a tickle of tang, and the starched laundry smell of steamed buns. Many who asked if Scarlett had a website were perturbed and intrigued when she told them no—a reaction she hadn't intended but decided to cultivate. A sense of serendipity if you discovered her *hanbaobao*, that set her apart from the humdrum dependability of a shop with a permanent address.

Daisy, with her superior English, had handled today's catering arrangements over the phone. She executed a contract that netted Hanbaobao a thousand dollars for three hours of work, and was now at home watching the babies. Tomorrow, she would turn eighteen, officially an adult and officially out of the reach of her parents. She could sponsor them and her younger sister for green cards, if she chose. If only she could have done so for Scarlett!

When Scarlett's tourist visa expired next week, she risked deportation. If the government forced her out, her daughter would also have to leave, losing the opportunities that were her birthright. Even if Scarlett escaped detection for months or for years, every day she'd live under that threat. The immigration authorities could raid her at work or stop her on the street. It had happened to other families. It could happen to Scarlett.

She didn't dare apply for asylum, not after Lawyer Loo's arrest. She could try for a student visa. A Chinese lady in the South Bay ran a sham university that collected tuition from foreign students but didn't require going to class. Cost: twenty-seven hundred dollars each semester. Or she could marry for a green card, but had no prospects. Old Wu had returned from China married, eagerly awaiting the arrival of his village bride. There were stranger pairings in Chinatown, where bachelors took wives young enough to be the daughters they never had.

For the Chinese—for most everyone, she supposed—nationality and identity used to be synonymous. You left your ancestral province only under duress, fleeing famine, bandits, and war. You were Chinese, would always be, and you'd no sooner swear allegiance to another government than give up your firstborn. No longer. You might change your citizenship to practice your religion and your politics, to become a voter in a new land where you were making a life for yourself and for your children. You might do it just to lower your taxes, and get ahead in the world.

Arms at each other's waists, the brides strolled through the crowd, passing under the banner—CONGRATULATIONS CASEY AND YING, in colorful patch letters, like a quilt. A musician in a straw hat tilted at a jaunty angle plucked on a banjo. Wind chimes tinkled. Like a country fair, but for the whine of the siren and hum of traffic far down the hill. Scarlett assembled Casey's usual order: double meat and extra green onions. Instead of plum sauce, ketchup, which her wife would consider an abomination.

"Surprise!" Casey said, leading Ying to the *hanbaobao* cart. Ying smiled tightly, preparing to be disappointed by Americanized Chinese food, too sweet and too bland. Scarlett selected the fluffiest bun and added each ingredient in the traditional order and ratio. She wanted a good recommendation, a referral that might land her on the lawn of a *lala* wedding every weekend. Ying took a bite and widened her eyes with delight and surprise.

"*Hen you ming,*" Casey said. Very famous.

"*Bu cuo,*" Ying said. Not bad. She licked her fingers clean. Her nails short, her hands muscled and wide-knuckled.

Casey squeezed her wife's waist, looking into her eyes with such ardor that Scarlett had to turn away, struck with longing. She and Boss Yeung once couldn't keep their hands off each other, once couldn't bear to be parted for the night.

In the village, *lalas* were alluded to only as a decadence an innocent girl should avoid.

When Scarlett was a teenager, her bunkmates at the factory dorm were rumored to be lovers. The pair spent all their free time together, and in the dark, if Scarlett heard fumbling, gasping, and the squeak of bedsprings above her, she popped in her headphones. In time, the curvy girl left, pressured by her parents to marry someone from back home. Scarlett always wondered what happened to the abandoned one. If she remained in the city, finding other women, unfilial daughters who did not bear children to continue a man's family line. Or did she give in and marry a man she could never love, suppressing desires that could lead to jail, a beating, or getting fired?

Scarlett tried to place Ying's accent. *"Ni cong nali lai?"* she asked. Where are you from? Which among Chinese didn't mean where you lived or had been born, but where your grandfather hailed from. Who were your people? Were they known for being crafty, for their sincerity and honesty, for their spicy foods and spicy temper? A standard question, one of the first asked when two Chinese encountered each other, before inquiring about marital status and the number of children. Ying didn't answer. Her expression turned shifty, as if she were hiding a secret.

Beautiful, Scarlett said, gesturing at their dresses, trying to change the subject. A friend brought the brides glistening Mason jars of cocktails, bubbly and garnished with sprigs of mint. The *hanbaobao* line never flagged, and not until the brides took the microphone did Scarlett have a chance to rest.

Casey turned teary-eyed, sharing how they'd met in the conservatory a decade ago. A violinist from Salinas and a pianist from Shanghai. Two only children. Ying got a laugh when she thanked the guests for coming to their special day, in a wedding season without end. After the court decision, *lalas* in the United States must have been marrying in droves.

A handful of celebrities in Asia had declared themselves *lala*, including the daughter of a Hong Kong tycoon. After she married her longtime lover, her father had offered $65 million to any man who stole back her heart. Ma had tried to rule Scarlett's life, but she had never been blind to her daughter's essential nature. Her mother's clear-eyed view of her was a virtue that Scarlett had never considered until now.

Her voice thick with emotion, Casey thanked her parents, plump and gray-haired, though a trace of cinnamon remained in her mother's curls. She thanked their friend who had played the banjo throughout the reception, the *lala* couple with a multitude of piercings who mixed a big batch of cocktails, as well as their statuesque neighbor, her mahogany hair knotted into squiggles, who had sewn the banner by hand. Scarlett's attention wandered until she realized people were looking at her. Casey was talking about the *hanbaobao* cart. "Get one—there's plenty!" Casey said. Was she planning to thank every guest individually while at the microphone? She was charmingly exuberant, but the crowd was beginning to fidget. Ying whispered in her ear, and Casey nodded, telling her guests she'd thank each one before the night ended. "I'll let you get back to dinner, so we can get on to dancing! But—just one more thank-you," she blurted, and named the guests who'd traveled farthest, from London and another from Sydney. "Soon we'll have a chance to visit. Some of you have been waiting a long time."

On their honeymoon, because they finally had enough in cash wedding gifts to buy tickets? Or was it possible, Scarlett wondered, that Ying didn't have her papers and hadn't been able to travel until now? During the first dance, under the glow of tiki torches and beneath the whir of heat lamps, the brides swayed to jazzy music, heads resting on each other's shoulders. If they met in school, Ying must have come on a student visa and stayed after it expired. Teaching piano lessons for cash and taking odd jobs allowed her to live in the shadows. Now that *lala* marriage was legal, maybe—most certainly—Casey could sponsor her wife for a green card.

Family, related not by blood, but by marriage. And if Casey could sponsor her wife, so too could Daisy.

On her walk home, Scarlett jingled the change in her pocket. She didn't have enough for a birthday cake or flowers for Daisy, who might well prefer a set of test tubes and chemicals to make more explosives. She entered a music shop and asked the clerk what he had on sale—cheap. The Guardian, Hong Kong's latest pop idol. The singer posed against a brick wall, his head turned to one side, his eyes distant and dreamy. He wore a black T-shirt, jeans, and stylish suede sneakers, his long bangs falling sideways into his eyes. On the track list, she noticed "I Love You Hot," the song she'd been hearing all over Chinatown. Until then, she hadn't known the name of the singer behind it.

Back in the hallway of Evergreen Gardens, Auntie Ng pulled out a jar of freshly squeezed ginger from the pocket of her cardigan. Despite the screw top, it smelled strong enough to clear out your sinuses. The babies had been crying all day, she said. "Sprinkle a few drops on their bellies, then massage. Move the wind down. Not up!"

In the apartment, she discovered Daisy passed out on their double mattress. The children were wailing in diapers heavy and wet as fresh cement, with an eye-watering stink that could strip paint off the walls. Scarlett changed the babies, nursed Liberty, and gave Didi his bottle. He reached for her nose and she let him tug, then reached for his, pretending to swipe it off his face. He lit up, as if there were no one else in the world he'd rather see aside from his mother. She rubbed his back in slow circles until he fell asleep.

She and Daisy had survived the first four months of motherhood, the hardest months of sleep deprivation, short tempers, and terrifying first fevers and falls that had humbled them. Neither of them was as self-righteous and unyielding as they'd once been. They had groped their way up, each pulling the other one to her feet, celebrating the first hundred days of their babies, and forging a bond that ran deeper than the ones they held with the men with whom they'd conceived. If Boss Yeung hadn't betrayed her, if William hadn't disappeared somewhere across a river of stars—kept apart as if by the Goddess of Heaven—she and Daisy never would have become sisters. Sisters not by blood, but by choice.

Soon both babies had nodded off, their deep breaths lulling Scarlett like crashing waves. Tucking the blanket around Daisy, Scarlett curled beside her. Even if they started off apart in bed, or back-to-back, by morning, Daisy's hand tangled in Scarlett's hair, and Scarlett's feet crossed Daisy's legs for warmth.

\* \* \*

The next morning, she presented Daisy with the CD. The printed cover, a smudged photocopy, featured the singer in profile. "You think he's my type?" Daisy asked.

"More than mine." Scarlett offered her daughter a mashed banana, its scent heady, overripe, verging on fermented. Liberty smeared it around her mouth. She was starting to enjoy solid foods, encountering new tastes daily: rice porridge, with its bland sweetness and slippery warmth, egg yolks rich and yellow as the sun, and mashed peas, green and bright. She often grabbed for the spoon. Crying, impatient, as if she were starving, as if it held the last bite on earth. Down the hallway, a toilet flushed in the communal bathroom. The building was otherwise silent, their neighbors using the weekend to catch up on sleep.

"Admit it. You bought it for yourself." She caught Didi before he rolled into the cardboard box that served as their dresser. He immediately started over again. Given the chance, he would have rolled across America, a kaleidoscope of sky and earth and light, of independence and exploration.

Scarlett laughed. "Don't talk nonsense." She popped the CD into their stereo, which needed a firm push to latch it. The babies were always reaching for its remote, studded with buttons and lights, lit with magical powers. Though it was scratchy, copied too many times, the singer's voice sounded silky and playful on the first track.

"Canto-pop," Daisy said with a dismissive wave of her hand. She hit the remote, clicking through the tracks, formulaic ballads swelling with orchestral emotion—"Love Is Dying"—and thumping dance hits—"Wanted Love, Not in Love." She had yet to reach "I Love You Hot."

She lingered on a song whose opening strains sounded familiar: it was a cover of the lullaby that she sang to her son, the lullaby that she'd performed with her boyfriend at karaoke. It didn't sound like the other songs on the album; his voice was earnest and unadorned, not slick and synthesized.

Daisy looked stricken. "It's him."

"You've heard of him? The vendor said it was new."

"William. My God—it's William."

Scarlett glanced at the cover, the singer's name in a scrawl, as if he'd autographed it. Her eyes met Daisy's, both women stunned into silence. After a few more beats, she asked, "Why is he called the Guardian?"

Daisy puzzled for a moment before laughing. She'd once asked him the meaning of his name. Guardian, he said. The record company must have translated it into Cantonese. He was named after Bill Gates, Daisy said, though he'd taken to calling himself William in a fit of rebellion, a version of himself free of parental expectations that he'd become a tech titan.

She'd searched online for Will Wan, William Wan, but never the Chinese translation. Sometime after he was told she'd terminated the pregnancy, he must have dropped out of school. She dug out her phone and uncovered an online encyclopedia entry that detailed his transformation and its timing. When Daisy had been sequestered at Perfume Bay, he had visited Hong Kong, with plans to backpack around China. Though raised with every modern convenience, he was fascinated by the old ways, Daisy explained. He was the kind who made pilgrimages to the villages that his ancestors had fled.

A photographer discovered him in the subway. That led to a modeling gig for canned ice coffee ("Mr. Espresso"), a small but pivotal role in a rom-com shot in seventeen days (*Delete My Love*), and from that momentum, a minor recording deal ("Introducing . . . the Guardian").

Daisy repeated the name of the debut CD, the one that she held in her hand. She studied the cover photo and looked back at the online encyclopedia entry. The album must have been pirated quickly, almost as soon as it had been released. Though "I Love You Hot" had been playing everywhere in Chinatown, she hadn't recognized his voice, processed so much it turned robotic.

"The last movie I saw in a theater was with him," she said. She laughed in disbelief. "And now—he's *in* one?"

In the haze of birth and its aftermath, she hadn't kept up with Hong Kong celebrity gossip—not that she'd ever paid much attention to the men with their dewy skin and foppish hair, or the starlets with their helium-pitched voices. She'd preferred American entertainers.

Daisy zoomed in on a movie still. "It's him." She shook her head, marveling. His abrupt change in fortune explained his disappearance from Cal and social media. Hidden in his stardom, hidden as much as a hermit in the mountains.

She scrolled through the bio. He'd studied wushu since he was eight, trained to perform in competitions, spinning and flipping. She showed Scarlett a picture of him as a child in a flowing satin outfit, brandishing a plastic sword.

"Why go back?" Scarlett asked. Why did Chinese Americans rush to the homelands their parents abandoned?

"He's been all over China with his family—Hong Kong, Beijing, Shanghai, Xi'an," Daisy said.

Places that Scarlett had yet to see. The package tours had stopped at every monument and museum, but what he remembered most were the crowds, the heat, and all those Chinese.

"Everyone looked like me," he'd told Daisy. He'd never blended in like that, his black hair, slanted eyes, and angular frame just like many people around him. No one stared or sneered at him.

It was a desire Scarlett couldn't comprehend. You could feel just as out of step surrounded by people with similar hair and height. "He could have gone to Chinatown," she said.

"Not the same. The people who left—they're not like the people who stayed," Daisy said.

She kept opening and closing the CD case. Click, click, click. Scarlett suspected that the Hong Kong entertainment industry's fascination with this newcomer would have made up for any of his inadequacies as a singer. His flaws were common enough to fix in post-production, but his smile, his build, and his look were rare: Chinese and yet not, American and yet not.

He and Daisy had talked about living and working in China someday, she said, after college. She found another picture of him at a movie premiere, a model on his arm with golden skin and feline eyes, a fierce beauty who called to mind Hua Mulan, the woman warrior who had taken her father's place in the army. Daisy

squirmed. Though the elasticity of her youth had helped her recover faster than Scarlett after giving birth, her body must feel ill-
fitting, and she glanced down at her baggy sweater, shapeless jeans,
and thick wool socks. Her grown-out pixie cut was a shaggy mess in
need of a trim.

"He never looked for me." Daisy couldn't hide her bitterness.
How quickly he'd tasted fame and forgotten his vows to her. Or,
Scarlett wondered, he might have given up on Daisy, thinking she'd
given up on him. Daisy should remember that she had borne his
child, a claim that no one else could make. Daisy ran her fingers
through her tangled hair. She must be thinking how he had once
pursued her, but no longer. She tapped another query onto her
phone. "We can get him a message."

To get the attention of a celebrity on social media, you had to be
loud and conspicuous. For now, Scarlett had to stay hidden. For
now, she needed Daisy to stay hidden, too.

A photo of Daisy snuggling with their son would catch her boyfriend's eye—and any detective's.

"Here!" Daisy scrolled through the posts, photos of him at various
premieres, a different woman on his arm every night. She frowned.
"This one is full of links to knockoff Gucci purses. And Viagra."

A fake profile. Liberty batted away the spoon, no longer interested in eating, and Scarlett set her on the floor. The threat of Boss
Yeung loomed until—if—she got her papers, Scarlett reminded her.

Daisy set down the phone. "I'd give you mine tomorrow, if I
could." Her citizenship.

Scarlett couldn't bring herself to propose. Throughout most of
history, marriages didn't spring out of romance, but grew from
practical considerations of family compatibility and future prog-
eny. She certainly didn't have any illusion that a man would ever
present her with a ring, on bended knee. But Daisy might still have
that hope, and who was she to sully that? That *lala* couple—for
years, they'd been fighting for the right to declare their commitment before the law, before God, before their friends, family, and
community. But Scarlett wanted to exercise that right in order to
deceive.

Music blasted unexpectedly, William rapping, loud enough to

rattle the window and send concentric rings through a mug of tea gone cold. Her daughter, clutching the stereo's remote, must have turned up the volume. In the apartment above, their neighbor rapped on the wooden floor—quiet! Scarlett slid the remote a few centimeters away and Liberty didn't crawl so much as drag herself toward it, grunting from exertion. Daisy snapped a photo with the phone. Liberty used her left elbow to travel across the floor, a movement as ugly and awkward and determined as Scarlett's own journey in life had been. It was the first time either baby had crawled.

Scarlett and Daisy locked eyes. This achievement summoned up everything they'd survived until now. For the sake of Liberty's forward progress, Scarlett had to do whatever necessary to keep their family together.

"You can help," Scarlett told Daisy. "If we—if we get married." Eyes averted, she explained in a rush that the wedding reception she'd catered had been for a *lala* couple, an American who married a Chinese.

Daisy stared at her. "You're *lala*? You want me—that way?" She grimaced. "I don't feel that way about you." She wrapped her arms around herself, probably questioning every glance, every touch that had passed between them, as if every kindness by Scarlett had been a seduction.

No, Scarlett said. She wasn't *lala*, and she knew Daisy wasn't, either. If they married for show, then Scarlett could get her papers fixed.

"I'm hardly an American," Daisy said.

Scarlett popped the lid off the tin where they stored their important documents. She handed Daisy her passport: brand-new, stiff and unscratched, embossed with a gold eagle, proof of her claim to this country. "You're American enough."

"What will people—" Daisy said. "I don't want them to think I'm *that*. I don't have anything against *lalas*. But I'm not *that*."

Because Scarlett had never married, because no one knew she was dating Boss Yeung at the time, some at the factory might have harbored such suspicions about her. A gossipy clerk had once mentioned how a *lala* couple in Taiwan had married in a Buddhist ceremony, exchanging prayer beads instead of rings. She had studied

Scarlett, as if to see if she might flinch, might grimace, might reveal her inclinations.

"But who paid for the reception?" Scarlett had asked. By custom, Chinese grooms paid. With two brides, who knew? The clerk had laughed, and Scarlett felt as if she'd warded off an attack. She was not the *lala* her co-workers might have supposed, who engaged in acts they considered unnatural, crimes against nature, acts that were none of their business, traditional or not.

"You can marry William. Eventually, after college," Scarlett said.

Daisy flipped through the blank pages of her passport. As much as she loved him, in their months apart, she must have realized how little she knew him, how little she could predict of the life they might lead together. Like Scarlett with Liberty, she must have fallen in love with Didi more and more every day, his fat big toe, like a ballerina's *en pointe*, and his easygoing laugh. Scarlett had caught Daisy sniffing his tiny sweaty socks, which had his stink and no one else's. She must crave him viscerally, just as Scarlett craved Liberty. She gazed at her son. "Didi needs his father," Daisy said.

He gnawed on a soft chew toy with the enthusiasm of a beaver. On the bed, Liberty used all her might to drag herself forward, throwing out her arm as if at the edge of a cliff, practicing her new skill over and over again. Standing, walking, and running would come next.

"If anyone finds out—" Daisy said.

"No one has to know," Scarlett said. "No one except the government."

"Won't they be suspicious?" Daisy asked. "Won't they wonder if we're really *lala*?" She listed the consequences if they got caught: She might get thrown in jail, fined, or maybe have her own citizenship revoked. And Scarlett would be deported and banned from returning to the United States.

"That could happen to me, either way. Getting married gives me a chance to stay," Scarlett said. She had to break the law to be within the law.

"Won't they ask who the fathers are?" Daisy closed her passport and smoothed the cover.

The immigration officer should understand that matters of the heart were complicated, and that relationships might take as many twists as a hero's tale. They lived together, had for months, unlike many partners in a sham marriage, and unlike the men and women who wed and divorced overnight on a drunken binge or the celebrities who took vows for the publicity while the cameras rolled.

Getting married was another act of devotion, of the many they'd shared in forming a family and starting a business together. Some *lalas* had children—didn't they?—with men playing a minor role at conception.

"I got pregnant with a friend who donated his sperm," Scarlett said.

Daisy stared at her, until she realized Scarlett was lying. She looked down, thinking, before she triumphantly announced, "And I hooked up at a party!"

Later that morning, when Scarlett rang Casey, the redhead bride, the call went to voicemail. An iron band tightened around her chest. The newlyweds might have left for their honeymoon, turned off their phones, parked themselves in the mountains or along the coast or on an island where they couldn't be found for a week or two. She needed a referral for an immigration attorney, one who didn't bilk his clients, who had experience with *lala* marriages, who wouldn't judge or gawk, and she didn't know who else to ask. Down the hallway, a door slammed and someone pounded down the stairs in a hurry.

If she hired a lawyer in Chinatown, word might get out, and she and Daisy and their children would be shunned. Old Wu would be heartbroken that she'd kept this secret from him. Shrimp Boy and Manager Kwok might turn the scheme into a money-making racket; they'd tell other newcomers in need of papers to do the same, in the hopes of doubling the bookings for wedding banquets at the Pearl Pavilion. Immigration authorities would question the uptick in *lala* marriages.

She didn't leave a message. A moment later, the phone rang.

"Someone called my number?" Casey sounded hoarse after a late night.

Scarlett almost hung up. She shouldn't bother them on the day after their wedding.

Daisy put the phone on speaker. "It's Scarlett and Daisy."

A pause.

"From the *hanbaobao* cart," Scarlett said.

"We had leftovers this morning for breakfast!" Casey said. "So good! Thank you—people kept raving about it. Did you leave something at the house? We're around, if you need to come by."

If they went by the house, Casey and her wife would sniff out their deception at once. Scarlett cleared her throat. "Your lawyer . . . ?"

"My lawyer? Was there a problem with the contract?"

"We're getting married," Daisy said.

Casey gushed out her congratulations, the phone's speaker crackling, and said she'd text the attorney's number. "Tell her you know me."

A muffled voice called out on the other end of the line—Ying. Scarlett started sweating as Casey told her wife. What did Ying suspect? Silence, followed by ominous whispers until Casey brightly asked if they needed referrals for a photographer, for a florist, she had a spreadsheet of vendors and they should book soon. A newlywed in such bliss she wanted everyone in the world paired off and married, too.

"We're going to City Hall," Scarlett said.

"You'll need a witness," Casey said.

"Witness?" Scarlett couldn't hide her dismay. She couldn't ask Old Wu, Manager Kwok, or anyone in Chinatown. She served scores of customers every day, including regulars like Casey she wouldn't call friends but looked forward to seeing. But no one she could ask to join them at City Hall.

"We don't know many people. Not so popular, not like you two." Scarlett laughed nervously. "You had so many guests!"

"You can get the clerk or someone waiting at the office to sign," Casey said.

Scarlett wondered if the immigration officials would question a couple who couldn't come up with a single friend to celebrate with them.

"With the babies, with the business, we don't have much time for friends," Scarlett said. She was sharing too much; she felt as if she were trying out what she'd say in her green-card interview.

"You have a baby?" Casey asked.

Her tone, curious and concerned, gave Scarlett an idea. What if Casey and her wife were their witnesses? A friendship with another *lala* couple would bolster her immigration case.

"Babies," Daisy clarified. "A boy and a girl."

More whispers on the other end of the line. Ying might remember being alone in a new country, ignorant of local laws and customs, hoping for the kindness of strangers—including the stranger who became her wife. And Casey might feel a kinship with newcomers to America.

"There's so much we don't know," Scarlett said. She hoped they could hear the invitation and desperation in her voice. "We're lucky we met you."

"We'll come," Casey said.

"Are you—what about your honeymoon?" Scarlett asked.

"We're waiting until spring break," Casey said. "We'll be your witness. If you'll have us."


The immigration attorney said their petition would likely be flagged, due to Daisy's short tenure in the U.S., and because Scarlett's visa was about to expire at the time of their upcoming wedding ceremony. During the interview, officials would grill them on the facts and circumstances of their relationship.

In this neighborhood, old fashioned streetcars, sleek as lipstick tubes, rumbled along the grubby block of check-cashing shops and liquor stores. Adela, the lawyer, had the glamour of a movie spy, all dark curls and a throaty accent, and the steel to stand up to a judge. She ticked off a list of forms they'd need—joint tax returns, rental agreement, and life insurance with Scarlett and Daisy naming each other as beneficiaries—and questions authorities might ask. "Where did you meet, and when? Who proposed, and where?"

"Last year, on a retreat for pregnant women," Daisy said. Her son nestled in her lap, drooling. Liberty squawked like a parrot until Scarlett handed her keys to jingle.

Daisy said she'd proposed in their apartment after dinner. She and Scarlett had agreed it seemed less suspicious if the U.S. citizen asked—and not the foreigner angling for a green card—but what did they know?

Adela didn't take any notes. Their answers had to hold up, and so did they. This consultation seemed like the first of many character tests. "What do you like to do together?"

They said nothing. They hadn't prepared for that question.

"We—" Daisy switched into Mandarin. "There are too many questions! We can't answer them all."

"We'll have time to get ready," Scarlett said to her. If Daisy was caving in under the lightest interrogation, they would never survive the years-long charade and scrutiny. "Say something!"

"It's your turn." Daisy jiggled her son on her knee. On the long walk from Chinatown, she'd been quiet, and her reluctance felt sticky as tar.

A streetcar clanged outside. "We take walks," Scarlett said finally. She didn't sound convincing. If she and Liberty were deported to China, Didi would lose the girl he knew as his sister, and the woman he knew as another mother. And Scarlett would lose the woman she'd grown to trust. To love.

For Scarlett to become a permanent resident, they would have to document their relationship, keeping records of their joint bank account, billing address, and tax returns for the next two years, the lawyer said. So many forms, so much paperwork, she was sure to slip up. Convinced their bid would fail, Scarlett was ready to leave when her daughter threw the keys on the floor. Cheeks burning, she reached down, but the attorney retrieved them for her.

"Everyone says it gets easier," Adela said. "They're lying. Not until they're four."

She checked her computer screen. "I'll get everything in order." Not a guarantee, not a prediction, but a promise that she would guide them through the process.

"Do you have kids? How old are they?" Daisy asked.

"A four-year-old." Adela smiled.

It felt like an inside joke, shared between mothers of young children who understood the struggles of getting through the day intact, and starting all over again at dawn. Scarlett had never felt like she belonged, but right now, what she and Adela shared as parents mattered more than what they didn't.

The thrift shop sold clothes by the pound. Babies strapped to their backs, Scarlett and Daisy squeezed past the racks of Hawaiian shirts, fedoras, and plaid hunting caps, past the mannequin's legs in fishnet stockings pointed seductively in the air, past the crumpled loafers and scuffed heels and in the back—dimly lit, dusty, and tinged with body odor—they found the deflated wedding dresses. Cream and ivory and snow white, edged in sequins and lace, poufy gowns and slinky sheaths in itchy polyester, satin, and sheer rayon with the mothball smell of decades past, of old memories and forgotten ones, the sour hint of broken engagements and jilted brides cleaning out their closets.

As they'd been leaving the attorney's office, Daisy had suggested coming here. Scarlett hadn't known such stores existed, not in China, where you spun and sewed your clothes yourself when you couldn't afford store-bought, and when you could, you splurged on the latest fashions. No one wanted to look poor. The factory girls would have passed up secondhand clothing as dirty, tainted with bad luck or with rejection, and Countess Tien and Lady Yu would have deemed it unfit to use as cleaning rags.

According to Daisy, Levi's, cotton tees, and other used clothes from America were popular in Taipei among the arty and rich. Even if all the garments were—as Scarlett pointed out—originally made in China, in a journey that zigzagged around the world, by cargo ship to the West and on a return trip to the East by air, stowed away in the suitcase of a jet-setting boutique owner.

In the mirror, Scarlett held a dress up to herself, the hem rustling on the floor, the lace scratchy as brambles against her neck. She twitched, her skin crawling when she pictured herself going into the dressing room, exposing her sagging belly, wide hips, and stretch marks on her thighs to the harsh lights, and tugging at the unforgiving fabric, the seams straining against her body.

Daisy had a silky frock draped over her arm that Scarlett could tell would flatter her, suitable for an outdoor wedding, for a bride barefoot with hair long and loose. With an expert eye, she plucked another from the rack, with a trumpet skirt, long sleeves, and empire waist, plain but elegant, and handed it to Scarlett.

The teenager loved to dress up, to consider the possibilities. Only this morning, she was a reluctant bride-to-be, but now excitement lit her eyes and flushed her cheeks. For a moment, it seemed she could forget her fears of getting caught in a sham marriage. A moment that Scarlett wanted to draw out to keep the game going, to coax Daisy into joining her at the altar. She reached for a dress festooned with bows and thrust the rustling cloud at Daisy. "In case the other one doesn't fit."

Daisy studied the dress and smiled, apparently understanding the rules without explanation. She selected one for Scarlett, with puffy sleeves and a bodice encrusted with fake diamonds that might have been stylish when she was an infant. They took adjoining dressing rooms, where Scarlett set her daughter on a blanket on the floor. She stroked Liberty's head. Had her own mother ever touched her with such tenderness? She must have, but Scarlett couldn't remember.

She wiggled out of her clothes with her back to the mirror, her nipples erect and tender in the drafty room. After slipping on the gown, tulle cascading over her like beer foam, she stepped out and discovered Daisy wearing her dress—or rather, the oversized dress was wearing her. She gripped handfuls of fabric to keep it from slipping off her otter's body.

They grinned, carefree and silly as they were only with their babies, never with themselves. They were infected by an air of mischief, as if pulling off a prank, or preparing for opening night of a performance. They linked arms and walked solemnly toward the full-length mirror.

She and her sister used to dig through their mother's closet, Daisy said. She'd been a bride many times. "I made veils out of toilet paper."

They poked at each other's skirts. "How do you get through a crowd in these big dresses?" Scarlett asked.

"You don't," Daisy said. "People get out of your way."

They changed into the gowns Daisy had picked. This time, when Scarlett zipped up the dress, the underwire stiff as armor, she no longer felt giddy, but intent, as if suiting up for war. The silky material felt light and soft against her skin. She inhaled, seeking a hint of the previous owner's perfume, but she detected only the chemical scent of dry-cleaning. No matter if the marriage had ended after three days or three decades, or if the couple was still happily married, the dress would lend its glamour to Scarlett. How would Boss Yeung react if he saw her now, dressed like a bride? Would he remember the salt on her skin, the sticky warmth of their bodies under clean cotton sheets, feel regret—or disgust? She'd take anything, anything but his indifference. Liberty was cooing, giggling on the floor, her hands reaching to stroke the satin. Scarlett picked her up and found Daisy in the hallway equally transformed—not a girl playing dress up, but a woman, a mother, a bride getting married, in the eyes of the law if not in God's. Her wife, her life.

They scheduled their ceremony at City Hall in the first slot available, just before Scarlett's visa expired. Because they couldn't walk through Chinatown in their bridal finery, they had to stuff their dresses into crinkly black garbage sacks and tiptoe past their nosy neighbors. Auntie Ng called out as they were exiting the building, asking where they were going so early in the morning. They slammed the door behind them.

At City Hall, they heaved their bags and empty strollers onto the conveyer belt at the guard station, and changed in the handicapped stall of the public bathroom. They couldn't both fit, and had to leave the stall door open for extra room. The floor was gritty and chilly beneath Scarlett's bare feet. She slid on her silver-sequined shoes, bracing herself against the handrail, trying not to drop the hem into the toilet, which reeked of disinfectant and urine. Old Wu had scavenged the shoes for her months ago, but she hadn't worn them until now. In his infatuation, he'd seen her as she couldn't see herself, as someone who would have occasions for such impractical, glamorous footwear. She felt guilty for hiding her marriage to Daisy, one of the many secrets she kept from him. If he'd known, he could have walked her down the aisle, given her away like in the movies.

She expected to get married in a dreary room with battered office furniture, but after they checked in, the clerk, a brisk black woman with ornate braids swept into a crown, informed them the judge was marrying couples under the rotunda that day. "Up the stairs and under the dome."

Each tucked a bouquet of wilting roses from the corner drugstore under her arm. With one hand, they pushed a stroller, and with the other, they hoisted the hems of their heavy, slippery dresses. A woman passing by exclaimed, "What beautiful dresses! Congratulations!" Scarlett forced a smile at the well-wishes of a stranger, but Daisy remained stone-faced.

They rode up one floor, the pulleys groaning and squeaking, and when the elevator doors parted onto the rotunda, a flash greeted them. Under the dome flooded with light like a cathedral, Casey snapped pictures and tied blue ribbons to their wrists. "For good luck," she said, explaining the old English tradition. It was too late for Scarlett to find something borrowed or new. She'd have to treat it like any other superstition: focus on what fell in her favor and ignore the rest.

For the album they'd present to immigration officials, she and Daisy would toast each other with plastic flutes of sparkling apple cider beside a frilly white cake. Chatter floated up from the ground floor, punctuated by the ding of the elevators.

While waiting for their turn, Daisy checked her phone. She'd been obsessively logging on to William's website several times a day. She gasped. He announced that he was taking a break, going home to the Bay Area for his mother's birthday.

She had to write him.

"Two months," Scarlett said. Two months until she received her conditional green card, but their attorney warned that the waiting period could be much longer.

"I'll send it in code. Something only he knows I know," Daisy said.

"He might already know," Scarlett said, something that only just now occurred to her.

"The detective almost found us. They must have found his parents."

Daisy frowned. Scarlett shouldn't have voiced her suspicion without knowing for certain, but she needed to stop Daisy from sending out a desperate new message that revealed too much— a photo of their son? their address?—that would lead authorities straight to them. He hadn't sought her out, for any number of reasons that must now worry Daisy. He might have decided against trying to find her because of his career, or maybe he'd fallen out of love with her.

Daisy's complexion had gone wan as a frog's belly. "He can't know. He doesn't know. Maybe his parents didn't tell him."

Their turn arrived. The judge peered over his black binder at them, his expression stern.

"I have to try," Daisy said.

The cellophane on the bouquet crinkled in Scarlett's sweaty hands. The judge was going to proclaim them frauds. "We're getting married."

"We're not married yet," Daisy said loudly.

A couple of meters away, Casey and her wife watched with concern. "Need a moment?" the judge asked. "But only a moment."

The next party waited behind a set of marble posts while a maid of honor fluffed the bride's train. Scarlett put her arm around Daisy and they turned their backs on the judge and their witnesses. Daisy trembled, Scarlett tightened her grip, and they both went still, amazed by the view down the broad staircase where a fleeing princess might drop her glass slipper. More flashes of light, snapped by Japanese tourists visiting San Francisco, entranced by the exotic sight of *lala* brides.

"Please." Scarlett held her breath. Every silent vow they'd made to each other had been building up to today's, the only one the bureaucrats recognized. Didi squealed and Liberty cooed, a reminder of the family Daisy had formed, whom she could count on and who counted on her.

Daisy nodded. They turned around to face the judge, who sped through the ceremony. He told them to join their hands, and Casey gathered their rings and roses. Daisy's hands in hers were small and sweaty as mice in a den, and they stared at each other in mutual terror as the gravity of this undertaking sank in. Boss Yeung hadn't remained faithful to his wife. Many couples didn't—maybe most— and yet dozens were gathering here to proclaim their commitment, among the hundreds, thousands who would marry across the country today. Tempting fate and staking a claim, an act of faith even for the godless.

"No words of mine or any other person truly marry you," the judge said. "You marry each other when you exchange your vows and commit yourself to this union."

Scarlett slipped the ring onto Daisy's finger, the cheap band tugging on her skin, pale as candle wax. Daisy did the same.

"You may now kiss," the judge said. They hadn't practiced, hadn't discussed it, though they had known of its eventuality. They leaned in and a flash fired. Their mouths brushed together with a lukewarm passion that Daisy remedied by cradling Scarlett's face in her hands. Her lips were soft and warm. Scarlett breathed in the deeper scent of her, the salt and heat that she had come to know in their months together, a scent that had become as familiar as her own.

# Chapter 22

**Boss Yeung** unlatched the cage and slipped the rat a treat. Sleek, spotted like a Holstein, it sat on its hind legs, gnawing at the oversized chocolate chip cookie that he'd saved from lunch. He never could abide wasting food, even if he no longer had much of an appetite. This rat had to be hungry, like all the specimens in this laboratory, where researchers were studying how starvation could lengthen life. The bony rats survived on a third of the calories of their typical diet, and must spend their days dreaming of gray-green pellets. Raised in the lab from birth, they'd never known the pleasures of their wild cousins who pawed through the trash eating pizza crusts and meat scraps, and died young, fat, and happy.

Uncle Lo's entourage had arrived yesterday and the university officials had arranged tours of the research facilities, a private session for his niece with the equestrian coach, a round of golf on the campus course, a private consultation with the chief oncologist for Boss Yeung, and a reception this evening at the museum.

It seemed Uncle Lo wanted to associate his family's name with Stanford, and burnish his reputation as pioneering and benevolent. But Boss Yeung had misunderstood how wide his friend's ambition stretched; Uncle Lo didn't want to live on only through his deeds. Like many a modern mogul, he wanted to live forever, to conquer death as he'd conquered his rivals, and the research he was funding at Stanford examined how a man might someday live for centuries. No doubt, Uncle Lo would be the very first beneficiary.

Despite the powerful ventilation system, the air was rank with rat urine and antiseptic, and the VIP guests hurried out of the lab, Uncle Lo in the lead, trailed closely by the development officer and the interpreter, a young woman who spoke rapidly with no emotion, her movements jerky as a windup doll.

Until the stop in the animal lab, Boss Yeung hadn't paid much attention to the tour. He'd missed Scarlett even more keenly since his arrival in California, a knot of longing at his throat. Everything he'd loved about her, her boldness and her determination, had come rushing back. This morning, he brought her childhood notebook onto the balcony of the hotel room, holding it out in front of him like a dowsing rod. No quivering led him to her or their son. After visiting her village, he felt closer to Scarlett than he had in months, closer even than when they'd been together, and yet she remained out of reach. She'd never forgive him for asking her to give up their son.

The lab would have amused her. Brilliant minds and tens of millions of dollars were devoted to investigating the lean meals of her childhood. He wanted her at his side, navigating, remarking. He missed those moments of content silence settling between them.

The rat finished off the cookie, twitching with frantic energy. Its brain must be short-circuiting with this blast of sugar and fat. Its saucer ears, veined and delicate as a fairy's wing, tiny paws that could have sewn a puppet's clothes, and shiny black eyes. Apparently, some Americans kept rats as pets, but you could never forget that these vermin snatched food from your mouth. You had to be vigilant. At Boss Yeung's shortbread cookie plant, the foreman kept the premises sanitary and secure from all such creatures.

"Baba?" Viann asked. Her first word, the tender name she had reverted to after he'd fallen ill. She asked if he needed to sit down; he looked as if he might faint. Uncle Lo had insisted they both come on this trip. A farewell of sorts, though none of them admitted it, the last time Boss Yeung might be continent and coherent.

It was early February, in the weeks following the Spring Festival, when their factories closed. Until the holiday, Viann had been traveling to mainland China at least once a week, lining up several deals with new clients. While he'd been under treatment, she'd dreamed up an anniversary marketing push for the shortbread division: a commemorative tin that doubled as a clutch, a raft of testimonials from Hong Kong's stars, and status as the exclusive tea time supplier for the national football team. He'd never doubted her, but hadn't known if the world would respect her. It turned out the world had changed, and he hadn't. He'd always viewed himself as a man who cast aside convention, but somehow, he'd gone backward. For too long, he'd hampered Viann, and soon enough she'd start her own empire if he didn't rethink his succession plans. If he survived, if he found his son, little brother would have much to learn from elder sister.

In the next lab they visited, a scientist—a woman with a skunk's streak of silver hair—explained how the gene sequencer worked. The machine, glossy white, striped with a pulsing, sapphire band of light, resembled a spaceship's warp drive and spent twenty-four hours a day sequencing DNA samples, drawn from blood or saliva and dropped onto a glass slide. The laboratory hummed: the sequencing machines, the stack of data servers guarded behind a cage, the refrigerator with the glass door filled with racks of test tubes, and the buzz of fluorescent lights. A song that sounded like the future, like the whoosh of a mother's blood flow to a baby in utero.

"You can clone me from a drop of blood?" Uncle Lo joked through the interpreter.

"Not quite," the scientist said.

"Not yet."

Didn't Uncle Lo realize that a gathering of his clones would lead to a bloody battle to the death? If they didn't first band together to rise up against him. Uncle Lo's brother yawned. Never Theodore or Ted, but still and forever Teddy, the younger brother. They looked nothing alike, Uncle Lo lean and pale as a fish, his brother dark, stocky, and barrel-chested—the differences that must have made people whisper that their mother had an affair. Infidelity might run in the family.

High on the wall, a painting featured futuristic skyscrapers at night, shining with green, blue, red, and yellow lights. Tokyo or Kuala Lumpur? Boss Yeung didn't recognize the skyline.

"Where is this?"

The researcher laughed. "It's me." A few of her DNA sequences had been isolated to create the image. "It's one of a kind."

Uncle Lo's eyes gleamed. "So you can tell me if I'm smarter than most people? Or if I'll live longer?"

"It's complicated," the scientist said. "Those traits aren't determined by any one gene. But we're looking into those questions."

"Can you tell if someone will come down with certain illnesses?" Viann didn't look at Boss Yeung. His chest ached. The sole blessing, if she wasn't his daughter—she wouldn't have to worry about inheriting this sickness. His son might.

"A few," the scientist said. She squared her shoulders. "More each year." A decade ago, it took nine months and a hundred million dollars to sequence a single human genome. Now you could sequence fetal DNA by sampling the father's saliva and the mother's blood. Another test used a drop of blood to detect every virus that had ever infected you.

Blood, saliva. The cigar he'd recovered didn't have enough to sample, but Boss Yeung had been harvesting more bodily fluids on this trip: Uncle Lo's crumpled napkin on the airplane, the plastic wineglass that he'd pinched from the flight, saved in a baggie for testing upon their return to Hong Kong. But he didn't have to wait, not with these machines, not in a lab designed to collect specimens tapped straight from the vein.

"Let's give it a try," Boss Yeung said. "Let's get sequenced." The ultimate vanity, to declare your body a continent worthy of exploration.

"It's not a toy," Viann said. "You can't interrupt their experiments."

"They'll do whatever we want." He looked at Uncle Lo. "When I'm gone, you'll have this. If you have a map of me, maybe you can find me again."

A map. Scarlett had treasured that view from above, charting their route, tracing her finger along hundreds of kilometers of roads. No doubt, she'd teach their son how to orient himself. Their son who might never know that his father had cherished him.

The interpreter's gaze ping-ponged between them until Uncle Lo told her, "You heard what he said!"

The development officer pulled the scientist aside. Though Boss Yeung couldn't make out the words, he could see her pleading expression, asking for a favor, a sacrifice for the sake of the university, for her research. The officer must have dealt with enough billionaires to know she couldn't buy off donors with a box lunch, souvenir T-shirt, and a visor. Until a donor's check cleared, she could never assume commitment.

A lab tech led them to a chair and drew blood samples from Boss Yeung and Uncle Lo. A familiar ritual: the rubber tourniquet and its powdery balloon smell, the tech gently tapping for a vein, Boss Yeung's hand clenched into a fist, and the pinch of the needle. Everyone else declined, including Viann, but he needed a sample from her to compare against Uncle Lo's.

"Afraid of the sight of your own blood?" Boss Yeung said.

She shook her head. "They've got enough to work on."

"They have the capacity." Boss Yeung spread his arms to take in all the machines in the lab. Teddy, stepping aside, knocked over a bottle on the counter, a cloudy white plastic vessel that bounced once and rolled underneath a cabinet. He flushed. He clasped his hands in front of him, and then behind him, with the resigned expression of a handcuffed suspect being led to a police car.

"This generation is afraid to spill any blood," Uncle Lo said mockingly, exasperated yet affectionate, a tone he employed when he expected them both to obey.

Viann and Teddy glanced at each other, and it seemed they didn't like getting categorized as cowards.

"You're always talking about the future, how we have to prepare for the future," Boss Yeung told Viann. "It will only take a minute."

She couldn't deny him his wish. She rolled up her sleeve, and after hesitating, Teddy followed. He didn't want to seem more cowardly than a girl. He presented his fleshy forearm, and looked away as the needle slid in. Viann bit her lip, watching as blood gushed into the vial.

* * *

Later, while everyone rested at the hotel before the reception, Boss Yeung hopped a cab back to Stanford. They drove slowly around campus, past the stately groves of eucalyptus trees giving off their menthol scent, the sandstone buildings and the red terra-cotta tile roofs that resembled an Italian prince's villa. It didn't take him long to spot the research building, a series of blocks in green glass, sandstone, and copper panels. He told the driver to wait.

The front door was locked. When a student biked up, she didn't question him following her into the building. He got into the elevator and tried to remember where the lab was located. They'd walked endless corridors today, ferried around the spacious campus by a fleet of golf carts. Students had zipped by on mountain bikes and joggers pounded past with the determination that plowed down the weak.

On the second floor, nothing looked familiar—or rather, everything did, and each lab could have been the one he'd visited. The next floor up, he wandered past the custodian, turned the corner and recognized the sign upon which someone had affixed a smiley face sticker. He knocked, but no one answered. Peeking into the window, he didn't see the scientist or her technicians, who might have stepped out for a beer to complain about having to satisfy the whims of a Chinese billionaire. He tried the doorknob. Locked. He was due in the lobby of their hotel in a half hour, and the cab ride back would take up most of the time.

The custodian must have keys. He found her emptying the trash in another lab, a sturdy coffee-colored woman who unlocked the door after he explained that he'd left behind his sweater. His English mangled, but she understood with the help of pantomime. The gene sequencers whirred, processing day and night the information coursing through his body. He felt as if he stood in the temple of a strange god for whom he'd left an offering. He spread his hand on the sequencer, cool to the touch, the vibrations purring through him.

The tech had explained that his blood would be spun down to extract a clear syrup of DNA, followed by another step to prepare it for the sequencer. The remainder of his DNA would be stored in the refrigerator until the lab completed testing. He pulled out a rack of tubes labeled not with names but barcodes. The tubes clinking, his hands sweaty. If he dropped it—disaster. Would the tech place the most recent samples in the front, or wherever there was space available? He couldn't steal all the tubes—the lab would notice the theft at once, and how could he carry them all?

He spied a red plastic biohazard box, a kind he'd come to know during his many injections at the hospital. The tech must have disposed of the vials that held their blood in here. He popped open the lid and with a pen, ferreted out the four labeled with today's date and their names. It seemed enough blood remained to test. He looked up to see the janitor, still standing in the doorway, staring at him. He apologized and stumbled out, the vials digging into his thigh, pulsing with a life of their own.

At sunset in the sculpture garden, the light fell low and flattering, and the crisp scent of cypress hung in the air. While a string quartet played, guests sipped wine and mingled with the jovial university president, two Nobel Prize–winning professors, and the trustees whose interest in China and its riches went far beyond the fiduciary. There was talk of the Great Wall, of pandas, of how both countries might prosper together. Boss Yeung sipped hot water with lemon, his body damp from the exertions of the late afternoon. When the waiter offered a tray of bacon wrapped shrimp, Uncle Lo cajoled Viann, "Eat! You look like a little girl."

"I'm full."

"Too thin!" said Uncle Lo, flush, vital, and impeccably dressed in a tailored buttoned-up shirt, his tie knotted tight as a fist.

She waved off the tray.

"No man wants a scrawny chicken."

"Enough!" Boss Yeung said.

Uncle Lo popped one into his mouth. "More for me." He clapped his hands and unveiled a surprise for his grandchildren: the Guardian, the brand-new American-born sensation, back home for a special private performance.

The next moment, a lean young man bounded in front of *The*

*Gates of Hell*, Rodin's sculpture of twisted bodies emerging from the weathered bronze. On top of the concrete pavilion, a stool, microphone stand, and guitar had materialized. He started off with an acoustic version of his hit "I Love You Hot." His falsetto had a mosquito's whine, but his voice was distinctive and Boss Yeung caught himself humming along. If his son remained in America, would he—like the Guardian—someday have such curiosity about China and things Chinese? If Uncle Lo hadn't told him, he'd never have known that this young Chinese fellow didn't even speak Cantonese. He must have memorized the sounds like a seal—er, er, er.

Uncle Lo's niece swooned, her hands clasped under her chin, swaying to the melody, while his nephew snapped photos—Teddy's children. Boss Yeung retreated into the garden, where the shadows of the statues were long and inky as wraiths. By tomorrow, he'd know Viann's paternity. The concierge at the hotel had been courteous and discreet, promising to find a local laboratory that could run a paternity test with utmost speed.

Though the information would bring Boss Yeung no closer to his son, he felt it would give him a measure of certainty and control now missing in his life. He studied a statue mounted on a pedestal: a frowning man, his hooded eyes staring into infinity. The statue's broad nose was as big as Boss Yeung's fist. He wanted to ask Scarlett what she thought of the sculptor's intentions, if he'd wanted to impress or to terrify. He stroked the statue's cheek, rippled and solid, still warm from the sun. The model had long since died, but his likeness lived on. Boss Yeung's thoughts went still; he felt suspended, floating in a depthless pool.

He heard the sound of voices carried on the breeze. Uncle Lo and Viann, standing by a tall hedge, their backs to him. Their absence must worry the development officer and the university president, but Uncle Lo abided by no schedule except his own.

Boss Yeung crept in a wide circle and positioned himself on the other side of the hedge. They were talking loudly, their tongues loosened by the glasses of champagne. He was jealous of their ease, of their banter, of their certainty in their continued existence. Even if he'd stood beside them, he might not have warranted their attention. He heard snatches of their conversation: a call from Mama Fang, traced to San Francisco, to Chinatown. The Pearl Pavilion.

"A dead end," Uncle Lo said.

Until now, he'd assumed that Uncle Lo kept the investigation confidential, but it sounded as though he and Viann had been discussing the case for months. He felt betrayed all over again, as if they'd cheated on him. Bile welled up in the back of his throat.

"Doesn't Mama Fang know anything?" Viann asked.

She was in delicate health after the amputation, Uncle Lo said. Her left foot. Boss Yeung's own foot tingled. It was the first he'd heard of her troubles. He despised Mama Fang, but never would have wished her such a fate.

"Scarlett is bad luck," Viann said. "For anyone she meets."

"After we find her, the only bad luck will be her own."

Viann said nothing, seemingly taken aback by this vengeful talk, and after a long pause, she outlined a new plan to ensure Scarlett and the baby never bothered the Yeungs again. Once they'd tracked down Scarlett, she could stay in the United States on a green card purchased for a half-million dollars through the immigrant investor program that was popular among well-to-do Chinese.

"I'll pay you back," Viann said.

"It's yours," Uncle Lo said. "The baby won't do much for your father, but will cause trouble for you." Maybe he'd had second thoughts about retaliation, or maybe he could tell how much Viann wanted a different destiny for Scarlett, one that kept her out of a labor camp, but put her—and her child—far from the Yeungs.

Viann exhaled, a shuddering breath of relief. They were conspiring against him, ignoring what might be his final wishes. Viann wasn't acting out of compassion, but out of self-interest. Boss Yeung's rage nearly lifted him out of his shoes, and he had to stop himself from tackling Uncle Lo and grinding his face in the dirt. His body was coiled, ready to strike, months of suspicions now culminating in his fists.

The song ended and the Guardian started another. Viann and Uncle Lo turned toward *The Gates of Hell*. Boss Yeung followed, his creaking bones rattling into motion. Their backs straight, arms pumping, their strides long enough to cross valleys. They out-stripped him and would go so much farther than he ever could.

Boss Yeung spread out three manila folders on his desk at the hotel. He'd obtained three copies of the paternity report, one for Viann and one for her father—for Uncle Lo.

He'd been preparing himself for this eventuality for so long he felt neither shock nor the heat of anger, only the bitter satisfaction that he had uncovered the truth. For decades, Uncle Lo had been dictating the terms and conditions of Boss Yeung's life. He wouldn't stop meddling, not until the end, not until he'd planned the parade route and musical selections for his funeral. Not unless Boss Yeung struck back as Uncle Lo had struck him.

The third copy of the report was for Teddy. The man wasn't Uncle Lo's younger brother, but his son. His son! He reeled at all the pos-sibilities this information presented.

Uncle Lo had fathered a legion of bastards: Teddy, Viann, and who knew how many more? Armed with the facts, Teddy might challenge Uncle Lo, might upset the precarious order that kept the twelve heirs in check and drag his newfound brothers and sisters into a palace bloodbath.

Viann was coming by shortly to take him to an appointment with a specialist at the university hospital, but he wanted no more of the pricking and prodding, no more experimental treatments. She had plotted with Uncle Lo, and that wounded him most of all. And yet, if she knew the truth, she'd cut her mother and Uncle Lo out of her life. When Boss Yeung passed on—and he would, he would—she would be orphaned.

He stacked the reports on the table, fanned them out, and stacked them again. Uncle Lo had promised Viann not to go after Scarlett, but what if he reneged? Boss Yeung could stop him by threatening to report him. The Party had been cracking down on the decadent and the depraved, after that eight-person orgy of officials went viral, and a spy chief had been caught with six mistresses, each in-stalled in her own villa. Uncle Lo, who seemed to be harboring po-litical aspirations, would want to protect his interests. If he agreed

to end his feud against Scarlett, Boss Yeung would keep the bastards a secret.

At last, his friend might respect him, for a game well played, a
final wrestling move that flipped him incontestably onto his back. A
move Uncle Lo believed only he had mastered, that he didn't think
Boss Yeung had in him. He locked the folders in the hotel safe, slid
on his shoes, and hobbled out.

# Chapter 23

A few weeks after she and Daisy married, they returned to the palatial City Hall for a *lala* festival. Scarlett had lived her life among the masses, chanting slogans with her classmates on National Day or packed into plazas singing the national anthem, but never like this, united in a purpose outside of the Party's. Rainbow flags snapped in the breeze. The crowd spilled over the lawn in a red-orange-yellow-green-blue-purple explosion, in their crowns of paper flowers, glittering plastic bead necklaces, tutus, knee socks, and feathers.

Daisy had insisted they attend. They needed more pictures to prepare for their immigration interview, and she could practice running the cart, whose income they would report as hers until Scarlett received a work permit. To build a paper trail, they'd filed for a permit for the festival, and set up the cart not far from the stage, tucking the babies in a playpen under a mottled sycamore tree.

William hadn't replied to Daisy's cryptic notes posted to his feed, which gave clues about McDonald's apple pies and the night market in Taipei. She'd suggested he perform at this rally in San Francisco and take part in this historic moment. A message in a bottle speeding along currents, with the chance of getting a response just as remote. Maybe he wasn't checking, or he thought it was a scam. Or he no longer cared.

Scarlett handed buns to the babies, who buried their faces into the softness of the bread. Liberty grasped the roll with both hands, her expression serious, methodically nibbling, while Didi nipped with the eagerness of a puppy. She piled toys and books around them, the stuffed caterpillar and a plastic mirror. Didi lost himself in activities, insisted on emptying a box of toys one by one, protesting if they ended his playtime. He wanted to see every task to its end and put everything in its place.

Liberty was curious and demanding, with an inherited restlessness that she wouldn't outgrow and would have to learn to resist. Sometimes when Scarlett interrupted, her daughter pulled away, eyes flashing with a thermonuclear defiance, a heat that fed off itself.

The sticky sweet scent of marijuana smoke drifted from somewhere in the park. Under the high blue dome of the sky, it felt like spring, not the middle of winter. Onstage, the speaker was talking about the fight that began ten years ago. Daisy was a quick study, careful not to dish up too much meat or slop on the sauce, topping off her attempt with an artful sprinkling of scallions. Some customers slid cardboard signs under their arms—EQUAL LOVE NOW! and NOW WE ARE MORE AMERICAN—as they ate, while others had attached fluttering Stars and Stripes and rainbow flags onto their backpacks. Once the line started getting longer, Daisy became flustered. When Scarlett touched her arm to put her at ease, Daisy frowned. Neither of them had been one of those girls who snuggled with their friends, or linked elbows while walking down the street, tilted their heads together at the movies; they'd have to work on their casual public affection.

In Chinatown, they hid their rings and their change in status. Another secret. A lie of omission that should have been easy to carry out, and yet Scarlett felt guilty for deceiving Old Wu and their neighbors. Elsewhere, she and Daisy had to remember to call each other *my wife*. Strange to say, but less strange than if she had used Chinese endearments, *laopo*—the woman she'd grow old with—or *haizita*, the mother of her children. Eventually, their marriage would end and she had no doubt Daisy would become another's *laopo*, another's wife. Scarlett might never again.

Daisy pushed back her bangs, smearing plum sauce on her forehead. "The steam trays should go in reverse, and customers could pick up from this side. Flow from left to right," Daisy said. Though she disagreed, Scarlett nodded. The more involved Daisy became in the cart, Scarlett thought, the less time she'd have to yearn for a ghost.

Didi studied the crowd with an intensity that could penetrate concrete and Liberty tugged at her socks. Daisy told Scarlett that she was leaving to take pictures of the festival for their photo album, to show they were part of the *lala* community. Scarlett called after her, holding up a *hanbaobao*. "You haven't had anything to eat."

"Later," Daisy said.

Unless Scarlett could summon Daisy's boyfriend out of the air, unless she could promise his love, nothing she did would soothe her. Scarlett fiddled with her wedding band, already tarnishing. The crowd smelled like the beach, suntan lotion, and sweat. Techno pumped out from the speaker, the beat throbbing through her. She checked her phone. She'd missed a call from Manager Kwok. A woman with hair dyed the color of whiskey asked if Scarlett had considered installing an online ordering system. Customers made suggestions all the time, asking for a chance to franchise, invest, or build a website; last week, someone had proposed serving *hanbaobao* on the jet of a tech mogul. Scarlett had a sheaf of business cards in bold colors on stiff and heavy paper from people who wanted to work with her—for her. Outlandish ambitions that grew less outlandish with each repetition, and if she wasn't careful, she, too, might believe she could achieve the wealth and might of an emperor. Here in America, she might change the world—but she had to hurry before someone else did.

The Pearl Pavilion neared the end of lunch service, its busboys clanking dirty dishes into the cart, the air thick with grease and the scent of chives and steamed dumplings. Spilled rice that resembled maggots and balled-up napkins littered the gold-and-brown swirls on the carpet. Boss Yeung had been sitting at a table for hours but hadn't found Scarlett here, not as a cart lady, not in the kitchen, not as a customer. He'd been foolish to think he could find her where the detective could not. The waitress dropped off his check. She was busty, the seams straining on her red satin tunic top. She caught Boss Yeung staring and snapped at him, asking if he needed anything else. He didn't want to ask about Scarlett outright. If she heard he was looking for her, she'd bolt, but he had no other recourse.

"Is there someone here named Scarlett? Who comes here, works here? She has a baby boy."

The waitress shook her head.

"Scarlett might not be her name." How strange he must sound!

A customer at the next table waved his order sheet at her, ready to pay. As she turned to leave, Boss Yeung showed the waitress the blurry selfie recovered from Ma's phone and uploaded to his own. The waitress seemed irritated, but did he glimpse recognition in her eyes?

"Is there anyone else who might know?" Boss Yeung asked. "The manager?"

No, she said.

From across the dining room, a man in a blue blazer stared at him, his gelled hair like the prow of a ship, his mouth in a tight line. He muttered to a busboy, who nodded and hurried away. Did he work here? Boss Yeung couldn't shake the suspicion that the man harbored ill will toward him. He loathed his shriveled body that made him the target of any would-be mugger or con man.

Walking through Chinatown, he searched the streets for Scarlett and their son, willing them to appear. He ended up by a Chinese dressmaker's shop, where a bridal cheongsam hung in the window, cavorting dragons and phoenixes stitched in gold on red silk. Scarlett used to work at a garment factory sewing evening gowns. Maybe she'd come here looking for a job. Besides, seamstresses gossiped, didn't they, in the long hours bent over their stitches?

Particles of dust and sheared cloth sparkled in a shaft of light coming through the shop window. The interior was hushed as a temple, the bolts of satin and silk and cotton absorbing every sound. The air smelled of chalk. The salesclerk ignored him until Boss Yeung announced in Cantonese that his daughter was getting married. He steadied himself on the counter, a glass display case of rhinestone barrettes. Would he live to see Viann married, to hold his first grandchild? Live to see his products sold in every country and on the moon under Viann's direction?

The clerk thrust a business card at him, curtly replied he'd have to get on a waiting list, and warned that his daughter might have plans of her own.

With his slumped posture and sickly complexion, Boss Yeung must seem an unlikely sales prospect, too poor to afford the services of a custom tailor. He assured her that his daughter was interested, but she was busy, with an important job, and had sent him to Chinatown to collect information on vendors, the florist, the invitations, and banquet halls.

"What do you think about the Pearl Pavilion?" he asked.

She sniffed that the restaurant was living off its reputation. "They skimp on the meat." The Pearl Pavilion must have fallen on hard financial times, she said, because the manager was letting a lady street hawker use its kitchen to make roast pork buns called *hanbaobao*.

"Are the buns any good?" Boss Yeung asked.

"Not for me, not for you," the clerk said. "For the young people."

She summoned her assistant, Windy, who emerged from the stockroom. "Where's the *hanbaobao* girl from?" Boss Yeung asked.

Windy didn't know, but was almost certain she'd seen the woman in Chinatown, shopping at a market with her baby.

Her baby. He swayed, his knees weak. The clerk asked if he needed to sit down, if they should call his daughter. No, he said. The cart, where could he find the cart?

At night, outside the bars and clubs a few blocks away in North Beach, Windy said. "But not always the same place, same time. You feel lucky if you find it."

"What nonsense!" her boss said. "Why would a business make it hard for you to find it?"

Boss Yeung had to agree. The *hanbaobao* cart was starting to sound mythical, Scarlett and their baby, too.

"Sometimes you can find it online." Windy tapped on her phone and showed him an app where people posted sightings of different food trucks and carts. If you were first to post it, you received more points. "It's like a game."

"Not any game I'd like to play," her boss said.

Windy scrolled through the entries. "I'm not seeing anything," she said regretfully.

He turned to leave and had reached the door when she shouted *"Waaaah!"* and called out the latest location of the *hanbaobao* cart: City Hall.


All around Scarlett, people snapped photos, overhead shots of the rally, of themselves, as if the moment didn't exist until it had been recorded. Towers of stereo speakers flanked the stage and at close range, the words coming out were more felt than heard. Two burly men bear-hugged, and a pair of women—both willowy, one copper-skinned, the other terra-cotta—swayed together, their eyes closed. In the midst of the crowd, Scarlett felt the rumble of a single heart beating, shaking her from the top of her head to the soles of her feet.

She didn't recognize the man until he said her name, his voice hoarse with illness or with emotion. He was scrawny as a baby chick, his face mottled, his back hunched, his step shuffling.

Boss Yeung.

Her body went heavy, filled with sand. She couldn't move, she couldn't speak, and the buzz from the crowd was suddenly coming from inside her skull. She'd feared this man, feared this day for months. She exhaled, her hands balled into fists. She'd never pictured him so fragile. If she shoved him—how she wanted to!—his rib cage might snap. She wanted him anguished and repentant, not dying. Not dead.

He was alone. She rushed over to the playpen, where Liberty gnawed on a rattle to block him from getting closer, planting her feet wide. She would fight him off and anyone else who dared to take her daughter away. He stared at Didi, the boy he believed his son and heir, and his yearning filled Scarlett with fury and sorrow.

"I never should have listened," he said.

To Mama Fang? Even if the idea for the bribe had originated with Mama Fang, he'd agreed to it.

"You could have listened to me," Scarlett said.

They studied each other. Her arms were meaty and her belly soft, that of a woman in her thirties giving in to gravity, of a new mother recovering from childbirth. His skin was the color of turpentine. The disease, whatever it was, had attacked him from within. She reached toward him, and then dropped her hands at her sides. She wanted to affirm the bony proof of his existence, and she could tell he wanted to touch her, too. She caught herself. She would never lose herself in him again.

"What is it?" she asked. "What happened to you?"

"Cancer. The kind that makes your blood sick."

She leaned against the playpen, the rough scratch of the canvas holding her together. She didn't know anyone who suffered from this disease. Not anyone who had admitted to it. Not her neighbor, curled over with cramps, heaving for months. Not her father, who returned from the mines coughing up blood. Not her classmate who burned with fever, who never came back from the hospital. Punishment, it was said, for an ancestor's wrongdoing. There was no escaping the blood of the people before you. She understood that now.

Liberty's cells sat in the deep freeze at the cord-blood bank. Technicians could fetch a cure born out of that very first cell, dividing and dividing as many times as there were stars in the sky to form a heart, brain, eyes, ears, fingers, toes. Their daughter held Scarlett and Boss Yeung within her, held multitudes infinite as the universe. He had to go at once. On the back of a napkin, Scarlett scrawled out the name of the cord-blood bank, Liberty's name and birthday, and the hospital where she was born. A slim chance, but all the chance he might have.

"What's this?" he asked.

Beach balls sailed overhead as the crowd cheered. "A cure,"

Scarlett said. "Stem cells. From the baby." A gift that she was giving freely and honestly, as Mama Fang—and Boss Yeung—never could.

"From our son," he marveled.

She'd dreaded this, Boss Yeung finding out the sex of his child and rejecting the flesh of his flesh. She accepted that he'd spurned her, but to witness him turning his back on their daughter—she would grieve all over again.

"From our daughter." When she picked up Liberty from the playpen, the baby squealed, craning her neck to see this stranger.

"The ultrasound—" he said.

Liberty rooted at her mother's chest, and though she had never nursed out in the open, Scarlett pulled aside her V-neck and let her daughter suckle. In that minute, the world held no one but them: Liberty's dreamy eyes, and Scarlett's head bowed over her in the only kind of prayer she knew. The next speaker took the microphone, a spark plug of a woman in a dark purple pantsuit. Liberty jerked her head up at the crackling sound. Scarlett straightened her shirt, and turned their daughter toward Boss Yeung. He didn't reach for her.

Scarlett ached, not over the loss of a lover, but the loss of a father for Liberty. Soon enough, Liberty would begin talking. Soon enough, she would ask for her father, hungry for how he might shape her. If Scarlett's father had lived, he might have taught her how to weave a basket to catch fish in the river, might have tempered Ma's rage and encouraged her as Ma never did. If he had lived, Ma never would have taken the job at the clinic.

Boss Yeung seemed stricken, his hands curled at his sides. His shock would turn to disappointment, to disgust. He pulled out a sheaf of papers tucked inside his coat—a contract, demanding custody? He smoothed the pages flat and presented it to her. The pages flapped open and Liberty reached for them, curious. Scarlett shifted Liberty onto her hip. He held a notebook, much like the one she'd had as a child.

She gasped. It *was* her notebook, the one in which she'd first written her English name, the one she'd saved from Ma's stove.

A cry escaped her lips and instantly she was that girl again, wanting so much more than the life handed down to her. Her feet fleet, determined not to let the earth—or her mother—break her. How many hours had she labored over that notebook? She could smell the chalk dust, the pencil shavings from the classroom. The pitted chalkboard and desks jammed with three students each. The whisper of her pencil across the pages flimsier than toilet paper. Her characters inside the workbook wobbly yet recognizable as her own. She'd assumed that Ma had turned the notebook to kindling. She'd been wrong. Ma hadn't been vindictive; she'd held on to it all these years, maybe because she wanted to understand the mystery of her daughter. A daughter she'd cherished after all. If she'd asked Ma for help while she was pregnant, she might have protected the baby as she'd protected the notebook.

Lost, now found by Boss Yeung. She sensed he'd made the trip to the village himself, out of desperation but also in atonement, and held her notebook close all the way here. The rally at City Hall erupted into cheers. Boss Yeung had tracked her to her origins. Did he pity her or think her backward? She found neither in his steady gaze. News helicopters hovered over the demonstration, and passing cars honked in support. Liberty grabbed the notebook and waved it, the pages snapping like a flag.

"What's her name?" Boss Yeung asked.

"Liberty."

"What's her name?" he repeated. "Her name in Chinese."

"She doesn't have one," Scarlett said. "She's an American."

He sounded out the syllables, "Lee-bu-tee." A name he wouldn't have picked, a name it appeared he wouldn't question. She slid Liberty onto her other hip, hugging her daughter with her left arm, her wedding band on display, where he couldn't miss it. When he recoiled, she defiantly stared back at him.

Onstage, the speaker rallied the crowd. "It started off as the winter of love, but let's make this the year of love!"

Daisy returned from taking pictures, her shoulders sagging, carrying herself as if bruised all over. She picked up her son from the playpen, nuzzling the top of his head. Boss Yeung seemed to catch sight of the matching ring on her finger, and then studied the other same-sex couples at the rally. Seeing Didi in his mother's arms, Liberty lit up. Daisy approached Boss Yeung, her expression wary, ready to fend off this stranger far too interested in their family.

Understanding appeared to dawn on him. Not that Scarlett was a *lala* but that she'd found a way to stay in the United States without him. In his eyes she saw what might be admiration.

"Anyone getting married next week?" the speaker said. Shouts rose up, jubilation like a shock wave. "How about just married? Anyone here last week—this month—please join us onstage with those who kicked it all off ten years ago!"

Scores of same-sex couples climbed the stage, beaming and blushing, fist-pumping and whooping. The afternoon light turned molten gold. Daisy, holding her son, tugged at Scarlett's elbow. Another photo to build their case for the immigration file.

"Go," Scarlett told Boss Yeung. He didn't move. She realized he wouldn't leave, not without his daughter, and not without her. He'd wait all day, all night—all week.

She and Daisy followed the other couples, rainbow as the backdrop: olive-skinned men with dapper matching goatees and slim dark ties, silver-haired pantsuit grannies with canes. Scarlett and Daisy cradled their children, who had gone quiet, captivated by the spectacle. They ascended the stairs.

The emcee started passing the microphone to each couple. "Thank you, thank you," Scarlett murmured, and she expected Daisy to say the same. Instead the teenager sang. "Good night, my love, to every hour in every day. Good night, always, to all that's pure in your heart."

Softly at first and then she belted the words, the crowd swaying and hugging in the sunshine. Daisy's voice caught in her throat and Scarlett nodded at her, urging her on. She swallowed hard and pushed through to the end of the song, the one she'd sung with William that night at karaoke in Taipei, that became a lullaby to their son, that he covered on his album. The song now served as her farewell, soaring with a determination that made it sound like an anthem. For Didi's sake—for her own—it seemed Daisy had finally accepted that he wasn't coming back.

Scarlett saw him before Daisy did. Tall, with the watermelon seed eyes Didi had inherited. He plowed through the crowd, knocking against a bearded man who stumbled, and a woman with a cascade of curly dark hair who fell to her knees. William must have received Daisy's messages, but too late to write back, or perhaps he wanted to see her in person before he knew if and how he wanted to respond. He was shouting Daisy's name, the tendons tight in his neck and his mouth wide. The crowd heaved, the roar loud as surf. Then Daisy was running off the stage, their son in her arms, great strides closing the distance that remained between them until there was none left at all.

# Epilogue

**Scarlett eased** Boss Yeung onto the bed, and Liberty climbed in, tucking her head into the crook of his arm. He stroked their daughter's hair, fanned out across his chest. Her cells had given him a reprieve, a year or so in which she learned to walk, to run, to leap, a year spent becoming the daughter of the man who hugged her tight, then raised her high into the air each morning.

His wife had renounced the world and spent her days praying at the Celestial Goddess's eco-luxury resort commune in Bali. He'd gradually turned over the company to Viann. At first she had been tentative around her baby sister, grateful that Liberty had saved her father, and grateful that Liberty wasn't a male heir. She'd become an indulgent aunt who could satisfy Liberty's fondness for sparkle. Viann still didn't know the truth of her heritage, but Boss Yeung had willed her a copy of the genetics report. Upon his death, she alone would decide her fate, which was what he wanted for her more than any revenge he might have exacted upon Uncle Lo.

Uncle Lo no longer sought to punish Scarlett, perhaps because she'd bestowed the gift of life upon his friend, or perhaps—for reasons known only to him—it had become counter to his interests. Whatever the case, she was out of his reach in America. She knew he remained suspicious she might disappear on Boss Yeung again, but what he thought no longer mattered.

Mama Fang was busier than ever. She'd sold Little Genius to Uncle Lo, and had hired a surrogate, who was now pregnant with her twins, a boy and a girl, conceived from donor eggs and sperm from Chinese Americans with Ivy League intelligence and movie star looks. One or both children might grow up to reject her, and so, she was preparing for her next venture: recruiting a network of top-notch Chinese donors and surrogates. In business alone, she might exercise the control that drove away those dearest to her.

Daisy and her son lived with William's parents in the suburbs east of San Francisco. After the paternity test eliminated their misgivings, they were involved in her life as her own parents never had been. They were pleased that she'd gotten into Cal, on the path they wanted for their wayward son. He remained in Hong Kong where stars were supposed to be chaste and filial. He wasn't the first celebrity to conceal his engagement and his child, to seem eternally young and eternally available. Still in love, Daisy struggled every day without him, their future uncertain but for Didi.

The bedsprings squeaked. Liberty was singing to herself about two little tigers, one without ears, another without a tail. Boss Yeung filled in the words that she forgot. Sunday mornings, she and Didi took a toddler music class in Chinatown. Afterward, they feasted on dim sum at the Pearl Pavilion, often joined by Old Wu and his wife and newborn son, who had a thatch of black hair and a roar loud as a jet plane; Little Fox and Joe Ng, together after her rogue of a husband ran off; Casey and Ying; and Auntie Ng, Granny Wang, and Widow Mok, busybodies still. The big round tables always had room for one more.

Scarlett curled beside her daughter. After his illness returned, Boss Yeung made a final decision as chief executive: establishing permanent residency for Scarlett by investing a half-million dollars in her name to open a *hanbaobao* pop-up shop, launch a wholesale business, hire a staff of ten, and refurbish a food truck that also hawked his family's shortbread. Following her divorce from Daisy, her application had sailed through, and she had just received her green card, marked by the hologram of the Statue of Liberty, smiling or frowning, depending on how the light fell. The fate Scarlett had avoided, the fate so many suffered—detained, deported, parted from their children—sometimes winged over her, a shadow she had outrun but would never forget.

Boss Yeung dozed off with their daughter, as the breeze drifted through the window. He loved Liberty more than any male heir, for sons carried the burden of expectation and obligation. A late-season fruit had never tasted sweeter. As the toddler's mobility improved, his had declined. Liberty might not remember the helium balloon he bought her every week or her hand clutching his, but Scarlett hoped their daughter would retain a sense of him, the feeling of his arms holding her, of his lullabies sung low and deep.

She reached for her phone and snapped a close-up of Liberty's lashes and her apple blossom skin. The time for naps would soon end, the nestling warmth and fluttering breaths of her daughter that she was already starting to miss. Liberty's pleasingly rounded limbs were lengthening into those of a girl, into the woman she'd become. Scarlett texted the photos to Ma, who had learned how to use a phone—her way of expressing the tenderness she couldn't put into words. The longer Scarlett had been a mother, the more she understood Ma and her decisions.

Once upon a time, the Goddess of Heaven, furious her daughter had fallen for a lowly cowherd, gouged out a river of stars with her hairpin. She stranded the lovers on opposite shores. Each year, on the seventh day of the seventh month, she relented, allowing the magpies to bridge the sky and reunite them. Love lost, then found, again and again. Now the legend held another meaning for Scarlett: a mother's forgiveness. In the story she would tell Liberty, not even the Goddess of Heaven could undo the past, but she'd commanded the magpies to complete her daughter's heart, by conjuring a flock that spanned the universe.

# Acknowledgments

I am grateful to those who read many drafts and provided advice along the way, including Maury Zeff, David Baker, Jane Kalmes, Angie Chuang, Yalitza Ferreras, Kirstin Chen, Angie Chau, and Kevin Allardice. Others who offered support, encouragement, and places to stay include Dawn MacKeen, Pia Sarkar, Josue Hurtado, Irene Chan, Jason Husgen, the Pak-Stevensons, the Taylors, the Freedes, Geoff Nilsen, Alicia Jo Rabins, Aimee Phan, Beth Bich Minh Nguyen, Reese Kwon, the other women writers of the Karaoke Book Club, and fellow debut authors Nicole Chung, Lillian Li, Lydia Kiesling, Ingrid Rojas Contreras, and Crystal Hana Kim.

Much love to the San Francisco Writers' Grotto, where I wrote much of this book, with special thanks to Bridget Quinn, Yukari Iwatani Kane, Mary Ladd, and Kaitlin Solimine. I am grateful for additional support from the Rona Jaffe Foundation, the Steinbeck Fellow Program at San José State University—especially Nick Taylor, Paul Douglass, Tommy Mouton, and Dallas Woodburn—the San Francisco Foundation, Aspen Summer Words, Bread Loaf Writers' Conference, Voices of Our Nation, and Hedgebrook, among others. While writing, I left my twin sons in the devoted care of Jaqueline Perez.

Mei Fong's *One Child: The Story of China's Most Radical Experi-*

*ment* and Leslie T. Chang's *Factory Girls: From Village to City in a Changing China* were among the most fascinating and useful books I studied while researching this novel. I'm also thankful for the editors at the *San Francisco Chronicle*, who backed my reporting in the villages and factories of the Pearl River Delta and in San Francisco Chinatown, and to the many migrants who shared their stories and dreams with me.

Early versions of chapters first appeared in *ZYZZYVA* and *Guernica*. A heartfelt thanks to *ZYZZYVA* editors Oscar Villalon and Laura Cogan, for their long-standing support of me and my work. They do so much to enrich literary culture in the Bay Area and beyond.

My agents, Emma Sweeney and Margaret Sutherland Brown, have championed this book, providing friendly, wise counsel and making my dreams come true. I am indebted to the Random House team for their expertise and generosity, including Emily Hartley, Susan Corcoran, Christine Mykityshyn, Stephanie Reddaway, Beth Pearson, Robin Schiff, Belina Huey, Madeline Hopkins, Chin-Yee Lai, Virginia Norey, Debbie Aroff, Colleen Nuccio, Toby Ernst, and others. Many thanks to publisher Kara Welsh, deputy publisher Kim Hovey, and editor in chief Jennifer Hershey for welcoming my debut novel. My deepest gratitude goes to my editor, Susanna Porter, who has tirelessly guided me through revisions with much insight and good cheer.

Thank you to my family for your enduring love and support—my mother, Sylvia, and my late father, Lo-Ching; my sister, Inez; my nephew, Declan; my brother, Lawrence; and my in-laws, Robert and Patricia Puich, and my sister-in-law, Kristine Puich, and her partner, Jeff Elmassian.

I was pregnant when I began writing this novel, when I began to discover how motherhood would open my eyes, my heart, and my imagination in ways I couldn't foresee. Every day remains an adventure with my sons. My husband, Marc, has been on this journey at each step, at each turn, and I thank him for everything, always.

# About the Author

VANESSA HUA is a columnist for the *San Francisco Chronicle* and author of a short story collection, *Deceit and Other Possibilities*. For two decades, she has been writing, in journalism and fiction, about Asia and the Asian diaspora. She has received a Rona Jaffe Foundation Writers' Award, the Asian/Pacific American Award for Literature, the San Francisco Foundation's James D. Phelan Award, and a Steinbeck Fellowship in Creative Writing, as well as honors from the Society of Professional Journalists and the Asian American Journalists Association. Her work has appeared in publications including *The New York Times*, *The Atlantic*, and *The Washington Post*. *A River of Stars* is Vanessa Hua's first novel.

vanessahua.com
Facebook.com/VanessaHuaWriter
Twitter: @Vanessa_Hua

## About the Type

**This book** was set in Aster, a typeface designed in 1958 by Francesco Simoncini (d. 1967). Aster is a round, legible face of even weight and was planned by the designer for the text setting of newspapers and books.